WITHDRAWN

THE
SOURCE

A WITCHING SAVANNAH NOVEL

By J.D. Horn

Witching Savannah

The Line
The Source

THE
SOURCE

A WITCHING SAVANNAH NOVEL

J.D. HORN

This is a work of fiction. Names, characters, organizations, places, events, and incidents are either products of the author's imagination or are used fictitiously.

Text copyright © 2014 J.D. Horn
All rights reserved.

Printed in the United States of America.

No part of this book may be reproduced, or stored in a retrieval system, or transmitted in any form or by any means, electronic, mechanical, photocopying, recording, or otherwise, without express written permission of the publisher.

Published by 47North, Seattle

www.apub.com

Cover illustration by Patrick Arrasmith

Amazon, the Amazon logo, and 47North are trademarks of Amazon.com, Inc., or its affiliates.

ISBN-13: 9781477820148
ISBN-10: 1477820140

Library of Congress Control Number: 2013955185

Printed in the United States of America

In loving memory of Quentin Comfort Horn,
the source of much happiness

THE
SOURCE

A WITCHING SAVANNAH NOVEL

ONE

"Hold the fire in your hand now, girl." Jilo's whisper washed over me. "Don't let it just take you in. You control it this time. Don't you enter its world till you ready to control your time there."

The small flame didn't burn me, even though I knew its heat must have been intense. It danced in my palm as it tried to pull my consciousness back—back into a memory of myself and my sister. Maisie had given me these enchanted flames, tongues of fire that allowed me to relive experiences from our childhood in vibrant detail. Now she was lost to me, torn not only from this world, but from our very reality. No one knew where she was, or even *if* she was.

These bright flickers were the last of her magic left on our plane, and they strained to touch their source like iron shavings reaching toward a magnet. They were my only hope of finding Maisie. I struggled against the flame's tug, trying to descend into the past, step-by-step, this time without getting lost in the memory. We had already used a dozen of the flames; the lights had given their lives one by one as they tried to guide me to her. They burned so brightly, but they flickered out too quickly for me to find the connection, to understand where I was being led. Counting this one, the flame that quivered in my palm, only five remained.

"Hold on to the light in your right hand, and you listen to Jilo's voice, hear?" She grabbed my free hand and squeezed it tightly. I squeezed back. "Let Jilo's voice be yo' anchor in this world. No need to rush, my girl, no need to rush."

Jilo's language and her insistence on speaking about herself in the third person belied her education. I knew for a fact that she had graduated from Spelman College with a degree in chemistry, but due to her sex and skin color, she had been born about two decades too early to follow her dream of becoming a medical doctor. Instead she became a Hoodoo root doctor, building a persona around herself that matched both the expectations and superstitions of those who sought her services. I was one of the few who had ever been allowed a peek behind this mask.

Jilo took a deep, slow breath, reminding me to emulate her. The waves of power washed up against me, but each came with less strength, and their frequency was diminishing. I resisted the gravity of the world that had begun to grow before me, trying to divert the energy of Maisie's spell from its intended use, turning it toward my own ends. The energy slowed and began to stretch out before me, bending. Frustrated by my resistance, it began to turn, stretching out and glowing like a comet nearing the sun. Just as I'd intended, the magic began to seek its source, reaching out in all directions until it found Maisie. I honed my consciousness, following the flame's path, but it was too late. The flame incandesced, expanding and brightening like a nova. An instant later it died. So, resisting the flames' pull caused them to burn out more quickly . . . This time, I didn't even get the joy of reliving a beloved childhood memory. Just blackness.

"We got closer that time," Jilo said, even though we both knew it was a lie. We'd made it this far twice before. She stood and hobbled over to the table where the Ball jar that held the remaining four flames sat and closed the lid tightly on them. "I can't do no more today. I ain't as young as you are," she said, but all the while her eyes never left my midsection. I knew she worried that too much of this walking between worlds might be bad for the baby growing there. I worried too, but I was also worried that I was running out of time to find Maisie.

"I appreciate what you are doing for me," I said, rubbing my palm over my ever-expanding stomach. I was just three-and-a-half months along now, but I could already tell that my Colin would arrive a very big boy.

"Jilo know you do, girl," she said, and then said again in a tender voice, "She know you do." She put her hand on her hip, rubbing away at some ache. "Jilo still think you should tell yo' family what you up to. They witches, they have a much easier time helpin' you find your sister than Jilo."

"I don't want to involve them. The other witch families won't even listen to a whisper about trying to bring Maisie back into our dimension. She damaged the line, they say, weakened it." Millennia ago, powerful witches, including many of my own ancestors, had woven a web of magical energy to protect our world. We called this barrier "the line." The beings who'd once ruled the earth—call them demons if you are religious, or transdimensional entities if you put your faith in science—had set themselves up as gods, meddling in human evolution, even more so in the genesis of witches than in that of regular folk. Eventually we witches rebelled, chasing the serpents out of Eden. The line prevented them from ever coming back. "My aunts and uncle would stop me too. They'd feel obliged to," I said, fearing that they might not have helped me even if the other families hadn't been opposed to finding my sister.

While my Aunt Iris wanted nothing more to do with Maisie, saying that she'd earned any punishment that had befallen her, Aunt Ellen was offering her usual blind allegiance to the united witch families. She didn't want to risk making waves. Uncle Oliver wasn't as dead set against finding Maisie, but he didn't think there would be much of her left to find. He had spent days ripping out the patch of lawn where Maisie had last stood before the power of the angry line threw her far from our world. He said the earth there had been burnt black several feet deep, and it wasn't even worth trying to plant anything. He'd returned the damaged soil, laid down pavers to cover the spot, and added a sundial. I guess it constituted his own form of a memorial. No, I knew my family would not support my clandestine efforts, and even if they did, the other anchors—the witches like myself who had been chosen to maintain and protect the line—had forbidden any efforts to bring Maisie back into our reality, fearing she would do more damage to the line.

"Jilo think maybe they *should* stop you. This sister of yours, she tried to kill you."

"She didn't know what she was doing," I objected. "She was under the influence of a demon, a boo hag. The boo hag you yourself nurtured and used to spy on my family." Maisie was more than a sibling, she was my twin. Fraternal twin, yes, but still we'd come into the world together. If I didn't look for a reason to forgive her, who else would?

"Jilo done told you she sorry about that. She had no idea that yo' sister had got messed up with that thing."

I still felt sick when I thought about how Maisie had taken the shadow entity and given it a form. Named it Jackson and took it as her lover. Allowed it to cut me and taste my blood. I felt even worse when I remembered how I myself had fallen in love with Jackson. A shudder ran down my spine.

"That right," Jilo continued as if she had read my thoughts. "That the sister you trying to find now. Jilo says you better off leaving the bitch wherever she landed. Sometimes you just gotta cut the cord, blood or no."

"Well, that sure isn't going to happen," I said sharply, but then regretted my tone. "I can't do this without you, Mother."

She shook off my frustration without even a grimace. "The families still chokin' off yo' power supply?"

"Yes," I said. "They don't think I'm ready to control it."

"And they still pissed you shared a little with Jilo."

"Yeah, they didn't seem too happy when they figured that one out." The other witch families had staged a kind of trial to determine if I was ready to assume the full use of my powers. The fact that I'd given Jilo just enough to keep her in business had actually been used as Exhibit A in the case against me, but I wasn't going to burden her with that fact. It was my power to give, and I'd done it of my own free will. "They say they're doing it to protect me from myself, that I don't know how to handle the power, that I'm not mature enough for it," I said, mentally ticking off their list of complaints, "and that I think too much with my heart instead of my head, putting my own desires before the greater good."

"Who the hell are they to judge you?" she asked, angry as a mother hen protecting her chick. "The line, it chose you, even without yo' magic. It knew you. It picked you."

"They said that letting me have access to my full power would be like letting a six-year-old play with an atomic bomb. I've got to ease into it, like I would have if I'd been able to access it since birth."

"What about the line? How you gonna anchor that damned thing if you don't have you full power?"

"I'm not anchoring right now. I'm connected to its power. I have to be, 'cause it chose me to help anchor it, but the nine other anchors are sharing my allotment of its energy and my portion of the burden of maintaining it. I'm sure if they could remove me as an anchor without bringing down the line, they probably would."

"Oh, they a way. They could kill you, just like yo' Ginny got killed."

My mind flashed back on the scene I'd walked into that summer. My Great-Aunt Ginny lying dead in a pool of blood. Bludgeoned with a tire iron. "They wouldn't do that," I said, praying that I was right.

"You sure about that?" Jilo asked. I said nothing, knowing that she'd read through any lie I tried to float. I wasn't sure. Ginny's murder had triggered the events that had led to the line's selection of me as an anchor. It had crossed my mind more than once that I ought to take care until I had my footing. Killing me would be the easiest way to create another vacancy.

Deep down I suspected that if I proved too inconvenient, too much of a handful, the families might decide to remove me from the scene entirely, and then congratulate themselves on being able to make the hard calls. I knew my aunts and uncle would go down trying to protect me, but some members of my extended family might even put their seal of approval on the decision. That's why I'd been agreeing to everything the families had asked of me, everything other than giving up on Maisie.

"Jilo, she don't get it," she continued, pulling me from my dark thoughts. "How is what they doin' any different from what old Ginny pulled on you? They stealin' what rightfully yo's. They know they a price for stealing a witch's power."

"They aren't really stealing . . ."

"They taking it from you without yo' permission," she said, but then read my silence. "Ah, Jilo see. You gave them permission, didn't you?"

6

"I did what I had to do. Maybe they're right. I don't know what I'm doing. I never had the chance to learn. I've got to catch up."

"The hell you say. Don't you see, girl? The line, it thought you ready. These other anchors, the families, they scared you into givin' over yo' power."

I knew she was right, but the truth was that I *was* afraid. I was terrified not only of the families, but of myself. I doubted I could control my magic at half power, leave alone full. I had missed out on my formative years as a witch, and now I was toddling along, taking baby steps. A magical infant who kept falling on her magical butt. The families had tasked Emmet with my education. Emmet had begun life as a golem, intended to house the consciousnesses of the families' representatives. But the same energy that had knocked Maisie into whatever place she'd landed had also fused the consciousnesses lent to Emmet's form into a single, brooding, pain-in-the-ass personality.

Happily, the energy donors were pretty much unharmed—they didn't seem to be diminished in the least by what they'd lost to their golem. Emmet still shared much of their knowledge and had retained a portion of their powers too. Since he possessed both wisdom and magic, the families had decided that he would be my teacher, and that he would show me how to harness my own power. Even though Emmet could be grating, I still felt sympathy for him. We had a bit in common. The families stomped all over him too, never even asking him if he had his own ideas about what he wanted to do with his life. They simply pointed him in my direction and told him to go to it. But even with Emmet as my capable tutor, I had only gained imperfect control over what little magic they'd allowed me. I shrugged.

"Fine. We keep lookin' for yo' crazy-ass sister together, then. Tomorrow," Jilo said, picking up the red cooler she always carried with her to Colonial Cemetery, where she met with her regular clientele. She slipped the Ball jar into the cooler. I had asked her to keep custody of it, to make sure no one intent on punishing Maisie could make use of its contents. "You better be puttin' some thought into what you gonna do with her if we do find yo' Maisie, 'cause Jilo ain't gonna be babysitting her." A sharp beam of sunlight found its way through one of the square, foot-long openings in the wall. The old woman of the crossroads stood there in silhouette, her features obscured by the bright light engulfing her. "I know you determined to do this—that why Jilo helpin'. But you don't owe yo' sister nothing. It that baby you carryin' you need to be worrying about." She opened the heavy door with a wave of her hand. "You ain't gonna be able to keep flittin' around on that bike of yours for much longer. If we gonna keep on with this, Jilo say you find us some place cleaner and closer to home." She let the door slam behind her, punctuating her point with the sound of metal slapping metal.

I looked around this forgotten room in the abandoned powder magazine where we'd been meeting. The gunpowder had long since been removed, but pointed and rusted objects still lay strewn everywhere, coated in decades of dust. Outside the redbrick fortress, heaps of garbage negated the medieval, almost fairy-tale glamour of the magazine's crenellated roofline. I would have been hard-pressed to find a more septic situation for my unborn child. "Maybe she's right, Colin," I said, addressing the child. I knew the baby was a boy; there had been no need for an ultrasound, since my Aunt Ellen always hit it dead on in these matters. I also knew I would name him Colin, after his father's father.

Aunt Iris was pressing me to go ahead and marry Peter Tierney, making it official before the baby was born. I had every intention of marrying him. I'd even accepted his ring, but I didn't wear it yet. Like the heart of a Russian nesting doll, I kept it stowed in its blue velveteen box in the jewelry case on my makeup table. I loved Peter, but every time I envisioned myself standing there before God and the world to say "I do," I remembered how he had gone to Jilo and paid her to place a love spell on me. He'd been desperate, terrified that I would leave him for Jackson. It bothered me more than a little that I'd actually considered doing as much. I'd forgiven Jilo, and on the surface, I'd forgiven Peter, but the betrayal had been so deep, so unexpected, that part of me wondered how far Peter would go in any situation where he felt hard-pressed.

As this thought registered, it made me feel a twinge of guilt. Peter was trying so hard to step up and be a good father and provider. In addition to his regular job, he'd gone back to working nights at his parents' tavern, and he was doing his best to start up his own construction business, taking on smaller jobs that he could do on weekends with a couple of buddies from his regular crew. I had reminded him that money was not a problem—ever since I had turned twenty-one, I'd been receiving a monthly stipend from the family trust—but he would have none of it.

"No," he had told me, holding up his palms toward me. "I can't take money from you. I don't *want* to take money from you. I want to know that I can take care of my wife, or soon-to-be wife, and my child. Without your money and without your magic."

It was a display of arguably antiquated male pride, but instinct and intuition told me not to challenge him on it. I simply nodded and smiled. "All right. I respect that," I said at the time, even though I was only humoring him. After taking some weeks to reflect on it, though, I had come to realize how much respect I did have for him. "You are one lucky boy to have a daddy like that," I told Colin, running my hand over the small bulge beneath my shirt.

I leaned into the enormous door, intent on opening it under my own steam. The seven-by-four-foot slab of steel cracked open with great difficulty. When I was a little girl, someone had managed to steal the massive door, taking it right off its hinges. That's about as far as they got, though, its weight causing them to abandon it by the side of a dirt road, leaving the city of Savannah with the task of rehanging it.

I considered using my magic to open the door, as Jilo had done, but while I might manage to swing the door open, I might just blow it off its hinges and into the next county. I decided to use my hands. I leaned into the steel, and was nearly blinded by the light that rushed in to fill the dark space behind and around me.

The day was a fabric woven from heat and humidity, the noises of nature, and the drone of traffic on Ogeechee Road. My bike was where I'd left it, propped up against the building. I could have used my magic to bring myself to the magazine, but had decided against it. The one "spell," for lack of a better term, I had managed to master so far was teleporting short distances. Not all witches could do it, but I could, and I could do it well. All the same, I didn't like the way it made me feel. Each time, there was an odd sensation that the person I'd been at Point A wasn't necessarily the same as the one who'd ended up at Point B.

"Mama needs her practice, but she also needs her exercise," I rationalized aloud to my son. A thrill ran through me as I sensed for the first time an intelligence on the other end of the conversation. Colin was there, connected to me. A feeling of love, unequal to any I had ever known, flooded through me. I realized that I would do anything to keep my baby safe. *Anything.* Then I wondered whether "anything" included giving up the search for Maisie. I decided to leave that an open question for now, but determined that I would find a cleaner and safer place to meet Jilo from now on.

I started for my bike, but then a noise came from behind me. Something close. I turned. A lonely clump of Georgia pines stood a few feet ahead on my right, and an older—no, *incredibly* old—man stumbled through them. He staggered and almost tripped, but then righted himself. He turned around in a circle, seemingly intent on finding his bearings. The air felt way too hot and sticky for the overcoat he was wearing, especially since the garment was several sizes too large. The hem nearly brushed the ground. In spite of his diminutive size, I began to feel uneasy. Something wasn't right.

This fear of strangers had only come upon me recently; I was no longer protected by any charms. When the line chose me, its power blended with my own, unraveling the protections that Emmet and my family had woven for me. Regular witches can't charm the line's anchors for good or bad. Now I had to stand on my own.

"Good morning," I called out to the man, but he didn't seem to hear me.

"*Ta me ar strae. Ta me ar strae,*" he repeated, circling once more before finally registering my presence. He made a rush toward me, and my breath quickened as adrenaline urged me to a fight-or-flight response. In his hurry, he nearly fell forward but managed to right himself at the last instant. He stopped and looked up at me. He had the most innocent face I had ever seen, his eyes wide and trusting. He was balding, and what tufts of hair remained around his temples were snow white. Deep wrinkles covered his face, but the folds there were laugh lines.

"Hello," I said again. "Do you need some help?" I asked, hoping he understood English.

"You must be the angel," he said, a thick Irish accent lending a lilt to his words. "They told me you would come for me at the end." He held his arms out to me in a gesture of welcome.

Any fear I had of this stranger dissipated. I took a few steps toward him. "Sorry," I said, "no angel here." Was that disappointment I saw in his eyes?

"That's just as well," he said, snagging his coat on some brush and nearly tottering over.

"Listen, are you all right? Can I help you somehow?" He looked up at me again with his sweet face. Something about him seemed to be touched by magic. He radiated a faint white light, a luminescence I wasn't sure I could have seen if I weren't a witch. I found myself wondering if he were indeed a man, or some kind of elemental masquerading as one. After recent experiences, I had grown much less inclined to accept things at face value.

He tugged at his coat, freeing it from the brush, and took another step toward me. He began rubbing his left arm with his right hand. "It's only that I am not quite sure where I am," he said.

"You are off Ogeechee Road," I replied. "Do you live around here?"

His answer came in the form of a short, sharp laugh. The laughter died as quickly as it had come. "I don't know." His knees buckled, and he fell to the ground. I ran to him, nearly tripping over my own feet, and knelt by his side. I gave him a gentle shake. He did not respond. I rolled him over with some difficulty. His skin was blue, and the radiance I had noticed only moments before had disappeared. Whatever magic had clung to him had deserted him.

"You're gonna be okay," I said and opened his coat, surprised to discover how slight his body was beneath it. I loosened his collar. He smiled up at me, but then his eyes glazed over. I felt for a pulse. There was none. I had taken a CPR certification course a couple of years before, and I did my best to remember the steps. Placing my right hand over his chest and my left hand over my right, I began compressions. Two inches deep, one hundred compressions per minute.

"Help!" I screamed, hoping that someone in one of the nearby businesses might hear. "Call an ambulance." I kept counting compressions as I listened for any response. There was none. I called out again. I had picked this place for my work with Jilo because the noise of a busy road drowned out most other sounds, and even though there were businesses in the area, large trees hid the powder magazine entirely. Now I cursed the noise and camouflage. He only had six minutes even with CPR. How long had I been pressing into his chest? Maybe only thirty seconds, but it seemed like forever. Should I stop CPR and call for an ambulance myself?

I gasped as a sudden realization shot through me—I was a witch now, but I was thinking like a human. What would a witch do? I knew that my resuscitation efforts alone would not bring him back. At best, the CPR would keep oxygen flowing to his brain until a defibrillator could be used. His heart needed to be restarted with a shock of electricity.

The moment this thought came to mind, a pulse of light shot down my arm, bright and blue like a tight ball of lightning. I hadn't consciously commanded it. My magic had interpreted my confused thoughts and taken over for me. The bolt shot into the man's body, and for an instant, his eyes flashed open, full of astonishment. His body lifted a few inches off the ground, and as I tried to pull my hands away, it followed me, the electricity between us attracting him like a magnet. Then the link broke at last, and he dropped to the ground, his eyes fluttering shut for the last time. The stench of burning meat rose to my nostrils, and I grew sick. The part of his chest where the energy had entered him had been burned black, and a gaping tunnel had been blasted through the space that once held his heart.

What had I done? I clawed at the sandy soil, scraping away the residue that clung to my palm, my fingers. My breath failed me, coming only in short gasps that couldn't fill my lungs. Hands reached out from behind me and held my shoulders. A calm, feminine voice spoke to me. "It's okay, baby. It's okay. But you have to come with me. We have to get you away from here." I had never heard that voice before, but I had known it all my life. I began shaking, my skin cold. The light reaching my eyes alternated between impossibly dim and painfully bright. I felt like the world had fallen away beneath me. I had to be hallucinating. I looked away from the damaged corpse I had created. My head turned slowly, knowing that once I laid eyes on her, nothing would ever be the same again. I looked up. A smile. Loving green eyes. A face so very much like my own.

"Mama?" my voice squeaked out of me, forcing its way between the walls of amazement and disbelief.

"Yes, baby. It's me," she said, and then seemed to read the next thought pressing on my mind. "It's me. I'm alive."

TWO

My mother guided me through the scrub-filled ravine that separated the powder magazine from the parking lot servicing the nearby businesses. A limousine waited there, and a liveried driver who was standing by its side jolted to attention, then opened the car's door. Together, my mother and he eased me into the air-conditioned cocoon, and then my mother slid in next to me. A dark privacy glass separated us from the driver's area, and even blacker windows, nearly onyx, protected us from the world outside. The car began moving, but I had no idea where we were going. Frankly, I didn't care. I held on to my mother's hands, grasping them so tightly it must have hurt. Her face held my eyes. It seemed so much like a mirror of my own, except that it held a couple decades more of experience, of sadness.

"I know you must have so many questions." Her words began to make their way through the haze. "And," she said as her eyes caressed me, "there are so many things I need to say to you. But we don't have time now." A pained smile formed on her face. She managed to extricate her right hand from mine, and ran her fingers through my hair. "I didn't want you to find out like this. I didn't want to just fall into your world, but I tracked you down at the powder magazine, and I had to get a look at you." She pulled my head to her bosom, pressing her cool palm against my cheek. "If only I'd arrived a few moments earlier, I could have helped, but I discovered you too late. The old gentleman had already . . . expired. You were so distraught, and I couldn't bring myself to leave you there."

"But how could you?" I asked. "I mean, how could you have left me before? Left Maisie?" I pulled back from her, a sharp and stinging anger cutting me to the quick. "How could you let us grow up believing you had died?"

"I had no choice," she said. "She wouldn't let me near you. She was working against me long before she plotted against you."

My mother didn't need to supply the name. "Ginny," I said. A slight nod confirmed my thought. "But why?"

"I'll tell you. I'll tell you everything. Only not right now. I've waited all your life to have a chance to explain things to you, and it isn't a story that can be rushed." She reached forward and pulled me into her again. I felt intoxicated by her scent—it reached all the way through the years and brought me right back to the cradle. For a moment, I let go of everything and just let my mother hold me. "I have to let you go for now," she whispered. "But I'll be near, and we'll talk soon. Very soon. I promise."

"No," I looked up to her, my heart in my throat. "No, you have to come home," I pleaded. "Come home now. We have to tell Iris and Ellen and Oliver that you're still alive. They are going to be so—"

Her body tensed and her eyes narrowed, small lines forming at their corners. "No," a barbed refusal tore from her lips. She drew a breath, forced her shoulders to relax. "No," she said more calmly. She pushed me away gently, but then patted my hand. "They can't know I've returned. Not yet."

"But they have to . . ." My words died in the air as the look on her face told me more than I wanted to know.

Her eyes had turned downcast and distant, as if she were reliving an unpleasant memory. A tremble danced at the corner of her mouth, and she clenched her jaw to regain control of the tic. "Oh, they know, my darling girl. My sisters know very well that I'm alive." Her voice broke, and she cleared her throat. "I'm not sure what they have told Oliver, but your aunts, they know." She leaned in and pinned me with her gaze. "Iris and Ellen took you and Maisie from me at Ginny's bidding."

"I cannot believe they would do something so terrible," I heard my own voice pleading with my mother. "Why would they?"

"The same reason Ginny stole your power and worked to turn your twin against you—yes, I know all about it. The line. Ginny justified all of her crimes by saying she committed them to protect the line. And in separating my children from their mother, Iris and Ellen were her willing accomplices."

I shook my head. I didn't want to believe, but there was something about my mother's words that I found so compelling.

She continued. "You think you know them, but you don't. Not really. You only know the side they have allowed you to see. If they realize you know . . . if they learn I am back, I fear for your safety." I started to protest that they would never do anything to hurt me, but she held up her hand to stop me. "They have always put the line before your well-being, and they always will. Deep down you know that, or you wouldn't be sneaking around with the old root doctor trying to find out what the line has done with Maisie. My sisters will not think twice about alerting the united families if they find out you know about me. The other anchors already have it in for you simply because you are my daughter. If they learn that I have made contact with you, they *will* make a preemptive move against you. I fear they may work a binding on you."

She waited until her warning had fully registered. Now that I was an anchor, a binding wouldn't merely strip me of my powers.

It would leave me to live out the rest of my life in a vegetative state—the power of the line would consume me, leaving me as nothing more than a receptacle. "You must say nothing. Tell no one. If you do, we will lose each other again, and this time it will be forever."

"But what could you have done to threaten Ginny so? I don't understand."

"I know you don't," she said and tapped once on the window that separated us from the driver. "And I'm sorry, but it isn't safe for me to linger. I'll explain everything when we see each other next. For now, promise me that you will keep this to yourself, for your own sake. For my grandson's sake." She smiled as she mentioned Colin. "Promise me." She placed her smooth, cool hand under my chin and tilted my face so that my eyes met hers. I heard the car's trunk being opened, then closed. That was when I realized we were no longer moving.

I found it impossible to refuse her. "I promise," I said, and she leaned in to kiss my forehead. "But how do you know what's happened to Maisie?"

"I have . . . *friends* who have kept me informed about my two daughters," she said. "I'm only sorry I couldn't prevent it all."

"Okay, but can you help me find her?"

She smiled at me one last time. "I already am, my girl." The door next to me opened, revealing the chauffeur. He stepped aside. I knew he expected me to exit, but I couldn't tear myself away. My mother touched my cheek and then moved her hands to her neck. She unhooked the necklace she'd been wearing and fixed it around my own neck. Something about wearing her locket made me feel so safe, so loved. She gave me a gentle push. "Go on now. You'll see me again very soon. This I promise you."

I climbed out of the car to find we had stopped not far from the southern edge of Forsyth Park. My bike, which had been in the trunk of the car, was waiting patiently on the curb. Suddenly a thought hit me, and I reached out to stop the driver's hand before he could close the door.

"The man, the old guy," I said, remembering that we had left the poor man's body lying in the weeds.

My mother leaned slightly forward. "It's already been taken care of," she said, and the driver closed the door. I watched the limo as it pulled away, leaning on my bike for support, putting all my strength into not letting my legs give way. The blare of a siren yanked me out of my fugue, and an ambulance and police car flew past me, heading, I knew, toward the old powder magazine. A second police car followed them a minute or so behind. This one had its lights and siren working too, but it moved at a less frenetic pace. As it passed, a passenger inside turned to look at me, and a flash of recognition crossed Detective Adam Cook's face.

THREE

As I walked my bike up our drive, it struck me that the house I'd grown up in had been really nothing more than a stage set. A theater of lies. The set may have been made of actual wood and brick, but nothing else was real. My mother's perfume still clung to me. She was alive. Alive! *That* was real. *That* was the truth. Everything I'd ever believed about her, about my family, about my life rang false now. A darkness squeezed my heart as a newfound hatred for Ginny took root. I had been working on letting go of my anger toward my great-aunt, but now any thought of forgiveness evaporated. Forgiveness, hell. I would go tomorrow and dance on her grave. She had stolen my power from me. I could overlook that. But taking my mother from me, from Maisie? That I could never forgive. I prayed that wherever Ginny's essence had landed, eternity would find her without one moment's peace.

How could Ginny have justified keeping my mother from me? But then what could she have hoped to accomplish by separating me from my birthright of power? She would have claimed she was doing her duty as anchor. Protecting the line. Protecting it from my mother. Protecting it from me. But the line had chosen me. It didn't fear me; it welcomed me. Ginny must have been wrong about my mother too. She must have been.

I touched the locket my mother had placed around my neck. The feel of its precious metal confirmed it wasn't merely a figment of my imagination. I leaned my bike against the garage and fumbled with the locket's clasp. It sprung open to reveal two tiny photos, one of Maisie and the other of me. We seemed such little things—there was barely enough hair on our heads to support the ribbons someone had put on us. How had she gotten these pictures? Had Ellen or Iris sent them to her to assuage their own guilt?

That my aunts had been lying to me yet again was obvious. My mother was still very much in this world, and they had spent the last twenty-one years reminding me to take flowers to her grave. My mother had told me point-blank that Iris and Ellen had colluded with each other and Ginny to keep the truth from Maisie and me, but I knew these women, and my heart would not let me believe that they had been anything other than Ginny's victims. The truth I needed to uncover was why they'd decided to lie to me. There had to be a reason—a good, strong, forgivable one—and once I got to the bottom of it, I would find a way to bring my family back together. We couldn't recapture the lost years, but we could recover and build a future. Together we would deal with the families. Together we would bring Maisie home.

I turned toward the house, but stopped dead in my tracks as another thought hit me. Had I been the only one kept in the dark? Up until a few months ago, they'd thought me powerless. Had Maisie known the truth this entire time?

A year ago, even a few months ago, I would have never entertained my mother's accusations. I would have rushed home and confessed everything to Iris in a single breath. But that was before I learned that my aunts had hidden the fact that Ellen's late husband, Erik, was my father; before Iris's husband, Connor, left me to burn in Ginny's house; and before my own beloved sister had turned me over to the hands of a demon. Now that the line had selected me as an anchor, I was on everyone's radar. I felt it in my bones that there were any number of witches, including members of my own extended family, who would jump at any excuse to remove me as anchor. I would keep my promise to my mother. I would remain silent about her return to Savannah. But I would do so only until I could get a better grasp on the slippery truth.

It took every bit of my self-control not to burst into the house screaming, demanding answers. I slipped the locket beneath my shirt and took a deep breath. I prayed that I would have the strength and the good sense to keep my fool mouth closed. My hand trembled as it opened the door leading into the kitchen.

"You're late," Emmet said without even turning to look at me. He sat at the table, staring intently at an apple that hung suspended in midair. The apple spun slowly, its peel coming off in one thin, clean strand.

"Yeah, sorry. Got distracted," I replied. I circled around and took the seat opposite him, unable to resist the pull of his gravity. Emmet was so dark, so intense. So lost. A mere few months ago, the man sitting before me had been nothing more than dirt in our driveway. As a golem, he had been well groomed, perhaps overly groomed, certainly overly self-confident. After a few months as a man, he had taken on a more feral look. The shadow on his cheeks pointed well past five o'clock, and his once closely cropped black hair had grown much longer, falling in thick, careless curls. He pushed them back from his forehead, and I noticed from the sorry state of his hands that he had picked up the habit of biting his fingernails.

"You are easily distracted," he said, and the apple stopped spinning and flew directly at my face. I held up my hand to repel it, and in a mere blink, it combusted and fell as ashes. Emmet looked at me, unimpressed. "Now was that really necessary? You used too much force to dispel such a tiny threat."

"Don't start," I said. "I am so not in the mood." His words cut too close. The smoke issuing from the apple's powdery remains reminded me of the scent of the old man's charred flesh.

"You are willful," he said ignoring me. "You are stubborn. You are unfocused. The families have asked me when you will be ready to take over as the line's anchor. I'll have to tell them I don't know. That you haven't given me any time. That you haven't given your magic any time."

I felt my temper flaring, heat rising up all around us. There was a rattling noise from behind me—the sound of the dishes in the cupboard beginning to shake.

"Good. Good," Emmet shouted and pushed away from the table. "You are full of power. Full of emotion. Now let's see you control either one of those things." He stepped up to me, getting right in my face. I clenched my hands, feeling a nearly electric fire build up in them. Cupboard doors opened and slammed shut. A glass fell to the floor and shattered, sending tiny shards into the air where they hung like deadly little prisms. I grew terrified of my own rage. I was acting out magically in a way I'd never allowed myself to behave before my magic had been returned to me.

Emmet reached forward and grabbed my wrists. He towered over me. His black eyes burned into me with a look of . . . what? Anger? He leaned in close.

"What's going on here?" Peter's voice shot into the room. I turned to see him at the doorway, and the shards of glass fell to the floor like so many raindrops. The dishes stopped rattling. Quiet returned.

Emmet released my wrists and spoke. "We are training. You should not be here."

Peter stomped into the room and put a possessive hand on my shoulder. "Don't tell me where I should and should not be, and don't tell me that what I saw going on in here was 'training.' I know Mercy, and I know when she is pissed. I don't need to see the kitchen getting shaken apart to know."

"She has to learn how to control her magic. To do that she has to learn to control her passions."

"She's pregnant. She doesn't need this kind of stress placed on her."

"She," I said, "is sitting right here. And she can speak for herself," I said to Peter, but caressed his arm while saying it. I loved the way he wanted to protect me, even in the face of something that I myself hadn't yet been able to comprehend or control. Deep down, I knew Emmet was right. I had to learn to control the energy flowing through me. The hole in the chest of the poor old man I'd been trying to help proved that well enough. I wished I could talk to Emmet about what had happened, but his disapproval would rain down on me. I wished I could share what had happened with Peter, but he would just worry for me.

"All the same," Peter said, "I'm getting you out of here." He pulled my chair back and lifted me to my feet.

"We aren't done. We haven't even really started," Emmet said. He crossed his arms and leaned casually against the refrigerator. He appeared thoroughly composed. Infuriatingly relaxed.

"Oh, you are done." Peter guided me toward the door. As he ushered me over the threshold, I turned back and caught a glimpse of Emmet. If I didn't know it was impossible, I would have sworn I registered a look of jealousy.

"I'm going to have to deal with him sooner or later," I said.

"But not now. I don't know what was going on in there, but I don't want you to spend any more time with that guy. It's not good for you or the baby."

"The families want him to work with me. Teach me how to use my magic. How else will I ever be able to take over as the line's anchor?"

"I don't give a damn what the families want, Mercy." He stopped walking and turned me toward him. "I care about our family. You and the baby and me. That's all I care about."

"Me too," I said, and then leaned forward to kiss him. His eyes lit up, green and blue and warm and loving. "But I need to learn how to control this magic inside me. You saw me in there. I need to step up and fulfill my duty. The line wanted me. It chose me. I know it sounds crazy, but it believes in me, and there haven't been many people in my life who do."

"I've always believed in you. Magic. No magic. I've always believed in you, and I always will."

"I know. I know that," I said.

"Good." He paused. "Listen, I am aware this isn't the best time to bring this up, but I came over this morning for a reason." He hesitated, trying to find the right words.

"Go ahead. Spit it out."

He nodded once. "My boss found out about the moonlighting I've been doing on the weekends, and he told me I had to make a choice. And I have. I've decided to leave my job and work full-time on my own company. I want to build a future for us, Mercy, create a legacy for Colin. I don't want to be somebody else's lackey anymore."

"That's great." I would have felt better about the decision if he'd discussed it with me first, but I would have encouraged him to do just that if he *had* talked to me about it.

"Well, hold on. There's a bit more." He took a few steps away from me and leaned against his truck. "I can handle small stuff by myself, but I'm not set up for the type of work I need to bring in. And I don't have the money to go out and buy equipment and hire folk on my own."

"That isn't a problem. Like I told you, I have plenty of money now that I get access to the family funds." I had been astounded by the size of the monthly checks. When the first one had arrived, I'd assumed it constituted payment for the full year. I had grown up without ever realizing how wealthy my family was. Maybe that was a good thing.

"No," Peter said, pointing his index finger at me. "I've told you how I feel about taking money from you. Please understand, I need your faith and support, but I need to be able to stand on my own two feet."

"Okay. I understand. At least I think I do." I couldn't help but smile.

A look of relief flooded his face, but then his brows knit back together. "I've found a partner. Someone who can back me financially. More importantly, he has a project, a big one, he wants completed. Immediately."

His hesitancy waved a red flag. *This* was why he had cut me out of the decision process. "And who is this 'someone'?"

"Tucker," he said as my mouth fell open. "Tucker Perry."

"You have got to be kidding me," I said, spinning around, about ready to storm back into the house until I realized Emmet would still be in there waiting for me and was probably enjoying every minute of this display. "That man is harder to shake off than a deep woods tick," I said, nearly causing a smile to form on Peter's lips. I flashed him a look that put that expression to bed.

Tucker was my Aunt Ellen's on-again, off-again boyfriend. Right now it was off, and I prayed to my maker that it would stay that way. Too suave, too sure of himself. Along with being a lawyer and a real estate developer, Tucker was a professional seducer. He had bedded a good percentage of Savannah's female population and a respectable number of the men as well. Once he'd even hit on my fiancé and me, prompting Ellen to threaten to turn him into a capon if he didn't leave us be. Tucker was a predator, a smooth and oily snake. It was fair to say I wasn't overly fond of him. The thought that Peter would take him on as partner fell beyond my ability to comprehend.

"No, listen," Peter said, reaching out for me. "It's not as crazy as it sounds. There aren't many people building around here these days, especially not people who are willing to take a chance on the new guy. Tucker may be a jerk, but he has money, and he has projects. Please support me in this. Please."

The thought of Emmet watching us made me capitulate more quickly than I probably would have otherwise. "All right. I will tentatively support this. But I am not convinced it's a good idea. For now, just get me out of here." I went to the truck and let him open the door.

"Where to?"

"It doesn't matter. Anywhere but here."

FOUR

"You said 'anywhere,'" Peter said as he turned off the truck's ignition. "Besides, Mom has been dying to see you." I looked up at the Irish flag that jutted proudly out toward the river. It stood as Magh Meall's sole sign, but that didn't matter. The tavern's honeyed dark-wheat microbrew and the small stage where local talent performed made Peter's parents' bar popular with both tourists and the local crowd. During the tourist season, the fire marshal himself would often pass out traveler cups to help ensure that the maximum-capacity law was being honored.

I was still in a mood over the whole Tucker bombshell, not to mention everything that had come before it. Compared to the rest of my morning, Peter's association with Tucker was nothing more than a minor irritation. Tucker knew how to make money, and I was sure he wanted his private parts to remain exactly where they were. I wasn't pleased, but it probably wouldn't be a total disaster in the end. I felt my shoulders relaxing. "Fine," I said. "But your mama had better not spend the entire visit talking to my stomach like she did last time."

Peter was fool enough to laugh, but he thought better of it and held up his hands, palms facing forward. "I'm sorry," he said, leaning in cautiously to kiss me. "I talked to her about that. She is just so thrilled about the baby."

"Well, in about five months she can spend all day making baby talk to Colin, but until then . . ."

"Gotcha." Peter hopped out of the truck and came around to open my door and help me down, an unnecessary but still appreciated gesture. He closed my door for me and took my arm.

"The only reason you're being such a gentleman is because you're afraid your mother is watching."

"Damned straight," he said, patting my arm as he led me to the tavern's door. I laughed in spite of myself. I went up on my toes and kissed him.

No sooner had we stepped over the threshold than his mother descended upon us. "Mercy! My beautiful girl! It's so good to see you." She forced herself to look me directly in the eyes rather than immediately going for my midsection.

"Oh, go ahead," I said, and she rushed forward and placed both hands over my stomach.

"And you too, my little Colin. Grandma loves you, little one."

"Okay, Mom. That's enough," Peter said. His eyes glowed with happiness, and my heart leapt a little at the sight. I did love him. And I loved the child I was carrying.

"You take a seat," she said to me. "And you take a hike," she said, addressing Peter. "I need a little 'girls only' time with your intended here."

Peter looked at me, the question about whether he should leave written across his face like a billboard. "It's okay," I said.

"You take it easy," Peter said to his mom.

"Go on, get out of here," she responded. Her tone was playful, but the command behind it was clear.

"I'll be back in an hour," he reassured me, and headed out the door.

Mrs. Tierney followed him, locking the door behind him. "Make sure we have a little privacy," she said. "I'll fetch us some tea."

I didn't really want tea, but I figured the cup would give me something to do with my hands. I dearly loved Peter's mother. I had known her practically forever, but she still made me a bit nervous. She had very clear ideas about what was proper and what was improper, and she enforced those ideas with an iron fist. Maybe she had developed the trait from dealing with so many drunk patrons over the years, but I always found it a bit disconcerting. "Thank you," I responded.

She returned in a few minutes with a pot of tea and two heavy mugs. The smell of mint turned my stomach a little, but I decided not to say anything. She too remained silent as she poured, but her eyes stayed fixed on me. She pushed a mug my way, and I clutched at it, grateful for the comfort of the warmth in my hands.

After a few moments, she took a sip and then placed her cup back on the table. "So, my girl. There have been many changes in your life recently." Boy did she ever have that one right. I said nothing, just bobbed my head once in agreement. "Any word from your sister? How is she enjoying California?"

We had spun a fiction around my sister's disappearance. According to the story, after breaking up with Jackson, Maisie had decided to see what life was like on the other coast. Even Peter didn't know the truth. I reflected on the family confab that Iris, Ellen, Oliver, and I had held. We'd agreed to keep Peter innocent of the truth for his own protection. I wondered if they might have even conducted a similar meeting some twenty years ago, pledging to protect *me* from the truth that my mother was still alive.

"She's fine," I responded. "Trying to decide whether she wants to settle near San Francisco or maybe down by Los Angeles."

"Well, it's a little odd that we finally get your uncle back from California only to turn around and lose your sister to the same state."

"Savannah's city charter only allows so many Taylors at a time," I joked.

Her lips turned up in a near smile. "Well, you aren't going to be a Taylor much longer, are you? You're going to be one of us. A Tierney."

I squirmed a little. Aunt Iris and Peter's mom had been openly colluding to pressure me and Peter to marry. They wanted the baby to be born into a married family, but the thought of organizing a wedding on top of everything else was overwhelming. "Mrs. Tierney . . ." I started.

"You don't have to call me Mrs. Tierney anymore. You're a full-grown woman, not a twelve-year-old girl. You don't have to call me 'Mom,' but I do wish you would call me by my given name." My own mother's face rose to mind as she said the word *Mom*. Would she be there for the birth of my son? I ached to see her again. I felt certain that if I could just convince her to come home and meet with my aunts, we'd be able to sort things out. Get to the bottom of whatever Ginny had done to trick or coerce them into going along with her twisted scheme.

I pushed the thoughts of my mother aside and focused on the current awkward moment. "All right, Claire," I said, tentatively trying the name out. It felt odd, but I committed myself to it.

"There, that wasn't so hard, was it?"

"No, it's just that I . . ."

"It's just that you don't want your future mother-in-law sticking her nose into your wedding plans. I get it. Don't worry. I

don't care where you hold the wedding. I don't care who offici-
ates. I don't care about the dress, the flowers, or the cake. I only
care that it happens soon. Your pregnancy will start to show
before long."

"I don't see why that should matter."

"Well, for the photos," she said, as if she were explaining the
obvious. "It may not matter to you. It may not matter to Peter.
But in a few years it may matter to little Colin." I said nothing, but
she read my reaction. "You do want to marry my son, don't you?"

"Of course I do." I hesitated. "But I feel a bit out of control
of my own life right now. I wish I could slow things down. Take
things more at my own pace."

"Sorry, dear, but welcome to the world of being a parent.
Your time no longer belongs to you. I won't push you, though.
At least for another week or two," she said and winked at me.

I took a sip of my tea and then regretted it. The smell was
what bothered me more than the taste. I fought a surge of nausea. Mrs. Tierney, Claire, reached out and pulled the cup away.
"It's all right. When I was pregnant I couldn't abide cinnamon."
She took the cups and moved them over to the bar, returning to
her seat with a much more serious look. "The baby. It's healthy,
right? Nothing unusual?"

"No, the doctor says everything looks really good," I said in
the most reassuring tone I could muster.

"I don't care what the doctor thinks. What does Ellen have
to say?"

I took her hand. "Ellen says the baby is fine. She swears that
she can hear him singing."

I thought this tidbit would entertain her, but her brow furrowed. "Takes after his father, he does," she said. "Well, good. So
tell me then," she said, changing gears, "this tall fellow who has

been staying with your family of late. The dark one who glowers all the time."

"Emmet?" I asked, even though I knew full well that he was the only one who could possibly fit that description.

"Yes, Emmet. Is he a relative?"

"No," I replied. "He's more of a friend of the family." I felt good about the level of honesty I could bring to that answer.

"So you've known him for a while then."

"Only a few months, actually," I said. "What about him?"

"It's only that he's been hanging around the tavern a lot lately. He spends his time nursing drinks and asking a lot of questions about our family—Colin, Peter, and me, that is. How did Colin and I meet? How long were we married when Peter was born?" She paused. "Are there any other oversized redheads in the family? That one almost earned him a sock in the eye."

"He offended Colin?"

"No, he offended me. Even if he wasn't implying anything by it, he still asked a whole lot more questions than a person might consider polite."

"He's a bit lacking in social skills, but he's harmless."

"I don't care. I don't like it, and I don't like him." Her eyes glowed with anger.

"I'll talk to him about it, tell him—"

"No. I'm being silly," she backtracked suddenly, waving a hand. "Don't mention it to him."

The door shook as someone tried the handle. "We're closed. Come back at five," she called out without budging from her chair. An insistent, authoritative knock sounded on the door.

Another knock came, this time much louder, and uniformed police officers appeared around the corner at the window. My heart rose in my throat as Claire and I exchanged a glance. Claire was a slight woman, but she pushed herself up from the table as if all the gravity in the world had dropped down on her. She struggled with the lock and then flung the door open wide. Detective Cook stood there, haloed by the sunlight that was pouring in around him.

"Mrs. Tierney," he began, "is your husband here? I'd like to talk to the two of you."

"Peter," I said, jumping up and rushing to the door. "Is Peter all right?"

"Hello, Miss Taylor," he said, obviously not thrilled to find me there. "Don't worry. This has nothing to do with Peter."

Claire let herself breathe. "Come in, officer."

Cook stepped into the room, followed by the same uniformed officers who had been peering through the window. "Your husband?" he asked.

"Colin isn't here right now. He's disputing a bill with a distributor. He'll be back before we open for the night. What is this about?" Cook looked over at me, and Claire surmised his thoughts. "It's fine. She's family."

I realized that he viewed me as every bit as much of a bother, an inconvenience, as I saw him. I felt a bit slighted, even though I had no right to. Adam looked at me, curious about how I'd managed to make the leap from a *kind of, sort of girlfriend* to part of the Tierney clan. We hadn't made the pregnancy public knowledge, and as yet there were no official wedding plans to relay.

"All right." He pulled an old Polaroid out of his coat pocket. The picture had been wrapped in a clear evidence bag. "Do you recognize this picture?"

Claire took the bag into her hands and focused on its contents. Her legs collapsed out from under her as she fell heavily into a chair. I took the one next to her and reached out without asking permission and snatched it from her hand. The plastic somewhat obscured the picture, but the image was instantly recognizable. It was a photo of Peter's father, Colin, and Claire holding a baby. It had to be Peter, but the child looked so scrawny and sickly I found it hard to accept that it could be. I focused on the background and realized that the photo had been taken in the very room where we sat.

Adam reached over and took the picture from me. "Mrs. Tierney?"

"Yes," she said, regaining her composure. "Obviously. I don't know who might have taken it, but it's from when we first brought the baby—I mean, Peter—home. Where did you find it?"

"Are any family or friends visiting you right now?"

"No. No one," she said, but then repeated, "Where did you find this picture?"

"We got a call this morning reporting that the body of an elderly man was found lying by the side of the road, just off Ogeechee. There was no form of identification on him, but we found this in his pocket. In light of certain unusual circumstances, we have to treat his death as suspicious."

I felt myself blanching. My eyes were drawn to Claire, who had turned equally white.

"I hate to do this, but I need to ask you to come with me. See if you can identify the body."

"Yes, of course," Claire muttered. "I'll call Colin. Tell him to meet us."

"I would appreciate that, ma'am."

As she stepped away from the table, moving over to the phone by the bar, Cook looked me deeply in the eye. "Do you know anything about this?"

"Of course not," I snapped at him. Too quick. Too defensive. I shook my head. "I have no idea what's going on."

The biblical adage "Be sure your sin will find you out" came to mind. Guilt and regret caused a trickle of sweat to roll down my spine.

Adam nodded his head, as if he accepted my words, but I knew he didn't. He forced his body into a more relaxed stance, and reached into his pocket for his omnipresent little black notepad. I'd witnessed this behavior before when he had come to question me about Ginny's murder. He used the notepad as a prop, drawing a witness's attention to it, leading him or her to believe that it contained a list of indisputable facts that pointed to that witness as the prime suspect in the crime being investigated. The pad could be considered an anachronism, but it was an effective tool all the same.

Claire hung up the phone, and Adam slid the pad into his pocket, his attention returning to her. Still, Adam had excellent instincts, and he was nothing if not tenacious. He'd circle back to me. I knew that much for sure.

"He's on his way," she said to Cook. "Mercy, will you stay here and help Peter open up if we don't return in time?"

"Of course," I said.

Claire leaned in to kiss my cheek as she passed me. "There's a good girl," she said. "Officers?"

The four of them left, letting the door bang shut behind them. I felt a sudden wave of panic rush through me, and I forced the door back open, nearly stumbling outside. The fresh air embraced me like a welcoming friend, but then a cloud passed over the sun, leaving me chilled and uneasy.

FIVE

I stood outside the tavern's door fighting off panic. I drew my arms up around myself, rubbing away at the goose bumps that prickled along them. Who was the old fellow who'd stumbled across my path? How could he possibly be connected to the Tierneys? Why had I been stupid enough to think I could resuscitate him?

"What's wrong, pretty lady?" a man's voice startled me. Muscle-bound; taller than me, but still short for a man; clean-shaven head. He wore a rebel-flag T-shirt cut into a tank top that revealed a sleeve of tattoos on his right arm. Even though my conscious mind failed to take in the many pieces that came together in the tattoo's intricate design, my subconscious registered a few of the symbols and interpreted them as bad news. His accent, the way he moved, everything about him said "backwoods."

I knew the first instant I laid eyes on him that I didn't like him or his entire gestalt, but I forced a smile. My instincts told me to be civil. Not to challenge him. "I'm fine, thanks. Just had a bit of a morning." His eyes—dark, hard, spaced a little too closely together, and shadowed by his brow—twinkled. He took a step closer. The sun glinted off the handle of a hunting knife, the kind you often heard called a "pig sticker," that he wore strapped to his leg.

A woman, homespun bleach job worn in a braid and makeup spackled over bad skin, stepped up to him and slung her arm around his shoulder. "Looks more like a little bit of morning sickness to me," she said. She turned her chin down and glared at me through narrowed slits. She was marking her territory. This man, she informed me wordlessly, belonged to her. Lord help her, she could have him, but he shrugged off her arm and drew up closer to me.

"Naw, that can't be. She ain't got no ring on her finger. You can tell by looking at her that she ain't the type to spread her legs just to say howdy. Am I right there, boy?"

In my peripheral vision, I noticed movement. Another of their group, this one much younger. High school age? He already stood several inches taller than the leader of the pack. The younger man's build qualified him as an ectomorph—very muscular, yet much leaner than his buddy. He skulked up behind the other two, hovering close enough to imply his complicity, but only just. Filthy jeans, dirty blond hair, angry blue eyes, a crooked smile. He was a good-looking kid, too good-looking to be theirs, and truth be told, a little too *old* to be theirs, even by bayou standards. A brother? Cousin? Cohort? Regardless of how they fit together, he still stood out as the prettiest of the trio. A look of excited expectation shone in those spiteful eyes. I felt my stomach drop when I realized that whatever excitement he expected had something to do with me.

"I should get back inside," I said, feeling behind me for the doorknob.

"Ah, no need to run off so soon," the older man said. "We were hoping to get to know you a bit. Learn a bit about your beautiful city here. Come on over here, Joe, and introduce yourself to the lady."

The kid stepped up and completed a semicircle, blocking my path. The single escape was back through the door to the tavern. "Hello," he said, and I could smell the excitement coming off him. Up close, I could tell he was a little older than my first impression had led me to believe. Sixteen? Eighteen? His eyes lacked any sense of empathy, humanity. He carried an aura that was exactly the right combination of innocence and danger to fascinate a girl who had a taste for crazy. I feared for any girl who'd let herself get caught up in his charm.

"See, that ain't so bad, is it?" the man asked, but I wasn't sure if the question had been aimed at me or at this Joe. "I'm Ryder. Ryder Ludke. This here is Birdy. Say hello, Birdy."

The woman stayed silent until Ryder tilted his head slightly toward her, a promise of uncontrolled violence concentrated in such a slight movement. "Hello," she said, cringing and taking a step to the side.

"Maybe you would like to invite us into your fine establishment and offer us a libation?" The question carried the weight of a command.

"Libation," Joe parroted, and then guffawed. He and Ryder shared a glance that celebrated Ryder's wit. These were train people, modern-day hobos with all of the nasty and none of the romance, I surmised. A race of panhandlers that had taken root in Savannah, taking over and occasionally scaring off the regular folk, the ones who sold palm-frond roses or picked out tunes on instruments. The train people used intimidation rather than souvenirs to liberate spare change from tourists' pockets.

"I'm sorry. I can't. I'm not the owner, and the bar doesn't open until five. We could lose our liquor license."

"Come on. You're free, white, and twenty-one, ain't you?" Ryder asked. "You can do whatever the hell you want."

"And what I want to do is get back inside and get ready for opening."

I found the doorknob and grasped it. The three were standing too close to me. I'd have to move quickly or they'd be able to rush the door. I twisted on the knob and forced my back into the door, but it didn't move. It had locked behind me.

"Here I thought y'all called Savannah the 'Hostess City,'" he said, taking another step closer. Following his lead, the other two constricted the circle. "You ain't being very hospitable. A man could take offense." His hand lowered, and his finger traced around the top of his knife's handle. Twelve and a half seconds ago, this place had been crawling with cops. Now that I could use one, there wasn't a single officer in sight. I wondered if my visitors had been watching for the police to take off before coming this way.

I considered using magic to open the door. But they'd still be able to follow me into the bar unless I moved fast enough to slam the door in their faces. They had ambled another few steps closer as I considered this. I'd be able to reach out and touch them in another step or two. Or they could reach out and touch *me*.

I considered using my best trick—well, truly my only trick—to slide myself out of there, but I figured it would be best to try something a little less overt. The last thing I needed was to piss the families off further with open displays of witchcraft. I pushed back a wave of anger at how the families stripped me of my ability to adequately defend myself. I had to keep a clear head, and anger at people who were not even present would not help with that. I decided to pull something from my Uncle Oliver's bag of tricks. Oliver reigned as the king of magic persuasion, half of which he seemed to back up with plain old self-confidence. "Well, on behalf of the Savannah Visitors Bureau, I apologize, but I do think it is time for y'all to move on." I pulled myself up taller and crossed my arms, trying to look firm but relaxed, like I was the one in charge. Joe and the woman called Birdy took a few steps backward, but Ryder didn't budge, "Go on now," I commanded.

Ryder chuckled and then used the back of his hand to wipe away his smile. "You, little miss, are a right piece of work, ain't you? You're a pretty little thing, but you done and picked yourself up some real bad manners. I'll gladly help you correct 'em."

Normally, two out of three isn't bad, but I had failed to compel this Ryder to take off. I'd have to talk to Oliver about it. Find out where I had gone wrong, but now I had a more pressing matter at hand. I breathed deeply into my diaphragm and envisioned a wall growing between us, not only separating us, but pushing Ryder backward, forcing all three of them to move on. Ryder's tattooed arm reached out toward me, but then quivered and fell to his side.

He gave me a dark look and stepped up with his arms held wide open, bumping his chest against the invisible barrier I had built between us. He was not in the least little bit frightened of my magic. Worse, the look in his eyes told me he was thinking of challenging it, but then he turned away and swaggered back toward the river. Joe followed him, tagging a few steps behind like an enamored puppy. Birdy stood her ground the longest. "I don't like you," she said, giving me one final, hate-filled glare. The feeling was more than mutual, but I didn't think it wise to antagonize her, especially since I had won this battle. I held my tongue.

"Birdy," Ryder commanded, and she scurried to his side.

I watched until they were gone, and then turned my attention back to the lock. I slid a smidge of energy into it, envisioning the force molding to the inner workings of the mechanism and then condensing, hardening. My heart was in my throat as I turned it. I was thrilled when I heard the click—for once, my magic had worked as I'd intended.

I hurried inside, slamming the door behind me and quickly turning the deadbolt. I leaned against the locked door and sucked in a deep breath, trying to calm myself. I nearly jumped on the bar when a bell rang out. The old landline phone, yellow with gray buttons and absolutely no form of caller ID, sounded again. I hesitated, but then answered.

"Hello, sweet girl," Colin said, the clunky receiver faithfully relaying the sadness in his voice. "I'm glad you picked up. I couldn't remember your cell number for the life of me, but this one's been in my head for thirty years."

"Peter isn't here yet, Mr. Tierney."

"Ah, I know that darlin', he's here with his mother. That's why I'm calling. The man who the police found. He was . . . he was family." I grasped the bar to keep from falling flat to the floor. Accident or no, the guilt of what I'd done squeezed my chest like a boa constrictor, pressing the air out of me. "We won't be opening tonight, so you best lock up and head on home."

"Wait, Mr. Tierney. I'll stay. I'd like to be here for you and Claire," I said, even though my head reeled at the thought. I had no idea how I would ever face Peter's parents after what had happened. Somehow I'd have to find a way to own up to it.

"I don't want to hurt you, my girl, but Mother and I need some time for private grieving. We'll be relying on you and my little grandson for comfort soon enough, but tonight, you'll have to leave us be. Mother wants her boy with her, so I wouldn't count on seeing Peter till tomorrow. I should get back to them now."

"Mr. Tierney," I called out before he could disconnect.

"Yes?"

"Who was he?"

"My Uncle Peadar, my father's brother. Here for a surprise visit, I guess. We haven't seen him in decades now, not since Peter was still in diapers, but Claire still felt very fond of the old fellow. Good-bye, Mercy."

"Good—" I began, but he had already hung up.

SIX

I spent a nearly sleepless night and was haunted by nightmares of Peter's great-uncle each time I drifted off. When I woke from the one that ended with a cottonmouth snake hissing out through the hole I'd left in the man's chest, I decided that enough was enough and that I'd rather stay awake to greet the dawn. I found my phone and saw that Peter had texted me at some point while I was wrestling with his relative's zombie in a dream. Peter's messages said that he loved me. That his mom was upset. *Really* upset, considering that they hadn't even seen Uncle Peadar in over twenty years. Maybe because the police thought he might have been murdered? He'd call after he finished the walkthrough with Tucker at the site of the job he was taking on.

First light found me up and heading to Colonial Cemetery, looking for Jilo. She did her magic a bit farther out, at a crossroads hidden off the dead end of Normandy Street, but she handled the money end of her business here in Colonial.

"Well you been busy, ain't ya?" she said as she plodded across the field toward me, using the lawn chair she always carried with her to Colonial as a makeshift walker.

"How did you know?"

"Girl, they a police station right next door to this here boneyard, and Mother may be old, but she ain't deaf. Now you tell her what you been up to."

"A man showed up after you left the powder magazine," I confessed, relieved to share with someone. Maybe it was unfair, maybe not, but I couldn't help resenting my mother for her silence. She had to know I needed her. I touched the chain of her locket and pushed the thought away. "The poor man was sick," I continued, trying to focus on the story I *could* share with Jilo. "Confused. I think he might have had Alzheimer's or something."

"Mm-hmm," she prompted me.

"I was talking to him, trying to figure out where he belonged, when he keeled over. He wasn't breathing. He had no pulse . . ."

"And you thought you would jolt him back to life with a wee touch of magic?"

I nodded.

"And ended up burning a hole clean through the old buzzard," she said, and then started laughing, that unnerving wheezing of hers that always ended up sounding like a death rattle. She winded herself, and leaned most of her weight against the folded chair while she wheezed. I reached out toward her, but she held up her hand. "Don't you go helpin' Jilo none. She done seen what yo' kind of help leads to, and she ain't ready to stand outside them pearly gates just yet."

She burst into another bout of laughter, but managed to gain control of herself again when she took note of the tears that were forming in my eyes. "Shoot. You stop worryin', girl. You didn't do nothin' wrong. Ain't got a thing to feel bad about. That old fella of yours, he already dead when you put your hands to him." Jilo did her best to offer me absolution, but it didn't stick.

"How could you know that? You weren't there."

"Did he have a pulse? Was he breathing?"

"No. He had turned blue."

44

"Well, there you go then. A blue cracker is a dead cracker." A smile of encouragement quivered on her lips. She reached out and wiped at my tears with her calloused fingers. "Hell, most folk would have never even stopped and tried to help him anyway. You a good girl. You done all you could for him," she said, but then gave me the stink eye. "They somethin' you ain't tellin' Jilo, though, ain't they. Get on with it, girl. You tell Mother."

She flipped the lawn chair open and eased her way into it. Sometimes she seemed like such a force of nature, but lately I could tell she was growing frailer. I sat down at her feet, and she pulled my head over to her knee, running her gnarled fingers through my hair. I don't know exactly when it had happened, but over the past few weeks, I'd grown quite attached to the old woman of the crossroads, and I knew that whether she liked it or not, she had come to feel the same way about me.

The secret Jilo sensed weighing on me was the truth about my mother. I wanted so desperately to tell someone. To try to get a bead on what had happened. Jilo knew my family's history better than anyone else. I felt certain she could help me understand the circumstances, but I wouldn't betray my mother —at least not yet. She had made me promise to tell no one, and that definitely included Jilo. Besides, I could tell that the help Jilo was giving me in my attempts to find Maisie was taxing her. So until I knew the lay of the land, I couldn't risk bringing her in on something that might just be more than she could handle. I offered up a lesser truth. "The man. When the police found him, he had a picture of Peter and his parents on him. Turns out he was some long-lost great-uncle. Peadar was his name. I guess they named Peter after him. Sort of, anyway. The Tierneys had no idea he was even in town."

Jilo cackled softly. "Well, my girl, if that true, then you in for a good surprise." I looked up at her. "That long-lost uncle you done barbequed? That picture not the only thing they found on him."

"What do you mean?"

"Police ain't tellin' nobody yet, but that old man, he had a damn fortune in jewels and coins sewed up in the linin' of his coat. Unless they prove it stolen, Jilo imagine it end up comin' to yo' brand new family, at least what the gov'ment don' see fit to keep fo' theyself, that is. The Tierneys, they probably don't even know 'bout it yet. You know how the police are. They always tryin' to figure out some motive, never figurin' that they might be some well-meanin' girl at the bottom of they troubles." I tried to glare at her, but she smiled at me warmly. When her eyes looked away from me and up over my shoulder, any kindness faded to concrete.

"Two of my favorite ladies." A man's voice came from behind me. I turned quickly to see that Tucker Perry had managed to sneak up on us. Jilo's hand gave me a gentle but firm push away.

"You best have the rest of my money to go with those sweet words, Perry," Jilo's teeth ground together as she spoke. She forced herself up out of her chair and strode toward Tucker, poking him in his chest with her forefinger. She had turned angry in a split second—angry at having been caught in a tender moment, angry at having been seen as anything other than the dark lady of the crossroads.

"You've been working spells for him?" I asked in disbelief.

"His money as green as anybody else's," she spat over her shoulder at me.

"Oh, Mother and I go a long way back, don't we?" Tucker asked, stepping around Jilo and coming closer to me. I struggled to stand, and he offered me his hand. I refused, and worked my way up on my own. My center of gravity had changed, and getting around had become a little harder than it normally was. All the same, there was no way I'd let that man taint me with his touch.

Tucker acted as if he hadn't noticed my refusal. "And now, the two of us have a long and mutually beneficial arrangement to

46

look forward to as well." I said nothing. I stared at him blankly, determined not to give him any satisfaction. "Thanks to your fiancé," he continued. "I am sure we will have many opportunities to meet up," he said and winked at me. "You sure are looking good, Mercy. I like you with a few curves." I was just about to lay into him but then he turned back to Jilo. He pulled out an envelope stuffed fat with bills and held it out to her.

Jilo snatched it from him. "Pleasure doin' business with you, Perry. Now get the hell out of here."

He smiled widely at the two of us. "Yes, a pleasure as always, Mother." He took his time making an exit, stopping once to examine one of the few remaining headstones.

"They say this cemetery full, but I'd gladly help free up a spot fo' that one," Jilo said, her expression as sunny as ever I'd seen it. Something about imagining the death of those who annoyed her brought out her best qualities.

"Why are you doing any kind of business for him anyway?"

"Like I done say, his money good even if he worthless hisself."

"But *what*," I emphasized the word, "are you doing for him?"

"Don't you pay that no nevermind. Ain't nothin' to do with you."

I kept my eyes glued on Tucker as he meandered out of the cemetery. "I don't like it. I don't like that you're doing spells for him. I don't like that Peter's doing business with him. Don't pretend you didn't already know *that*," I said, pointing at her.

"Jilo ain't pretending nothing," she said, "so you better get that there finger out of her face."

"I'd hoped to have seen the last of him when Ellen cut him out of her life."

Jilo looked at me, her expression inscrutable. "So you think Ellen has kicked him out of her bed?"

"Yes, she's done with him," I replied.

"Well they is done, and then they is done," Jilo said. "And you can take what you like and don't like and put it in yo' hope chest, 'cause Jilo, she don't care. She do business with who the hell ever she like." Right on cue, Tucker circled by in his convertible, honking his horn and waving. Ellen sat by his side. She raised a hand too, but her greeting was halfhearted at best. She lowered her head and turned toward Tucker, probably reading him the riot act. She hadn't wanted me to know she was spending time with him. Jilo let out one more cackle. "Now ain't you sorry you made Jilo promise not to kill anyone?"

SEVEN

"Ellen is out with Tucker," I said, suddenly feeling as if I were tattling on her. I stood in the doorway of our library, remembering a moment from childhood when I had complained to Iris about my sister.

"Yes, I know," Iris said, looking up from the mahogany writing table where my grandfather's old journals and files were spread out before her. She no longer wore her long blonde hair in a chignon as she had while her husband, Connor, was alive. Now it hung loose, falling just below her shoulders. She wore very little makeup, which she didn't need, and had on black yoga pants and a pink hoodie—my pink hoodie, I realized. "I had hoped that she would make a clean break with him," she said, "but there's not much I can do about it. God knows I don't have much room to criticize her taste in men." Iris had been putting her best foot forward, but she still mourned her husband, or at least the Connor she had thought she knew. There hadn't been enough time for either of us to process the fact that he'd plotted to kill me. I wasn't sure there was enough time in creation for me to process it. Iris mourned a double death: Connor's physical demise and the loss of the false image of him she'd held. Still, unlike

49

Ellen, who clung to her married name, "Weber," Iris had wasted no time dropping "Flynn" and returning to her maiden name.

I went to her and wrapped my arm around her shoulder. "What are you doing?"

She sighed. "I'm digging through your granddad's notes, trying to see what he can tell us about the situation at Old Candler." My first experience with having the power of a true witch, when I had been allowed to borrow Uncle Oliver's magic, had led me to the old hospital. That was when I had become aware of the spirits that were trapped there by my grandfather's spell. I guess Granddad counted them as collateral damage in his war to protect the children of Savannah.

After the old hospital closed, children began disappearing in the night. My grandfather tracked the source of these disappearances down to Old Candler, and after weaving a protective barrier around the building, sort of a miniaturized model of the line itself, he'd walked away, not realizing that he had built a pressure cooker with no safety valve. Jilo had alerted me to the need to open a tiny hole in the spell, as too much pressure had built up inside the place. She had intended to tap into it, channeling the energy that escaped to replace her then-waning power.

Jilo had agreed to abandon this plan after I gave her enough of my own power to keep her going for another decade or so. If the old hospital had remained as empty and unused as it had been for decades, my family and I would have had plenty of time to work out the logistics of how to free the human spirits trapped there without letting loose whatever dark forces had been responsible for taking the children. The building's sudden and expedited transformation into a law school was forcing our hand and making us act more quickly than we would have liked.

"Found anything?"

"As a matter of fact I have, but I keep misplacing things just as quickly as I find them. I swear, either these papers have a mind of their own, or I am going soft in the head." Iris glanced down at a stack of files; her head tilted to the side and she pursed her lips. She appeared surprised by what she saw there, but then casually moved the files off to the side and began riffling thoughtfully through the other papers neatly displayed on the desk's surface. A foreign word—*Lebensborn*—had been written on the top file of the stack she'd pushed aside. I didn't speak a word of German, but I recognized it. *Lebensborn* was the Nazi breeding program that had aimed to increase the birthrate of their favorite flavor of Aryan. When they hadn't been able to breed blue-eyed babies quickly enough to feed the Nazi machine, they'd started kidnapping them from neighboring countries.

I reached for the file. "Why would Granddad have a file on *Lebensborn*?"

"He had a taste for what he considered the *oddities* of history. You might enjoy looking through his papers when you have time." She took the file from my hand and put it back where it had been on the stack. "Just please keep them in order if you do."

"Did he ever mention Mama in his writings?" I watched her closely for a reaction, but rather than betraying any kind of shock, her face relaxed upon hearing my question.

"Of course he did. He mentions all of us, but his journals aren't like personal diaries. They're filled with history, ponderings, and his theories about magical processes. All the same, his personal life crept into his writings from time to time. Is there something in particular you were wondering about?"

"No. Just curious."

She looked at me, and her lips pinched together, causing lines to form around them. If she knew my mother was alive, her face did not betray her. I saw only a well-worn sorrow there. "Here," she said, handing me a journal bound in marbleized paper. "This is where he wrote about what he found at Old Candler."

My eyes scanned down the page, taking in bits and pieces of the meticulous script that covered it. "Jilo was wrong in one sense," Iris said. "She assumed that a collection of minor demons, perhaps even common boo hags, were behind the unpleasantness." Iris seemed to remember my own *unpleasant* encounter with a "common" boo hag as soon as the words slipped off her tongue, but it was too late to swallow them. She took the tack of moving on quickly. "But it wasn't. It was one single entity. A demon called Barron."

"So this Barron is what Granddad trapped at Candler?"

"It's all here," Iris said, taking the journal from me and flipping a few pages, "in your grandfather's journal. He did a lot of research into this beast before he confronted it. The demon we're dealing with has quite a pedigree. He was brought to the New World by a slave trader—well, actually, *in* a slave trader. That's one superstition with a grain of truth to it. Demons can't cross running water on their own."

"Good to know," I said, meaning it sincerely. "But how did he—it—manage to get into our world in the first place? Isn't the line supposed to protect us from creatures like him?"

"He was summoned. The line is like a net in more ways than one," Iris continued. "It protects us from the most intense evil. But if a practitioner of magic—and note that I am not saying a witch—is powerful and determined enough, he can pry open a hole big enough to bring a smaller, less powerful force over the border. Barron was smuggled into our world by Gilles de Rais, an associate of Joan of Arc."

I can describe what I knew about de Rais in a string of words: aristocrat, war hero, squanderer of one of the greatest financial fortunes of his era, pedophile, and serial killer. I shuddered at the thought of the scores of children he had slaughtered to feed his twisted desires; it was no shock that he'd seek to align himself with a demon. "If Barron was small enough to slip past the line, he should be easy to handle, though, no?"

"Please remember, when we speak of this demon as being *small*, it doesn't mean that he'll be easily managed or dispatched. It means that while he's a murderer and defiler, he isn't necessarily capable of ending the world as we know it. Barron's power has grown during his time in our world. Our goal is to return him to where he originated, but we will not find it easy to send him anywhere he doesn't want to go. I'm beginning to see why Dad settled for containment versus expulsion. His research led him to the conclusion that it would require the sacrifice of an innocent to even get Barron to appear for the banishing spell." My hand slid protectively over my stomach. "Precisely," Iris said.

She returned the journal to the table and went to sit in one of the high wingback chairs. "Enough about this demon for now. How are you doing?" Her body language was textbook perfect. She leaned back comfortably, placed her arms on the chair so that her upper body remained open and her shoulders relaxed. She tilted her head slightly to the right and focused on me. Whether her posture was contrived or sincere, she was showing that she was there for me, present, listening, nonjudgmental.

"I'm fine. I'm good."

Iris nodded to acknowledge my reflexive response. "It's only that I sense there's something you might want to share with me. Unburden yourself, perhaps?" My mind jumped first to my mother, and it took all of my self-control not to parrot Iris's words right back at her. I couldn't bring myself to believe that betraying my mother's confidence to my aunt would bring me harm, but it bothered me more than a little that I couldn't completely shake the fear—no matter how small—that my aunts might turn my mother over to the families. Whatever Iris's reason for doing so, be it mendacity on Ginny's part or duress, she had sided against my mother before. I bit my lip. Hard. Then my memory rewound further to the incident with Peadar. Did Iris know about any of it? Or maybe she was just fishing, like she used to do when Maisie and I were young? She'd sense something wasn't quite right, and let on that she knew what the issue was, tricking us into spilling the beans.

I smiled and shook my head. "No, I'm good." I could have, maybe *should* have, told her about Peadar, but I was afraid of where the discussion might lead. I had begun accumulating all these little bits and pieces of my life that I didn't feel safe sharing, and I hated that.

Iris stiffened a little and then stood, returning to her work table. "All right. You'll tell me when you're ready. Until then I'm going to get back to work," she said, waving me from the room, dismissing me from the awkwardness of the situation.

The shade of the library had chilled me, so I decided to head back out into the warm sunshine. I sat for a moment in the garden, but felt the need to get a bit farther away. For the first time since Connor's face had covered the front page of the newspaper, I felt comfortable enough to return to River Street. Most of the people there would be tourists anyway, I reasoned. They wouldn't know me from Eve. I found a bench by the river and watched a freight ship maneuver the dredged side of the waterway until it negotiated its way under the bridge. I accepted a graciously offered sample from one of the candy stores, then headed back up the bank, letting my feet carry me where they would. I found myself wandering without any real destination, just following a tug I felt. I cut through Warren Square and followed down East Julian, the tug growing a tad stronger with each step.

"It's a classic five-four-and-a-door," Oliver's voice called out to me. He sat on the steps of a beautiful yet modest example of Savannah architecture, dressed only in running shorts and shoes. Oliver seemed to defy the passage of time. His youthful appearance caused most people to suspect that he'd hired Dorian Gray's portrait artist. He had the flat-muscled stomach, slim hips, and broad shoulders of a much younger man. He was my uncle, but he could easily pass for my brother. I used to think that he used his magic to create a glamour for himself, making people perceive him without the scuff marks of time. Now my witch sense told me that his power had somehow preserved him, aging him at a much slower rate than the rest of us. "I made an offer on it this morning," he said, running his hand over his new buzz cut. He'd just gotten back a few days earlier from closing up his home in San Francisco, and had his hair cropped close in order to ease his adjustment to Savannah's harsher clime. "I'm pretty sure the sellers will accept," he said, smirking. He read the disapproval on my face. "Oh, come on. I made a fair offer. Didn't use a single smidge of magic." He held up two fingers, making the Boy Scout oath. "Do you like it?"

"Of course I do. I've always loved this place, but why would you want to buy it?"

"Because I'm a grown man, and I need my own space. A space where my big sisters are not constantly sticking their noses. I can't even set something down in my own room without having it up and disappear on me. And you can forget *entertaining*, if you know what I mean." He stood and turned to take the house in. "This place is perfect. I can run my business on street level and live upstairs." He turned to me and raised an eyebrow. "All business on the bottom, and party on the top."

"Oliver," I said, blushing.

He burst out laughing, thrilled to have embarrassed me. "So, tell me," he said, switching gears without warning. "How goes the magic?"

"I don't know. I kind of feel like I am standing in the middle of a hurricane."

"And the Sandman?" It was his nickname for Emmet.

"He's a huge pain. He criticizes and complains constantly, but he never gives me anything I can use."

Oliver just nodded. Then he shifted gears again. "Anything else you'd like to talk about?"

"No," I responded too quickly.

Oliver had always been much more direct than Iris. "Nothing at all?" he prompted. When I didn't respond, he continued. "Nothing like punching a hole through some itinerant's chest?"

The blood drained from my face. "How did you know?"

"How did I know?" he asked and reached out to tousle my hair. "Gingersnap, we all felt the burst of power. Wild, uncontrolled, amazingly strong. It had your pretty little fingerprints all over it. As far as knowing about the 'mysterious' death of the old man, the story was all over the news." He tapped his forehead. "I used my astounding powers of deduction to tie the two together. Iris was hoping you'd open up to her, but I understand she couldn't get a squeak out of you."

"I didn't mean to hurt him . . . I was trying to help." I heard the petulance in my own voice.

"Oh really, so you haven't turned into a serial killer stalking old men?" He grinned at me. "Come on, let's walk." He took my hand and began leading me down East Julian toward Warren Square.

"Where are we heading?"

"Home for us to change and pick up your aunts, and then off to Elizabeth for my official welcome home dinner."

"You know how thrilled I am to have you home for good," I said as he tugged me along. "I just don't know if I feel like going out tonight. I've got nothing to wear. I'm too fat for my nice clothes. Besides, people are still looking at us funny because of what happened to Connor and Ginny. I'm not up for being on public display." And if those objections weren't reason enough, there was also the fact that I'd be more comfortable eating glass than I would, sitting across from him and my aunts without being able to demand the truth about my mother. I couldn't give voice to that, though.

"Well, I hear ya, but you are coming with us tonight for a couple reasons. First of all, you are paying. Second of all, I am back in town." Oliver's return to Savannah had been heralded in the society section of the newspaper, the focus being placed on the success of his public relations firm rather than on any superstitions surrounding the Taylor family as a whole. "That means the Taylors are back."

The reporters at the paper had been trying to do us a favor by shifting the focus off the recent scandals that had rocked our clan. Maybe it wasn't fair that we'd pinned Ginny's attack on Connor, but—as I'd learned firsthand—my uncle had been more than capable of killing. Besides, even in Savannah, we would be hard-pressed to find a grand jury who would believe she had been killed by a boo hag masquerading as a man.

"People can't talk about you behind your back if you are constantly in their faces." Oliver punctuated this thought by calling out to one of the city council people who was passing us on the other side of the street. "We are *back*, Gingersnap. Now, regarding your clothing issue, Ellen has you covered. She has been out all day scouring maternity shops to build you a brand new wardrobe."

"Not all day," I said. "I saw her with Tucker this morning. I think she's seeing him again."

Oliver nodded. "Yeah, she is, but that situation is out of your control, Gingersnap. You might as well surrender to that fact and the fact that you are doing dinner with us, 'cause you are not going to win in either case."

"I saw Detective Cook yesterday," I said, surprised by my own mean streak. I wanted to derail Oliver, make him a little less in control, but it amazed me that my first resort was punching below the belt.

"Yeah, me too," Oliver said, not perturbed in the slightest. "He came by to see us. Adam figured he might as well pay us a visit sooner than later, since the stranger who died mysteriously is from the family you are marrying into." Silently, we cut through the south end of the square and continued west on Congress, swinging south on Habersham.

"I didn't know they were related," I blurted out when the silence got too heavy for me.

"Mmm" was Oliver's only response.

"I didn't . . . not at the time. He showed up from nowhere, and he needed help."

"And you tried to help him, but you aren't in control of your power yet, so you overdid it."

"Yes," I admitted.

"But rather than taking your time to learn how to control your power, you're blowing off Emmet, whose sole purpose at this point is to train you, so that you can hang out with Mother Jilo." I pulled my hand out of his, ready for a fight.

"There's that redheaded temper again," he said with a smile. "What? You're surprised that I have been keeping tabs on you?"

"No, I am not surprised. I am downright pissed."

His laughter made me even angrier. "I know what you're up to. You and that old scarecrow."

I just glared at him.

58

He turned and started walking away. "You aren't going to find Maisie. Not on your own, and not with Jilo's help either."

"Well I can't just forget her," I snapped. "I can't turn my back and walk away like all of you have done."

"I haven't walked away," Oliver turned back, his face flushed red, his fists clenched by his sides. "I have been doing everything in my power to find her."

I crumpled. Maybe my hormones had gotten the best of me. Maybe I just felt relieved to know that Maisie hadn't been completely deserted. Oliver reached out and pulled me into his arms as I started sobbing.

"I could never walk away from Maisie. Any more than I could walk away from you. Neither can your aunts."

"But Iris said—"

"You forget what Iris said," he interrupted me. "And you forget what Ellen said too. There's a difference between what we say around the house, where we suspect the families are listening, and what we say when we are pretty sure they aren't." He paused. "We will find her. We will," he said, tilting up my chin so that my eyes met his.

I was thrilled by this proof that my aunts were willing to put Maisie's welfare before their allegiance to the families. There had to be a reason why they'd separated my mother from us. One that even my mother herself didn't understand.

"But you do need to prepare yourself," Oliver said, perhaps mistaking my relieved reaction for overconfidence, "because we really do not know what shape she'll be in when we do."

"But how will we find her?"

"We'll start with the one thing that should have been obvious to that old root doctor, Jilo. Dirt."

"Dirt?" I knew that Jilo often used soil in her mojo bags, using the energy to draw like to like. Soil from a bank for money, soil from a graveyard for death.

"That's right. The dirt from where Maisie was standing when she disappeared. Why do you think I dug it up? Why do you think I put a sundial out there?" I shook my head. "Have you ever really looked at it?"

"No, not really," I replied. Honestly, I'd avoided the spot altogether.

"Take a good look when we get home. You'll notice something interesting."

"Tell me," I begged him.

He smirked and raised his eyebrows. "The shadow never moves. It isn't a sundial. It's a time lock that's keeping that little patch of earth nice and fresh and as close to how it was the moment Maisie disappeared as possible. Now tell me, do you feel a little more like celebrating?"

I went up on my toes and kissed his forehead. Maybe, just maybe, everything would end up all right after all.

EIGHT

We needed a large space, one where we could work magic without attracting the prying eyes of the other witch families. To my surprise, Jilo volunteered the use of her haint-blue chamber, a magical hall that existed just outside our dimension but could still connect to any place within it. It stood as a testament to Jilo's skill that she, a non-witch, could use borrowed power to build such a thing. For years, she had secretly connected it to a room in our own house, making her capable of coming and going as she pleased. Not that she'd snooped around too much on her own. She'd relied on the boo hag who had camouflaged himself first as Oliver's imaginary friend, Wren, and then as Jackson. Wren had manifested himself in our home for decades, but my family had never caught on to his true nature, assuming he was a *tulpa,* or a thought-form, a thing so well imagined that it had separated itself from the one who'd originally envisioned it.

I hadn't been inside Jilo's haint-blue room since the night I'd found Wren there holding a knife to Jilo's throat. Walls, floor, everything had been colored the same aquamarine that was prized for its efficacy in repelling unfriendly spirits. That being said, if you invited the spirits in, the way Jilo had done when she'd made her pact with the boo hag, the haint blue wouldn't do you much good.

Today, Jilo's cerulean throne was missing, and in its place Oliver had drawn a chalk sigil. The etching consisted of a crisscrossed combination of lines and circles that took up a good portion of the room. Walking around it, I counted ten circles, and I noticed that a pentagram had been inscribed in the centermost one.

"Jilo told him, he oughta use blood, not chalk, but that sweet uncle of yours would have none of it." Jilo's voice echoed around me, although my eyes couldn't get a fix on her yet. To me, the room looked completely empty. Then the air in one corner rippled, like August heat coming up off the highway, and there she stood. "He," she said, punching the word into the air, "say he know what he doin', though, so Jilo need to stand back and let the expert handle things."

"What is it supposed to be?"

"He say it the 'Tree of Life,' but it sure don't look like no tree Jilo ever lay eyes on. We didn't talk much. He just pranced in here, made his scribbles, and took off."

Disdain for my uncle dripped from her every word. That Jilo would ever allow Oliver into her sanctuary, that she and Oliver would or even could work together, amazed me. "Thank you for helping us, Jilo. Thank you for letting us use your . . ." I struggled for a term. Room? No, it wasn't a room. Rooms remained stationary, but this space could coexist with any other point on the earth. Right now it hovered over our own garden. The pentagram at the center of Oliver's drawing overlaid the point where he'd placed the sundial. "Well, just thank you. And thank you for putting up with Oliver's ego too."

Jilo's creased face smoothed as much as her advanced years would allow. "You welcome, girl. All the same, Jilo like to buy you uncle for what he worth and sell him for what he think he worth."

A humming filled the air, and the lines on Oliver's diagram
began to glow. I was focusing so intently on them, I didn't notice
the shimmering air that signaled his arrival. I sensed his presence—a tingling that ran down my spine—and looked up. He
stopped dead in his tracks and took a moment to absorb the
haint-blue chamber. "I failed to say so last time, but this truly is
impressive, Mother."

I was grateful that he'd used the term of respect when
addressing Jilo.

"I don't think many of those born of the power could con-
struct a chamber like this."

He had meant it as a compliment, but to Jilo's ears, it
sounded like another reminder that she had no power of her
own, only borrowed power. "Well that is mighty 'witch' of you,"
Jilo said, her eyes narrowing.

"I meant no offense," Oliver said, offering a courtly bow.

"No need to bend over for Jilo. You ain't her type," the old
woman sniped and then chuckled at her own barb. "Let's get on
with this."

"You have the jar?" I asked, meaning the Ball jar where we'd
been storing the remaining flames.

"'Course," she said, her voice laconic, cold. Her eyes looked
in our direction without focusing on us. Her mouth was set in a
straight line. I hadn't seen this look on her in quite a while. I had
grown unaccustomed to Jilo's reptilian mask. She had allowed
Oliver into her realm, but she would not display any sign of gen-
tleness that he might mistake for weakness. She pulled her red
cooler literally out of thin air, its color a vibrant contrast to this
turquoise world.

Jilo opened it and passed the jar to me. Bright little sparks
flitted about inside, bright little sparks that would hopefully lead
me to my twin. I watched them interact for a moment, changing

colors briefly as they bumped into one another and then flew apart. I offered the jar up to Oliver's outstretched hands.

"So how will this all work?" I asked, as he placed a satchel that I had not previously noticed on the floor next to him.

He knelt and set the jar down next to the satchel, then opened the bag. "Earth," he said as he pulled a brown paper sack out of it. He gave Jilo a taunting look. Dirt played such a great role in her form of magic, but she and I had completely overlooked its power up until now. Jilo grunted to show that he had not managed to impress her.

"That's from beneath the sundial?" I asked.

"Yes," he nodded. "It's the earth where Maisie was standing when she disappeared." He sat the bag down. "Air," he continued, pulling out a perfume atomizer and giving it a quick spray. Maisie's favorite scent rose up around us, summoning an image of her face as clearly as if she'd appeared before me.

"Fire," he said lifting up the Ball jar. "And water." He produced a bottle of scotch and three glasses. "Single malt, twenty-one years old. I'd intended it as Maisie's birthday present." He lined the three glasses up on the ground next to the satchel, filling them without spilling a drop. He held a glass up. "Mother?"

She hesitated, but only for a moment. She took the glass from Oliver's hand. "Thank you," she said, and then knocked it back in one gulp. "Amen," she said, sucking in a deep breath. Oliver saluted her with his own drink and downed it in the same manner.

"I can't," I began. "Baby and all that."

"Oh, this one isn't for you, Gingersnap. We need this for the spell. You've had a chance to check out our workspace here?" he asked, pointing at his chalk sigils.

"Yeah, but I have no idea what it means."

"It's known as the Tree of Life, and much ink has been spilled in trying to describe what it means. Most of that ink died in vain."

"All right, professor, why don't you enlighten us?" Jilo said, but there was no real rancor in her words. It must have been very good scotch.

"No. I don't want to color Mercy's perceptions. I'm going to let her do all the enlightening today." He made quite a show of moving his elemental markers over to the diagram, placing earth and fire at the lower part of the pentagram and air and water at its hands. "And now for 'spirit,' or perhaps, more correctly, 'power.'" He motioned for me to join him, and I went and stood at the head of the star.

"I don't know what I'm supposed to do here. I don't understand any of this." I started to step away, but his hand shot out and held me in place.

"Don't move. Don't tell yourself what you don't know. Now, Mother, would you stand next to Mercy, right outside the pentagram?" Jilo shuffled her way into the diagram, keeping a wary eye on Oliver the entire time. "Thank you," he said as he stepped outside the chalk lines and pulled a metal bowl and a short stick from his satchel. I shook my head and started to speak, but his look stopped me dead. I acquiesced.

"What in the hell are you up to?" Jilo asked.

Oliver responded by hitting the side of the bowl with a part of the stick that was covered with felt. The bowl rang out as clear as a bell. "This," he said, using his palm to stop the ringing, "is a singing bowl."

"Mm-hmm," Jilo hummed, "sho it is."

Oliver sat down cross-legged on the floor, taking the bowl onto his flattened right palm. He closed his eyes and breathed in deeply, straightening his spine, and then he struck the padded portion of the mallet against the bowl a second time. This time, he contracted his hand and curved it, causing the sound to change. He started to rock the bowl gently between the heel of his palm and fingertips. The sound modulated, higher, lower, the ringing actually quite lovely and calming. I relaxed into the sound, which was exactly when Oliver smiled.

"That's right," he said, striking the bowl again. "Listen. Try to detect where the sound begins and ends." He struck the bowl again and again, a rhythm building itself from the repetition. The ringing washed in and out, and I both heard and felt the vibrations. They layered over each other, growing wider and deeper, forming a wave that carried me away. I could no longer sense a beginning. I could no longer perceive an end. Oliver's body began to sway, and before I knew it, I felt my own body weaving in the air that moved to make space for me. My breath slid in and out in time with the reverberations.

I no longer heard anything except the bowl, but Oliver must have somehow communicated with Jilo, because she opened the Ball jar, and the flames floated out to land in my outstretched hand. Then nothing existed but the chiming and the light. They merged together and flowed as one, and the Tree of Life that Oliver had etched in chalk entered into the realm of my awareness again, glowing and singing to me. I realized this sigil was not merely a drawing, not merely a diagram. It represented a two-dimensional expression of something so very vibrant and large that it could not possibly fit into our world. I watched as the lines folded up on themselves, an autonomous origami bending into dimensions far beyond any I had ever imagined or experienced. The circles began to overlap one another, linking together into the most perfect sphere, tinted the same haint blue as Jilo's chamber. I hovered in blackness next to it—*becoming* the blackness. "What is this place?" I said aloud to no one. The globe spun at a maddening pace as images leapt out to me. Epochs and moments and every single possibility that each contained.

The scent of Maisie's perfume hit me again, and my thoughts turned to her. Something was in my left hand. I looked down and realized the burnt earth had somehow been placed there. Liquid flowed over the earth, causing it to filter through my fingers. Thoughts of Maisie consumed me, and the flame in my other hand grew into a sun, the earth into a mountain, the liquid into a sea, her scent blossoming like a flower where the two met beneath the star's warm rays. The rotations of the blue sphere began to slow, and it came into greater focus as it condensed into a single door, painted with bright red panels and black stiles and rails. Something brushed up against my leg, and then wove between them, circling in a figure eight. I looked down, amazed to find Jilo's three-legged cat there with me.

"Schrödinger," it said, and then wound back off into the darkness. I was puzzled at first by the one-word message, but then I understood. Like the cat in Schrödinger's famous thought experiment, Maisie was frozen in a place where the possibilities were limitless. The line had locked her in a state of flux, like some kind of sleeping beauty awaiting rescue. I felt my sister's presence. The line had encased her in a sense of awe, a sense of wonder—she was lost in a sense of ecstasy very much like what I had felt when the power of the line first settled on me. The ringing lessened. The sphere began to dim, and then it unfolded, circle by circle, line by line. I stood again in Jilo's chamber, the Tree of Life now nothing more than a chalk drawing beneath my feet. Oliver was knocking back scotch straight from the bottle.

"You did it," he said, his face flushed. "You opened the Akashic records, kid. The universal knowledge of every event that ever has occurred and ever will occur in all of its squiggly and mutable glory. You got a peek into God's very own diary." Another swig. "I'd always heard the right witch could."

"Wait," I said, trying to clear my head. "You've never done anything like this before?"

"Of course not," he said with a sad smile curling his lips. "The records won't open for just anyone. I've never met a witch for whom they would. I knew it, though. I knew if anyone could access them, it would be you." We had used the rest of Maisie's flames in this experiment. What if it hadn't paid off? I halfway wanted to throttle him, and I more than halfway expected Jilo to beat me to the punch, but when I turned to look at her, what I saw surprised me.

She was trembling, her eyes focused on something far away. I crossed over to her and took her hand. She jerked awake from her reverie, her eyes full of panic and sorrow. "I have seen it now," she said, her voice soft. "I have done wrong. I have worked evil in this world," her words called out to ears other than mine, begging for absolution. "You have to go. You both have to go," she said, waving her arms, shooing us away like noisome children. Haint blue burst like a bubble around us, and in an instant Jilo and her world had gone, leaving Oliver and me standing in our own garden. Oliver was still clutching the bottle of scotch. As he took another swig, the empty Ball jar fell from nowhere and shattered at his feet.

NINE

Iris knelt beside the flowerbed closest to the sundial, making a great show of deadheading flowers that in truth had not even begun to fade and pulling out the sparse weeds that had managed to take root under her vigilant care. The sunhat she wore had belonged to my grandmother, and, combined with the soiled floral-print gardening gloves she had on, it enhanced the more than casual resemblance that old photographs showed she bore to her. My aunt had not been the least surprised by our sudden arrival. "How did it go?" she asked as if we had just returned from a trip to the grocery store. "You can speak freely," she said, pointing to a large crystal, the biggest rose quartz I'd ever laid eyes on, that had been placed in the flowerbed, apparently as decoration. As she spoke, the quartz gave off a faint glow.

"What's that?" I asked, drawing cautiously toward it.

"That, my dear," Oliver said, "is a little charm your Aunt Ellen came up with for us."

"Okay, but what does it do?"

"It keeps the families from being able to listen in on us, or spy on us with remote viewing. She's planting one in every room in the house. She'll join us when she has finished." We had no definitive proof that we were under surveillance, but when the families

69

convened to discuss managing me and my access to power, they seemed very certain of details none of us had discussed with them. Even conversations to which Emmet, whom Oliver openly suspected of being a spy, hadn't been privy. "Before you share anything with one of us that you wouldn't want the families to know, make sure one of the crystals is present and glowing."

"But won't the families know we're blocking them?"

"Of course, Gingersnap, but they sure as hell can't complain about it, now, can they? They have no right to spy on us, and they sure as hell don't have the right to spy on you. You are after all an anchor now, aren't you?"

"Go on, tell me what you have learned," Iris said.

I looked deeply into her eyes. I knew she was capable of lying. She and Ellen had lied to me about my father with a naturalness and ease that worried me. When you're lying to protect someone, there's a certain sense of nobility to it—you know, or think you know, that you're freeing your loved one from the weight of knowing. I myself understood this from having lied to Peter about Maisie. But I felt a little less noble about it with every other falsehood that had followed.

Lying didn't come easily to me, which surprised people given the way I'd made my pocket money up until recently. I used to lead tourists around Savannah on the Liar's Tour, making up lies about famous people and places. The fun of the tour came from the fact that everyone knew I was making the stories up. True deception was a different matter. My aunts had much more talent in that arena. They had lied both actively and through omission about knowing the identity of my father. They claimed to have done this to protect Maisie and me. And together, with or without Ginny's coaching, they had concocted the story of how my mother had died at my birth after begging Ellen to use all her power to save me rather than herself. I deeply wanted to believe that their horrible lie about my mother had come from a place of goodwill. Remembering that my mother had seduced both their husbands, I felt a pang. I wanted to believe that Ginny hadn't left them with a choice, but when my aunts had helped drive my mother away, piety may not have come into play at all.

"She did it," Oliver said, the glint in his eye showing the great pride he took in my accomplishment.

Frankly I had no idea why what I had done was so special. "I did nothing. I just stood there," I said.

"Well, just by standing there, you did something most witches could never dream of doing. The Akashic records don't reveal their secrets to just anyone." Iris removed her gloves and hat. "Where is she?" she asked under her breath.

The smile fell from Oliver's face. "She's nowhere." I knew then he must have seen what I had seen, felt what I had felt.

"I see," Iris responded, her voice catching. "I guess it was too much to hope that she could have survived the blast that took her."

"No," I said, and helped Iris to rise. "She isn't dead . . . not yet, anyway. She's kind of 'on hold.'"

Iris looked at me blankly and then turned to Oliver for clarification. "I guess you could say she's frozen among a number of possible outcomes. It's like the line tucked her safely away until it could figure out what to do with her."

"Is she in pain?" Iris asked.

"No," I said. "I'm sure of that." I wasn't just telling her this to ease her mind. The line hadn't chosen to punish my sister; it had chosen to protect her. "Listen, I know how crazy it sounds"—I hesitated, and the two drew closer to me—"but while I was near Maisie, Jilo's cat appeared. It spoke to me."

Iris and Oliver stared at each other for a moment, their expressions inscrutable. "Okay, I missed that part. What did puss have to say for itself?" Oliver asked.

71

"'Schrödinger.' That's all it said."

"Let's not take the cat thing too literally. The spell took you to a place where language is less effectual than symbol. I think we all get what message the symbol tried to convey to you."

"Yes," I said. "Schrödinger's cat. It's like Oliver said: Maisie's been locked in a state of flux."

"Perhaps you can spell it out for the kids at the back of the class?" Ellen asked as she approached us, carrying a tray filled with glasses and a pitcher of sweet tea. Over her shoulder I could see Emmet staring at us through the kitchen window. "Quietly?" She set the tray down on the table near us and began to pour. We joined her. Ellen glowed with vitality. She sported a fresh bob haircut and had been experimenting with new makeup. Her face was relaxed, her eyes glimmering. My aunt had finally pulled herself together and was beginning to overcome the double tragedy of losing her son and husband on the same day. She had decided to reopen her flower shop, and had even begun scouting around the City Market for an open space. And she had put alcohol behind her, although I noticed that Oliver had surreptitiously whisked away the bottle of scotch he'd been clutching. If only she could put Tucker in her rearview mirror once and for all . . . She beamed at me. The love she held for me was real, even though I was her husband Erik's daughter by her own sister. All the same, as badly as I wanted to believe in her, I knew that sweet Ellen was just as capable of deceit as the rest of my relatives. "So?" she raised her eyebrows and asked, an impatient shake of the head punctuating her request.

"Cat in box. Neither dead nor alive, but in a state somewhere between the two possibilities, until an observer opens the box. The observer plays a role in determining the fate of the cat," Oliver summed it up and took a glass of tea.

"Maybe I am a touch too blonde," Ellen said, "but I don't see what this cat has to do with our Maisie."

I smiled. It felt good to hear her refer to Maisie as *ours*. "Whoever gets to Maisie first will free her from her limbo. Right now she is nowhere. No when. Just a point among possibilities. The observer won't merely free her, he or she will determine from the many possible outcomes what happens next for her."

"But how do we make sure we get to Maisie first? With all this talk of nowhere and no when, for heaven's sake?"

"I don't know. What I saw seemed purely symbolic," I said. "I mean, talking cats and a black-and-red door hanging in thin—"

"Black-and-red door?" Ellen interrupted me, her voice carrying louder than she'd intended. She hushed herself, glancing back toward the kitchen. "What did it look like?"

"It looked like any other regular panel door. It had red panels, but the rest of it was black."

"Why?" Oliver asked. "Does that mean something to you?"

Ellen looked from one of us to the other, finally settling on Oliver. "Yes," she said. "Tillandsia." She lowered her eyes. "Tucker and some of the others recently purchased a large house out in the country to use for gatherings. It's just past Richmond Hill. That's where we were heading when we passed you in Colonial."

I said nothing, but she looked directly at me and started defending herself. "I'm no longer part of Tillandsia. It's only . . ."

"It's only what?" Iris asked, her voice steely.

"It was just a ride. A chance to get out of Savannah for a few blessed minutes, to go somewhere no one's watching me, expecting me to hit the hooch or go whoring." She spat out the words, but then calmed herself. "I'm sorry, but Tucker never judges me. Nor does he hide his whiskey the second I appear," she said with a glare at her brother.

"Okay, fair enough," Oliver said. "It was a platonic, lily-white outing . . . So why do you think this has anything to do with Tillandsia?

"The house. It's huge, badly in need of a lot of repair and renovation. The single thing that's in decent shape is the front door. It
was freshly painted. Red panels set against a black background. It's
hideous. I told Tucker it would have to be the first thing to go, but
he just laughed. He said he kind of liked it and would probably keep
it that way." I tucked away the realization that this new Tillandsia
house was Peter's project until I would have time to process it.

Oliver shook his head. "Could be coincidental."

"It could be," I responded as the truth hit me, "but we all know
it isn't. Maisie and I came into this world as a result of Tillandsia's
'activities.' Tucker himself told me that my mother was the one to
introduce him to Tillandsia. She inducted Uncle Erik"—I still
found myself calling him that—"into the group as well. Didn't
she?"

"Sweetie—" Ellen began.

"Yes," Iris interrupted her. "But not for sex. Emily had a different agenda." Iris turned on her siblings, anticipating that
they'd protest. "The girls are somehow linked to Tillandsia. If we
are ever to get Maisie back, Mercy must know what Emily was
attempting."

"You're right," Oliver said. Ellen nodded her assent, but
pulled her arms around herself. She went and took a seat in the
sunlight, nearly turning her back on the rest of us. Oliver followed her with his eyes, but when he spoke, he was addressing
me. "Your little 'incident' the other day. With the old fellow," he
added, as if there were any chance that accidently burning a
man's heart out wouldn't be the first thing to leap to mind. "It
took a bit of power to deliver that jolt. When you drew that
power, we all felt it. Any witch around here would have. Kind of
like an electrical brownout."

"That means," Iris said, "that whenever you do something
that draws a lot of power off the line, other witches will know

you are up to something. If you want to do something big without setting off a magical blow horn, you have to find another way
of harnessing the energy."

"Okay, how would you do that?" I prompted when the two
fell silent.

"Well, Gingersnap, it depends on the size of the thing you
are attempting."

Iris put her hand on my forearm. "If you can't draw off the
line, you are basically left to resort to your friend Jilo's tactics.
Using sympathetic magic, drawing like to like. That's fine for
tricks. In reality, though, there are only two ways outside the line
to get your hands on real, big power: blood magic and Tantra,
sacrifice and sex."

"So she used Tillandsia to build up a battery of power," I said.

"Yes. I believe that you and Maisie represent an unexpected
by-product of Emily's use of sex to amass magical energy."

"But why? What was she trying to do with it?"

"We don't know for sure. I guess we never will," Iris said and
shook her head sadly. "She died before we could get it out of her."

"Oh." My breath failed me, and the word stuck in my throat.
Iris sure was doing a fine job of sticking to her story. "Not even
any guesses?" I asked, and winced at the sound of my own
pathetic laugh.

"We could speculate all day," Iris said, reaching out for me. I
did not take her hand. "But what we need to do is try and understand how this all relates to what's happening with your sister."

"But if you are right, and Maisie and I are somehow linked
to whatever our mother joined Tillandsia to accomplish, we have
to figure out what that was. How else could we begin to figure
out how it relates to Maisie?"

"She's right," Oliver said. I felt apprehension flare off Iris in
an almost palpable wave. "But where would we start? After Emmy

died, Ginny claimed her journals." I don't know what it was—a
lack of finesse in his tone, the absentminded way I could feel him
flipping through the alternatives, or the way he didn't even try to
act smooth—but something told me he really didn't know my
mother was alive. I felt a pang of relief, but that was derailed by
the massive doubts I still felt about Iris and Ellen. "And you, Gingersnap, are all too aware that those have been reduced to ash."
He paused. "We could try, and I do mean try, to search for echoes,
but it all happened so long ago now."

"Search for echoes?" I hadn't heard of that before.

"Charge the atmosphere of the places Emily spent the most
time. See if we can replay any memories the surroundings might
still hold."

"After all this time?" Iris asked. "No, I don't think it's worth
the trouble or the risk of drawing the golem's attention to what
we're doing." She looked directly at me. "You know he's here to
spy. That's the sole reason for his presence. It's ridiculous for the
families to insist that he's somehow more qualified to train you in
the use of magic than we are."

"It's true, Sandman is under foot, but what better way to
keep him occupied than to have him show Mercy how to sift for
memories?" Oliver said. "He doesn't have to know the real reason. Just that Mercy would like to know how."

Ellen turned in her seat. "I agree with Iris. It's a bad idea." I
saw her eyes telegraph Iris a quick look of concern, but Iris
remained stoic.

"Do you have a better one?" Oliver asked, but didn't wait for
a response. "No, I didn't think so. It's settled then," he said, and
then addressing me, "Let's go find Emmet. Oh, wait"—his voice
dripped with sarcasm—"here he is now." He saluted the window
where Emmet had been standing stock still the entire time.

TEN

Emmet stood as still as a statue when we entered the room, turning only when Oliver called out, "Hey, Sandman. You ready to teach our girl here a trick?"

"Of course I'm ready to assist in Mercy's education. It's my sole purpose for being in your home," he said, and then his dark eyes burned into me. "It's my sole purpose for being period, as best as I can reason." A certain heaviness, manifested by a physical darkening of the air around us, filled the room.

"Not awkward at all," Oliver said under his breath, and even though I felt sure Emmet had heard, his expression didn't change. "All right then, Mercy here wants to learn how to shake loose some memories from this old house. Charge the atmosphere and see what pops out. Maybe get a glimpse of her mom or her grandparents."

"I"—Emmet looked directly at me, acting as if he had forgotten Oliver was even in the room with us—"would be more than happy to show you. I've been thinking that perhaps I've been approaching your education in the wrong way, trying to teach you what I think you should learn instead of what you'd like to learn. The families have perhaps objectified you in their rush to have you meet the responsibilities of being the line's anchor. They, *I*, have forgotten that you are a person and a witch in your own right."

"Thank you," I said, touched by his words. They summed up so much of the way I'd been feeling lately; the families merely saw me as a seat of power, and to Peter's parents, I was the incubator of his child. Somewhere in becoming who I was going to be, who I was had been getting lost.

"However," he continued, "I have been forbidden to assist you—any of you, for that matter—with any attempt to reach Maisie."

"We aren't asking you to do anything like that," Oliver said. "I mean, I could teach her what she wants to know myself. We merely thought it would make you feel like you were serving your purpose here." His tone grew heated. "And we hoped that it might get you to knock off the skulking a bit." I realized he wasn't trying to provoke a reaction from Emmet; he still considered the big man a walking hunk of clay, unworthy of his consideration, perhaps even incapable of feeling any barbs.

"I was unaware that I have been 'skulking.' My sole intention was to keep myself available to Mercy." His voice was measured, unflinching. Only his eyes revealed that Oliver had struck a nerve. Emmet annoyed me, it was true, but I had no desire to see him in pain.

"Come on, Emmet," I said, taking his hand and drawing him away. Oliver's tone was growing more sardonic by the moment, and I knew that if he stayed around Emmet, he'd use the former golem as a whipping boy, taking out all his anger and frustration on him. In truth, Emmet and I had much in common. The families saw both of us as pawns, means to their desired ends. Truth was, he was every bit as lost in all of this as I was.

The heat I felt in Emmet's hand surprised me; he burned a bit more brightly than the average man. He followed me dutifully, so I let go of him. When I did, something tangible came over him. Disappointment? Lately I had felt buffeted by others' emotions. Their feelings would try to take me over, and that constituted a major part of the reason I'd felt so lost lately. I had to talk to Emmet or someone else about this problem, but I doubted that this was the best time.

"The memories of your mother, your grandparents," he said as we reached the second-floor landing. "They may be more difficult to summon, since a bit of time has passed, and since they are . . . gone."

"Okay," I prompted him.

"Perhaps we could start with something a little easier," he said, and for the first time since he had become *real*, I saw the shadow of a grin on his lips. "And have you work your way up? I want you to have a sense of accomplishment," he explained. "Success will provide a much stronger encouragement for you to continue your studies than early failures."

I laughed. "You have been reading books on teaching, haven't you?"

"Well, yes," he said, lowering his eyes and stepping back a bit, acting as if I'd stumbled upon an embarrassing secret. "Does that offend you?"

I shook my head and rolled my eyes at him. "Come on. How do we start?"

"Follow me," he said, leading me to my own room. He stepped inside, and I followed. "May I close the door?" he asked.

"Of course. Why not?"

"I thought you might feel vulnerable, being in here alone with a man. A stranger."

"You aren't a stranger," I said. "I've known you all your life."

His broad shoulders relaxed and his full lips curved into a smile. The sadness that haunted his eyes dissipated, if only for a moment. "You are the only one who sees me as real. Everyone else—your aunts, your uncle, and the other families—sees me as an empty shell. An automaton."

"We know different though," I said. "And sooner or later, the rest will see too." I touched his arm, and felt a jolt run through him. For a second, his face flushed and his lips quivered. I stepped back, and the moment passed.

"I am sure you already know," he said, his tone turning distant, professorial, "that everything is made of energy. Living energy. Everything around us here. The walls, the floor, your bed and desk. Actions, circumstances are made of energy too, and energy can't be destroyed. Even so, the way energy organizes itself changes over time. This house is well maintained. The roof is fairly new; the paint is fresh. Your family continues to pour new energy into it to keep it in the condition they desire. If they did not, the house would eventually decay and fall apart." He paused and sat at my desk. At nearly seven feet tall, he was strangely oversized for the seat. "Do you understand?"

"Yes, I think so. Entropy and all that." I'd taken a steady progression of university classes in physics, math, languages, art, and literature. Aunt Iris had long since become frustrated by the fact that I'd never earned a degree, even though I had credits enough for three. I loved the learning, and I think a part of me felt afraid that a diploma would symbolize that my learning days had come to an end. My rational mind told me that I owed it to myself to finish my degree, and I also needed to set a good example for my son. I wanted him to know that his mama always finished what she started. I promised myself that I would do just that after Colin was born.

Emmet looked at me with pride. "Yes. Things fall apart. The same thing holds true in regards to events. We build the events in our lives. We furnish them with our intellect and decorate them with our emotions, but then we walk away. We never bring new energy to them, and with time, they fade and disappear from our senses. That's what leads to the sense that time is passing, what we call 'the present' simply reflects where we collectively are focusing the most energy."

"So the daily events of my mother's life are still available to me if I can bring enough energy to them?"

"Yes, to a certain degree, but time has passed. More importantly, you have a deep-seated sense of having been separated from your mother." The irony of Emmet's words nearly took my breath from me, but he was too caught up in his lecture to notice. "The memories that are closer to you are easier to revive—they're simply awaiting a burst of energy that's strong enough to jar them loose. Perhaps that's where we should start." Emmet stood and walked up to me, standing so close the heat from his body radiated into my own.

"You appreciate this vessel," he said after staring at me for a long moment. "You respond emotionally to it, perhaps even physically as well." Strong hands grasped me and pulled me into steely arms. His mouth found mine and forced it open, his tongue, a flickering flame, forcing its way inside. A burst of fire shot down my spine, and I would have been jolted off the ground had his arms not been holding me so tightly. I was breathless when he finally released me. I reached back and slapped him as hard as I could. My hand left its mark, but Emmet didn't even react. Instead, he grabbed me and spun me around again.

There before me sat a much younger version of myself wearing a pink sundress I'd hated. I had been way too much of a tomboy for Iris's liking, and she'd been on a constant mission to get me to dress like a girl. The pink-dressed me sat at the table, crayons in hand and an angry expression on my face. The sight made the present version of myself smile. Emmet loosed his grasp on me, and I drew nearer. I remembered this moment now. Iris had put me in a time-out because I had thrown a fit over having to wear that very same dress.

"When you imagined your father, you drew my form, my body, for him," Emmet's voice came from over my shoulder. "With your crayons."

I was shocked, but I knew he was absolutely right. The sketch showed large and sturdy hands on a man as big and strong as a tree. I had imagined someone to whom I could appeal the injustice of pink dresses and time-outs. I had forgotten the image as I had grown past my childish hope of finding my dad. In broad strokes, that image stood behind me now. I turned to face him.

"This vessel could have taken any shape—a child, a woman, a common household pet, even. When you came across it rising from the earth, it contained nothing but pure potential. Your consciousness cast it in this form. As you dealt with Ginny's death and the issues between you and your sister, your longing for a father figure resurfaced, perhaps not consciously, but strongly enough to give birth to this image. You provided the mold into which the energies flowed. They simply responded to the need you projected onto them."

Oh, no, it didn't make me feel in the least little bit icky to realize I was attracted to my idealized paternal figure. Well, maybe Emmet was only a manifestation of my childhood perception of the idealized *male*, I quickly rationalized. Satisfied with that extenuation and deeply determined never to consider the issue again, I said, "I didn't know," and took a few steps back from him.

"And then you named me," he responded, regaining the distance I had put between us. "Like it or not, you have made your mark on this body. You've put your stamp on me. The line selected you and turned me into a person, a man, in the same instant, I cannot believe it happened by accident or chance."

He knelt before me, bringing his eyes more in line with my own. "Mercy, I remember the incidents from the lives of the nine who made me. All their joys and shames, their accomplishments and little infidelities. But, Mercy . . . Seeing your face is *my* first memory."

"Get up, Emmet," I said, trying to diffuse the passion I felt in his declaration, but he reached out and took both of my hands.

"Mercy, the line didn't make a mistake. The line made me *for you*. You are my only purpose and my only passion."

I might have felt threatened or uneasy, but I knew that Emmet spoke nothing but the truth. "For now, maybe, but you'll find others." His face grayed; he was stricken. I didn't know why he had chosen this particular moment to make his declaration, but he had offered all he had and all he was to me. Completely. This had been his big gamble, the moment when he put all his chips on the table. It broke my heart to reject him, but we both knew I was saying no. "I'm pregnant. I'm marrying Peter."

"If you wanted to marry Peter, you already would have." Anger crept into his voice. My choice had stung him. "He had to rely on the old woman's magic to reach you."

"No. I was confused," I said, speaking calmly, ignoring the heated resentment I heard in his voice. I didn't want to hurt Emmet. I had never even considered that he might have feelings for me. "I was deceived by Jackson. I would have turned to Peter anyway. I *have* turned to Peter. He's my oldest friend. I love him. I am carrying his child."

"I would gladly raise your child as my own," Emmet vowed to me.

"Enough," I said, shaking my hands from his. "Get out of my room." I should have ordered him out of my house, out of Savannah, but in spite of what my good sense told me, I didn't have the heart. He had nowhere else to go.

"As you wish." He stood, reaching his impressive full height. "At least you've learned how easily passion can lend itself to use in magic, and why your mother would have used it to reach her goals."

At first I couldn't find the words. Ellen's crystal had been out there with us, but that only prevented remote spying. I stood there with my mouth open. "You were listening to us . . . You could somehow hear us."

"Not exactly. One of the witches who created me is deaf. From him, I received the ability to read lips. For the record, the families have forbidden me to help you in any way with Maisie, but they said nothing about your mother." He started to leave but turned back to face me again. "You think you know Peter, but perhaps there are things he doesn't even know about himself."

"What is that supposed to mean?"

"Don't you find it strange that he has been the sole suitor to knock on your door, the sole *human* suitor?"

"Regular guys tend to get freaked out by my family. By the magic."

"That's why witches tend to marry other witches, but our Peter was never put off by the magic. Has this never struck you as strange?"

"I will not discuss Peter with you," I said, my loyalty and love for Peter raising my ire against the golem. Emmet nodded and left my room quietly, leaving the door open behind him. I crossed to close it, but Ellen appeared before I could.

"Did you get what you needed from the golem?" she asked, crossing the threshold to my room without waiting for permission. "If not, you know I'd be glad to teach you."

"No," I said. "I think I understand how to charge the room now. Thanks." It wasn't exactly the truth, but I was not in the mood to provide her with any details about my lesson. Ellen turned the chair by my makeup mirror around and sat down facing me. "I'm sorry," I said. "I was planning on heading out."

"You can spare me a few minutes, can't you?" She straightened her skirt and smoothed down her chic haircut. "Please."

"All right," I said and sat on the foot of my bed.

"I know you are not happy that I intend to continue spending time with Tucker . . ."

"No, indeed I am not," I said, my words coming out more sharply than I had intended. "You are doing so well. I don't want to see him drag you down again."

"Oh, Mercy, from your perspective, I can see why you think he drags me down. That's because you are only judging on what is visible from the outside. You don't know the innumerable times he has pulled me up." She tilted her head, her blonde hair falling at an angle around an angelic face. Her cornflower-blue eyes were no longer looking directly at me. Instead, they fell to a spot on the floor between us. "I was nearly mad. No, I *was* mad with grief after I lost Erik and our son. I didn't want to live in this world without them anymore. I tried to keep things together, at least until they had been buried. The night after the funeral—" She stopped talking as large wet drops fell from her eyes. "I took a razor and slit my wrists." I gasped at this revelation. "I wanted to end it. I wanted to die so badly I didn't mind the pain. I didn't mind the blood. I didn't mind the thought of one of you finding me. I was in such torment, I couldn't find a single ray of light to pierce it."

She looked up at me, the horror in her eyes cutting into me as a razor had once cut into her flesh. "I couldn't die, Mercy. My own powers wouldn't let me. The cuts healed almost as quickly as I could make them." She stood and walked over to my window, looking out on the perfect day. "After four or five hours, I gave up. I poured myself a drink. I cleaned up the mess. I went to bed." She turned back toward me. "The next day, I ran into Tucker down on River Street. He was in the process of moving into his office."

"And he took advantage of your pain."

"No. No." She rushed forward and sat next to me and grasped my hands. "Look at me," she commanded, and I did. "He didn't take advantage of me. He let me take advantage of him." I said nothing, but my doubt must have been obvious. "Not that it is truly any of your business," she said, "but we enjoyed almost two years as friends before we ever acted on our attraction to each other."

"He didn't need you for sex. He had Tillandsia for that."

Ellen's eyes flashed wide with anger, but she regained control. "You're right. He didn't need me for sex. He didn't need me for money. He didn't need me for anything. He wanted me. He has been a true friend to me for years."

"A true friend who hits on your nieces."

"I've spoken to him about that. He has promised me that he will never approach you to participate in Tillandsia again. He's leaving the group himself. He's organizing the renovation of their new meetinghouse, and then he's done."

"Ellen," I said, exasperated. "His promises are worth nothing. He's not a good man. He is just no good, plain and simple."

"Peter thinks he's good enough to take on as a business partner."

"Yeah, and I am not thrilled about that either, but at least it's only business. There are laws to help keep him in line, but you gotta know Tucker will never be faithful to you. He's incapable of it. It isn't in his DNA."

"Yes. I know that. I know exactly what kind of man I am getting with Tucker. I don't have to question if he's lying to me. I know that he *will* lie if it is more convenient for him than telling me the truth." She laughed at a joke she hadn't shared. "And I sure as hell don't have to lie awake nights crying and wondering if he's cheating on me, because I know that if he is not in bed next to me, he is making love to someone else." She paused and looked deeply into my eyes. "That's who he is. He is a liar and a cheat, but he is also so kind and loving toward me. When he's with me, I know it's because there is no one else he'd rather be with at that moment. When he makes love to me, it's truly me he wants. With Erik, I knew his body would be with me, while his heart and mind were with your mother."

It nearly took my breath away to hear her say that; I hated that my very existence was due to her husband's infidelity, but I knew she wasn't saying it out of cruelty. "Besides, he doesn't run from the magic like most men. I think the strangeness he senses around me is part of what attracts him to me. Don't judge me, sweetheart. And don't judge Tucker. It's true he's a bastard, but he isn't hiding any kind of ulterior motives. With Tucker, what you see truly is what you get."

"But Ellen, you deserve better."

"Oh, sweet girl, you have no idea what I deserve, but I need you to understand something. Tucker is nowhere near perfect, but he makes me happy in ways no one else can."

"I don't want to hear any more of this," I said and stood, heading for the door.

"Mercy," Ellen called out, sharply enough to get me to stop in my tracks and turn back toward her. "Tucker has asked me to marry him." She gave me a few seconds to register her words fully. "I've said yes."

ELEVEN

Ellen stood and left me standing there, my mouth still hanging open. I decided that getting out of the house was indeed the best thing to do. I spun the chair she'd been sitting in around and sat down in front of the mirror. I ran a brush through my hair as I argued with people who weren't even there. Peter held the first position on my list. Tucker had managed to manipulate my fiancé into going into business with him. Tucker was looking to worm his way into the family, and their partnership had helped *legitimize* the bastard. In a separate confrontation, I had an imaginary conversation with Ellen, telling her that she was out of her cotton-picking mind if she thought I'd act as bridesmaid. Then I realized that I was acting petty, even if only in my own imagination.

I put down the brush and looked at myself in the mirror. The woman I saw squinted angrily back at me. I didn't like what I saw. I didn't like how my feelings toward Tucker affected me. Maybe the man truly was trying to change? Maybe he was helping Peter get started in business as an olive branch to me? Ellen seemed to think he was worthy. Maybe I should do my best to accept him? Then the wave broke, and my dislike for the man washed over the levee of tolerance I'd started to build. *Anyone other than Tucker.*

I needed a quiet place to stop the noise in my head. I put on some sunscreen and moisturizer, a touch of pink lip gloss, and then drew on a little eyeliner. I changed into a very modest, nearly formal sundress with a collar that covered me up to the clavicle and a skirt that fell a tad below the knee. Then I went to church.

Other buildings had jostled their way in, robbing the towers of St. John's Cathedral of their position as the most prominent feature in the Savannah skyline. None, though, had matched their soaring beauty. However, like an allegory in stucco, the French Gothic beauty of the exterior couldn't begin to match the grace of the vaulted interior. I stepped through the doors, instantly comforted by the haint blue of the cathedral's spangled ceiling and arches. I took a seat in the second row behind the font, and sat quietly, enjoying the play of the light that was filtering through the stained glass windows. My family and I weren't Catholic. We weren't Protestant. Frankly, we weren't allied with any formal religion, but I had always loved St. John's. Regardless of your religious affiliation, a sense of peace and holiness filled the cathedral. Tourists filtered inside, most of them appropriately respectful of the sanctity of the place, others a tad too boisterous as they snapped their photos. Loud or quiet, all were struck by the beauty they encountered. I closed my eyes, letting their exclamations and the sound of clicking cameras weave into a tapestry of prayer. A prayer for guidance. A prayer for humility.

"Pardon me, miss." A voice startled me. My eyes snapped open. "I am so sorry to disturb you," a congenial-looking grandfather in a straw fedora and plaid shorts said. "Is your name Mercy?"

"Yes," I said nodding, confused.

"Your mother asked me to tell you that she is waiting outside for you."

"Thank you," I said, my heart leaping. I jumped up and hurried out of the church. I stood on the top step and scanned the camera-toting crowd at the foot of the steps for my mother's face, but I couldn't spot her. I looked up and down the road, trying to catch sight of her car, but it was nowhere to be seen.

"Don't you look pretty?" My mother's voice projected itself out of another woman's mouth. I rushed down the steps and up to a plump, middle-aged woman wearing an oversized neon-green St. Augustine T-shirt.

"Mama?" I asked, trying to reconcile the sound of my mother's voice coming out of the stranger's bright mauve lips. I looked deeply into the woman's eyes, the lids of which had been painted nearly to the brow in dark turquoise.

"Yes, in a way. I'm *borrowing* this body for a few moments. I cannot hold it for long, but I needed to tell you I am thinking of you always. I am creating a sanctuary for us, a place where we can speak freely, and I can take the time to get to know my beautiful daughter. I will send for you as soon as I can."

This was ridiculous. She had to come home and face her sisters. She couldn't keep running. "But I have so many questions now. I need to understand what happened. I'm confused, Mama." I said, but the woman just shook her head, looking at me as if I were mad.

"If you think I'm your mother, you sure are." She walked several feet away from me, keeping a concerned eye on me until the friends she'd been waiting on made their way out of the church. She whispered to her cohorts, and the other two turned to glance at me. "Don't look at her!" the first woman said. "Let's just get out of here." At that, the other two started laughing, and all three made their raucous way to the next stop on the tour. I'd just been marked down as another of Savannah's oddities, but frankly that was the least of my concerns.

TWELVE

As we pulled into the parking area next to Magh Meall, I spotted a sign on the door reading "Closed for Private Function." Most of those attending the wake had never met the guest of honor, but I had more reason than most to raise a toast to Peadar. A week had passed since the old man's eyes had closed for the last time. I pushed away the memory of how it had felt to have his body rise beneath my magic only to fall charred to the ground. I knew that many of the tavern's regulars would be here tonight: those who came to drink, those who came to play music, and those who came to do both. Claire and Colin had drafted Peter to work behind the bar, so I had caught a ride with Iris and Oliver.

Ellen and Tucker's wedding announcement had been published on the society page the previous day. "People will expect us to arrive together," she'd said to explain why she'd chosen to ride with Tucker rather than the rest of us. I hated to think of her permanently attached to the man, but at the end of the day, I didn't get to have a say. I prayed she would find happiness and adjust as well to married life as Iris had to being single.

I could not help but admire the way Iris had blossomed since Connor's passing. Her style no longer reflected his insecurities, but instead the beautiful woman she was, inside and out. Tonight she wore a new black dress that hit her slightly below the knee, modest in cut and color, but seductive in the way it clung to her trim frame.

Oliver had donned a black single-breasted suit and a thin black tie; the two shades of black matched to a degree that only Oliver's expert eye could have managed. I wore a sage-green tea-length dress Ellen had picked out for me. Not the best shade for mourning, but the dress flattered me, fitting my growing stomach perfectly. It made me feel pretty, and by God, that would be enough for tonight.

Oliver parked our car very near the entrance but in a no-parking zone. He looked over his shoulder at me and winked. "They don't mean us," he said. I knew for a fact that the man had never had to pay a parking ticket in his life. Since we hadn't blocked a fire hydrant or anything, and since my feet were swelling in the shoes I'd let vanity talk me into wearing, I met his wink with a smile. "You two stay put," he said, as he hopped out and opened first Iris's door, then mine.

"It's wonderful to have you home," Iris said, affection for her little brother suffusing her voice and expression. He closed the doors and offered each of us one of his arms, leading us toward the door that swung open as we neared it.

"If it isn't my beautiful soon-to-be daughter-in-law," Colin said, leaning forward to plant a wet, whiskey-laced kiss on my cheek. "It means the world to Claire that you and your family are here tonight. It means the world to both of us." Another kiss, and Oliver maneuvered me over the threshold. "Ellen will arrive shortly," Oliver explained.

"We got the beautiful flowers she sent—they are over by the display Claire has set up for our Peadar." He forced a smile onto his face. "And speaking of Ellen, I look forward to congratulating Tucker on finally getting her to make an honest man out of him."

92

"That would indeed count as quite a feat," Iris said. She felt no more enthusiasm for the impending nuptials than I did.

"Perhaps we could make it a double wedding?" Colin asked me good-naturedly.

"Not a chance," Oliver responded. "You never want to see two Taylor women competing for the same spotlight. Trust me, it's easy to get burned." He put his arm around Colin's shoulders and led him toward the whiskey.

I looked across the room, to where Peter was beaming at me from behind the bar. Our eyes met, and I felt the baby move. "That's right, little man," I said. "That's your daddy." I moved toward the bar, and he leaned over it to kiss me deeply, hungrily. Another taste of whiskey. His face looked a little flushed, and his eyes were moist. His Irish was showing.

"There you are, my love," Claire said, coming over and taking me in her arms.

"Can I help somehow?"

"Oh, no, we've got everything under control. Have you seen the memorial to Peadar?"

"No, not yet," I responded.

"Here, let me show you." She led me across the bar to a long table that had been draped with a white tablecloth. Two large vases of white roses paired with blue lisianthus and yellow irises, one of Ellen's favorite bouquets, anchored the ends of the table. A large black-and-white photo of a young man, dark with a mischievous grin, stood in the middle, flanked by white column candles and smaller photos of Peadar from over the years (the 1970s?—the '80s?), the dark hair graying, and crow's feet lining the corners of his eyes. There was also a Polaroid similar to the one found by Detective Cook, this one showing Peadar standing between Claire and Colin and holding his infant namesake, Peter.

"It's hard to believe that scrawny little baby grew into the man behind the bar," I said, as I could find nothing else to say about the older stranger whose life we had gathered to celebrate.

Claire's face darkened for a moment, but then she glanced over at her son, and her smile returned full force. "Isn't it, though?" She turned back to the memorial. "We didn't have many photos to use. That one was the day we brought Peter home from the hospital. This one here," she said, touching the Polaroid's thick bottom border, "this was the last time we saw Peadar. He and Colin's father had a falling out, and then . . . well, then nothing." She tried to choke back tears. "I'm sorry. I can't bear the thought that he may have been murdered." I wanted to tell her that he hadn't been murdered. That he hadn't died alone either. I would have to soon, but not here and certainly not now. "He was so dear, so innocent."

"I could tell," I said, prompting a look of confusion from Claire. "From the photos," I said, although the photographs reflected none of the innocence I'd seen in Peadar's eyes. "He looks like a very nice man."

She pulled a tissue from her pocket and dabbed at her eyes. "I should get back to the kitchen, see how things are going there." She gave me a quick hug and a pat on the stomach. I noticed that Ellen was arriving with a sheepish Tucker in tow. He wore a canary-swallowing smile and was readily accepting the many handshakes and pats that were coming his way. In that moment I hated myself. The man did look happy. He did seem to be in love. Who was I to question Ellen's choices? I realized that I had to put on my big-girl pants and apologize to her.

A chorus of "The Girl I Left Behind Me" broke out near the bar, being led, much to my amusement, by Oliver. A player near the bandstand whipped out a mandolin. Uilleann pipes droned awake and moments later a fiddle joined in, followed by a banjo.

Voices from every corner joined in. Iris had put down her drink and was dancing with Colin. Now *this* was an Irish wake. I hadn't managed to save Peadar, but looking around, feeling the music move through me, I felt happy. I took a seat near the memorial that gave me a decent view of the bandstand.

A hand touched my shoulder, and I looked over to find Detective Cook standing behind me. "Still the life of the party, isn't he?"

It felt somehow disloyal to discuss Oliver with Cook. "I don't think you should have come tonight," I said. "This is a private event, and I didn't see the name 'Detective' on the guest list." I was all too aware that the two had been involved. Their secret romance had ended in tragedy years ago, a tragedy involving Jilo's granddaughter, Grace. For years, Oliver's guilt had driven his whole life, and even though he would never confess it, I knew that he would give his own life to right the wrong he had done. I saw no such remorse in the detective.

"Oh, I was invited, all right," he said, showing me the pint of beer in his hand.

"So you are here as a private citizen, not a policeman, then?"

"That depends on whether you have something you are trying to hide," he said, but the twinkle in his eyes indicated that he was pulling my leg.

"Oh, Detective Cook, my life is nothing these days if not an open book."

He took a sip from his beer. "You know, you could call me 'Adam' if you'd like. I'm not your enemy. Matter of fact, I am one of the best friends you have in this room."

"I will reserve judgment on that." I paused. "Adam. However, I'm more than willing to do away with formalities if you will quit calling me 'Miss Taylor.'"

"Deal," he said. "But no one is going to call you 'Miss Taylor'" for much longer, huh? Claire told me," he said in response to my unasked question. "When's the wedding?"

"Soon. Why, you angling for an invitation?"

"I'd be honored," he said and looked over at Oliver. "I assume your uncle will give you away."

"Yes, and someday I hope to return the favor." Cook—Adam—laughed. Disloyal or not, it seemed like the right time to do a little meddling. "So, how much longer are you going to punish him? It's obvious you still have feelings for each other."

"Ah, Mercy. If it were only that simple. I'm not punishing him . . ."

"No?"

"No. The world isn't as simple as you seem to think it is. I'm a policeman, a detective . . ."

"Oh, so you aren't vindictive, just a coward."

He stepped back and his eyes widened, filling with fire. He teetered only a thumb's breadth away from telling me off, then his shoulders slackened and a grin returned to his face. "Damn, you Taylors sure know how to push my buttons."

"You got such big ones, and they are so darned shiny," I said.

He took a few more sips of his beer and looked around. We both watched as Oliver grabbed Iris and spun her around the room, expertly landing her into the arms of a dark, much younger stranger. "I'm not a coward, Mercy, but folks around here, hell, folks in this room even, if they knew about me . . ."

"They'd what?" I said and slugged my fist into the rock that was his stomach. "Try to beat you up and take your milk money?"

"They'd lose respect for me. I've worked my entire life to become somebody in this town. To use my life as an example for others."

I had no desire to argue that point. "You're right. Some will lose respect for you. They'll call you names. Laugh behind your back. I guess you aren't a big enough man to handle that, huh?"

"That isn't fair," he said. His lips tightened, and he surveyed the room. I watched as he looked around the bar, examining every face, trying to decide how each would react to the gossip.

"No, I guess I'm not being fair. I don't really understand what you've done to get to where you are. I don't understand what you might have to face or what you might lose. But I do understand one thing."

"And what is that?" He stopped scanning the crowd and fixed me in his gaze. The tempo of the music fell off a bit. A twin-fiddle waltz brought even some of the shyer folk in the room to their feet, pairing off two by two. It surprised me to see that Iris was still in the arms of her handsome stranger, and by the look on his face, he had no intention of letting go. Oliver had gone behind the bar to take over for Peter, and he was helping Colin fill pints and distribute shots of Jameson.

"That no matter how much he protests to the contrary, Oliver will spend the rest of his life waiting for you unless you do something about it."

"So what do you propose I do?"

"Make up your mind. Either he's worth the risk you'll have to take or he isn't. If he isn't, tell him that, and make it clear so that he'll finally move on. For real."

"And if he is?"

"I think you can figure that out on your own."

"That I can," he said, and then drained the rest of his beer. "You'll excuse me."

"Of course." I watched him as he weaved his way through the dancers and approached the bar. Oliver reached out to take Adam's glass, but the detective shook his head and took Oliver's hand. I had never seen my uncle look so completely shocked. His face went white and then flushed red, the goofiest smile possible growing on his face as Adam led him around the bar and took him into his arms. A hush descended on the guests as Adam started to move, but the music grew in enthusiasm if not pace as the two began waltzing.

From behind me I heard a loud snort, and then, "Well would you look at that." Phil Jones, one of the hard-assed guys from the dock, started laughing so hard that he spilled his beer. I turned, ready to pounce and claw his eyes out. "Looks like Cook finally grew a pair," he said, shaking the spilled beer off his hand.

"About time," his buddy answered. "Listen, I got an early morning tomorrow. Do me a favor and say good-bye to Colin and Claire for me, okay?"

"Sure thing," the other dockworker said. "Take it easy." Noticing that I was watching them, he smiled and gave a quick wave before tottering off to replace his spilled drink.

Just goes to show, you never know, I thought, kicking off my shoes and wishing that Peter would put down his guitar and ask me to dance. As I watched him play, I did my best to will it to happen, without actually "willing" it to happen—I did have to take care with my newfound powers. That was when I felt someone's stare on the nape of my neck. It settled there, burning me with its intensity. I turned to face Emmet, his dark glare pinning me, cutting me off from the rest of the crowd.

Without changing his expression, he approached me and held out his hand. "I've actually never danced before, but one of my makers teaches ballroom. Will you join me?"

"No," I said, a tinge of regret coloring my refusal. I wanted to dance, but not with Emmet. It would be unfair to him, and without a doubt, Peter would see it as a betrayal. Besides, I knew Claire would not be happy to see him here, considering how close she'd come to punching him the last time he visited the bar. The waltz ended, and both the pace and the volume of the music jumped way up as the older folk returned to their seats or the bar.

"May I get you something to drink, then?"

"Listen, Emmet," I shouted over the music, "it's really nice of you to offer, and very sweet that you would come out tonight, but . . ."

"A little water, then?" He tilted his head and smiled. Any other woman in the place would have gladly been his in exchange for that smile.

A little flame lit up in me. I could use the water. "All right. Yes, thank you."

Emmet managed to get himself served quickly, probably because he stood head and shoulders over the other patrons. I looked away and focused on the bandstand, on Peter, but from the corner of my eye, I saw Claire heading straight for Emmet from the kitchen. I couldn't make out what she said to him over the din, but it didn't take any magic powers to sense her agitation. She knocked the glass from his grip with the back of her hand, but he quickly reached out and caught it, snapping it up with the speed of a cat. I sighed. It looked like I'd have to put my shoes back on.

By the time I'd managed the task, Claire had guided Emmet to the door, following him out of the bar. I forced my way through the crush. "Pardon. Excuse me," I called, bumping into people, knowing the band was playing too loudly for them to hear my apologies, but making them all the same. I opened the door, surprised to see that Claire had already led Emmet nearly a block away, the two of them too caught up in their conversation to notice my presence.

It had gone dark while we were inside the bar, and I trod carefully as I wobbled my way toward them. Even though Claire was whispering, her words became steadily clearer. "I am warning you." Claire punctuated each word with a fisted blow to Emmet's chest. "You stay away. I know who you are. I know what you are." Emmet's face remained inscrutable, even though Claire had cornered him under a streetlight. "When I gave my son over to the care of your people, I was promised that he'd have a good, long, healthy life. That I'd get to see him again before I died. And you sent him back a dried-up husk. You murdered him." Her words came out in a hiss. "But you had better listen up, 'cause I will not tell you again. You aren't getting Peter, and you sure as hell are not laying a hand on my grandbaby. I will see you and all your kind in hell first." Emmet stayed silent, undoubtedly as much out of his laconic nature as his apparent confusion. He clearly had no idea what Claire was talking about. His silence infuriated her. She reached up and brought her nails to his cheek, clawing out five angry red gouges.

"Claire," I said, coming up and pulling her hand away before she could strike him again. "What are you doing?"

"Stay where you are, Mercy. You don't understand what's going on here. You don't know what this . . ." She hesitated and then settled on the word: "'Man' is capable of."

"I assure you, I'd never harm you or your family," Emmet said, his hand touching his bloodied cheek. "I'd certainly never hurt Mercy." He drew back his hand, looking at the blood on it like it was a curiosity. Pain, I realized, was a novel experience to him. He was a babe in the woods. In that moment, I felt responsible for him.

"Shut your mouth, you dark devil," Claire sneered.

"Let me take you back to the bar," I said, pulling her quivering body to me.

"Stay away from him, Mercy," she said, her expression akin to that of a cornered and wounded animal.

"All right," I said. My eyes met Emmet's. He shook his head to indicate that he had no idea what was wrong with Claire, and I gave him a pointed nod. He understood the meaning: *Make yourself scarce.* "He's leaving, and we should go back inside. We'll get Colin and Peter, and we can talk all about—"

"No. Peter mustn't know. You can't tell him."

"I won't. I won't say a word," I said, mentally crossing my fingers. "We'll get you inside, and I'll tell Colin to take you upstairs until you feel better."

Claire managed to pull herself together. "I'm sorry. I know I must look like a mad woman to you, but you have to listen to me. If you love that child in your womb, hear me. That man. Emmet. I know it sounds crazy, but he isn't a man."

"What do you think he is?" I asked cautiously. I had no idea what she believed him to be, but it disquieted me to hear her hitting so close to home.

"Just believe me. He's . . . he's something else. I've known his kind before, and now I know they are full of lies. I know why he came. They want Peter, and worse, I think they want little Colin."

"No," I said, trying to calm her. "Emmet is harmless. I don't know what you think he is, but I assure you that you are wrong."

"And how can you be so sure?"

"You're going to have to trust me on this one," I said, suspecting that learning Emmet had risen to life from a mound of Georgia dirt would push her completely over the edge.

"I love you, Mercy, like my own daughter, I do," she said, reaching out and grasping my hand. "I'd trust you with my very life, but I am not willing to trust anyone's judgment, even yours, when it comes to that baby you are carrying. I'm telling you. If I ever see Emmet near you again, I will find a way to kill him or at least make him wish he were dead. You hear me now?"

"Yes, ma'am," I said, trying to calm her. I didn't think it wise to point out to her at just that moment that Emmet was still living with us, and I couldn't exactly send him away. I'd save that discussion for when she was thinking a bit more rationally.

Great—another wrinkle in my already complicated life. Now in addition to finding my emotionally unbalanced sister, uncovering the truth about what had caused my mother to desert me, and, oh, having a baby, I'd have to find a way to protect Emmet from my future mother-in-law. "I do. I hear you. Now let's get back inside and find Colin, okay?" She nodded and walked back into the bar with me.

THIRTEEN

At the end of the wake, Peter was not fit to drive, and Iris and Oliver had both disappeared. For some reason, Claire's meltdown around Emmet left me in no mood to use magic as a means of transportation, so I called for a taxi and made my way home like a regular person. When I arrived, the house felt deserted; I sent out a psychic ping to see if Iris had perhaps beaten me home, but it came back empty. No one was around, not even Emmet. I experienced a strange combination of loneliness and elation; I had not found myself alone in the house in forever. I realized that now was my opportunity to charge the atmosphere to see what memories I could make rise to the surface. My goal would not be, as Oliver had suggested, to try to get to the bottom of what my mother had been attempting through Tillandsia. Uncle Oliver meant well, but I really had no idea where I would even start on that. I suspected I could spend a lifetime sifting through the echoes that the house held, trying to find a few needles in a century-and-a-half's worth of haystack. No, I had one specific event I needed to witness: my own birth. Once I had found my answers about that, everything else would fall into place. I was sure of it.

Even a novice such as myself should be able to shake a few lingering impressions loose, especially since I had such an exact target. I made sure the doors were locked against any nonfamilial intruder, and then I went a step further, charming all entrances so that no one, including family, could come in without my being alerted. It was a sad state of affairs, but I wanted to make sure my mother's siblings wouldn't discover what I was up to until I had answers.

I hoped that by holding something that belonged to my mother, I would have an easier time of honing in on the particular energies I needed to tap into. I would use my mother's locket. That it had until recently been in her possession should be a plus. Tonight had been the first time that I hadn't worn the locket since she had given it to me. It would have been too noticeable given the neckline of the dress I was wearing. I didn't want to risk one of my aunts noticing it, or worse, recognizing it. I had left it in my jewelry box, mixed in with the few other pieces I had: the pearls I had received on my eighteenth birthday, the small diamond studs I'd received two years before that, the smaller blue box that held the engagement ring I still couldn't bring myself to wear regularly—even tonight. I pushed away the emotions that reached from the ring to grab me and extricated my mother's necklace. Something about touching it caused me to question my earlier optimism. Could there really be any hope of a familial reconciliation? Could separating a mother from her daughters truly be an explainable, leave alone pardonable, act?

I closed my eyes and took a cleansing breath. I had to keep an open mind. I couldn't let my fears prejudice me. Still, my previous exhilaration had turned to a heaviness of heart. I put the necklace around my neck and snapped the lid of the jewelry box closed.

Iris had taken over my mother's room, the room where Maisie and I were born, as a painting studio. She said she liked the golden late afternoon light that filtered through its windows, but she'd once confessed that being in this space comforted her and made her feel closer to the dear little sister she had lost too soon. I wanted to cry as I remembered how sincere she had sounded when she shared this with me. I pushed the sadness away and took a good look at the space.

My mother's lesser belongings had long since been given to charity, her more personal and precious items boxed up and stored in the attic for the day when Maisie and I chose how to divvy them up. But Iris had not erased my mother from the room. Far from it. A large, and now I knew firsthand, exquisitely accurate portrait of my mother dominated the room's southern wall. I didn't come in here often, but every time I did, I walked away feeling somehow touched by my mother's presence.

A large easel stood in the center of the room. It held a canvas, but the canvas had been covered with a tarp. I decided to respect my aunt's privacy. Now I wished I hadn't so stubbornly refused taking pointers from Ellen. I really didn't know how to proceed.

Emmet had used a combination of surprise and passion to surface the memory he had helped bring to life. I needed to get in touch with a powerful emotion, but I worried that my confused feelings about my mother's return might color my perceptions. So nothing about my mother. Probably better to steer clear of anything about my aunts too. My mind floated over my recent history with Maisie. Too fresh. Too painful. These emotions might bulldoze over any more subtle energies.

My feet were tired. I kicked off my shoes and took a seat in an awkwardly placed armchair. For some reason, Iris had left it turned at an angle, away from the portrait of my mother, away from the easel. The only thing it faced was a bit of blank wall. A sense of familiar resentment started to rise up in me as I reflected on Ginny and her manipulations. I remembered how Ginny made me wait in the entrance hall of her house, staring at nothing but a blank wall for hours. I had dealt with it by making up stories for my own entertainment. Stories that would later serve as the backbone of my Liar's Tour. The hall and the chair I had been forced to sit in were now both gone, burned away to nothing by the same fire that had consumed Connor. Resentment flared into anger, and then I heard voices behind me.

I whirled about quickly. There was no image, only a murmuring. I strained my ears to try to make out what was being said, but the voices were so faint, seeming to come from worlds away. And then they stopped altogether. I rose and crossed cautiously to the center of the room. Again, I could make out the faint but distorted sound of feminine voices. Was that a cry of pain? Desperation? I recognized Ellen's voice and could almost make out her words. I caught an image of her and Iris huddled over my mother, but the vision looked like a poorly preserved kinescope being projected onto the room's current reality. The image froze and then stretched like a rubber band, wrapping around and going through itself, reaching up and feeding into the portrait of my mother. I realized that any emotional imprint made on the day of my birth had long ago been channeled into the painting.

I tried to focus, to tune into the faint energies. I grasped the painting's frame, pressed my hands against the lacquered oils. I could feel small eruptions of energy flare off the painting, but what I had come for was locked away—the energy that had been channeled into the work had been permanently transformed. I took my hands off the painting and put them over my face. A sob formed in my breast, but I stifled it. I didn't want to cry. I wanted to know the truth.

My arms trembled, and my hands quivered, but I would not give up without making one final effort. I forced my anger and disappointment into a hard, tight ball and raised my hands. The orb shot from my fingers, landing right where I had aimed it: the spot where I had seen the three women together. I stalked forward, focusing all my power on expanding the sphere of energy. I could see the flickering image from the past stretch distortedly across its surface. I fell to my hands and knees, leaning in to try to interpret the jerky movement of the grainy, bulbous vision. The room around me crackled with my magic, and the smell of ozone flooded my senses. I forced myself to ignore these distractions. I channeled more and more energy into the orb. Distorted sounds, out of sync and incomprehensible, arose in waves. Then, with no warning, the glowing sphere collapsed in on itself and was gone. I had forced too much energy into a fragile moment. I heard wailing, and it took me a moment to realize that I was the one making the sound.

I fought a growing sense of hopelessness. I held my hands out again, trying to build up more energy for a last-ditch effort, but my concentration was broken when my peripheral vision alerted me to something floating down from above. I leaned my head away, but a soft speck landed on my cheek. I reached up and tried to brush it off, managing only to smear it. I looked at my hand and realized that it was ash. My mind had no sooner registered this realization than other flakes began to descend from above, thick and heavy, covering me like dry, gray snow. The ashes formed a thin powdery layer all around me, but rather than resting where they lay, they lifted back up, whirling around me like a slow spinning dust devil, some of the ash working its way into my nasal passages. I jumped up and ran to the easel, whipping off the cover to use as a shield against the ash. I froze at the sight of Connor's face staring back at me.

The easel held more than just a simple portrait. It was a triptych—the canvas had been divided into three equal portions. Both side panels had been completed; the one on the left showed

Connor as he had been in his youth, and in the one on the right, his face had been turned into a demon's, the same hate I had witnessed the night he died shining through the image's eyes. The center panel was still inchoate. A few layers of paint gave the impression that Iris had made many attempts at beginning this portion. I realized she was using her art in an attempt to reconcile the two images she held of her dead husband: the man she thought she had married and the monster he had proven himself to be. My eyes glided straight over the reflection of his youthful glow on the left, drawn to the image of the flames I had seen devour him. Here on the canvas they were frozen in time. We had held no funeral for Connor. There had been no remains to bury; no body had been found. The fire elementals had feasted well. Ashes were all that had been left of Connor.

Ashes. I began swatting at the dust with the tarp, trying to wipe Connor's remains from my skin, shake his ashes from my hair. Then I heard Connor's laughter. I spun around toward the sound. The ashes coalesced before me, taking on a definite form. A hand, smoldering, reached out of the dusty cloud and grasped at me. I leapt back.

"I will live again. I will live through you." I felt his words more than I heard them. The hand fell formless, and the cloud of swirling ashes rushed up in an attempt to surround me, envelop me, enter me. His spirit was attempting to possess me. No, it wasn't me he wanted; his spirit was trying to supplant that of my unborn child. That simply was not going to happen. I forced myself to regain control of my magic. I slid away from Iris's studio and into my own room.

For once I was ready. I had been preparing for this moment since the day after Connor's death, when I'd witnessed his essence lurking in a mirror. An attempt had been made to cleanse the house, to balance out its energies and remove anything with evil intent, but somehow I'd known the sneaky bastard would manage to slip through. Neither of my aunts nor Oliver had mentioned sensing his presence, but for months I felt him lurking on the periphery, just beyond capture. Angry. Jealous. A black cloud of hopelessness that fed on its own shadow.

I threw open my closet door and dug deep behind the shoes and boxes of high school memorabilia. I grasped the cool neck of the bottle I had hidden there. I shuddered a little at the sight of my creation. It had started out as a simple cobalt-blue glass bottle, but Jilo had coached me, showing me how to clothe it in clay and paint it with natural pigments. What had once been a simple container was now an effigy. A crude but recognizable image of the man who had been so willing to sacrifice me for power, even though he believed himself to be my father. "When you make a spirit trap, the image don't have to be dead on," Jilo had told me. "It just got to be the image you hold of him."

And it certainly did reflect my image of him. I'd captured his smugness. His rapaciousness. His cruelty.

I felt my blood pulsing in me. My temperature alternated cold and hot. My focus narrowed, blocking out everything but the burning anger I held for Connor. I felt confident. I felt in control. The door to my bedroom shook, then began to bend in and out as Connor tried to force it open. It looked for all the world like the door was breathing, expanding as it gasped in air, flattening as it let it go. I stood there in the silence. Waiting. Listening. My pulse pounded in my own ears. I took a step toward the door, and it began to shake so hard I halfway expected it to pull off its hinges, and then it stopped cold.

"Come on, you son of a bitch," I muttered under my breath. "This time I am ready for you." I pulled the cork out of the neck, grasping the stopper in my sweaty palm. I felt his sudden panic. I knew he had realized that the balance of power had completely changed. I was no longer the powerless girl he could injure and leave to die. He moved away from my door. I could feel his energy retreat. Instead of pursuing me, he began to flee. At that moment I realized Connor's spirit had no power outside of what I myself had loaned to it. By charging Iris's studio with magic, I had given him enough energy to manifest. And I had just shut off his supply. I grasped the spirit trap tightly with both hands and used my magic to swing the door open.

I strode through it and into the hall. "Spirit without body," I called out as Jilo had taught me, "this is your body." I held the effigy bottle up high. "Spirit without breath"—I lowered the bottle and blew across the lip of the bottle, causing it to emit a whistle—"this is your breath. Spirit without blood"—I spat into its neck—"this is your blood." I chased his dusty shadow back to the door of Iris's studio, and I stood back from the door, willing it to open. It did, but it did so slowly, a weakening force on its other side trying to force me back. There was a sound—maybe it was only the door's hinges protesting their being at the center of this war of wills, or it might have been an expletive shrieked by Connor's wilting spirit.

"I command you, spirit, enter your body." I tilted the bottle of the neck toward the door and took a step forward. "I command you, spirit, be filled with your breath." I crossed over the threshold into the studio. "I command you, spirit, bathe in your blood." The ash again lifted up and began to swirl, but I knew it was under my control now. "I command you, spirit, enter your body." The ash pulled together into a gray ribbon, just thin enough to penetrate the bottle's opening. I focused on seeing every last particle rise and take its place inside the effigy. Within moments the room was clean, the bottle full. I smiled as I plugged it with the cork.

"You know, Connor, I expected you to put up more of a fight, but I guess in the end you always were a *disappointment*."

I turned the bottle in my hand. Yes, I had the foresight to prepare the trap and learn how to use it, but now that I had deployed the necessary magic, I had no idea what to do with it. Jilo probably would have buried it at her crossroads, along with God only knows what else she had deposited there over the years. But it would be foolish to inter Connor's hungry ghost at the epicenter of Jilo's magic. If it ever managed to free itself from the trap, it would certainly make use of any magic it could find to wreak havoc. No, it would be better to weight it down and drop it into the ocean. But tonight, that was not an option. I needed a place where I could keep it safely, someplace that would allow me to take the time to think about what to do with it in the long run. *Time.* The word turned around in my brain, like the bottle turned in my hand.

I hurried downstairs and out into the garden. The sundial Oliver had placed there would keep anything it touched in stasis. Connor wouldn't just be locked in the trap I'd made for him—he'd be trapped in the moment as well. I could take as long as I needed to decide how and when to address the problem. I looked at the sundial and silently commanded it to rise. It vibrated, its own gravity making it much heavier to lift than I had anticipated. I tried focusing harder, putting more juice into my efforts, but the more magic I hit it with, the heavier it seemed to grow. Exasperated, I closed my eyes. "Please," I asked. I heard a humming sound and opened my eyes. To my amazement, the dial had floated up and was hanging at eye level. "Thank you," I said as relief rushed over me. Leave it to Oliver to rebel against even his own nature and create an enchanted object that must be asked to cooperate rather than compelled. I sat the spirit trap on the blackened soil the dial had been covering, and the ground opened up to swallow the bottle whole without my even asking. The dial descended back into place.

FOURTEEN

I went back to Iris's studio, replaced the cover over the nightmarish triptych, and looked around the room. Even my witch's eye couldn't notice anything that might alert Iris to the night's activities. I knew I had to tell Iris what had happened. It was her right to know, and I would tell her. I would. In the morning. But I didn't want to risk her stumbling across the truth in the night. I turned off the light and closed the door. I climbed in the shower and stood in the hottest water my skin could stand. I wanted to wash off even the memory of Connor's residue touching me. As I slid between my sheets, I remembered to undo the charm I had placed on the entrances; I didn't want the charm to wake me as my family came creeping in.

I was exhausted both physically and spiritually, but sleep did not come easily for me, and when it did, it brought dreams of a faceless creature that slithered on its stomach even though it had the shape of a man. Obelisks shooting lightning and stone circles humming to life surrounded me, making a sound that constantly rose in pitch and intensity. Shattering glass fell, raining down on the whole wide world, and then I heard my mother screaming. I was up and out of bed before the approaching sun could ripen the morning sky.

I sent my thoughts out as I went down the stairs, checking to see who had made it home from last night's wake, and who had found a better place to spend the night. Given the way Adam and Oliver were getting on last night, it surprised me to sense that a sleeping Oliver lay beneath our roof. I was a little more surprised, but also kind of relieved, to pick up no sign of Iris's presence.

For some reason, I couldn't get a clear reading on Ellen, so I stopped by her room and cracked the door open. The bed had been slept in, and the twisted sheets and pillows that spilled onto the floor told me that Ellen had not passed a much more relaxing night than I had. Unless, of course, she had brought Tucker home with her. If so, then the bedclothes told a very different story. Her absence bought me a bit more time before I had to make an already overdue apology.

I went to the kitchen and put on a pot of coffee for the others. After last night, I suspected that Oliver would welcome a cup when he awoke, and Iris might too, whenever she came dragging herself home. In spite of the news I had to share with her, a small and mischievous part of me felt glad that I was up early enough to witness her walk of shame. Of course, the whole unwed mother thing made it impossible for me to give her too hard of a time. Besides, I didn't want to do anything that would discourage her from getting out and living her post-Connor life. In the bright light of day, my resolution to inform her about last night's encounter was wavering.

I made myself a cup of decaffeinated tea, and headed out to the garden to greet the sun. I suddenly realized that my psychic headcount hadn't marked Emmet as present. Maybe he had taken off early this morning, or perhaps he hadn't come home last night, either. Emmet was a full-grown golem, though, so I had no doubt he could take care of himself for one night. Or maybe someone else had taken care of him. I felt an odd and unwelcome twinge of jealousy at the thought that some other woman might have welcomed him into her bed. I pushed the feeling away and told myself that it would be the best thing for all of us if Emmet moved on. But then another thought hit me. Maybe Claire had scared him off? No. That was unlikely.

Again I felt anger and misplaced jealousy toward the faceless and most assuredly imaginary woman who had seduced him. "Get a grip," I said to myself. I truly did love Peter. I forced myself to look at this possessiveness I'd begun to feel toward Emmet. Was I just being protective of him? In spite of all the years of knowledge and experience lent to him by the witches who had created him and his manly body, he was somehow still an innocent. I wanted to go along with that rationalization, but then my more honest side spoke the truth. This jealousy I felt truly had nothing to do with Emmet or his emotional well-being . . .

I might have learned that I was not the odd woman out when it came to magic, and Peter had never failed to make me feel beautiful and special, but I still struggled with a poor self-image. Emmet's declaration of love had flattered me, bolstering the unhealthy side of my ego. I could follow these emotions where they might lead me and break Peter's heart—again—ruining my life, and both of theirs, just to feed an emotional black hole. Or I could own up to the fact that I still had a lot of growing up to do. I sighed. Self-awareness sucked. I thought about what my mother had done . . . how she'd had an affair with Ellen's husband. Maybe that choice had sprung from a similar place?

My thoughts drifted from my mother to Peter's mom. I was worried about Claire. I had no idea what had set her off against Emmet. Perhaps Claire herself had a strong enough psychic ability to sense his otherworldliness? But that didn't explain the history she seemed to think she had with the golem, who she thought his people were, or, most importantly, what had happened to Peter's brother, the son she had turned over to them for safekeeping. I felt certain of one thing: It was a pure fiction that the old man was some long-lost Great-Uncle Peadar. This man, this "dried-up husk," as Claire had called him, was somehow Claire's son and Peter's brother. Logically, I couldn't account for how Peter's brother could be older than his parents, nor could I imagine the circumstances that had inspired Claire and big Colin to give up their boy, but there was no question that Claire believed him to be her long-lost son. "Peadar," the name of the missing uncle, was only a convenient label to hang on the body that had been found. Something for Detective Cook to chew on.

After Claire and I had returned to the bar, Colin came and whisked her upstairs to their living quarters. She hadn't made another appearance. I had joined Peter behind the bar, and we'd worked together until last call. "This is nice," Peter had commented at one point, his mismatched eyes, right blue and left green, misty with drink. I knew without asking what he meant by "this," and part of me agreed. Even so, the revelation that the Tierneys—a family I had always thought of as being the most normal family in the world—had been touched by some form of magic was making me ask the same questions Emmet had raised. How could it be that Peter was never bothered by my family's magic, and now by my magic, for that matter, when most *normal* people were at least a little unsettled by it?

The sound of a car pulling into our drive pulled me from my thoughts. A door opened and softly closed, and then the car reversed back onto the road. High heels moving cautiously across stone told me one of my aunts had returned.

Iris's eyes widened, and she stopped in her tracks, clutching her purse to her chest, when she registered my presence in the garden. In spite of her air of guilty surprise, she looked radiant in the rosy hues of early daylight. I knew it meant I was both a hypocrite and a liar, but I realized in that instant I'd never speak to her about Connor. I couldn't bring my heart to do it. I couldn't risk the fragile renaissance I was witnessing any more than I could rip the wings off a butterfly. I would take this secret to my grave. I made this decision in the full knowledge that my own weakness would make it a heck of a lot harder for me to judge either of my aunts. I raised my cup. "Morning."

"Good morning." She gave me a smile that tottered between embarrassment and hubris. "I guess this old girl still has it in her," she said just in time for Oliver to arrive, shirtless and wearing baggy sweatpants, a mug of steaming coffee in hand.

"Well, she sure did last night," he said with a smirk, "and by the looks of you, all night long too."

"Oliver," we gasped in unison, and he let loose with a full-throated laugh. He came over to the table and joined me.

"When do you close on your new house, again?" Iris asked before shaking her head and going inside. In spite of her embarrassment, there was a sly and satisfied look on her face.

"Surprised you are home," I said.

"And why do you say that?" He held his mug in both hands and leaned in as if I were about to tell him the juiciest of secrets.

"Well, you know. After last night. You and Cook. I mean Adam."

He feigned a look of shock. "Well, my dear, we don't all have the alley cat morals of your Aunt Iris."

"You'd better not let her hear you say that," I said.

"Point taken." He took a sip of coffee and leaned back in his chair.

He grinned. "We danced a little. Drank way too much. Talked a little. Then I walked home. I was in no shape to drive, I'll tell you that."

"Wait, that's it?"

116

"We are having lunch today," he said. "I want to take our time and make sure this is right. We were kids . . . before. I don't want to rush things. I want to go slowly and enjoy it."

"You, Oliver Taylor, want to take things slowly?"

"Is that so unbelievable?"

"Yes. Who are you, and what have you done with my real uncle?" He blew me a very wet raspberry in response. A question rose to my mind. "How is it that Adam doesn't react poorly to your magic?"

Oliver raised his eyebrows and frowned at the same time, considering the question. "He did at first, when we were young, back when we first met. But I *suggested* that he not 'react poorly to it,' as you so quaintly put it."

"You compelled him?"

Oliver nodded. "Yeah, but that was the one and only time. I owned up to him that I had done it, and I promised us both I'd never suggest anything to him again." He took a sip of coffee and then looked at me over the rim of his mug. "Adam is worried about you, you know?"

"Worried about me? Why?"

"'Gut feeling,' he says. Peadar Tierney showing up with a hole punched through him. You've been acting all cagey around him, he says. Don't worry; I didn't say anything about the old guy."

"Is it hard for you, keeping secrets from Adam?" I found myself piling up secrets in my relationship with Peter: my mother's return, the truth about Maisie, the incident with Peadar, Emmet throwing himself at my feet, *my liking* that Emmet had thrown himself at my feet.

"Honestly, I don't know, but the way things happen around here, I am sure I will have many opportunities to find out. Tell me, Gingersnap. What was all the commotion with Claire last night?" He sat down his cup and leaned his chair back so that it balanced on its hind legs. "No, I was neither too wasted nor too preoccupied to notice."

"You tell me. Claire thinks she knows Emmet or at least 'his people.'"

"People?" he rocked his chair back on all fours and tilted his head.

"She says he isn't human. She thinks he is something other-worldly, but other than that I don't know more than you do."

"But you will get to the bottom of it?"

"Of course. I have ideas, but they sound crazy, even to me." My instincts told me to hold off on sharing more than I had to, at least until I knew the full story of what was going on with Claire. "I love Peter, and I want to marry him, but I want to know what I'm getting into with the Tierneys. You know?"

"Indeed I do. Let me know if I can help." The sun had made its way high enough in the sky to illuminate the whole of our garden. "Lord, doesn't that feel good?" Oliver asked as he stretched up into the golden light. He stopped mid-stretch and stood, walking over to where he had placed the sundial. He held out both hands, palms down, toward the marker. "Someone has been messing around here." He turned and regarded me, his right eyebrow raised. "*You* have been messing around here. Just what have you been getting up to, Gingersnap?"

My mind breezed over a thousand lies, none of which I had the heart to tell. I rose and rushed over to his side. "Connor," I said and gave a slight nod toward the dial. So much for taking the secret to my grave. "I was trying to resurrect a memory of Mama," I said. "He hijacked the energy."

Oliver's face turned gray, somehow understanding the whole of the situation from these few words. "I'm sorry. I had no idea. Say nothing . . . to anyone. I'll handle this. Okay?"

I felt myself begin to tremble in spite of the sun's warm rays. I drew my arms up around myself and nodded once. And with that began yet another Taylor family conspiracy. That's all it took. A secret and a shared desire to protect the ones we loved. Oliver put his arm over my shoulders and led me back to my chair.

"I've been giving a lot of thought to what the Tree of Life told us about your sister's situation," he said in an obvious attempt to pull my thoughts away from Connor. "I think we ought to consider borrowing from your mother's bag of tricks. We need Tillandsia."

"What do you mean?" I asked.

"I think it's what the Tree of Life was trying to tell us, *you*, when you saw the doorway to the new Tillandsia house." He leaned in toward me. "We need power. Big power that the families cannot trace, power that the anchors can't just switch off if they figure out what we are doing."

"And you think we can get this power through Tillandsia."

"Think about it. We may not know what Emily intended to do with the power she was summoning, but we know that she spent years using the Tillandsia 'gatherings,'" he said, and I felt grateful for the euphemism, "to build up a battery of power. Power that the united families could not control."

"Assuming that power still exists, that it hasn't all been used up or dissipated, how would we access it?"

"If I knew my Emmy, and I do believe I did, that power is still locked up tight somewhere. We, however, don't stand a snowball's chance in hell of getting at it."

"Then why even bring it up?"

"Because *we* don't, but *you*, Gingersnap, do. I'm sure Emily put some kind of lock on it, so that only she could access it, but you carry a bit of Emily in you. I'm willing to bet that it will make itself accessible to you."

"You don't know that."

"No, I don't, but don't you think it's at least worth a try? For your sister's sake?"

I turned my face toward the sun and closed my eyes, letting myself hide behind the flamingo color of my eyelids. "Of course I'll try, but I don't have a clue as to how I'll do it."

The brightness faded, Oliver having stepped between me and the light. "'Fraid there is only one way to get ahold of the Tillandsia power."

"And that would be?" I asked, opening my eyes to see him standing there, haloed like some earthbound angel.

"The only way to access the power built up through Tillandsia is by 'participating' in their activities." This time I didn't appreciate the euphemism. Not one little bit.

The thought of participating in a Tillandsia gathering—or, throwing all niceties aside, *orgy*—was repellent. Growing up, I had thought Tillandsia was merely a private group where public people gathered to get their party on without having to worry about headlines. Now, I knew it was oh so much more. My heart broke at the thought that my lovely Ellen had been a willing participant in the group during the years after Paul and Erik had died. She said that even though she knew it was wrong, Tillandsia had somehow eased the pain of her loss. Still, I doubted she had ever used it as more than an anesthetic. It seemed unlikely that she had a hidden agenda like my mother had had, or possibly still had.

A freshly showered Iris rejoined us in the garden. I forced my full focus on her, not daring to let my eyes even stray toward the sundial. Her hair was damp and pulled back into a ponytail. She wore no makeup, but in spite of that fact, she looked younger than I'd ever seen her. She had on her favorite yoga pants and my favorite T-shirt. "Hope you don't mind," she said, noticing my noticing.

It had grown way too tight for me these days anyway. "Not at all. It looks cute on you."

She smiled and blinked slowly, like a happy cat. "Thank you. I thought so too. Have you told her?" she asked Oliver.

"No, not yet. We were discussing other things." He winked at me.

"Told me what?" I felt a tingle run down my spine.

"We have a plan," Iris said, "to deal with the situation with the demon at the old hospital. Well, actually, it is Emmet's plan, but I think it's a good one. I'll fill you in later, but clear your calendar tonight, because we are going demon hunting."

FIFTEEN

My phone rang, and I looked at the number. It was Claire. "Hello?" I answered.

"Oh, Mercy dear, I'm glad you answered," Claire said, her voice betrayed her anxiety. "Listen, we need to talk. Any chance you could drop by?"

"Of course. I'll come right over." I knew she would try to convince me not to share the encounter I had witnessed between her and Emmet with Peter. I felt Peter should know about his brother. Still, I hoped it wouldn't fall to me to do the telling, as once again, I'd probably lose my nerve. I hoped that his parents would in time come to terms with their grief and tell Peter themselves. In the meantime, I had to set Claire straight about Emmet. She knew he wasn't exactly human, but still I knew he couldn't be whatever she believed him to be. To begin with, he had no *people*. He had donors, the witches who had made him. My family was as close as it came to his having people.

I left Iris and Oliver in the garden and went inside to change into a more presentable outfit, a pleated cerulean blouson sundress Ellen had bought for me. My inner tomboy fought back, so I paired it with some beat-up tennis shoes. I was glad Ellen wasn't around to catch me pairing the dress with this footwear. She'd never let me out of the house this way. It hit me that I hadn't yet thanked Ellen for all the trouble she had gone to on my behalf. I decided that I'd at least pick her up a card before returning home.

Stepping back outside, I decided the temperature had risen too high for me to walk, and for the first time, I felt too pregnant for my bike. I grabbed its handlebars and wheeled it inside the garage. "See you later, old friend." I couldn't help but give it a pat. An eerie sense of finality washed over me, and I started to cry. "So silly," I said to myself, shaking off the tears. Hormones and capricious magical abilities made for some very intense, if peculiar, emotions. I closed my eyes and felt my body slipping. My one attempt at keeping my eyes open while jumping from one place to another had made me sick and dizzy. When I opened my eyes, I was standing in the alleyway behind Magh Meall. I rang the delivery buzzer and tried to collect myself, still feeling an inexplicable sense of loss.

I waited as I heard the sound of the large steel bar that secured the back door being removed from the brace that held it. The deadbolt turned and the door opened. Even though Claire had been expecting me, she looked surprised. "Oh, dear, it's you. That was fast."

I worried about rubbing her nose in my magic after the meltdown she'd had around Emmet. So I fibbed a little. "I was nearby when you called." I entered and watched as Claire returned the steel bar to its place and flipped the deadbolt.

"I appreciate your coming by," she said, weaving her way through the kitchen and out to the bar. I followed on her heels. "We need to talk about what happened last night. I must explain to you . . ."

"About Peadar, and about this preoccupation you have with Emmet."

"Yes, Emmet," she responded, taking a seat at the table with the best view of the front door. She motioned for me to join her, and I sat across from her. "I cannot warn you away from that one firmly enough. He isn't what he appears to be."

"And what if I told you that I already knew that?"

Her head tilted back slightly and her eyes widened as she took in my words. "You know?"

I knew Emmet was not human, even if I wasn't sure what she believed him to be. "Yes," I said, justifying my half-truth by holding it up against the years Claire had been keeping secrets from Peter and me. "But I don't understand why you think I should be afraid of him."

Her face grew taut, and she leaned into me, grasping my hand in hers. "Because he'll try to take your son."

"Don't be ridiculous."

"Mercy, hear me. I knew the first time I saw Emmet that he spelled trouble. I should have come to you then, but I had hoped to deal with the situation myself, sparing you. I thought I'd found someone who could help me. Someone who could convince Emmet to take off and leave our family alone. When they found Peadar's body, I knew I couldn't keep it from you any longer. I had to share the truth with you, for the baby's sake. I don't understand why his people need our children, but they find you when you are hopeless. They come to you when you are too desperate to tell them no. They come with their deals and their promises and their lies."

I pulled my hand from her grasp. "What did they offer you in exchange for your son?" I, of course, had no idea who *they* even were, but now that Claire was finally sharing her secrets, I wasn't going to say anything that might stop her.

She was taken aback by my words. Her skin grew ashen, and she leaned forward suddenly, almost as if she were about to pass out. "They promised me," her words came out in a ragged whisper, "that he would live." She raised her eyes to meet mine. "He was dying. Blood cancer. The doctors could do nothing for him. Only their kindness forced them to admit this to us and let us bring him home at all. When we got to the bar, she was waiting here for us."

"She?"

"I have no name for her. Never laid eyes on her before and never laid eyes on her or her kind since, until this Emmet. She was such a beauty. A beauty so perfect I found it impossible to believe her to be anything but good. I thought we'd left her kind back in the old country, but it looks like they followed us here too. She said it was our music that had attracted her to Magh Meall. When she spoke, her words had such power over us." Claire paused. "Or maybe it was only the hope they offered that affected Colin and me so. She promised us that our boy would live. He would know a life of love and luxury. Her people would raise him as a prince," she said, her eyebrows knitting together over her sad smile.

"She promised us we would see our son again before we died. It never occurred to us that they would send him back to us a shriveled-up old man. A desecrated corpse." She began to shake, and I reached out to her. "I don't know why they would have done that to him, my girl." She shook her head, her eyes imploring me for an explanation, even though she couldn't really think I had one to give. But I did, and I could not let her go on thinking her son had been murdered in cold blood.

"They didn't," I said, the weight of my guilt collapsing my fear of confession.

"But how could you know that? How could you know what his last minutes were like? What he was thinking as they ripped his heart from him?"

"Because, it didn't happen like that." I got up, and then knelt before her. "You know that my family is different, that I am different."

Her expression turned wary as she looked down at me. "If by that you mean you are a truckload of witches, yes, I've always known. I've got a bit of the sight myself."

"Peadar, your son, he didn't die alone," I said, reaching up to smooth her hair. "And no one murdered him."

"Then you tell me what happened to him." Her voice grew stern. She stopped my hand from stroking her.

"He was lost, confused, and dying when I found him."

"You found him?" she echoed me.

"He wasn't alone. I was with him," I said, trying to ease her pain. "I tried to help him. To restart his heart."

She pushed herself back with great force, knocking her chair over as she stood. "You? You did this to him?"

"Not to hurt him. To help him," I pleaded. I stood and took a step toward her, but she raised her hand as if she would slap me.

Her palm quivered as her fingers curled in toward it, leaving only the pointer aimed at me. "Don't come near me. Not right now. Don't come near me."

"Claire, you must know I'd never intentionally hurt your son. I didn't kill him. I swear. He had no pulse. I was only trying to help. You have to believe I'd never hurt Peter's brother."

Her hand fell to her side. Her mouth fell open, and then she laughed. A hard and bitter laugh. "Oh, you stupid girl. You stupid girl. You don't understand at all."

"Understand what?"

"The deal Colin and I made. That's what," she said and drew nearer. "Peter has no brother. The man whose heart you burned out, *he* was my son. My only son. My Peter."

SIXTEEN

Shock sent the sensation that I was falling from my head to my feet, and then back up again. My mouth gaped open, but no words came out.

"That's the deal we made, my girl. They'd take our Peter, and in return for keeping him alive, we would raise her son. The boy we raised, the boy we love as if he were our own true son, the boy you let fill your womb, he's one of them, the *daoine sidhe*. One of the gentry. That is why he can never know any of this."

"Come on. This is crazy. It can't be true. There's no such thing as fairies," I said. The words came out by reflex, but I myself had encountered stranger things. Even so, even if fairies existed, it was not possible that my Peter could be one of them. 'That my baby could be half Fae. I placed my palm over my stomach. Ellen had not sensed anything unusual about my son. At least nothing she had told me about.

"And there is no such thing as witches either, but here you stand before me."

I couldn't argue that away. "Okay." I said. "Accepting for the moment that this is possible, how can I keep it from Peter? If it's true, he has the right to know."

"But there's the rub. If you tell him, if he ever learns the truth about his nature, we will lose him. He will go to them. He won't be able to resist, no matter how much he may love you and his son. Trying to resist would only drive him mad or kill him. No, Mercy, you have to lay aside your opinions of right and wrong and do what I tell you. This secret, the truth about Peter—whom I very much consider my son in spite of it all—you have to take it with you to the grave." Wow. Twice in one morning. I was still trying to process the fact that Emmet had been right all along when a loud knock rapped the door and both our eyes darted toward it. "They're here. They don't know about Peter, so keep your mouth shut about him."

"Wait. Who are *they*?" I halfway expected King Oberon and Queen Titania to be waiting on the other side of the door.

Claire didn't respond. She righted the chair she'd knocked over, then crossed over to the door. She undid the deadbolt and opened it, but my view was blocked until she swung it wide and stepped aside.

"Hello again, pretty lady," the man who called himself Ryder greeted me, stepping over the threshold. I recognized him immediately—he was the leader of the trio of "train people" who had accosted me outside the bar. Ryder's companions, Birdy and Joe, followed him, Birdy making quick furtive glances around the room as if she halfway expected an ambush. Joe sauntered in behind her and flashed me a big toothy smile before taking a seat at a table near the door. Claire closed the door behind him and reset the deadbolt.

"You've met?" Claire asked.

"Yeah, we've had the pleasure," Ryder responded.

"Wait," I said, focusing on Claire. "You know these people?"

Claire looked at me. "Don't be afraid, Mercy. Ryder's here to help us."

"Help us what?"

"He knows about Emmet. Ryder has experience with the supernatural. I was researching the gentry, trying to figure out why Emmet had come nosing around. Most of what I read was nonsense, but when I found Ryder's website—"

"Wait. You found him *online*?"

Claire winced at the sound of my outrage. "He's offered to help. He's come all the way from Louisiana." When these points failed to move me, she leaned in toward me, her tone conspiratorial. "He's dealt with the *daoine sidhe* before."

"What do you mean dealt?"

"Dealt," he said tapping the top of the knife he wore strapped to his leg. "And with other supernatural creepy-crawlies too. Skinwalkers," he continued, "demons, blood drinkers . . . witches." I flinched, and he laughed.

"But you aren't a witch yourself. You must borrow the power." As Jilo had taught me, some non-witches were extremely talented at channeling energy, so I didn't doubt his story. I forced myself to shake off my fear of the man and looked at him through the lens of my own magic. An aura of scattered and violent energy surrounded him, flecks of red emitting from a black hole. I sensed the darkness inside him recognizing my own power and tugging at it, trying to swallow it.

Ryder held up his forearm, and the tattoo that covered him from wrist to shoulder began to glow, a pulse of energy racing along its lines. Its design began to change, becoming animated before my very eyes. He held his arm up, proudly displaying it. "You got some juice in you, girl," he said with a leer. "I'd sure love to squeeze it out."

"What are you?" I asked, unable to tear my eyes away from the morphing design. As I watched, the ink transformed itself into an expertly rendered etching of my own face.

He lowered his arm, and I flicked my eyes from his tattoo to his face. The smile I saw there sickened me. "I'm just an ordinary guy. A man who has accepted a mission and been given the power to carry it out. I see a problem, and I do my best to deal with it. One of your kind, one of you witches, appreciated my efforts enough to give me this here tattoo. It not only gives me a bit of my own magic, but it makes me pretty much immune to most other magic. That's why you couldn't just shoo me away the other day. I could've had you then, but it wasn't the right time. She's a beauty, ain't she?" He laughed, rolling his forearm around to compare the ink rendition of my face to the real deal. "Started out as a band around my wrist, but it's growing nice." The tattoo flashed and returned to its original pattern.

"Those symbols in your tattoo, they help you steal others' power. There's a price for that, you know? You'll burn for it. I've seen it happen."

"Oh, I will burn all right, girly, but not today."

"I think I've made a mistake inviting you here." Claire began crossing cautiously toward me. I figured that she had probably just made the biggest understatement of her life. "I think you all should leave."

"Now, y'all ain't gonna make the same mistake twice, are you?" Ryder asked, and in a blink Joe had crossed the room and was cradling Claire in his arms, the serrated blade of a hunting knife similar to Ryder's pressed against her throat. "Maybe you'd like to try this again?" the ringleader asked, looking at me. "How about that drink you refused me the other day?"

"Don't hurt her," I pleaded. I went behind the bar and found three glasses, filling them with sour mash. Could I do something to take out Joe without hurting Claire? I could feel my magic rise in waves around me, my panic pushing it to limits I doubted I could control with any kind of precision. I had to find a way to reach them without harming Claire. As I carefully set the glasses on a tray, the flimsiest of tactics formed in my mind.

"No. You stay where you are, Ryder commanded, and then, "Fetch, Birdy." She jumped at his words, eager to please. She was so grateful to count Ryder as her man that she didn't seem to mind being ordered around like a dog. Our eyes met as she collected the tray. Hers hardened at the sight of the pity in mine.

"Emmet isn't what you think he is," I said, hoping I might think of a way to convince them he wasn't worth their trouble.

"He isn't human." Ryder said. "And he's just burstin' with magic." He took a drink from the tray. "So what is he?" I remained silent and stared at him, my mind rushing over plausible tales. For about the millionth time, I cursed my inability to out-and-out lie. "You want her to keep her tongue, you better start wagging yours."

Joe pried Claire's mouth open and shifted the blade. Her eyes had grown as wide as silver dollars with panic. "He's a golem. A golem. Let her go."

"Well I will be good and damned," Ryder said, tossing back his whiskey. "They still makin' them things?"

"He's more than that, though. He's alive for real. I don't understand it myself, but he's alive."

"Hear that, Joe? A patch of dirt has turned itself into a living, breathing man." Joe nodded at him. Birdy dropped the tray on a table and stood by the younger man's side as he took a swig of his whiskey. She downed her own in one gulp and threw the glass at the bar, where it shattered into a thousand pieces. Claire jumped at the sound, and the blade sliced a shallow nick into her neck.

"Easy there," Ryder said to her. "You're my collateral in this here transaction." He turned back to me. "It ain't natural, a golem with a mind of its own," he said, addressing me. "A golem needs a

131

master. Your boy is probably aching for someone to take control of him, help rid him of that pesky free will, that conscience."

"So you want to turn him back into a puppet."

"No." He laughed and in a single movement slid his knife from its sheath and sliced through the air. "I want to skin him, that's what I want. Real magic, witch magic, has been bound up in his body. I'll turn his pelt into objects of power, *talismans*," he said, as if repeating a recently learned word. "Turn his bones into relics, cook his marrow into *unguents*." He mispronounced the word, but I still got his meaning. "Ain't a wannabe witch in the world who wouldn't give me their firstborn for a piece of your golem's magic. Including that old darky you been hanging with."

How did he know about Jilo? That was a question for another time. "Listen," I said. "If it's money you are after, I have plenty . . ."

"No, darlin', I ain't doing this for money. I'm doing it for power. The trinkets I'll make out of your golem's hide will come at the price of *fealty*"—a medieval oath of loyalty, another word intended to impress—"and a sacrifice of blood. The power of that blood will become mine." He nodded at me once. "Now you call him. You tell him to get himself on over here, and once we have him, we will leave you lovely ladies to get on with your day."

"Enough," I said. "I am not helping you hurt Emmet to power some magic Ponzi scheme."

"Oh, missy, I ain't asking for your help. I've been keeping an eye on you for a while, and maybe you ain't noticed it yet, but wherever you are, that golem of yours ain't never too far behind. He may not give a damn about your friend here, but I am pretty sure he gives one for you. Maybe if I start to cut that little bastard out of you, he'll show hisself instead of hovering invisible behind you like some kind of limp-wristed guardian angel. How about it, golem? When the bough breaks, it's all gonna fall down anyway," he said and parted his lips into a sneer.

"Call him, Mercy. Call him," Claire keened. Blood had trick-led down from the wound on her neck, dampening her shirt.

"No need," Emmet's voice came from behind me. "I am already here." I turned my head for a quick look, relief flooding me as Emmet materialized behind me. He reached forward and placed a hand on my shoulder. "I promised I'd be here for you if you needed me."

"She needs you all right," Ryder said, sneering at us. Emmet pressed his body up against my back. His arms hooked around me. "You know what I am, don't you, golem?"

Emmet tightened his grip on me. "By your markings, I can tell you are a collector. You kill, and with each death you cause, you gain power. You are a scavenger of the potential energy of others. You are the bottom feeder of black magic."

"Yeah, that's right," he said, sliding his knife from its case. "You can insult me all you want, but I am still gonna wear your skin. Joe," he commanded, but the boy didn't obey the unspoken order. He swayed on his feet and then fell backward, Claire dash-ing from his faltering grasp. Birdy rushed to his aid, but then she crumpled over too. "The bitch doped us, baby," she managed to call to Ryder before losing consciousness. The spell I'd placed on the whiskey had worked. I'd hoped it might take out Ryder too, but he lunged at me with his knife, seemingly unaffected.

My fear and anger bound themselves together and I poured my focus entirely into the blade in his hand. The knife glowed red and then blue, the metal losing shape and transforming into a molten glove that charred the flesh beneath it. He howled, and then grasped his wounded hand. Rage burned in his eyes. His jaw unhinged like a snake, and he vomited foul-smelling black orbs that fell to the floor. Unrolling, they revealed themselves to be horrible little creatures, rats with nearly human faces that scurried along the floor, surrounding me. Razor-sharp claws protruded from their very human fingers and ripped into the bar's wooden floors. Claire screamed and climbed up on the bar. I let my magic slide me over to her side.

"Burn them, Mercy," Emmet said, his tone so free of fear, so matter-of-fact. Without a further thought, without the least concern for Birdy and Joe, who still lay unconscious where they had fallen, I raised my hand and sent out a bright and searing blue flame to encircle the vermin and the mad man who had summoned them. The creatures drew in closer to Ryder, protecting him, trying to extinguish the flames, but they failed. The fire rose like a wall between us, the rodents popping like frying bacon, releasing the stench of sulfur as they were incinerated. As his last defender fell, Ryder roared, but to my surprise, he raised his arms and began to summon the flames to him. An old lesson, the first Jilo had taught me, surfaced in my memory. I had sent the energy to him, and now he could do with it as he willed. Stupid. Stupid. Stupid.

Emmet flung himself in front of Claire and me, and threw up a shield of light separating us from Ryder. As I watched from behind the energy I prayed would keep us safe, Ryder pulled the flames into himself, screaming in agony but welcoming the power all the same. As he consumed the last of the fire, he drew the supine figures of Joe and Birdy toward himself. Their bodies constricted and shot up in the air, disappearing before our very eyes.

"They've escaped," Emmet said, turning toward us.

I nodded, trying to take it all in. The floor where Ryder had been standing was scarred by scorch marks and gouges left by the creatures' claws. The scent of sulfur, burnt skin, and ozone nauseated me. I fought the urge to vomit.

"But I am still proud of you," he continued. "You defended yourself admirably."

"But if you were here all along, why didn't you help us sooner?"

"It presented you with an opportunity to learn. I stepped forward when they threatened you."

"But they were hurting Claire."

"She is not my concern." He lifted me off the bar and set me on the floor. He didn't remove his hands, even though I had my footing. He looked at me with gentle eyes. "You are my . . . *charge*."

"She was in danger," I said, breaking free of his grasp. He towered over me, and I strained my neck to look him in the face. His expression was so calm, so matter-of-fact. Emmet could be exasperating. If he hadn't just saved me, I probably would have punched him. "You should have helped."

"She wanted me killed and my skin to be worn as a garment."

I looked at him. I looked at Claire. He had a point. "Emmet isn't out to harm me or the baby," I said, addressing Claire. "He isn't a threat to you, Colin, or Peter," I continued.

"But can I trust him not to share what he has learned about Peter?" she asked, and then, "Hell, can I even trust you?"

"I will keep your trust if Mercy wishes it," Emmet said. "As long as Peter's true nature does not pose a threat to her."

"Peter could never be a threat to me," I said. "Yes. I want this kept between us."

"But does it not change your feelings toward him, knowing he is no more a normal man than I am?" Emmet asked, a certain wistfulness in his tone.

I felt Claire's eyes fix on me like a drill boring through metal. "I think deep down, I've always known he was something more than that. So, no," I said as I met Claire's gaze, "my feelings for Peter haven't changed." Her face softened at my words, but Emmet's self-satisfied smile told me that he felt he had found a foothold.

SEVENTEEN

The door began to shake as the sound of a fist pounding against it echoed through the room. I jumped. "Open up," Peter called out, sounding like he was scared out of his wits. He kept up the pounding as Claire shook herself from stunned silence and crossed the room to open the door for her son. Peter lunged through the doorway as soon as she undid the deadbolt. He grabbed her upper arms and pulled her to him for a quick squeeze. When he pushed her away, she stood there covered in plaster dust, as if she didn't quite know what to do. His eyes darted around the room and found me, and within seconds he had swept me into his arms. I could feel his heart pounding. "Are you all right?" he asked, loosening his grip on me enough to examine me.

"I'm fine. We're all fine," I said, trying to calm him, but his eyes fell to the ruined floor.

"What the hell has been going on here?"

"Your mother has been a foolish woman," Claire said as she closed the door. "She has been mistaking friends for foes and enemies for allies."

"Okay, but that still doesn't tell me a damn thing." I had never before heard Peter use even the mildest of profanities around his mother. I suspected Claire's own shame was the only thing keeping her from giving him a good round swatting.

"We're okay," I said again.

"I should have known you were here," Peter said, finally taking note of Emmet's presence. "If there is trouble, you are bound to be nearby."

Emmet held his tongue, but his dark eyes cut into Peter like daggers.

"Mr. Clay just saved the lives of your mother, your wife, and your child," Claire said, collapsing into a chair. "You owe him a debt of gratitude. As do I. He's a man of honor."

Peter's face began to soften when Emmet chose the worst possible time to make a point of clarification. "She is not his wife yet," he stated in a matter-of-fact tone. Peter's face flushed candy-apple red and his eyes nearly bugged out of his head.

"Maybe not legally," I jumped in, holding Peter's forearm tightly, "but in every other way." The men's faces reacted in a see-saw fashion, with Peter's forehead relaxing as Emmet's eyebrows pinched together. A question hit me and drew my full attention to Peter. "How did you know to come? How did you know we were in trouble?"

"Colin called me."

"But your father's out fishing with friends. He couldn't have known," Claire said, looking up at him.

"Not my father," Peter said. "My son. I know it sounds crazy, but I felt him calling me. I knew he was here, and I knew he was afraid. I dropped everything and ran." My hand fell to my stomach. *Half witch, half fairy—oh my, little one, you are truly going to be a wild card. Has there ever been another like you?* Peter smiled and placed his hand over mine. "I guess my boy takes after his mom." His smile faded. "What is that smell?"

"It's a long story," I began.

"I have time." Peter escorted me to the chair next to his mother's. "Out with it."

"Your mother believed I posed a threat to Mercy and your child," Emmet said without a shred of emotion in his voice. He might as well have been reading ingredients for a recipe.

"I'd like to hear it from them, thank you," Peter said, his fists curling tight and his shoulders tensing.

"Let him talk," Claire said.

"Sit," I said, hoping that Peter would let the tension leave his body if he did. He spun a chair around, placing his forearms on the back of it, but he didn't relax one little bit.

"I am, of course, in no way a danger to Mercy or your child. I have vowed to protect Mercy until she can protect herself."

"She shouldn't have to protect herself. I should be the one to protect her."

"You have no magic, but you are marrying a witch who is one of the anchors of the line. The dangers she will face require great power to stave off, and again, you have none."

Peter started up from his chair. "Sit," Claire commanded. Peter hovered, not sure whether to obey her or toss Emmet out of the bar. "He's right, son. I'm sorry. I know you'd like to be the one to keep Mercy safe, but today I've seen what she's up against. You're a good man—a strong man—but you are *only* a man." She rushed through the words as if she feared either Emmet or I might object to them. "The things I've seen today . . . There are monsters out there. You owe it to Mercy and your son to be man enough to let Mr. Clay teach her what she needs to know. Don't get in the way. I did, and it almost cost us everything. If you love her, you are going to have to let her be the strong one."

"I gotta get back to work." Peter pushed away from the table and left the three of us staring at the door as it slammed shut behind him.

"He'll be okay," Claire said after a moment of silence. "I know my boy. He's frightened, but he'll come around. You're his world."

"Frightened people do foolish things," I said, not even really thinking about how this could be applied to what Claire had done, inviting Ryder and his gang into our lives, but once the words had been spoken, I couldn't call them back.

"Yes, we do," she said. "I must apologize to you, Mr. Clay. I was wrong about you, both about what you are and about your intentions. I hope you can forgive me. I pray that you will keep your word and remain silent for my son's sake as well as Mercy's."

"You have already suffered a much more severe punishment at the hands of the collector than I myself would have ever meted out. In regard to Peter, I will kneel at the altar of Harpocrates."

Claire looked at me for clarification. "That's Emmet for 'We're good.'"

She nodded. "I think I'd like a bit of a lie-down," she said. "I don't know how we are even going to open tonight with this mess. Good Lord, the smell. It may take days for it to fade."

"Rest," Emmet said, addressing Claire. "As a sign of good-will, I will repair the damaged floor and rid your establishment of this scent. It will be a way to 'clear the air' between us once and for all." Emmet tilted his head to the side and smiled. He seemed quite pleased with his pun, but Claire was too over-whelmed to even notice. She just nodded and left the room.

As soon as she was gone, Emmet set about restoring the damage that had been done. The floorboards seemed to rearrange themselves on a molecular level, the deep gouges welcoming the returning wood dust that had until recently filled them. The burn marks lightened in color and faded to match the original shade. He stopped a moment before finishing the restoration. "As a point of clarification," he said, "a fetus's ability to call to its father in times of danger is not a witch trait. That magic belongs to the *Fae*."

EIGHTEEN

My family and Emmet were wrapped up in the final preparations for the cleansing of the old hospital, but I was distracted.
Iris had warned me that ridding Old Candler of the demon
would be a challenge, but now I could barely concentrate on
anything other than my son. What his life would be like. What
he would be like. How could I find out if there were any records
of a hybrid witch and fairy birth without raising some very difficult questions from my aunts and uncle? Even if I were certain I
could trust them, I felt I had to honor my promise to Claire. I
regretted having told Oliver as much as I had about Claire's mis-
givings about Emmet. I could come up with a cover for that. I
didn't know what that cover would be, but I'd find something. I'd
recently promised myself there would be no more lies in my life,
but that promise was probably the biggest lie of them all. To try
to escape the labyrinth of my thoughts, I made a stronger effort
to concentrate on Iris's words.

"A hundred years ago, such a thing as a witching hour still
existed," Iris said as she removed a few essential items for the
cleansing ritual from the cupboard and put them into a grocery
bag. "Electric lights, night shifts, twenty-four-hour restaurants.
These things have pretty much done away with it."

"How so?" I asked. After waiting a lifetime, I had finally made it to the inside track of the world of magic. In spite of other concerns, I wanted to soak up as much information as I could, as quickly as I could.

"Well, because the witching hour has never had anything to do with a certain time on a clock. It isn't midnight. It isn't three in the morning. It's simply the time when the majority of conscious minds are sleeping. Reality becomes a bit more *pliant*, more *flexible*, when the world around a witch is dreaming. It made it easier for him or her to work magic, imprint his or her will on reality using much less energy. Now folk are up at all hours. The world is always awake—calculating, measuring." She consulted her list. "Sage, lavender, and cedar oils." She looked at me. "You do get that these things have absolutely no effect on spirits, leave alone demons, right?"

"Then why are we using them?"

"They might not have any effect on the bogeys," Oliver chimed in, "but they affect the people who enter the environment where the spirits have been."

"Okay," I said, shaking my head at the same time to show I didn't follow.

"Sage doesn't chase away spirits," Iris continued, "but it does mask their scent. Spirits carry an ozone scent, and demons smell like sulfur or rotten eggs. A person might not even consciously register the smell, but they'll sense it on some level. It's that awareness that the spirit can use as a doorway to return to the environment."

"So you are telling me that what you don't know really can't hurt you."

"Only after the spirits have been removed, sweetie," Ellen said. "The herbs and oils just make the place more pleasant. The less creepy the vibes are in a place, the less likely a person is to go looking for shadows and inadvertently invite them back in."

"Now salt does affect demons directly," Iris said, and Oliver chuckled, as though her words had summoned up a memory. "When one does manage to materialize in our reality, it usually starts out quite small, with a body made up of a mucus-like substance."

"Think snails or slugs," Oliver said, shaking the box of rock salt that Iris had placed on the counter.

"Ugh," Ellen said. "I always hated salting. That sizzling and whining sound those things make."

I stood there staring in disbelief at the three of them. "Your grandfather used to take us out with him when he went *hunting*, as he liked to call it," Iris explained.

"Ellen was a bit too girly to enjoy the finer aspects of the catch," Oliver said. She waved off the memory, giving a shudder. "Your mama, on the other hand, she was what the itty-bitty baby demons had nightmares about."

They all laughed at once, and then said, "The old saw mill," in unison. I loved these three so much, and they seemed to love my mother so much . . . I kept forgetting that she herself had implied that they'd kept her from me. The affection they appeared to share for my mother didn't at all match her version of events. I felt sure there was enough love there to right Ginny's wrongs. That was *if* I could ever manage to get my family all together. But there would be time to reflect on that later. Within the hour, I'd be facing a demon. I set all thoughts of my mother to the side.

"Honestly," Ellen said, "I wish we didn't have to deal with this now. We have enough on our hands."

"I feel the same way," Iris said, "but the people renovating that place are the ones setting the schedule. We need to dispatch Barron before Candler is turned over to its new purpose. I wouldn't want to risk what he might do otherwise."

Emmet entered the room, carrying a dusty box that looked like it had been rummaged from a far corner of the attic. "I beg you all to reconsider the wisdom of the jocular tone of these preparations. You should not risk lulling Mercy into a false sense of security about dealing with Barron. It's true that he is not the greatest evil this world has ever known, but he is a parasite that preys on the weak and the young, those who cannot defend themselves. Remember, Mercy, this demon feasts on children."

"You're right," Iris said. "It is certainly not our intention to make light of the evil this demon has done, but I have already made it clear to Mercy how dangerous it will be to deal with him."

"It's only that we are so happy to have her with us," Ellen said, "as one of *us*." I knew what she meant. I felt it too. For the first time, they could include me, rather than mislead or misdirect me for my own protection.

"But you are right, Sandman," Oliver said. "Fun and games aside, this is serious business. Are you sure you are up for it, Gingersnap?"

"She is ready," Emmet answered for me. He raised his chin and looked down at me proudly. My efforts with Ryder had impressed him much more than they had myself. All the same, I'd asked him not to share the details about our encounter at Magh Meall with the others. We'd share our agreed-upon version of events when we were through dealing with Barron. "But she needs your sober example."

Oliver looked at me for a response anyway. "He's right," I said. "I'm ready to do this. I know it is serious, dangerous, but we *will* do this together."

"All right then." Iris addressed Emmet, "Have you chosen a poppet for us?"

"Yes," Emmet said, producing an antique porcelain doll from the box he had been carrying. He placed it on the counter next to the supplies Iris had gathered together. I noticed that the doll's hands had been bound with a red ribbon. "It is ready for animation, but I feel it's best to wait until we are closer to the time of use."

"Oh," Ellen said. "Do we have to use that one?"

"It's the only one made entirely of clay. The vessel must be made of earth."

"Wait," I said, "what are we doing with the doll?"

"Your grandfather trapped Barron in the hospital," Emmet said. "We need a vessel to transport him to his new home. An enticing vessel. A living vessel."

"You are going to bring the doll to life?"

"To a semblance of life," Iris said.

"In much the same way my body was at first animated," Emmet said.

"We're all going to give it a share of ourselves, Gingersnap, just enough for the combined energies to confuse Barron, making him believe it's a human child."

"And then?"

"Then," Iris said, "when he comes to take the child, we will trap him inside the doll. Then we can remove your grandfather's spell, free the spirits trapped there, and remove Barron to a safer location until we figure out how to return him to where he lived when Gilles summoned him."

"And you are okay with this?" I asked Emmet. It sickened me that we'd be using as bait something so close to what Emmet had been.

"What else would you propose?" Iris asked. "That we use a flesh-and-blood child? Or that we visit the pound and find a puppy?"

"Of course not," I gasped. "But Emmet . . ."

"I am touched by your concern, but this doll will not contain the vital spark that the line has given me. It will be as I was before the line touched me, an empty vessel. Nothing more." I still wasn't sure how I felt about it. Even before the line had coalesced the nine essences of Emmet's makers into a single personality, I had considered him more than just an "empty vessel." Had my own feelings led me to project more onto him than had truly existed? Had my own perception of him influenced the line to free the golem as it had?

"Shall we load up then? Head over to Candler?" Oliver asked, interrupting my reverie. I nodded, and my aunts grabbed their purses as Oliver took charge of the supplies Iris had pulled together. I grasped the doll. I knew my resistance was irrational, but I couldn't bear the thought of Emmet carrying the poppet to its sacrifice.

"It was my idea," he assured me once more.

Oliver and Iris drove together, and Emmet and I followed with Ellen. We had planned for Oliver to arrive first so that he could charm the newly instated security guards. It bothered me to see that Candler was no longer deserted—the first visible evidence of the restoration work was the light that shone all around the building that had been dark my entire life.

I hadn't expected to see that the parking lot had already been extended, and the opening into which I had descended in search of Jilo was now paved over, sealed for good. "Rumor has it they wanted to cut down the old oak to make space for a few more cars," Ellen said as we followed Oliver. "I thought Iris would die from a fit of apoplexy. She's put a curse on the oak now, you know. Anyone who attempts to harm it will be sorry they tried." My aunt smiled at me in the rearview mirror. "You know Iris and her love of history."

"Good for her," I said. The Candler Oak was sacred to me as well.

Thanks to Oliver's powers of persuasion, both magical and his plain inborn sense of entitlement, we were not only allowed access—we were actually escorted inside by the guard on duty. "You'll keep everyone else out of here tonight, and tomorrow morning, you will forget we were ever here, please."

"Of course, Mr. Taylor," the man responded. "Y'all have a good evening now."

I still wasn't totally comfortable with Oliver's ability to compel others, the way he would impose his will on them without the slightest twinge of conscience. Maybe it was my conscience that kept me from being able to work this skill as well as my uncle could.

The door hadn't finished closing behind us before Emmet spoke up. "I sense that something is wrong here." We all stopped in our tracks, and I watched as my family tried to sense what he had.

"I don't feel anything," Ellen offered, shaking her head at me.

"No," Iris said. "Emmet is correct. Someone has been here tonight. Magic has been worked."

"Blood magic," I said, feeling the horror of the victim rush up around me.

"Yes," Emmet said, pride for me, his prize pupil, showing in his eyes. It was intriguing to watch him learn how to connect to human emotions. He seemed to feel love, perhaps anger, but his response to the victim's pain was clinical at best. Empathy hadn't caught up to him yet . . . at least not empathy for strangers. I could sense the pain and fear she had experienced. I knew it without a doubt—the victim had been a woman. The sense of betrayal she felt toward the man who had brought her here broke my heart. I found myself clutching the doll I carried for comfort.

"I'm afraid it's worse than that," Oliver said, getting a full fix on our surroundings. "There's something missing, something that should be here but isn't."

"The demon is gone," Iris said, her tone revealing that she herself could not as yet wholly accept that fact. "I sense a blankness, a hole where its evil was."

I began walking, following my witch's sense that had little if anything to do with the normal five. My family and Emmet

146

followed me, a tightly knit shield of our combined magic protecting us as we continued down the main hall and to a stairwell that had been blocked off for decades. The steel door had been removed, no, blown from its hinges, and it lay several feet from where it had once hung. "Down here," I said, my feet leading me down the stairs to the basement. The door at that end had also been ripped from its hinges. It lay several yards away, bent into the shape of a U. The hall was bathed in shadow, only a single naked bulb shedding an insufficient circle of light. Splinters of glass running the length of the ground showed where the other bulbs had been broken. As my eyes adjusted to the dim lighting, I saw the body that was only partially hidden behind the bowed metal door. A pair of denim-covered legs stuck out, one foot covered by a dirty sneaker, the other bare and twisted toward us so that even in the shadows, I could make out the neon pink polish on the toenails.

The smell coming from behind the door was impossible to bear. I brought my hand up to my nose. I wanted to stop, but my body continued to carry me closer. As I drew near enough to see over the door, I cried out involuntarily, "Oh God," and stopped. The body had no torso, only a ravaged stump that stuck out a few inches above the top of the blood-soaked jeans. There, through the redness that colored the remaining flesh, I recognized the remaining part of a tattoo as the orange feet of a famous cartoon bird. Without my consciously attempting to do so, my magic charged the room, awakening a vision of the violence that had happened here.

I saw the train people. Joe held Birdy, while Ryder cut into her with an athame, a ceremonial dagger. He held it in his left hand, manipulating it clumsily. Birdy's screams echoed in my ears—heart-wrenching wails of pain and unheeded pleas. Joe's face tilted up and strained in an expression of sexual, nearly religious ecstasy as he assisted Ryder in this act of treachery. I turned and started swiftly back toward my family, but tripped over something. The doll flew from my grasp and shattered as it hit the floor. I fell to my hands and knees as Emmet rushed up in an attempt to catch me. I looked over my shoulder to see what I'd stumbled on and gasped in horror as Emmet pulled me into his arms, holding me tight to shield me from the horrors I had seen. I'd tripped over an arm, a familiar hand and tattooed forearm that was partially covered in the molten steel of a hunting knife.

"He offered up Birdy," I spoke in Emmet's ear. "He offered up Birdy for power."

"That appears to be the case," Emmet said, releasing me into my Aunt Iris's outstretched arms, but taking his time about it.

"You know this person?" Iris asked. I calculated how much I could tell her without exposing the truth about Peter. "She was a friend of yours?"

"No, not a friend. She and her associates tried to use Mercy and Claire as bait to capture me," Emmet said. "This woman's mate, a man named Ryder, has been consorting with a witch, a true witch who placed the mark of the collector on him. In her efforts to protect me, Mercy damaged his mark. I suspect he summoned the demon, offering it freedom in exchange for the power Mercy took from him."

"But how could he use Birdy to summon it?" I asked. "I thought the demon was only attracted to children and innocents. I wouldn't have considered Birdy either."

Ellen and Oliver had walked away from us, crossing over to examine what remained of Birdy's body. "I'm afraid, sweetie," Ellen said, tears welling up in her eyes, "that there was a baby. This Birdy of yours was pregnant."

NINETEEN

I retreated to my room the second we returned home. I was morally drained and physically exhausted. In spite of the horrors of the day, I slept like a stone. I didn't make it up and out until after noon the next day, but as soon as I did rouse my sorry self, I made a beeline to Colonial Cemetery. I needed to find Jilo and talk all of this through with her. She'd had far more experience with conjured demons, borrowed power, and misdirected love than anyone else I knew. She'd enjoy chiding me about a "mud pie" falling in love with me, and I could sure use the laugh her wicked comments would bring us both. Besides, I hadn't seen her since the Tree of Life ceremony, and I missed her.

Nearer the opposite end of the park, where the paths intersect in a V and become one, sat her battered green lawn chair, her red cooler balanced on top of it. The top of the cooler leaned against the side of the chair, leaving its contents exposed. I could make out a sheet of yellow paper that had been taped to the cooler's side. The writing was too distant for me to make it out. I kept an eye on the horizon, scanning for Jilo as I drew near her ersatz office, but I couldn't catch even a glimmer of her, visually or otherwise. It startled me when my eyes registered the rolls of cash stuffed into the open cooler. I'd never seen that much money in one place before. I reached out for a roll of hundred-dollar bills. A shot of energy stung my hand and burned my fingers. I looked at the note. "Out of business. Take what you gave me and not a penny more."

"It looks like Mother Jilo has closed up shop." A deep voice came from behind me. I turned to see Adam towering head-and-shoulders over me. He worked out of the police station on the other side of the cemetery's wall, so I wasn't surprised to meet him in Colonial. "I saw you at the gate. Thought I'd follow you in and see if you knew anything about this, seeing as you and Mother have grown so close over the last few months."

How or why he kept tabs on me and Jilo didn't seem as important to me as what was up with her. "I don't know," I said, more to myself than to the detective. "The other day, she wasn't quite herself, but I never expected her to pull something like this."

"She was upset? Maybe someone's been threatening the old lady?"

At this I burst out laughing. "Have you ever known Jilo to run from a fight?"

Adam smiled. "I reckon as not." He held a hand out toward the cooler, but I swept it away.

"I wouldn't do that," I said, "unless some of that money belongs to you."

"No, no. I never came to Mother for 'professional' services. I just like to keep an eye on her to make sure she's getting along all right. She was nearly family after all."

"I kind of feel like she's family myself," I said, amused to see he was somewhat taken aback by this.

"The Taylors joining forces with Mother Jilo? Lord help us all." He shifted uncomfortably and shrugged his shoulders, turning his torso a bit away from me. His posture told me that he would be happier if what he perceived as the traditional balance of power was kept in place. "Well, if you talk to Mother, you tell her I asked after her. Let me know if she's doing okay, right?"

"Sure." I could do that. I was worried about Jilo's sudden abdication, but I kept telling myself that steel doesn't dent easily.

Adam raised his right hand in a brief wave. "Okay, I will catch you later," he said and started down the V's right fork, which ran parallel to the wall of tombstones. I sighed quietly. It wouldn't be long before what was left of Birdy was found, and then Adam would be paying us yet another official visit. To my surprise he stopped in his tracks, turned, and took a few quick steps back toward me. "Oh," he said in that innocent tone that I had come to learn meant he was about to spring something big on me to try to get a reaction. *I am hiding things from him, and he is dropping bombs on me. So much for our newfound friendship.* "The old man we found. Peter's great-uncle." I said nothing, forcing my face into a question mark. "We've pretty much finished looking into the items sewn up in his coat lining."

"I don't understand." I pretended Jilo hadn't already told me about the small fortune that Peadar carried on himself. "What was in it?"

"Uh, just a few personal belongings," Cook said. "We'll pass them on to the Tierneys soon. You take care, okay?"

I nodded, and he took off again. I was happy that the Tierneys would receive the treasure Peadar had left behind. I fought off the wave of guilt that blamed me for being the agency by which he had left the world. I didn't have the luxury of wallowing right now. I glanced around the cemetery, miraculously free of tourists at the moment, then closed my eyes and envisioned home. The sliding sensation made me feel giddy and a little light-headed, but when I opened my eyes, I stood near the garage. Easy enough, but so far I had only attempted sliding short distances, and to places I knew well. I had never before attempted to find a person, and even as close as Jilo and I had grown, I still had no idea where the old woman kept her residence.

I focused on her, envisioning her face's tight lines and the way they crisscrossed one another, the ebony beads of her eyes. I got the impression of a room, not her magnificent haint-blue chamber, but a sitting room, the shades pulled tight. I sensed cool and shadow, the hum of a box fan, a shade being blown open by the outside breeze, an inch of sunlight piercing and then disappearing from the room. A voice, Jilo's voice, humming a tune I did not recognize. A heavy book resting on her lap. The sensations sharpened.

"You leave me alone, girl," Jilo said. "I don't want none of you today." She waved her hand, and the room warped before my eyes, nearly fading. I was in no mood to be dismissed, and I felt no small sense of pride when I managed to hold my focus. Jilo and I arm wrestled for a few moments; she tried to force me away, but I insisted that she allow me to draw near. Her world floated up like a bubble, popping open and spreading around me as the sense of sliding fell away. I'd won the fight, but Jilo had managed to hold me off well enough that instead of appearing before her in her room, I found myself standing outside an old farmhouse that could have been situated anywhere between Valdosta and Florence for all my eyes could tell. A rusting red tin roof. A wide wraparound porch, shimmers of fading haint blue on the overhang, and the same shade peeling from the frame of the front door and window casings.

Four of my five standard senses told me that I recognized the place, though, recognized the crunch of the gravel beneath my feet as I took a few steps toward the house, the spring of the steps as I climbed to the porch. I realized this was the house where Jilo had brought me the day of Ginny's funeral, when she'd had me blindfolded, kidnapped, and driven here by the ghost of

Detective Cook's grandfather. I had been so terrified of Jilo and her magic then. Now, instead of being afraid of her, I feared for her. Funny how quickly your world can change. I reached for the screen door, but the front door opened before my hand could make contact.

A very tall young man, a much younger and somewhat more masculine version of Jilo, stood in the doorway, blocking my entrance. He was dressed plainly in a tight white tank top and too-loose jeans. A wide leather belt held the pants in place, a full two inches below the top of his boxers and only an inch or so above indecency. "She says that she doesn't want to see you." His accent struck me, bereft as it was of the Southern softness my ears had become accustomed to.

"And who are you?" I asked, trying to make it sound as if I really had the right to ask any questions.

He threw back his head and laughed. "That's right, you wouldn't recognize me, would you?" He stepped out of the house, closing the door firmly behind him. "Truth be told, I barely recognize you. You were such a frightened little mouse the last time you came here. Now look at you, all full of the magic and not in the least little bit scared." He stepped closer, standing only a few inches from me, trying to use his height to intimidate me.

The house's front door flung itself open. "Martell," Jilo's voice thundered.

The young man deflated at the sound of her voice. "Ah, I was just messing with her a bit, Gramma."

"Martell." I spoke his name, realizing that this was the great-grandson Jilo had helped escape from jail after he'd been arrested on suspicion of having murdered Ginny. To help him break out, she'd bent light around him, making him invisible, but then she had trouble mustering enough power to unbend the light. She had confessed to me that her first use for the power I'd given her was to make Martell visible once more, but I hadn't given him much thought. "Nice to finally see you. Now back off and let me talk to Jilo."

He hesitated, but Jilo called out. "Let 'er in. She a Taylor, and Taylors don't understand the word 'no.'" My eyes locked with Martell's. One last challenge, a warning that told me he loved his great-grandmother, and then he stepped aside.

I opened the screen door and stepped into the darkened room. All the shades were closed, and the lights were off. The way Jilo had banished light seemed less an attempt to keep out the day's building heat, and more as if she were in mourning. "Now what the hell you want?" The question came to me from the room's darkest corner. The hum of the box fan was silenced as Jilo's knobby fingers slid out of the shadow and switched it off.

"I want to see you. Make sure you are all right." I took a couple of steps toward her, but stopped, shocked at the sight. She seemed to have shrunk somewhat, crumpled in on herself. Her hair had turned a confrontation of steel and snow, without even a memory of the jet it had been only a few days before. It appeared that the years she had managed to forestall had caught up with her overnight.

"You ain't got to worry none about Jilo. She just tired. She tired of silly people and they silly desires. The way they so lazy that they come to Jilo for magic, rather than tryin' honesty and hard work to get what they want. She tired of the diggin' and she tired of the Hoodoo. She don't want the power no more. She tired of the magic, and she sure enough tired of the Taylors," Jilo said, and then stopped herself. "Jilo don't mean you, girl." Her voice softened. "Jilo will never get tired of her Mercy."

A lump formed in my throat, and I rushed over to her, sitting cross-legged at her feet. Her hand, cold and nearly leathery, reached forward and began to stroke my hair.

"Tell me what happened, Jilo. What really happened," I said.

Silence settled between us for what seemed like several minutes. "That damned uncle of yours" was all she said.

"Oliver?" I asked, confused.

"You got any others?" she asked, causing me to realize that with Connor and Erik gone, the list had indeed been whittled down to one.

"What did he do to you?"

"Nothing," she said, "and then again, everything." She began humming again, stroking my hair. "Jilo saw it," she said finally. "She saw the whole damn thing."

"I don't understand."

"Oh," she said shifting stiffly in her chair, "he ain't meant to do nothin' to Jilo, but he had Jilo stand there next to you in that tree of his. Jilo didn't see anything at first. She just did what yo' uncle told her to. She sprayed the perfume. She put the dirt in yo' hand and poured the whiskey over it. But she didn't see nothing. Not until she look in yo' eyes. And then she saw the whole thing. Jilo's entire life, it done flashed before her, just like she was dyin'. And Jilo saw. She saw every single choice she made. How every single action tied into every other single action. Every single wrong. Every single harm. Jilo done saw herself from the outside in, and what she saw was wrong. Jilo saw the beast there waitin' for her. Just waitin' there with it sharp teeth to gobble up her sinful heart. It too late for Jilo, my girl. She done the harm she done. She know she gonna have to face up to that. But she ain't diggin' herself no deeper. Jilo's done with magic."

I should have never waited so long to check in on Jilo, but I'd always thought of the old woman as being carved from granite and dipped in steel. It hadn't occurred to me that *she* might need *me*. I sat up straight, seeing her more clearly now that my eyes had adjusted to the shade. She looked fragile, if not already broken. I had to choose between coddling and tough love. I decided on a delicate balance of both, starting with the latter. "So you are planning to hole up here between now and death?"

She gave a sad cackle. "That comin' for Jilo sooner than you think, girl."

"No," I said as I stood and glared down at her. "You aren't deserting me like this. I have no doubt you've done some things you should be ashamed of. But it seems to me that rather than sitting on your butt and moaning—"

"Now you watch how you talkin' to Jilo—"

"And feeling sorry for yourself," I continued even more forcefully. "It seems that while there's still some breath in you, you should get out and try to mend some of that damage you've done."

"Jilo . . ." She fumbled with a button on her dress as her lower lip poked forward. "She too old. Too tired. What's done is done."

"But what isn't done isn't," I said sharply. My voice caught in my throat. "I need you, Mother. I need you."

She looked up at me, a moistness forming around her eyes. "And what do you need a broken-down old thing like Jilo for?"

I reached forward and took both her hands. They were oh so cold, as if life had already begun to desert them. "Because you are the only one I am sure I can trust. Completely."

Her eyes looked me up and down. "You so sure about that?"

"Yes," I responded without hesitation.

"Well maybe you shouldn't be," she confessed, pulling her hands out of mine.

"What do you mean by that?"

"Well, 'cause we both know they is outright lyin', and then again, they is not tellin' the whole truth. Jilo know something about you. About yo' family. That little bastard, the one you called Wren. Don't forget, he was keepin' an eye on yo' family for

Jilo long before you born. If Jilo told you what she been keepin' from you, that trust of yours might up and disappear."

I fixed her with my stare, causing the old woman to squirm for perhaps the first time in her life. "Tell me." My heart beat a wild tattoo, but I forced my voice to remain level, calm.

Her eyes darted around me, then fell to her lap. "Those pretty aunts of yours been lying to you, girl. Not like Jilo been by holdin' back, but outright lyin'. Jilo think maybe Ginny figured it out too, but she not sure about it. Iris and Ellen, though, they know. They had to know all along."

"They know what?" I asked, growing impatient. My magic reached out to her as I fought the urge to break in and read her thoughts. Deep down, even without rummaging through her memories, I knew what she would say, but still, I had to hear her say it.

Her eyes fluttered up to meet mine. "Your mama, Emily. She didn't die having you. She ain't dead at all."

I never thought I'd be happy that Jilo had used Wren to spy on my family, but finally I had the opportunity to learn the truth from a somewhat objective witness. I sat back down at her feet. "Tell me everything."

TWENTY

Jilo licked her dry lips and readied herself to speak. "You know Wren was keeping an eye on yo' family for me."

I nodded, noticing that she had repeated herself but not pointing it out.

"Well, he the one that told Jilo. He saw yo' mama wandering around this house the day she was s'posed to be getting planted in the ground. Said she was goin' through the place lookin' for something." Under its own volition, my hand flew up to touch the chain of my mother's locket.

Jilo started to say something more, but before she could, Martell barreled through the door. "Gramma, you gotta come see this." He ran back to the porch. "Damn," his voice carried to us through the screen door. Our eyes locked, and I scrambled up to my feet. I stopped to help Jilo hoist up her light and brittle body.

I let Jilo come under her own steam as I hurried outside. I didn't see anything unusual from the porch, nothing that would get Martell going like he was. I walked out into the yard after him and followed his eyes to the sky. A dark arc, like a rainbow drained of its colors, had stretched across the western horizon. In the few moments I stood watching it, its color changed from steel to granite to coal.

Jilo had found her way to the porch and was leaning out to examine the phenomenon. The arc began to unfurl, forming a curtain of dusk, not so much hiding everything on the other side as draining the color, fading it to black and white . . . and then all light disappeared, leaving only darkness. "You two come up here. Get out of the yard." Jilo's voice quivered. "Go on," she commanded when we didn't move. Martell stood where he was, entranced, frozen in place like a statue. I grabbed his hand, my own fright giving me the strength to drag him across the gravel, up the steps, and into the house behind Jilo.

We watched through the window as the veil against the sky began to close in on us. It grew in both proximity and length, the edges curling up toward each other, encircling us. "Gramma, what is it?" Martell asked, his face trembling, fear stripping him of the contrived swagger, revealing the innocent little boy behind it. In spite of my own fear, my heart went out to him.

"It's going to be okay," I told him, and then found myself looking to Jilo for confirmation. She said nothing. She went from window to window, opening the blinds. Each window framed a growing shadow. The band of darkness had changed, becoming a devourer of light. I shuddered, realizing that it had stopped growing and had begun contracting, like a serpent squeezing tighter. The world beyond its grasp had ceased to exist for us. On its inner edge, the side that grew ever nearer, the last bit of bright blue summer sky was being drained of color and light. The sky began to press down on us, its heaviness palpable, and the ground beneath our feet trembled. Like a bubble rising to the surface, the world around us lifted up, forming an ever-contracting sphere. It was like a black hole sucking everything into it.

Jilo turned to me, and I saw true terror in her eyes. "It coming for Jilo." Her voice was a dying whisper. "She sorry it catching you too," she said, still looking at me. "Yo' granny, she sorry," she said, reaching out and pulling Martell to her. I glanced out the windows, but nothing was visible beyond them. The world stopped at the panes of glass, and then the windows themselves began to crack under the growing pressure. All sound stopped as gray seeped in through the walls, draining the already faded flowers of Jilo's wallpaper to nothing.

Walls began to curve around us, and the baseboards warped before our eyes. I ran to Jilo and took her and Martell in my arms. The boy was trembling, but instead of resisting, he clung to me. I didn't know if it would work. I wasn't even sure a world still existed outside this quivering bubble, but I grabbed them both and held them tight. I closed my eyes and focused on home.

The next thing I knew, I felt the sun on my face and heard the sounds of birds and traffic. I opened my eyes, and there I stood in the garden, still holding my hitchhikers in a death grip. Martell broke away, stumbled a few feet, and began to wretch. Jilo looked at me with something that went past respect and spoke of wonderment. "Bless you, baby," she whispered, and then went and stood beside her grandson, patting her hand on his shoulder to comfort him.

"I'll get him some water," I said, heading to the kitchen door.

"If yo' uncle has any of that scotch left, I'd be much obliged," Jilo replied, giving Martell a final pat. I smiled. The old girl was nothing if not resilient; she was already on the mend.

Walking into the silent house, I sent out a psychic ping to see if it would bounce back to me from any of the house's corners. Nothing; no one was home.

I went into the library and found some whiskey for Jilo, then passed through the kitchen to grab a couple of glasses, filling one with water and one halfway with the stronger stuff. I returned to the garden, almost dropping the glasses when I found Iris standing next to the table across from Jilo and a defiant-looking

Martell, who sat slumped into his chair. He was pointedly look-ing away from my aunt and feigning boredom. I handed him his water, which he took silently.

"Martell," Jilo said.

He sat up a little straighter. "Thank you," he said without much feeling and began to nurse his drink, eyeing the glass I handed Jilo with covetous, underage eyes.

"Thank you, my girl," Jilo said.

"Oh, my goodness," Iris said. "Have I taught you nothing? Those are the everyday glasses, not the ones we use for guests. This young man here, Martell"—she raised an eyebrow, probably recollecting where and when she'd first heard the name—"he looks hungry to me, and the best you can offer him is water?"

"I could eat," Martell said.

His grandmother tut-tutted him. "Martell, you a guest here."

"But Gramma, I was just saying—" He stopped as Jilo's eyes opened wide, and she pointed her index at him.

"Thank you, Miss Iris, but they no need to fuss over Jilo and the boy."

Iris laughed. "Pardon me, Mother, but there we disagree. If after all these years, Mother Jilo Wills is gracing this home with her presence, it is indeed an occasion worth a bit of fuss." She looked at me with a wide, lopsided smile that caused the corners of her eyes to wrinkle. I could tell she had always hoped for the chance to start putting the bad blood behind us all.

Jilo remained silent. She took a deep sip of her drink and slowly closed and reopened her eyes, as happy as a fat cat by a warm fire.

"Martell, hon," Iris said, and Martell regarded her with a coolness he must have spent hours practicing in front of a mir-ror. "Why don't you come into the kitchen with me and tell me what you'd like."

Martell was not stupid. He looked to Jilo for approval this

time. She nodded once and waved him ahead. "Go on, boy. Don' you just be hangin' around in there neither. You help Miss Iris."

"Yes'm," he responded, and actually rushed up to hold the door open for Iris.

When the door closed behind them, I went and sat next to Jilo. "What was that? What force could possibly swallow the world around us like that?"

Jilo wouldn't look me in the eye. Her eyebrows were lowered, and her right hand quivered and reached up to touch her hair. "That Wren, he ain't the only demon Jilo had truck with over the years. She honored most of the deals she made, but she might've cut corners on a few of 'em." She cleared throat. "Ever since yo' uncle and his tree, Jilo ain't had the heart to take the steps she need to keep the angry ones in line."

"What would those steps be," I asked warily.

"You gotta offer up appeasement, sacrifice," she said.

"Blood," I said, my mind flashing back to the first time I had encountered her at her crossroads, how she'd been carrying a live chicken in a burlap sack.

Jilo looked up, shaking her head and holding her hands before her, palms up. "Too much blood. Too much blood on these hands."

I grasped her hands and squeezed them. "It may be what you think, and if it is, we'll figure out how to handle it, but I'm not sure if the attack was aimed at you or me," I said, thinking of Ryder and Joe and what they had done to Birdy. "The one thing I do know is that this house is the safest place for you and Martell to be right now. At least until we figure out what happened back there."

"Are you plumb out of yo' mind, girl?" Jilo laughed. It was not a happy laugh. It sounded much closer to the ones I used to hear when she was still hiding her gentle side from me. "You tellin' Jilo that you want her to spend the night beneath the Taylor roof?"

"Yes, that's exactly what I am saying."

"They ain't no way that gonna happen."

"Why not? Are you too good for us, or are we too good for you?"

Her face bunched up into a mass of wrinkles, and her eyes drew together into tight little slits. "Yo' family will never allow it."

"Oh, I think what my family will allow would surprise you. You see how Iris is falling all over herself at the sight of you."

"Jilo in her yard, she ain't under her roof. They's a big difference in those two things."

"I don't know about that. She just dragged your grandson inside, droopy pants and all. Listen, do you really want to go back out . . . out there while you think something has it in for you?"

She sat there, honestly weighing whether the danger she might face would merit sacrificing her pride. "I don' know. Jilo, she has history with the Taylor—"

"And history is all it is. You tell me, which of the still-living Taylors does the great Mother Jilo Wills have a score to settle with?"

"She gonna have one to settle with you if you keep talking at her with that tone."

I couldn't help it. I laughed, and then she began chuckling too. "Come on," I said to her. "Come on inside." I stood up and went over to the kitchen door, holding it open for her so that she could go in before me.

"No," she said after a few moments. "Jilo ain't going in through the back way." She pushed her chair back and leaned into the table to prop herself up. "You raised in a very different world than Jilo. When Jilo young, that back door was the only way she could go into a fancy white house." She struggled around the table until she got a firm footing. "When Jilo a girl, she done made herself a promise, and by God, she gonna keep it."

"What promise was that?" I asked, letting the door close.

"Jilo done promise herself that if she ever step foot in the Taylor house, she was going to go in through the front door. You hear me?"

"Yeah. I think I understand." I took her arm, and then led her through the gate and around the side of the house to the front entrance. We went up the steps until we were standing before the door. "Well, go on, then," I said nodding at the bell.

She reached forward. The way her hand quivered touched me, her index finger shaking as if she expected the bell to shock it. She gave it a quick poke, and then a more forceful one. Jilo pulled her hand back, and stretched as tall as she could make herself. She held her head up as high as her neck would allow when my smiling, but slightly confused, aunt answered the door. Iris looked at me for explanation. I would have shrugged, but somehow this moment struck me as solemn. "Jilo always promised herself that if she ever entered our house, she would go in by the front door."

A look of understanding registered in Iris's eyes, causing them to appear a little sad in spite of her smile. "Well, of course," she said. "Do come in, Jilo," she said and stepped back.

"Before she do, Jilo has to make something clear," she said and shot me a look that told me I'd better hold my tongue.

"Yes?" Iris asked, the smile fading.

"Before she come in, it only fair you know. Jilo, her sins, they comin' home to roost. You offer Jilo sanctuary, and you might find yo'self caught up in her mess."

"Sanctuary?" Iris looked at me, trying to glean information from my expression. She must have accepted whatever she saw there. "The Taylors can take whatever the world tosses at them. Come in, Mother."

"Thank you," the old woman said, gingerly lifting her foot over the threshold.

TWENTY-ONE

A fine morning followed a mercifully uneventful night. Iris served us the Southern breakfast Connor had always demanded, fried everything with a pat of butter on the side. Martell tore into his plate, and after a few thank-yous and compliments, Jilo tucked pretty well into hers as well. My stomach was having none of it, so I made myself a bowl of plain oatmeal with brown sugar. Pleased that our guests were happy, Iris kissed the top of my head and excused herself to head out and tend to the flowerbeds.

"It was mighty gracious the way yo' aunt allowed us to spend the night, oh, and that uncle of yo's too." She truly meant what she'd said about Iris, but her comment about Oliver had come more grudgingly, I noticed. Last night he had returned home and come to the library to pour himself a drink, only to find Jilo, Iris, and myself discussing the events of the day, Jilo clad in one of Iris's robes. "All right, then" was all he said, pouring himself a double and exiting the room without another word.

"Trust me," I said. "As far as you and my uncle are concerned, that counted as a brass band welcome." If Ellen had come home the previous night, she had done so long after the rest of us had retired, so I hadn't had a chance to gauge her reaction.

I was anxious to get back to the discussion Jilo and I had been having before the world literally began to collapse in on us. I did not, however, feel comfortable picking up where we'd left off in the family kitchen, especially with Martell listening in. I would have to be patient. I stood and went to the sink to rinse out my bowl before putting it in the dishwasher. When I looked out the window, I saw that Adam Cook was talking to Iris. He was wearing his serious face; Birdy's remains must have been found.

"It's Detective Cook," I told Jilo and crossed the room to open the door for Iris and the policeman. "Adam," I acknowledged him. "Two days in a row."

"Indeed," he concurred. "I'm pleased to see you've caught up with Mother." He addressed Jilo. "I have been worried about you."

"No need to worry about Jilo," she said, cackling.

"It's good to see you well all the same." He paused, nodding slowly in her direction. He turned back to face me. "Actually though, I had a different reason for dropping by this morning." I motioned him to the chair next to Jilo's, and then pulled out the remaining chair for myself. I said nothing, just arched my eyebrows as a sign he should continue. He shifted in his seat, his legs a bit too long not to bump into the bottom of the table as he did so. "Miss Taylor—Mercy," he corrected himself, "were you by any chance down by the river last night? Maybe out near Elba Island Road?"

I shook my head, relieved that the God's honest truth would serve me well this time. "No, nowhere near it. Why do you ask?"

"All right," he responded without answering my question. "Is Mrs. Weber home, by any chance?"

"No, not right now. Aunt Ellen's probably out exercising or maybe at City Market," I said, and Adam wrinkled his brow. "She's reopening her flower shop."

"Ah, good for her," he said.

"Yeah, I think it really is, although right now she's her own biggest client given all the bouquets she's planning for her wedding to Tucker."

"Do y'all have any idea where she spent the night? Do you know if she might have been out with Mr. Perry?"

"That's exceedingly possible," Iris said, "but not certain. She told me Tucker had unexpected business to attend to in Atlanta, and she didn't know if he'd make it in time for the menu sampling she'd arranged for their wedding reception."

"And did this upset her?" Adam asked.

A pinched smile formed on Iris's lips. "Inconvenienced, yes. Upset, no. Adam, perhaps you should tell us what this is all about."

"All right," Cook said. "Mr. Perry's boat ran itself ashore about an hour ago out near the bend by Falligant Avenue. A couple of kids spotted it and went to take a look."

"Oh, for heaven's sake," Iris said and laughed. I sensed her relief that this visit wasn't connected to the grisly discovery we had made at the old hospital. "So Tucker failed to secure his boat, and some teenagers took it for a joyride. Probably the same kids who reported it."

"No," Adam said. "I have reason to believe that's not the case." He looked at me. "You've been less than supportive about Ellen and Tucker's marriage, haven't you?"

"Listen," I said. "I have accepted his relationship with Ellen. I have far too much going on in my own life to run around committing acts of theft and petty vandalism. You can assure Tucker I didn't have anything to do with it." I shook my head in disbelief.

"I'm afraid I can't do that," Cook responded. "The boat wasn't empty. Mr. Perry was found inside. I'm afraid he's dead."

I jumped. I watched as Iris turned gray and rocked a little from the shock. Jilo reached out and took her hand. "I'm sorry to hear that," I said, although the truth was I felt more sorry for Ellen than for Tucker. Guiltily I wondered how Tucker's demise would affect Peter's fledgling business.

"That sounds very close to sincere," Cook said. I suddenly realized we had gone back to Cook and Miss Taylor. "I always got the feeling that you didn't care much for Perry."

"Well, sure I never liked the guy much, but . . . well, I'm still sorry. I didn't wish him any harm. Ellen's going to be devastated." I wondered if she could find the strength to make it past another tragedy. "What happened to him?"

"I'm not at liberty to share the exact details with you as yet." He paused, fixing me firmly in his gaze. "But we are treating the death as suspicious, in a large degree because it bears some striking similarities to another case we've seen recently. Another death to which you, Miss Taylor, have a connection, albeit tangential."

I blanched. I was happy that I had been sitting, because otherwise I might have keeled over. Jilo rose to my defense. "If you gonna go about tryin' to hang this on anybody who disliked that smarmy son of a bitch, you should be puttin' Jilo on that list long before any of the Taylors. That jackass been gratin' Jilo's last nerve since he turned nineteen."

"I wouldn't have thought so right off the bat, Mother," Cook said, a cool smile forming on his lips, "but finding y'all here like this, looking so close and cozy, I will very much take that under consideration." He pushed himself away from the table and nodded once at the three of us. "Mother, Martell," he said in farewell. "Miss Taylor, you tell Ellen to give me a call when she gets in, okay? It'll save me the trouble of having to hunt her down." He nodded once more and exited through the back, leaving the door open behind him.

I could hear Jilo's teeth grinding together. "Okay, girl," she said with a final clack. "Jilo think she wrong yesterday. This ain't about her. This about you. You know you can count on Jilo, even though she ain't sure she can do you much good no more. She got to think about her grandbaby here," she said, nodding her head at Martell. He started to protest, but she held up a finger in his face, effectively silencing him. "Jilo got people over on Sapelo. She gonna take the boy there, make sure he safe. They still things you gotta know, and Jilo tell you once she had a chance to get a bit of rest herself. All that gonna have to wait fo' now. If you need her, she come running, but she can't help you or your family no more with getting back that sister of yo's. Jilo thinkin' they somebody who jus' plain don' want that girl brung back." She faced Martell. "You help Gramma up," she said. He did as she told him without protest. "Thank you for your hospitality, Miss Iris."

"Of course, dear. You are always welcome here. Both of you."

"Martell." Jilo lifted her arm. He took ahold of it and maneuvered her slowly toward the door. "You take care, girl," she said, looking over her shoulder at me.

"Jilo," I called, and she stopped and turned toward me. "The spell. The one you worked for Tucker. What did you do for him?"

"Jilo don't guess it matter much now." She reached out and pushed gently past her grandson. "Fool came to Jilo and said he wanted to do right by your auntie. Spell he asked for would make sure he see her face every time he was thinking about cheatin' on her."

She turned and shuffled through the door. Martell reached back and closed it firmly after them. I hung my head between my hands and began to cry. I had been so terribly, terribly wrong.

Iris leaned over me and hugged me. "I need to track down Oliver and let him know," she said. Oliver had made himself scarce this morning. I reckoned he hadn't relished the idea of breakfast with Jilo. "Are you going to be okay?"

Before I could answer, the door opened and Ellen entered, beaming sunshine and happiness as she clutched a bouquet of flowers. "Am I hallucinating," she said as she shut the door behind her, "or did I just witness Mother Jilo Wills leaving this very house?"

"No," Iris said, "your eyes are not deceiving you. Please." She tapped the chair next to mine. "Come and sit down."

"Well, then, I guess this is a day of miracles all around." Ellen said, ignoring Iris's request. "First of all," she said, handing the flowers over to Iris, "I ran into the delivery boy on the way in, and these are for you. A rather more fandango combination than I will be sending out once my shop is open, but . . ." She stopped herself. "Expressive." She turned quickly toward me and her eyes flashed wide. "I'll bet you anything they are from that young buck she danced with at the wake." She slapped at my hand and giggled like a schoolgirl. "Iris has a boyfriend," she sang out. She winked at me, but then the smile fell from her face. "Sugar, what is wrong? Aren't you feeling well this morning?" She reached out to touch me, but read something in my eyes. Her hand stopped a little short.

"Ellen," Iris said.

Ellen ignored Iris's tone and forced a smile back to her lips. The smile did not reach her eyes. "It is such a beautiful morning out there. You just need to get out of this house and . . ."

Iris and I looked at each other, neither of us sure of what to do. "Aunt Ellen," I said, "you should listen . . ."

"No," she said, shaking her head once and turning away. She had sensed that we had bad news. I could see she was shutting down, pulling away, trying somehow to keep the moment from happening.

Iris reached out and grabbed Ellen's hand before she could make her escape. Ellen turned back to face her sister. "Detective Cook came by a little while ago. I'm afraid there's been a mishap . . ."

"A mishap . . ." Ellen echoed, the color leaving her face as she pulled her hand away.

"I'm sorry, Ellie, but Tucker, he's dead."

Ellen's knees started to give at the word.

"Maybe you should sit?" I asked, rising myself.

"No. No. No," she said, shaking her head. "This cannot be happening. This cannot be happening again." She pulled her arms in around herself. "Not again, not again," she kept repeating. I was reaching to put my arms around her when the bouquet on the table caught my eye. The flowers had all withered away.

TWENTY-TWO

At Ellen's insistence, Iris drove her to meet with Detective Cook. I stood in the kitchen, staring out after their car and trying to take it all in. The air in the house felt thick with tension, so after a few moments I went out to the garden. I found a place at the table and first rested my chin on my hands, then leaned back, placing my right hand as a protective barrier between Colin and the world around us. I couldn't believe Tucker Perry was dead.

I tried Peter's number for the third time, but it went straight to voicemail again. I hoped to catch him before he heard from someone else. I texted him, telling him to call me.

Adam had intimated that Tucker's death seemed somehow similar to Peadar's. I could only surmise that meant Tucker had been left with a hole punched through him. Tucker had without doubt made plenty of enemies over the years, but how many of them had access, natural or borrowed, to magic? And why was his murder made to look like the accidental harm I caused Peadar's body? Was the intention to implicate me or just toy with me? Who might have connected the dots between me and the body left at the old powder magazine?

Ryder's face, twisted in rage, rose up in my thoughts. I'd humiliated him and cost him an appendage. On top of that, he probably blamed me for what he'd done to Birdy. Could he be trying to seek revenge? I'd assumed he'd arrived in Savannah after Peadar's death, but he'd been awfully proud about his ability to follow me around without attracting my notice. Maybe he'd been here early enough to witness what had happened at the powder magazine?

I needed to find out just when Claire had contacted Ryder. I reached for my phone and almost clicked on her number, but was derailed by the thought that Ryder had been granted the powers of a collector by a witch. A real witch. And there were so many witches who had been unhappy to see me chosen as anchor. If I were somehow Ryder's true target, there was any number of witches, half of them from my own extended family, who might have sent a collector to do their dirty work for them. Maybe Claire had just been a puppet? Had she somehow been influenced to contact Ryder? Had her distrust of Emmet been fed by magical means? I hated myself for making Tucker's death, Ellen's tragedy, all about me, but I suspected due to the circumstances, it might actually be all about me.

My left hand sought out the locket my mother had given me, pulling it out from beneath my shirt. The feel of it caused my analytic mind to switch off and my emotions to take over. I knew I had to be strong for Ellen, but I was deeply afraid. I craved my mother's comfort and wanted the reassurance of her scent, her embrace, but I hadn't even heard from her since she'd spoken to me through a tourist's borrowed mouth outside St. John's. I loosed the locket's clasp, wanting to take a little comfort in the baby pictures of myself and my sister.

The locket popped open, but to my surprise, it did not hold the same pictures I'd seen before. Maisie's had been replaced with the photo of a man. Confident blue eyes beneath a shock of blond hair. Lean face with sensuous lips and a dimpled chin. He looked familiar, but I couldn't place him. The picture that had replaced my own I immediately recognized as a miniature version of the photo Ellen had given me of Erik's grandmother, my own great-grandmother, Maria.

Using my nail, I carefully peeled out the man's photo. It came out of the locket with minimal effort, but nearly fluttered past my hand to the ground. I reached out and snatched it up. The man bore a certain undeniable resemblance to Erik, although I remembered my uncle, my *father*, as being more robust, more virile than the young man in the all-too-small oval. Carefully, I turned it over in my palm. The ink on the back had blurred and faded with age, and the script was painfully cramped and foreign-looking, but I could still make out a word, a name: Careu. I returned the picture and closed the locket. Grabbing my phone, I did a quick search on the name. The results came back with a definition in Romanian ("square"), and several options for health care, but nothing that provided any insight.

The skin on the back of my neck began to tingle. Sensing that someone was watching me, I turned, expecting to find Emmet. "Your mother has requested that you come with me." The words came from my mother's driver, the man I'd only seen for a few moments a couple of weeks ago. Now he stood on the other side of the gate that opened onto our garden. This time, maybe because it was the first chance I'd had to observe him in full sunlight, I realized something was off. His complexion was gray and waxy in appearance, and the muscles in his jaw didn't seem to move enough to produce the words he said. It seemed almost as if someone was projecting words through him. The out-of-sync way his lips moved, combined with the synchronicity of his arrival and my thoughts about my mother, prickled my intuition.

I had been waiting, day after day, for word from my mother. I had heard nothing from her since the cathedral, and now her driver was showing up right after news had broken about Tucker's death. As badly as I wanted to see my mother, I didn't feel right about the situation. I didn't like her driver's vibe. I didn't like the way she'd implied that my aunts had made her desert Maisie and me but refused to divulge any details. Iris and Ellen and, to a lesser degree, Oliver, had taken care of me my entire life. When it came right down to it, I didn't know my mother. Besides, I'd grown wary of getting into limos alone after the last spin around town I'd taken in one.

"I tell you what; I need a few minutes to get ready. You give me the address, and I'll meet her there." He stayed where he was by the gate, not stirring. My phone began to ring. No number showed, but I answered anyway. I could use this as an opportunity to create a cover story for why I couldn't go with the driver.

"Please get in the car with Parsons before the family comes home," my mother's voice commanded. "You aren't safe there, darling girl. Let Parsons bring you to me. Please come." The phone clicked off at the same moment the driver reached over and unlatched the gate.

An unexpected arrival. An ambiguous threat implying that the people who had raised me might want to harm me. Neither of those things felt right. On top of it all, I couldn't shake the feeling that this Parsons was being held up by invisible strings, and should they be cut, he'd fall immobile to the ground. I wondered if my mother herself was the puppeteer, using Parsons much as she had controlled the tourist outside the cathedral. Still, my need to see my mother and get some answers trumped my inhibitions, so I did as she told me.

The drive led us out of Savannah proper, and I squirmed as we passed the old powder magazine on Ogeechee, the memory of my last visit there making it impossible for me to take an easy breath until we entered Richmond Hill, where Ogeechee changes into the Ocean Highway. Richmond Hill came and went. We passed a small graveyard to my right, and shortly afterward, we turned off the highway and entered into a maze of country roads, more of them gravel than not.

I felt a bit claustrophobic behind the tinted glass. I pressed the window button and was relieved that it opened, relieved that at least something in this world remained under my control. Dusty, dry air hit me. Outside the limo's arctic twilight, a fine early fall day was taking place. The blue sky and warm air worked together to help unwind some of my tension. I hung my hand out the window, enjoying the feeling of the air rushing around me. It reminded me of Iris, and how she could use the air currents to fly. I was more than a little disappointed that that particular trick didn't seem to be in my repertoire. If I could let myself be taken and carried by the wind, I'd probably never come down. I couldn't understand how Iris could have voluntarily put that ability on hold during her entire marriage to Connor. He had been weak but extremely prideful, and Iris had managed his resentments by dumbing down her abilities.

One thought of Connor led to another, and my blood began to boil as I considered the way he'd planned to let Ginny's house burn down around me. Even though the son of a bitch had believed himself to be my father, he'd been ready to kill me to get his hands on a little more power. I trusted that Oliver would dispose of the spirit trap in a way that would free us from Connor for good. I looked down and realized that blue sparks had begun to form on my fingertips, my magic ready to strike out and protect me from a danger that was no longer there. I closed my eyes and leaned my face into the breeze, letting it calm me. The car hit a rough patch in the road, jarring me back to attentiveness. That's when I realized that I could be heading into another, very similar confrontation right now. As badly as I wanted to trust my mother, experience had shown me the importance of remaining vigilant. I wanted to believe she wouldn't expose me to danger, but only a little over three months ago, my own sister had turned me over to a boo hag for sacrifice. If it weren't for the betrayals I'd suffered at the hands of my uncle and my sister, I would never have entertained my mother's insinuation against my aunts and uncle. Maisie and Connor had both betrayed me, though, so I needed to hear my mother out. I was running a little low on trust all the way round right now.

We slowed as we approached a private drive, framed by stone gates and canopied by parallel rows of ancient live oaks. The driver eased between the gates, turning off the rough public road and onto the newly paved roadway. The smell of creosote perfumed the air. I leaned out of the car to get a better view of the house—no, mansion—at the end of the lane. The words "decrepit grandeur" came to mind as we came nearer. It was a fine old house. Georgian, with a nearly square base, stretched into a rectangle by the addition of a wide porch at both the entrance and above that, on the second floor. Four windows down, four windows up, with a door dividing each row. Six Doric pillars, obviously intended more as decoration than support, stood guard, wearing their badly battered and peeling coat of white. Various pieces of construction equipment staged around the house promised that better days would be coming. In front of the house, the straight drive intersected with an oval. The fresh soil in the oval's center was clearly destined to provide nourishment for flowers, perhaps a young magnolia? Was this to be my mother's house? Had she truly come home?

The car came to a full stop, and I swung my door open and hopped out before the driver could reach it. "You should have allowed me to assist you, miss," he said, the words sounding again as if he'd swallowed someone else's phone. I gave a weak smile in answer, and let him push the door closed. I took a few steps back, away from the house, so that I could take in the full effect. I backed up without looking behind me and bumped into a sawhorse, surrounded by very fresh sawdust. My eyes had started back to the house when they got stuck on a name stenciled on the sawhorse. "Tierney Construction" leapt out at me, and I swung around surveying the rest of the equipment that had been left in place. Everything that wasn't large enough to have been rented had Peter's name stenciled or otherwise inscribed on it. The unexpected connection between my mother and my fiancé didn't sit right. My instincts had kicked in again, doing their best to warn me away. Something was not right.

"Mercy," my mother's voice called to me from the porch. "Come in," she said, and stood there waiting at the top of the steps, her arms wide-open for an embrace. As confused as I felt, the sight of her buried my apprehensions. I wanted so badly to believe in her. I couldn't resist it. I ignored the pavement and took a straight line across the oval's unplanted garden. "Careful, careful," my mother called out, laughing.

I flew up the steps and into her arms, spinning her around. The joy was undeniable until it up and winged away when my eyes landed on the house's black-and-red door. "Tillandsia," I whispered into her ear.

She pushed her way free of my weakening embrace. "Yes, my darling girl, Tillandsia." She took me by one hand, and with the other, turned the knob on the very door that I had seen in my vision. The improbable hope that Maisie would be standing there, safe on the other side of the door, flooded through me, but when the door creaked open, it revealed nothing but a freshly sanded wood floor and two comfortable and modern armchairs that looked hopelessly lost in this enormous space. As my eyes traced the lines of the entranceway, I wondered what furniture could possibly be consequential enough not to be dwarfed by such a setting.

The area in front of me was immense and hexagonal. A dome skylight, which had not been visible from the house's exterior, hovered above it. A set of stairs to my right carried on past the second floor to a gallery, which probably allowed a 360-degree view of the surrounding landscape, thanks to the dome. I realized the Georgian exterior was merely a façade. Symmetry played a very small part in the house's interior. My mother closed the door behind us and took her place in one of the easy chairs. "Spectacular, isn't it?"

"Yes. From the outside, I would have never guessed."

"I'm afraid there isn't much more to show you yet. The entrance here is the most complete portion. All the same, your fiancé's crew is doing a wonderful job."

"Peter doesn't know about you, that you are involved with all of this?" I asked, cautiously taking the seat next to her, almost as if I were expecting it to bite me.

"Of course not," she replied. "As far as he knows, he's handling the work for a group of Tucker's friends."

"Tucker's dead." I said, collapsing into the cushions.

"I know." Her voice broke as she said the words. "That's why I knew we could meet here. When the news spread, Peter sent the crew home."

"You're using magic to spy on Peter?"

She laughed a slow, sad laugh as tears came to her eyes. She raised her finger at a security camera neatly hidden in a corner. "No, my dear one. I am using technology to keep an eye on progress." She took a breath and wiped her tears. "Tucker was a dear friend. My oldest and perhaps even my last in Savannah."

"I'm sorry. I didn't know you two were close."

"Of course you didn't," she said and folded her arms across her chest, bracing herself. "You don't know anything at all about me. Thanks to Ginny and my sisters." I felt a pain in my chest as she lumped Iris and Ellen in with Ginny.

"I promised to tell you everything, and I plan on doing it now. Tucker's murder has convinced me that it's urgent for you to know the full truth."

"But what does he have to do with any of this?"

"Tucker has been helping me . . . helping me take the steps I needed to make my way home to you. Someone has been working against us."

"Ellen would not have killed Tucker," I said, my loyalty kicking in. "He and Ellen were engaged."

"Keep your friends close, and your enemies closer. Everything Tucker did, he did to help us, including proposing to Ellen."

"He was lying to her?" My emotions ran along a zigzag path; I could not find a firm footing. Just when I had begun to believe that Tucker really loved my aunt, a new reality had been revealed to me. "How could breaking Ellen's heart be of any help to us?"

"Breaking Ellen's heart?" She raised her eyebrows and lowered her chin, looking at me with astonished distaste. "Your concern is touching," she said, looking down her nose, "but your loyalties are misplaced." It was all too much for me. I could not bring myself to think of either of my aunts as a murderer. My mother seemed to read my thoughts, whether through magic or because they were telegraphed by my face. "I am not making any accusations. I am only telling you that the man who has been helping me in my return, in reaching out to you, has been murdered. And that is a sign that someone knows I have returned and is working against me. The way Tucker was murdered tells me that that same someone has it in for you as well. They are trying to fit you up for Tucker's murder."

"I don't think I really have to worry about the police," I said, reasoning out loud. "I only have a tangential relationship to Peter's great-uncle, and of course I know, *knew*, Tucker, but . . ."

"It isn't the police I am worried about. It's the families. They are of course aware of your mishap with the old man. They must have felt you draw on the line's power, but even if they did not, their golem spy would have reported it to them at the first opportunity."

"I don't think Emmet is spying for them," I said.

She paused to consider, and then nodded. "Perhaps, perhaps not. Maybe I've grown too suspicious over the years, but soon you will understand why. All the same, I am sure the families know of the incident."

"You're probably right about that much," I agreed.

"So now Tucker has been murdered, his heart burned out of his chest just like with the old man. This time, though, there was no tug on the line's power."

"So the families should realize I had nothing to do with it."

"Or perhaps they will decide that you have been practicing magic using other means to gain the power. They are aware that you have been holing up with Jilo, that you and the crone have been up to something together."

"But we've been trying to find Maisie."

"Something that they have expressly forbidden. I don't believe that they're aware that's what you two have been up to, but they smell rebellion brewing."

"I'm not rebelling . . ."

"Then what would you call it? You are simply doing the exact opposite of what they have told you to do."

"How could you know what the families are thinking anyway?" I asked.

"I have my resources, and I know their concerns about you." So she had her own spy among them. I wondered who might be filtering information to her. "You have been refusing to spend time under the tutelage of their golem," she said, "preferring the left-handed training you can get at Jilo's feet. You are not knuckling down and taking the steps you need to assume your position as an anchor of the line. If that wasn't enough to convince them that trouble is nigh, there is the final and most damning point of all. You are my daughter."

My heart warmed at the sound of pride in her voice, but I could not make the leap she seemed to want me to make. "I still don't see how any of this relates to Ellen and Iris," I said. "How you could possibly think that they are attempting to set me up? Why would they want to?"

She placed her hand on her chin, her flawlessly manicured index finger resting against her lips. Her eyes looked down and away. She seemed to be considering events long since passed. She looked back up at me. "So much history. So many secrets. I've been keeping them for so long, I don't quite know how to start."

"Tell me what happened," I said, kicking off my shoes and drawing my legs up under me, making a conscious effort to appear more relaxed than I was. "If Ellen and Iris are so horrible, how could you possibly have left Maisie and me with them?"

Her perfect complexion turned gray. "What have you been told?" she asked. Her lips pressed together into a tight line.

"The short version? You seduced Connor and Erik, got pregnant by Erik, and then died giving birth. You were noble at the end, though, and you put me before yourself. You begged Ellen to use the last of her power to save me."

"You poor child," she said. "Hanging the responsibility of your own mother's death on you." Our eyes met. It felt wonderful to be validated, to have her see things from my perspective. The comfort did not last long; I found myself wondering if she were mirroring me, trying to say what she knew I'd want to hear to gain my confidence. She pressed her hands together as if preparing to pray. "Okay," she continued. "Let's start with the easy part: Connor. What do you know of my powers?"

"Nothing. We never discussed your powers."

"Of course they wouldn't have been discussed with you." She concluded a train of thought I hadn't yet boarded. "Still, your mother has a few tricks up her sleeve. One of the most useful is that I can create a double of myself. A doppelgänger. As outwardly real as I am before you now. I cannot maintain the double for long, although I have over the years gotten much better at it."

"Kind of like Wren."

"Kind of like my parents supposed Wren to be. They weren't at all shocked when Oliver showed up with his new playmate. Projecting energy as matter was something they had already seen from me. Maisie used a similar skill when she helped Wren grow into Jackson. Yes," she said after a pause, "I am aware of it all."

I squirmed as she reminded me of what Maisie had done to me. I had very little solid emotional ground to stand on, and now this stranger, my mother, was causing it to quake.

"I'm sorry," she continued. "I know it's unpleasant for you to dwell on that, but I have so many unpleasant things that I must share with you."

I nodded. "Connor?"

"Yes." She paused. "Connor. You know what he was like. Weak, greedy, and lecherous. It's true Iris wasn't meeting his needs. She'd had so many miscarriages, and she reacted by shutting him out. When they returned to Savannah, Connor became fixated on me. Always there. Always reaching out to touch me. I tried to divert his sexual energies into Tillandsia." She paused and gave me a cool look. "You know I participated in the group. I will get into my reasons shortly, but for now, please understand that I did all I could to turn Connor from me. In spite of my best efforts, he only grew more eager. I think it was more than sex, more than obsession. He had caught on to what I was trying to do with Tillandsia." She paused. "But I don't want to get ahead of myself."

"I spoke to Iris. I reasoned with her. I pleaded with her to handle her husband. She refused to believe me. One morning I woke up to find him sitting at the foot of my bed. Staring at me and . . . well, touching himself." Her face tightened with distaste. "I moved out that very day. Rented a little place near the river, but he followed me there too. Always waiting for me the second I came out the door. Telling me how I was the one he loved, not Iris. Going on about how deeply he needed me. I knew what he felt for me was not love; what he called 'love' was the desire to possess. Finally I decided that the only way to get rid of him was to give him what he wanted. I hoped he would eventually tire of me and move on to someone else." A smile curved only the right side of her mouth. "I created a double, and I sent her to him. Once he had satiated himself and was asleep, she, it, would dissipate. He carried on a hot little affair with a series of my doubles, but he never touched me."

"And Erik?" I asked and watched her face soften at the mention of my father's name.

"Erik was different," she said. "I am guilty of having an affair with Ellen's husband, but I'm not ashamed. The times I spent with Erik were the happiest of my life. I never meant to hurt Ellen, but as I hope you will understand, I was in love with Erik and he with me."

TWENTY-THREE

"Erik was the love of my life, only Ellen found him first," she said and flushed. Her composed exterior melted, and I saw a flash of the woman she must have been at my age. I understood what she had been through, the pain that cut her on both sides for hurting her sister and not being openly able to love my father. I knew now that I had never "loved" Jackson, that the emotion I'd felt for him was actually my reaction to the power that had been used in his creation, the power that should have been mine. All the same, I didn't think I stood in any position to judge my mother.

"Here is where it all becomes so terribly complicated and murky," she said, and her eyes looked beyond me toward an unreachable past. "Do you believe in fate?" she asked me, regaining focus.

"I don't know. Sometimes, I guess."

"Sometimes?"

"I guess I use it as a rationalization. When things end up like they did with Maisie, part of me wants to believe that there was no other way for them to turn out. That Maisie never had a choice, and was only playing the role written for her."

"And the other times, when you don't believe?"

"When I want to take things into my own hands and make a difference."

"Like you are trying to do now for Maisie."

"Yes, I guess so."

"But which would be better? If you had to choose? Control or chaos?"

"Honestly, somewhere in between," I said and smiled.

She returned my smile. "I see you have Oliver's way of worming yourself out of committing," she said, the criticism hit me as a warm one, filled with pride. "But now the line has chosen you. It has made the commitment for you, without giving you a choice in the matter." She shifted in her chair and leaned forward. "The line is an awesome power, but never for a moment think you control it. It controls you. It owns you." She let the words hang between us, giving them time to soak fully into my consciousness. I knew she was right. I'd always thought that having access to magic would mean true freedom, but ever since the line had chosen me, my life no longer felt like my own. The families, the other anchors, they all seemed to want a say.

"There are those who chafe against its ruthless control. Those who at one time assisted in its creation, but who would now like to free themselves of its tyranny."

"The other three families," I volunteered.

"Yes. Renegade, traitorous, evil. I'm sure you've heard these words used to describe the families who have balked."

"But what they want *is* evil," I protested. "To bring down the line, to subject us to the control of monsters."

She shook her head sadly. "Monsters, indeed. Consider the world around us, Mercy. Wars and famine. People killing one another and ruining the planet to drain it of the last drop of fossil fuel. It hasn't always been this way. The monsters, the demons, are nothing but bogeymen, created to keep witches, the strong ones like me and you, in place." She had gotten caught up in her own tale and wasn't picking up on my growing wariness. "Those beyond the line are not demons. They are creators, teachers, and the most merciful of judges. They placed the thirteen families in positions of trust, but we grew greedy and willful. We betrayed them." She stood, and paced for a few moments. "Your father, Erik, he came from one of the three families."

"Yes, I know, but he turned away from them and joined with the other ten."

"No." She stopped and faced me. "He never betrayed his family. His allegiance to the ten was a fiction."

"But why?"

"There had been a prophecy . . ."

"Yes, I've heard about the prophecy that was made when the witches created the line. It was said that one day there would rise a witch who would unite the thirteen families again, and together they would bring down the line. That witch would come through a union of Erik's family's blood—"

"And the Taylors'." She rushed over to me and took my hands. "The ten anchors saw this prophecy as a dark and fearful thing, but the other families, including your father's, saw it as the sole glimmer of hope in a universe gone mad. I'm sorry. I know it makes your father sound cold-blooded and calculating, but he never loved Ellen. Their meeting. Their courtship. The way he disowned his own blood. He was playing his role in a carefully choreographed scheme with the goal of creating a child."

Calling his behavior merely "cold-blooded" was being generous, and I shuddered at the thought that my father could have been so calculating and heartless. I felt ashamed of my connection to him.

"A child," my mother continued, not seeming to notice that I'd checked out emotionally, "who could restore order and bring peace. Ellen knew nothing of this prophecy at the time. The few witches who did know of it considered it more or less a fairy tale, but then Erik and Ellen married. The mere possibility was enough to give those anchors loyal to the line pause. They conspired to prevent her from conceiving, but her own power to heal kept setting her body to right. That's the real reason Ellen's powers began to fail her for a time. After Paul was born, Ginny turned Ellen's ability to access the line's power down to low, low enough that Ellen's body couldn't keep the families' magic from making her incapable of conception. They would never have allowed Ellen to bring her child to term, except that the prophecy called for a female child to be born. Paul owed his life, short though it proved to be, to a Y chromosome."

"But wait," I said as I struggled with my own sense of history. "I remember a time when Paul was still alive. A boy was hit by a car outside Ellen's flower shop. He was dying, and she managed to bring him back. It scared the crap out of me. If Ginny had already been tampering with her powers, how could she have managed it?"

"The adrenaline? The emotion? Something kicked Ellen into high gear and allowed her power to loosen the valve Ginny had put on it." She paused. "I'm sure you remember that Paul and Erik died only a week or so after the incident."

"But that really couldn't have been connected to Ellen's saving the child."

"Ellen had proven that she couldn't be controlled, at least not with one-hundred-percent certainty. The families felt justified in stepping in and dealing with the matter." The blood drained from my face, and nausea washed over me. "You think that wreck was an accident?" She shook her head. "No, the families arranged the crash to make sure that neither Erik nor Paul would ever sire a daughter."

My mouth fell open. It was too horrible. I didn't want to believe a word of it, and yet it explained so much. I weighed the doubt I felt toward what my mother was saying against the way the pieces fit so tightly together. "Did Ginny know about this? Did she help kill them?"

She returned to her chair and took a few moments to collect herself. She wrapped her arms around her torso and looked past me. "I don't believe so. Ginny was a great many things, but she fell short of being capable of murder." Her tone seemed to imply that she was being magnanimous in her assessment of my great-aunt. "They would have kept the deed from her until it was done, and then found a way to convince her they'd done it in the line's best interest. It wouldn't have taken much convincing, of that I am certain."

"But what about Maisie and me?" I asked.

My mother relaxed and leaned forward, a mischievous look in her eye. "In spite of all their magic, the ten families and their anchors, they are still just people. They are neither omnipotent nor omniscient. They believed that you were Connor's daughters," she said and then shocked me by throwing back her head and laughing. "As if that weakling bastard could ever engender girls like mine, like you or our darling Maisie. Anyone with half a brain could see that your blood is far superior to any Connor had to offer. You come from a much purer stock."

"But Iris and Ellen knew," I prompted her.

"Yes, they knew." She licked her lips. "Your aunts are very much like this house, I'm afraid. What you see on the outside is very different from what you'll find within. They are capable of actions you might never believe."

"Such as what?" I asked. She was very likely right that I wouldn't believe, but I had to know what she'd say. "Tell me."

"They were both very angry with me. I think it's fair to say they hated me. Iris blamed me, rather than her own frigidity, for her marital problems. Of course, that couldn't be further from the truth. On the other hand, where Ellen was concerned . . ." She paused. "Please remember that Erik and I had fallen very much in love with each other. Desperately in love, the way I hope you and your Peter are, or at least may someday be." I remained silent. She kept pointing out similarities between our experiences, as if she was trying to trick me into identifying with her. "We knew it would hurt Ellen, but we had decided to run away together. Leave Savannah and return to Erik's home in Germany. Raise our children there, where we could protect them, you, from the line's anchors. Somehow, Ginny learned of our plans, and she put all the pieces together.

"She and my sisters conspired against me. They came to me with the proposal that they would protect you and Maisie. If I left, letting everyone, including Erik, believe that I had died, they wouldn't turn the two of you over to the ten families. Oh, it worked out great for each of them. Iris could hold on to Connor because he believed himself to be your father. Erik was happy to remain with Ellen, knowing that she would be a good mother to you even though she had divined the truth about your parentage, especially since I had *died* and could no longer threaten her marriage. Ginny got to get rid of me, the only member of the Taylors who didn't kowtow to her and accept her slavish support of the line."

"But they held a funeral. The whole of Savannah came. They buried you," I said, not as statements but as a demand for explanation.

"It wasn't me they buried. They buried a doppelgänger your aunts and Ginny forced me to create. That coffin they buried has been empty for years."

"How did Tillandsia play into all of this, though? You were trying, weren't you? You and Erik? You were trying to build up enough juice to bring down the line."

"Yes," she said, "your father and I wanted to bring down the line and rip our world out of the anchors' grasp. To let love and light find its way back in. Now I know that I was naïve," She stood and came to me, kneeling before me and placing her hand on my cheek. I felt torn between the impulse to cling to her and the urge to pull away. "The united families, the ten who maintain the line, have shut us off from those who would help us. Those who would teach us how to live peaceably together, heal the sick, feed the hungry. The knowledge and the technology the elders want to share with us would create heaven here on earth. Imagine a world with free energy, without famine or disease. The line supposedly protects us from demons, but the truth is it imprisons us. Tell me, Mercy, where does a real witch, such as yourself, get her power?"

"From the line, of course."

She looked at me sadly. "So it's true. The other anchors, they haven't shared with you how the line was created. They don't trust you." She shook her head. "No. True witches never got their power from the line. It is the line that derived its power from witches. That's the anchors' big secret. A secret that most witches who support the line pretend not to know, and if they admit to the knowledge, pretend not to believe. Witch magic, *our* magic, was the gift of the very beings we drove out. They empowered us, entrusted us, and we betrayed them."

I held up my hands. I had no more patience for politics. "Okay, even if this is true, you haven't begun to explain why either Iris or Ellen would want to kill Tucker, leave alone frame me for it."

"I believe Ellen caught wind that Tucker was loyal to me."

"Or disloyal to her, you could say."

My mother nodded her assent. "That would be Ellen's view of the situation." She took a few steps away from me, and then turned back, holding her hands out toward me, her palms turned upward. "That would be Ellen's motive," she said, "at least as far as removing Tucker is concerned."

"What about where I'm concerned?" I asked.

"My dear, as you know, the line has a taste for Savannah Taylors. With you out of the way, there is at least a thirty-three-percent chance Ellen would be chosen as the next anchor. She couldn't ask for a better position from which to seek revenge for the death of her son."

I leaned back and considered what she had said, and as I did, I noticed that the dome above us had been covered with frost. "Look," I said and pointed up. My mother raised her eyes to look at the dome, and I heard a loud *whumpf* as if something heavy had been slammed against it. Tiny lines formed across the glass, and the sound of stressed panes cracking echoed all around us in the hexagonal hall. Wordlessly, my mother raised both hands toward me, and a force shot from her that knocked me and my chair several feet back. The chair tumbled over me as I landed a little beyond the entranceway, in a side room. The music of a thousand singing shards nearly drowned out my mother's gasp. I bounded to my feet in time to watch a transparent stake tumble from above, impaling her through her eye. A total collapse followed, the whole weight of what remained of the dome tumbling down and sending shards like fireworks shooting through the hall. I wasn't screaming. The sound wouldn't come. I wasn't moving. My body wouldn't budge. I didn't use magic to protect myself. I could not process thought, let alone channel energy. In the instant before the nearest shards sliced through me, hands reached out from behind me and whisked me from the doorway. I heard the door slam behind me and innumerable strikes as the tiny projectiles embedded themselves into its wooden skin.

Strong arms held me, sheltered me. Shaking, horrified, I looked up into Emmet's face.

TWENTY-FOUR

I didn't know how I came to be home, or in my room. When I came to myself, a different pair of arms, just as strong, just as sheltering, held me, rocking me gently.

"Peter," I breathed his name, and his arms tightened around me. He planted a kiss on the top of my head. Images of my mother's torn body nearly sent me back into shock, and I struggled against his embrace. "My mother, my mother," was all I could say.

"It's all right, honey. Everything's going to be okay. I'm here. Your family is here." As he said the words, my family's presence filtered into my awareness. Ellen stood over me, at the foot of the bed. Oliver had positioned himself near the window, facing me, with his back toward the light. Iris sat by Peter's side of the bed.

"I am here as well," said Emmet, a tall shadow in the far corner. Strangely, his presence reassured me the most.

"You should sleep now," Ellen said as she came around to my side. Her voice sounded hoarse and lacked its usual warmth. Dark circles had formed under her eyes. I realized she had been crying. Of course, Tucker. She reached out.

"Please don't touch me," I said, and she pulled her hands away as if they'd been burned. Her eyes, already red, moistened. I had both shocked and hurt her. A part of me felt bad for causing pain to the woman I had thought I knew, but the image of my mother's final moments had been burned into my mind. I couldn't bear Ellen's touch. "I'm sorry. I would just like everyone but Peter to leave. And Emmet," I added.

"Of course, Gingersnap." Oliver stood. His face showed concern for me combined with a touch of confusion and hurt.

"But sweetheart, you have had some kind of shock," Ellen protested. "I should stay and keep an eye on you. Make sure you are all right."

I found myself balling up, moving away from her touch, pushing myself more securely into Peter's arms. "I'm fine. The baby's fine. We're both fine."

Ellen stopped dead in her tracks and looked to her siblings for guidance.

"You need to take care of yourself. I'm sorry about Tucker."

Her eyes flashed at me, showing an emotion that fell somewhere between ire and despair, but then her lids tightened and her expression hardened. "Thank you. I assure you I will find out who did this to him."

"Come on, let's leave the girl to rest a bit," Oliver ordered, drawing Ellen away from me and heading to the door. "Iris?" She stood without saying a word, but reluctance was written all over her face.

She joined her siblings at the door, but turned back to me. "We love you," she said and followed the others out. Emmet crossed and shut the door behind them.

I struggled in Peter's grasp enough so that he loosened his hold and I could face him. "My mother," I started, "I think they killed her." No, I was suddenly certain they had killed her.

Peter's face broke into a worried smile. "Mercy, you don't know what you're saying. They didn't kill your mother; she wasn't killed at all. She died." He paused. "I know you're worried about having the baby, that you will be like your mama and you won't make it, but that isn't going to happen to you. You are so strong."

"No." I looked over at Emmet, but his face remained a blank slate. "My mother didn't die giving birth to me. She was murdered at the Tillandsia house. Today."

"The Tillandsia house?" His forehead creased, and he shook his head to show he had no idea what I was talking about.

"The big old place, past Richmond Hill. With the black-and-red door. The one you have been working on for Tucker. The dome skylight in the entrance. It shattered and collapsed on her. They caused it to collapse." I shuddered at the thought of my mother's bloodied body.

He brushed the hair from my forehead. "That place is just a big old dilapidated Georgian. It only has regular old windows. No dome. No skylight. Not even any higher windows that could be mistaken for a skylight. Nothing modern like that at all. Nobody's been hurt there. I was there myself until a half hour ago when Oliver called to tell me you weren't well. You had a bad dream, that's all."

With wild force I twisted from his embrace and tried to sit up. The room spun around me, but I managed to lean up on my elbow and face Emmet. "Tell him," I commanded. "Tell him what happened. You saw it. You saved me."

"I'm sorry. I can tell him nothing. You had fallen over in the garden, and I found you there. I carried you up to your room, and then called your family. I am afraid whatever you experienced was a hallucination."

"Why are you are lying?" I shouted at him.

He reacted as if he were dealing with a sick child. He shook his head silently at Peter, and then looked at me with soft and sympathetic eyes. "I don't mean to cause you further upset. I would confirm what you are saying if I were able to do so."

195

I knew I hadn't dreamed or imagined it. Peter was wrong. My mother hadn't died giving birth to me. It was a blatant falsehood. I had a sudden inspiration and felt around my neck. My fingers found the locket, proof that my mother was alive, or at least had been on the day she'd given it to me. In my vehemence to show it to Peter, I broke the chain that held it. My certainty of what I'd witnessed faded instantly. "Here. Take this. Open it."

I dropped the locket into his palm and leaned against my pillows. His fingers were too large, too calloused to open the locket easily, but after a few tries he managed to work open the clasp. "What can I say?" he asked. "You sure were a beautiful baby. You and Maisie both."

I reached out and swiped it from him. I looked down on the pictures, one an image of my infant self, the other of Maisie at the same age. The photos of my great-grandmother and Careu, the golden young man with the confident eyes, had disappeared. I snapped the locket shut and held on to it for dear life.

Another wave of vertigo washed over me, forcing me to close my eyes. "I must be sick," I said, more to myself than to my companions.

"I'm afraid so," Peter said. "And it's been making you have some terrible dreams. Now would it be all right to call Ellen in? Let her do what she does to make you better?"

Even with my eyes closed, I could feel Emmet's gaze boring into me. "Don't you see how magic never daunts him as it would a normal man?" they demanded silently. "Don't you see that he is no more *real* than I am?" The question quickly faded, only to be replaced by a sense of his concern for my well-being.

I didn't say a word. I nodded my assent, but in truth I wasn't sure if the question I'd answered was Peter's or Emmet's. Exhaustion overtook me, and I had fallen dead to the world by the time Ellen reentered the room.

TWENTY-FIVE

I climbed out of bed and caught sight of myself in the mirror. Someone had removed my clothes and slipped me into a seafoam-colored silk nightgown. The kind you get for a holiday present and never end up wearing. I sat down on the foot of the bed, trying to pull together the pieces of yesterday, the same as if I were trying to rebuild the shards of glass into the dome that had crushed my mother. Or had maybe crushed my mother. My own reflection faded as the image of her bloodied body rose to mind. I muffled the cry that tried to fight its way out of me. Even if the whole thing had been a hallucination, the fear and sense of loss were real enough to me.

I prayed that the others were right, and I had somehow dreamed up the whole day. That my mother was still alive and I could somehow find an explanation for all of this that would allow me to have her in my life without rejecting my aunts, without rejecting the line.

The robe that went with the gown had been laid out over the chair. In spite of everything, I realized that I was starving, so I pulled on the robe and headed downstairs to find some breakfast. As I came to the foot of the stairs, I heard my name being spoken, but the hushed sound of the words that came after told me that I was being discussed rather than addressed. I crept along the hall toward the voices and found myself by the swinging door that opened into the kitchen.

"I blame myself," Oliver said. "It isn't enough that she's pregnant and has just gotten in touch with her magic, I had to encourage her to go and play librarian in the Akashic records."

"I disagree," Iris said. "It was much better that you stepped in and controlled the situation, rather than letting her and Jilo stumble into something neither of them could handle on their own."

"But to hallucinate that Emily is still alive and we are trying to kill her . . . She's under too much stress, and I've done my share of placing it there."

"She was determined to find Maisie." Ellen tried to ease his guilt. "And you had nothing to do with her pregnancy or the fact that the line chose her as anchor."

"But you can't possibly think she had anything to do with Tucker?"

Ellen's silence lasted a moment too long. "No, not intentionally. Not even consciously. But she's not truly in control of her powers. Maybe her guilt over hurting Peter's great-uncle blended with her desire to push Tucker out of my life. Maybe she thought she was dreaming. You saw how she dreamed up this whole scene with Emily." I crept nearer the door, trying to decide whether I should keep silent or burst in and let them have it.

"Oh, Ellen, not even then," Oliver defended me.

"You saw how she pushed me away. She isn't herself. Maybe this sudden influx of power has hurt her, changed her somehow. Maybe toying with the Akashic records did something. Maybe there's a part of her that can no longer discern the difference between real and fantasy."

"I think it might be for the best," Iris said, "to support the families in their proposal to send her to visit Gudrun. Let Gudrun teach her how to handle her powers, and then share the secrets of the anchors with her. At least Mercy will be safe there." Gudrun's name caused me to flash back to the day when I'd first tasted magic, when a splinter of wood soaked with Oliver's blood had been turned into a talisman that allowed me to borrow his power. The hardened face that had glared back at me through the mirror when I'd tried to reach out to Maisie.

"No," Oliver said, and then, "I don't know. Gudrun proved to be of little use in helping Maisie. There's also the baby to consider."

Talking about me behind my back was one thing, but no one would discuss my son without my input. I barreled through the door, leaving it flapping behind me. "Good morning, y'all. What have I missed?"

"Well, from your behavior and the tone you are taking, young lady," Iris replied, "I don't imagine you have missed much." I stopped for a moment, taking in the room's strange rosy glow that emanated from the pink crystal at the center of the table.

"Sit down, Mercy," Ellen said. The hurt she had carried with her since yesterday blended with her doubts about me, darkening her eyes. I stayed still, ready to take on my three relatives, but I was a little disarmed by the pain I saw written on their faces.

I had so desperately wanted to believe that the woman who found me was my mother. I still did. However, I also wanted to believe that she was still alive. That we would get the chance to know each other. That my son would get to know her. All the same, I did not want to believe the stories she had shared with me. I didn't want to believe that Iris and Ellen could have committed such crimes. Beyond that, I still struggled with what struck my heart as my mother's heretical statements against the line. Could it possibly be true that the line imprisoned us rather than protected us? I was still trying to process the images she had drawn of the benevolent teachers who wanted nothing more than for mankind to return to their waiting arms. Something about all of this struck me as too neat. My mother's return. Her version of what had led to my birth and her disappearance. Her sudden death in a room that, as far as I could tell, had never existed on this plane. I posed the question to myself. Could these three people before me, imperfect as they certainly were, commit such monstrous acts?

"Take a seat," Iris commanded, a chair sliding out for me seemingly of its own accord. Magic had become much more evident in our house, much more openly practiced since my own power had been returned to me. I knew that Iris had been holding back on Connor's account, but I had to wonder if they'd been holding back to spare my feelings as well. Somehow their desire to save my self-esteem didn't mesh well with what my mother had told me about them. I took the proffered seat, but leaned back and folded my arms across my chest. I wasn't quite ready to let go of my indignation over catching them gossiping about me.

Iris did not care. "You are feeling better, I trust?"

"Yes." I offered nothing more.

"What, are you twelve?" Oliver burst out and walked over to the counter. Even though he'd protected me when I wasn't there to speak up for myself, it was clear that he too still smarted from my rejection. He tossed a bag of chamomile tea into a mug and added hot water. My eyes fell to the table. I didn't want to look at any of them. After a few moments, Oliver slid the tea in front of me. I grasped the mug in my hands, grateful for the comfort of its heat.

"You accused us of some pretty wicked crimes yesterday," Iris said, her tone measured, even. She had obviously practiced saying these words many times during the night. "We know something happened, something that was upsetting. However, instead of coming to us, trusting us, you sent us away. You told Peter and the golem that we lied to you about your mother's death. Then you went one step further and said we killed her."

"And you are in here talking about how I killed Tucker and need to be shipped off before I start taking out the whole of Savannah one by one."

Ellen threw her hands over face. Her shoulders hunched up and convulsed as she sobbed.

Iris reached over and put her hand on her sister's shoulder. "No one said that."

Ellen lowered her hands. Her face was grief stricken, puffy, and red, and dark circles stood out beneath her eyes. "I loved him," Ellen's voice warbled. "I really did." She looked at me through heartbroken eyes, mascara clumped and eyeliner dripping in watercolor rivulets down her cheeks.

My anger started melting. "I know that. I do," I said. There was no way she had harmed Tucker. No way. "I swear I didn't do anything to him. I would've never done a thing to Tucker, because I know you loved him."

"And you don't think we loved our sister?" Ellen asked. "Do you really think that Iris and I killed her in cold blood? Do you really think we could have? Do you really think I could have?"

Emotion overwhelmed me, and I too burst into tears. "I am so sorry about Tucker." I reached out and took Ellen's hands.

"I know, baby. I do believe you are."

"You have to know I wouldn't hurt him. Intentionally. Even if I thought I was dreaming. I just don't have that kind of hate in me."

Ellen looked at me, the storm clearing from her eyes. I knew she realized that this was true. "No. You don't. I don't know why I let my heart think that you might."

Iris came around to me, pulling my head into her bosom. "There, there, there." She stroked my hair and bent over to kiss the top of my head. When I managed to pull myself together, she tilted my face so that she could look me directly in the eye. "I don't know who or why, but I believe someone is trying to sow the seeds of doubt and mistrust among us. Someone who wants the four of us to battle each other. Someone who wants it bad enough to kill to make it happen."

"Okay," Oliver said, his tone telling us that he planned to take control of the situation. "The Taylors have an enemy. That isn't exactly a new item for the family history book. What do we know about this enemy? Only one thing, and that is that he or she knows they don't stand a chance against us if we stay united."

"That was your pep talk?" Iris asked as a palpable sense of relief settled over the four of us. Even Ellen smiled at her big sister's sarcasm. She wiped her eyes with the back of her hand.

Iris turned to me. "So now you tell us what happened. What could have possibly made you think we killed your mama?"

I drew a breath. I couldn't believe anyone would have been so cruel as to toy with me this way. To offer my mother to me and then snatch her away. "She found me," I said. "Right after the accident with Peadar. She came and took me away."

"Who did, darlin'? Who found you?" Oliver asked. Even through the maelstrom of emotions that whipped through me, it amused me to hear his accent coming through so heavily.

"My mama. Emily."

"Now, Mercy, that isn't possible," Iris said. "You know she's been gone for quite a long time now. Someone is playing some kind of cruel and horrible joke."

"Perhaps she came to you in spirit? A ghost?" Ellen offered.

"No. She was real. She felt solid," I said, even though my own experiences told me that didn't really count for much. "She said she was alive. That she didn't die having me."

"Oh, Mercy," Ellen breathed. "If only that were true, but I was there. Iris too. You know. We've told you what happened."

"She said you lied. That you took Maioio and me from her, and then forced her to create a double that you could bury." I lowered my eyes. "Besides, Wren told Jilo that he saw Mama here in the house on the day you all supposedly buried her."

"Whoa, whoa, whoa." Oliver held up his hands. "Let's slow down a bit here and start over at the beginning. Someone—someone pretending to be Emily—came to you—"

"Maybe, but I'm not sure she was pretending."

"You think it really could have—"

"A double, you say?" Iris interrupted him.

"Yes. She said that she can create doppelgängers."

Iris and Ellen looked at each other. "Do you think it's possible?" Iris finally asked. "We were so focused on the girls," she said to her sister. "Could Emily have managed to give birth and then switch places with a double?"

Ellen paused before answering. "Yes. It's possible," she finally said. "By the time I knew that Mercy would live, and I could turn my attention back to Emily, she had passed. I'm not sure that I'd sense the difference between a dead body and a body that had never had any life."

"But even if Emmy had the magic to do that, why would she?" Oliver asked.

"Tell us what she said. All of it," Iris commanded, ignoring her brother. "Don't skip anything, even if you are afraid it might hurt us."

"Go ahead, sweetheart. Tell us exactly what's been happening." Oliver nodded, telling me to go on.

I dug deep into my gut, asking it to tell me whether I should put my trust in these three. I wanted—no, needed—to believe in them. But I'd also needed to believe in Maisie, and I had learned the hard way that my desire to trust someone didn't make them trustworthy. Someone was lying to me, be it my mother, someone pretending to be my mother, or one or more of the three sitting before me. In the end, I decided to offer my family the benefit of the doubt. I took a deep breath and told them everything. Almost.

TWENTY-SIX

Iris and Ellen both retreated to the places they felt most comfortable, Iris pulling on my grandmother's sunhat and heading to the garden, Ellen opting for the darkened library and an open bottle. Now, however, didn't seem like the appropriate moment for any kind of intervention.

Oliver sat deep in thought, staring down at nothing, wiping his hand down his mouth and chin. I could practically hear the wheels spinning in his head. He looked up at me. "I have an idea of how we might find out who is behind all this."

He paused as if he were reconsidering. "I'm listening," I said, prompting him to continue.

"I can't read your mind like I used to, you know?" he asked. I had suspected as much, so I just nodded, even though the statement struck me as a non sequitur. "Non-witches, though, it's a bit of a struggle *not* to read them."

"So, what? Tucker, Emily, Ryder. There has to be a witch at the bottom of it."

Oliver ignored me and grimaced. He was still wrapped up in his own train of thought, and his smooth forehead pinched into an uncharacteristic worry line. "We'd have to do it without telling

Iris or Ellen. Iris would think it *unseemly*, even if it proved effective. And well, Ellen, she couldn't know."

Great, another secret, I thought. "Exactly what is it you are considering?"

"Going to the morgue and paying Tucker a visit."

"What?!"

"No, listen. If you can channel enough energy into him to fire him back up, even for a few moments, I should be able to read his thoughts."

I shook my head and felt a chill travel down my spine. Ellen would be devastated to know we were even considering it. "No, even if it were possible, Tucker had a huge hole punched through him. The only thought you are likely to pick up is 'Ouch.'"

Oliver shrugged. "Or we might just find out who killed him. We might just find out who took one more bit of love from your Aunt Ellen. Who has sent her back into the downward spiral I thought she'd finally shaken off. Who is trying to turn you against the family who loves you."

"You say we should do this for Ellen and me, but we both know Ellen wouldn't want us to disturb Tucker's body. I'm not sure if I'm okay with it either. I don't know if it's the right thing to do. Meddling with the dead."

"I don't either, but I do know it's wrong for me to sit here and do nothing while someone is attacking my family and those they love. Besides, I'm not suggesting a séance. It's more like when you were in school, and the teacher had you touch a severed frog leg with a battery to make it contract. We won't be disturbing Tucker. Just applying a little jolt to see if we can trigger a reflex. Come on. We go. We try. Either we get somewhere, or we don't. Let's do this. Tucker's not getting any fresher." He paused. "It could be Peter next, you know." He was hitting me below the belt with that one. "Or Adam." There lay his real concern.

"Oliver," I said. The thought of Tucker's decaying body made bile rise up in my throat. I lowered my head and took a deep breath, hoping the nausea would pass, "I'll gladly help you set up charms to protect Adam," and I'd toss in a few for Peter just in case, whether he was already protected by *Fae* magic or no. "But tinkering with Tucker's corpse?" I hated the word *corpse*—the way it felt on my tongue, the way it sounded in my own ears.

"We both know there are many ways around charms." I had learned that firsthand when Jackson moved me into a nearby dimension, just outside of the reach of the charms Emmet had set up to protect me. "They are good for fending off non-magical folk, maybe even magical small-timers, but someone with real mojo? Not so much." He scanned my face. "What are you really afraid of?" I looked up to find Oliver's eyes searching me the way they used to, when my thoughts were an open book to him.

"Mama said Tucker was killed because he had been helping her."

"Listen, we don't even know if that was Emily. And if it was, then we aren't just looking for Tucker's killer. We're looking for whoever killed her too. This may be our best way, our only way, to really get to the bottom of things. How about it?"

A sigh escaped me. I caved. "All right. Let's go before I change my mind."

"That's a girl," my uncle said, striking me as just a tad too pleased to be visiting with the dead.

Oliver held his tongue during the drive to the morgue. Besides magic, one of his greatest strengths was that he knew when to stop selling. He wasn't going to risk saying anything that might cause me to question the wisdom of what we were about to attempt. I found it disconcerting just how near to the coroner's office Peter's house sat. Growing up in Savannah, I had adjusted to the knowledge that bones were buried just about everywhere, but I still felt squeamish at the thought of newly minted corpses being autopsied just a few blocks away from Sackville. "Looks like an office," I said as we parked.

"You were expecting Castle Frankenstein?" Oliver turned off the ignition and opened his door. "Let me do the talking," he said, as if I'd been about to offer. In the time it took for that thought to cross my mind, he'd circled around and opened my door for me. He followed behind me a step or so as we walked toward the building, as if he were anticipating that I might turn at the last moment and run. The door opened, and climate-controlled air mercifully engulfed me. Only then did Oliver step around me to approach the man sitting at the reception desk.

The thought that a morgue would have a receptionist struck me as the setup for a bad joke, but Oliver had already started his delivery. "Hey, Don!" he said, sounding for all the world as if the man behind the desk were a long-lost friend. "How's Jen doing?" Don was a bit taken aback. His eyebrows raised and his lips puckered as he tried to place Oliver's face. They were total strangers to each other, but Oliver was using his mindreading skills to pluck random bits of information from the man's consciousness. To my own surprise, I realized that Don was an easy read even for me. It felt a bit like going to a party and sneaking a peek in the host's medicine cabinet.

"Um, she's real good," Don replied.

"Good, real good," Oliver echoed. "So how's life under the new regime?" It had been a teapot-sized scandal a few months ago when the longtime coroner had resigned under a shadow of alleged misuse of county funds. "Meet the new boss, same as the old boss?"

I could feel Don's mind landing on the name Taylor. A remembrance of a newspaper photo. Once again my family's notoriety raised its head. "What can I do for you, Mr. Taylor?" he asked.

"Well, we were hoping to visit Tucker Perry."

Don's eyes narrowed and a smirk came to his lips. "This is the coroner's office, Mr. Taylor. We don't exactly have visiting hours."

"Still, you can make it happen," Oliver said, as if he were simply stating the obvious.

"Well, of course I could, but there are procedures. Rules. We can't just let people come traipsing through here to see the bodies."

Oliver mirrored Don's expression. "Has there been a lot of that going on?"

"Well, no, but . . ."

"Don, take us back and show us Tucker's body." His tone was still reasonable, but this time it was unmistakably a command. Don wavered between his sudden need to do as Oliver wished and his long-ingrained fear of breaking the rules. "Come on, you know you want to."

Oliver and his magical coercion. I knew he couldn't read my mind as easily as before, but it did make me wonder whether he had convinced me to come with him the same way he was convincing Don to show us Tucker. Were anchors really immune to being charmed, or was that simply a bit of propaganda? I really had to wonder. Don got up from his desk and held the door to the morgue open for us.

"Doesn't it bother you?" The words jumped out of me of their own volition. Oliver lowered his chin and tilted his head to the side, the very image of innocence. He had no idea what I was talking about. "This. Compelling people to do things."

He shook his head. "No," he said, and then, "should it?" I said nothing, just stared at him with my mouth open.

"Do you really want to do this here and now?" he asked. "I mean, it's kind of rude to keep Don waiting." He poked his head closer to me and raised his eyebrows. Sometimes I loved him so much, and other times I could just throttle him. It struck me that the interval between those times just kept getting shorter.

We stepped into the most thoroughly tiled room I had ever seen. Gray tiles on the walls, tan tiles on the floor, the ones on the floor slanting in slightly around drains. I shuddered at the thought of what had been washed away through those drains over the years. Several doors lined the beige wall of refrigerated units. I knew Peadar's remains still lay sealed behind one of those doors. Jilo had tried her best to convince me that I shouldn't feel guilty, but I was still awash in regret.

"Tucker?" Oliver asked, prompting Don to open first one door and then a second. He closed each in quick succession. Even though there'd been nothing in the news, it occurred to me that what was left of Birdy might be here as well. "Third time's a charm, Don."

The man smiled nervously and nodded, pulling open another door. He checked the toe-tag on the body and nodded again, pulling the body tray out of the refrigerator. Oliver assisted him in shifting the body to a gurney; then he pushed the tray back and shut the cooler's door.

"You can return to your desk now. We'll put him away when we're through here."

"Good. Real good," Don said, practically bowing as he returned to the door without ever turning his back on us.

Oliver crossed over to the gurney that held Tucker's body, but then called out, "Oh, Don?" The man stopped in his tracks. "Let's keep this little visit between us, okay?"

"Sure thing. Of course," Don said and left the room.

I joined Uncle Oliver near the body. I'd hoped to have a few more seconds to prepare myself. I'd expected that the sheet would have been pulled up over Tucker's face, but it was turned down around his clavicle, leaving his neck and head exposed. His skin showed a light purplish-blue cast.

"Ah, Tucker, you bastard," Oliver said, an odd affection for the deceased playing in his voice. "You were a total prick, but who would've wanted to hurt you like this?" His lack of respect for the dead made me uncomfortable. I looked at Oliver, and he read the distaste on my face. "You of all people are telling me you didn't think of him as a jerk?"

"Well, yeah, but he's dead now."

"So he's a dead jerk."

"Ellen loved him," I said. The regret I felt for the way I had acted about their engagement weighed heavily on me. Another stone of guilt pulling me down. Silently, I apologized to Tucker. Later, I'd do the same to Ellen, this time out loud.

"And we love Ellen, and that is a big part of the reason why we are standing here now. Shall we?" He stepped away from the tray so that I could position myself between him and the body.

"Are you sure we should do this? I mean, when Iris laid hands on Ginny, it opened a door for Grace's spirit to come through."

Oliver winced at the memory. "It isn't quite the same thing, Gingersnap. Ginny was a powerful witch, an anchor. Tucker, he was just an ordinary guy. But you are right, we need to be mindful of what we are attempting here." He pointed his finger at the floor, and a beam of blue light emanated from it. He paced around, drawing a glowing circle on the floor. "In case anything does slip through, this will contain it until we can send it back." He guided me to the head of the table. I looked down at Tucker. His trademark gold curls, strong forehead, and full lips. Now that his eyes were closed and he wasn't leering at me, I could take in the full effect of his features. "He was a handsome man."

Oliver nodded. "Until he opened his mouth." I shot him another warning glance. He shrugged an apology and moved on. "You'll need to touch him. Probably best if you put your hands on his head. You okay with that?"

I nodded and reached forward to place my fingertips on his temples, but I couldn't complete the action. I stopped with my hands hovering a few inches above Tucker. "What about . . ." I started, but then hesitated, feeling a little foolish.

"What about what?"

"What about his soul?"

A smile curved on Oliver's lips. "You still believe in the soul, Gingersnap?"

I considered his question, feeling somehow unsophisticated, but then nodded. "Yes," I began, my voice trembling, then said it again with the force of conviction. "Yes, I do."

Oliver reached out and touched my cheek. "Yeah, I kind of do too. But we aren't trying to pull his spirit back to his body. We are just going to hit it with a little juice, just enough to spark up his hard drive, get his synapses firing long enough for me to look around."

I let my decision filter down from my head to my gut. I owed it to Ellen, even if she might not like what we were doing, to find out who'd done this to Tucker. And I owed it to myself to get some answers too. I nodded and breathed deeply, calming my mind, focusing on the few positive thoughts about Tucker I could mine from my heart. I touched his temples, and his body pulsed and lurched up into a sitting position. A guttural sound issued from his throat. It might have been a full scream if his trachea had not been destroyed. His back faced me, and I shuddered as I saw the light shining through the hole burned through his body. I saw Oliver's eyes dart up to meet Tucker's, and I felt grateful that I didn't have to see his dead eyes myself, that I didn't have to witness whatever was written in them. Tucker's right hand shot up and clamped itself over mine. Cold. Dead. But still trembling. An image rose up in my thoughts. A large and terrifying dog. No, a wolf. My conscious mind rejected it as ridiculous. There were no wolves in Savannah. Perhaps we had waited too long to attempt our grisly task. Maybe the physical damage had been too great, or perhaps decay had closed off Tucker's circuits. His body convulsed once, twice, and then went slack in my hands, his head banging down against the metal table. I was still holding my hands out before me. They felt soiled, and all I could think of for a moment was my desire to run them under hot water until the coldness of death had been washed away. Small sparks shot from the fingertips of one hand to the other. I clenched them into fists and brought them down to my sides, just as the door to the morgue banged opened.

Adam entered the room, shaking his head, his own fists clenched. "Just what in the hell are you two doing in here?"

TWENTY-SEVEN

Adam grabbed Oliver by the collar and gave him the bum's rush out of the morgue. As they approached the door, Adam turned back to glare at me. His face was a mask of anger—horizontal wrinkles lined his forehead, his eyes glared at me, and his jaw jutted forward. I could see the pulse at his temple. He lifted one eyebrow, and that was enough to communicate that if I didn't follow, I would be the next person to be dragged from the room. I shot one last look at Tucker, feeling ashamed of leaving him uncovered and sprawled awkwardly, one arm flung back over his head. I turned to set him right. "Mercy." Adam's voice turned my name into a one-word command. I turned back and followed.

Adam left us waiting in a small gray room in the mortuary for at least an hour. I suspected it was taking him a good while to calm himself. "He spotted my car." Oliver had gleaned as much from Adam's thoughts. "Stupid of me not to park farther away." Oliver seemed cool as the proverbial cucumber, so I tried to follow his lead.

I had no idea how many laws we'd just broken, but I saw no camera or taping equipment in the room we were waiting in so I knew it wasn't an actual interview room, just a private place to talk. Satisfied that Adam wouldn't hear us, I turned to Oliver. "I saw a wolf."

"So did I, Red, but I don't know what to make of it. Keep it under your riding hood for now, okay?"

I let it go, but another worry rose to mind. "Do you think they've found Birdy?" I fought against the memory of her anguished face, against reliving her sense of terror and betrayal.

"No," Oliver said casually. "And they won't. Sandman and I went back last night and cleaned things up, but the less you know, the better."

I felt too nervous to sit still, so I stood and started looking at the wanted posters pinned to a bulletin board on the wall. Each photograph was of a wanted murderer. I reckoned that made sense at a coroner's office. One guy had a face that was covered with tattoos. His crazed eyes reminded me of a photo I'd once seen of Charles Manson. It only took one look into those eyes to know they belonged to a man who had committed many violent acts, one who took his pleasure in the fear and despair of others. A shiver ran down my spine, and I returned to my seat next to Oliver.

"Those people," I said, nodding at the photos, "are horrid."

He looked up from his phone, which he'd been using to answer emails. "Those people are dead. It's a collection of mug shots of known killers whose autopsies have been performed here."

Lovely, I thought to myself, and at the same instant Adam stormed into the room and slammed a manila folder down before us.

"Open it," he commanded.

Oliver did, but then snatched the folder from my view. "She doesn't need to see this," he said, shoving the folder back at Adam.

"She's seen worse." He opened the folder and slid its contents before me.

"Oh my God," I said in the instant before the bile rose to my throat. They were morgue photos of Peadar, or the "real" Peter, as

I'd come to think of him, versus the changeling I'd agreed to marry. Regardless of what Adam thought, this felt much, much worse than seeing Tucker's body. I had been the one to do the damage to Peadar. I couldn't help myself. I began to cry.

"Adam, stop it," Oliver said, snatching the photo out from under my face.

"Then tell me what's going on," he said. Oliver's eyes told me to keep quiet. "Come on, y'all. Talk to me. Tell me the truth for once." Adam looked from me to Oliver, and then settled on me. "No lies, no half-truths. For once, don't prevaricate. Don't dissimulate. Lay it out for me."

"I'm not sure what you are looking for from us," Oliver said, causing Adam's gaze to dart back to him.

Adam blinked, then looked away. He lowered his eyes to his folded hands and clenched his jaw. "All right. Let's play it your way. I have two mutilated bodies in this morgue." That told me that they hadn't discovered Birdy yet. Whatever Oliver had done had kept her out of sight, at least for now. "One of which I just walked in to find you messing with. Although the coroner cannot say with absolute certainty that they were killed using the same weapon, it's pretty damned obvious they were killed with the same type of weapon. That being said, he doesn't have a good half damn of an idea what that weapon could be." His hands clamped into fists and he banged them both down on the table between us. In spite of myself, I jumped. Oliver didn't flinch.

Adam stood and walked to the corner of the room. Keeping his back to us, he lifted his hands into the air, the fingers twisting out like branches. He sighed in frustration before turning to face us. "I may be many things, but I am not a fool. I know magic when I see it, and in this town, the Taylors are magic central." Oliver leaned back in his seat, crossing his arms over his chest. I noticed that the air conditioning had raised goose bumps on his arms, and the blond hairs covering his forearms were standing at attention. "Oliver, you can't keep shutting me out, not if we are going to have hope for any kind of future together."

Oliver went from calm to livid in an instant. He stood up, leaning into the table and pointing at Adam. "Do not try to use emotional blackmail on me. If I keep something from you, it's because it's beyond what I can possibly tell you."

"Oh, it's over my pay grade, is it?" Adam asked, storming over.

"Precisely," Oliver said and looked at me. "Come on, Gingersnap, we're done here. We are leaving."

Both of them stood over me, seething, ready to rip apart everything they had just started to piece back together. "Sit down, Uncle Oliver," I said. He looked at me, not quite comprehending. This time I took a firmer tone. "I said 'sit.' You too," I addressed Adam. They hovered, each waiting for the other to make the first move. "Well, if you two aren't perfect for each other. A matching pair of jackasses. Now, I said 'sit.'"

Energy burst from me, a little stronger than I had intended, but I had grown tired of this nonsense. My feet were swelling. My pants chafed my stomach. And damn it, I wanted ice cream. With barely a wink, I lifted around four hundred or so pounds of man up into the air and slammed both of their hardheaded selves back into their respective chairs. "There," I said to Adam. "Now that there is magic." His eyes opened wide as he looked at me. He sat up straight and ran his hand across his mouth, trying to wipe away the look of shock, trying to regain composure and a sense of control.

"You can't," I said.

"I can't what?"

"Control the situation," I said. "You keep trying to poke your nose behind the curtain that Oliver works so hard to keep in place for you, just so you can keep thinking that you are in charge, that you aren't in over your head. Well, you are."

"Mercy," Oliver tried to stop me. "You cannot un-tell something that you've told."

"Oh, I know that. I do." I nodded my head at him, and then turned to Adam. "And that's why I am giving Detective Cook the chance to decide. Looks to me like the slightest show of power has left him trembling." Adam started to protest. "Shut it. I'm not through. You think you know things about the Taylors, about witches, but I'm here to tell you that you don't know a damned thing. How can I be so sure? 'Cause I am a witch, and I don't even know a damned thing. I know what you are feeling, that queasiness in your stomach, that cold sweat between your shoulders. No, it isn't the air conditioning. It's what you feel when you see a spirit, when you cross an elemental's path, or when you feel a witch's magic. It feels like what to you? Jarring? Unnatural? Terrifying?" I glared at him. "Answer me."

He drew a breath. "I find it unsettling."

"Yes, you do," I said. "So if you are 'unsettled' after a little taste, are you sure you want to heap a full serving onto your plate?"

"Yes, if it means I can get to the bottom of these murders. Prevent another from happening."

I laughed, but it was not my usual laugh. The cackle I heard shocked my own ears. "Adam, you could know every single detail of our lives, and it still would not help you to prevent any crime that a witch has her heart set on committing."

"So," he said, his color returning to him, "you are telling me that the rest of us . . . the real humans—"

"Witches are real humans," Oliver said as flatly as if he were playing a taped response.

"You know what I mean: regular folk. Non-witches. You are telling me that we regular folk are pretty much in control of nothing, if one of you decides to meddle."

218

"Yes," I said, a calm filling my voice, "that's exactly what I am saying. How does hearing that make you feel? Powerless? Hopeless? Do you want to dig any deeper, or should we stop here?"

He ran his hands over his head. His elbows went to the table, and then he held his head between his hands. He remained still and silent for a few moments. "I have to know," he said. "I need to know."

"Why?" Oliver cried out. He slapped his palms down on the table and leaned in toward Adam.

"Because, everything else aside, I want to build a life with you. We can't do that if you always have to keep me in the dark."

"We can," Oliver protested, but then he smiled. "I don't ever want to see you looking at me like you looked at Mercy when she slammed your sorry ass in that chair. Leave it, please."

"I'm sorry," Adam said. "I can't."

Oliver nodded and bit his lower lip. "All right then." He looked at me. "I don't think y'all really need me for this, do you?"

"No, I don't think so," I said. Oliver stood and patted my shoulder before exiting. I watched Adam's face, the way his eyes followed Oliver as he left. There was a confused mixture of tenderness and annoyance in them. That's when I knew for sure that he felt real love for my uncle, and bringing Adam into the know was the right thing to do.

When the door clicked closed, I held my hand up before Adam's face, making my best effort to copy a sideshow magician's fancy feat of prestidigitation. Before his sharpening eyes, I produced one of Ellen's charmed rose quartzes. Better safe than sorry in case anyone decided to listen in with magic.

"What's that?" he asked. He squared his shoulders, and relaxed in his chair, trying to appear casual, unimpressed.

"This is a little something to make sure what we say here stays here. You have to understand, Adam. Even though I am

sharing with you, you can't share any of what I tell you with anyone else. Outside this room, you can't even discuss it with Oliver,
not unless he tells you the coast is clear. Got it?" It felt odd but
exhilarating for *me* to be the magic expert. I'd do my best not to
talk down to him the way other witches had always talked down
to me before my powers manifested.

"Got it," he said and nodded his head. "Where do we start?"

I stopped and considered this. There was still so much I was
only now learning myself, so much I didn't understand. "Well, I
think the best place to start is with Ginny. You see, Connor didn't
kill Ginny." His eyes narrowed; he had been oh so certain of
Connor's guilt from day one. With only a few words, I had completely wiped away his smug sense of self-validation. "It was a
demon, a boo hag, if you will, who did the killing. You knew this
demon as Jackson."

TWENTY-EIGHT

Some might have considered it a misuse of county equipment, but I didn't object when Adam offered to have a uniformed officer drop me off downtown, and the officer did not object to fulfilling a childhood fantasy when I asked him to put on the sirens and lights. Cars pulled over and pedestrians stopped to wait for us as we flew down Waters to Wheaton to Randolph, finally arriving on Broughton. The officer stopped beneath the SCAD Theater marquee and turned off the siren and lights. He put the patrol car in park and got out and came around to open my door.

"Thanks for the ride," I said.

"Sure thing, Miss Taylor," he replied before shutting the door.

"Can I treat you to something?" I asked, nodding toward the ice cream shop.

"No, thanks, ma'am," he said, patting his stomach and returning to the car. He pulled out into traffic.

The siren had caused a number of people to gather outside Leopold's, and I jostled my way through them. A group of children in the shop's party room still had their faces pressed against the window, trying to spot the cause of all the excitement. Behind them, the party's hired entertainment, a man wearing the odd combination of a pirate outfit and a white clown's face looked a little less than happy to get second billing.

"Everything okay, Mercy?" asked Josh, a student at SCAD and part-time scoop jockey, as I came through the door.

The worry melted from his face when I replied, "Emergency ice cream craving."

"*Craving*, huh?" he asked as he rolled up a sleeve and exposed a tattoo, one undoubtedly of his own design. I repressed a shudder—his innocent tattoo brought to mind the markings on Ryder's arm. I acknowledged his underlying question with a smile and nod. "Well, congratulations," he said, seeming truly happy for me. "Might I recommend our newly created mother-to-be tasting menu?"

The squeals and laughter from the birthday party made me smile. I'd had more than a few of my own celebrations in the side room, and hoped to have many more here with my son. "Oh, yes, that sounds perfect. Newly created?"

"Yep. About seven seconds ago. Grab a seat." He nodded at a table near the window. "Not doing your tour anymore?" he called out as I took my seat.

"No, I think I've told enough lies about this poor old town," I said and smiled at him.

He had arranged a dozen or so small paper cups on a tray and was digging away in the cooler. "Mind if I take up the mantle, then? It would be a shame for a good idea like that to go to waste."

"Not at all," I said, feeling only a twinge of sentimentality. I'd been doing the Liar's Tour since I was twelve. Giving it up to someone else would mean closing a door on a big chunk of my past. Deep down though, I knew that the door had already closed. "Come by the house sometime, and I will give you the leftover souvenirs." I had about five hundred Liar's Club to-go cups, or "walkers," as we called them around here, stashed in my closet. A few T-shirts too.

"Sweet. Thanks. Here, on the house," he said as he walked over and placed the tray in front of me with a flourish, then returned to the counter to help another patron. As I ate my ice cream, I was flooded with memories of the days I'd spent leading groups around the squares and coming up with the most audacious lies I could think of. A couple laughed as they walked down Broughton, and the sound pulled me back to the present. I gazed out the window, my eyes settling on the library across the street, an unremarkable building that had once been a department store. Special to Savannah in that there was nothing visually interesting about it. Architectural white noise, wallpaper.

As I scanned the building's lines, I became aware of a figure leaning up against the gray kiosk that stood before it. He wore a dirty red baseball cap, the bill of which he had pulled down to hide his eyes. His clothes were worn, his jacket torn on the shoulder. By outward appearance, he could have been one of Savannah's homeless. Even though he didn't look directly at me, I felt his interest in me, his intention that I should notice him. He lifted his cap and ran his hand through his hair. My heart pounded when I recognized him. It was my mother's driver, Parsons.

I pushed away from the table and darted out the door. Parsons had already made it halfway down the block, and he raised his hand and waved, signaling me to follow him. I felt like I was walking in a dream. Uneasy memories of his masklike face and out-of-sync voice warned me to turn around. But still I felt compelled, whether by magic or curiosity, to follow this odd man, disguised as a homeless man to avoid notice. Parsons turned at Habersham and laid an envelope on one of the benches in Warren Square. Without pausing or giving me another glance, he pulled his cap tightly over his eyes and headed over to a rusted Impala parked at the far end of the square. The car shot out black puffs of exhaust as it fired into life. I watched Parsons pull away, and ran to the bench to grab the envelope he had left behind.

My name was scrawled on it in unfamiliar cursive. I ripped the envelope open, and a piece of card stock fell to the ground. I picked it up without looking at it, then pulled out a folded sheet of paper from the envelope and read:

> My dear daughter,
>
> If you are reading this, then our time together has been cut short, and my most trusted servant, Parsons, has been obliged to risk his own life to deliver this to you.
>
> I returned to Savannah in the hope that I would find a way to make things right. To make peace with my family. To help you save your sister from the hell to which the line has sentenced her. To reclaim our lives together. To watch your child grow in the way I was denied the joy of watching you and Maisie as you matured into the strong, beautiful women that you are.
>
> I failed to protect your sister, but I have not failed to protect you. The witch families have used your fear to extort most of your rightful powers from you. They have also constrained your direct access to the energy of the line, but I have created another source of power for you, one over which they have no control. I grant you now the only inheritance I can, the full use of the power I have collected through Tillandsia. Use the enclosed invitation to gain entrance to Tillandsia and claim your birthright. Protect yourself. Protect your child. Trust no one.
>
> With more love than words can express,
> Your mother

I refolded the letter and returned it to the envelope. I felt the card in my hand, letting my finger run over the engraving. "Tillandsia," I read aloud. The word and a two-color drawing of the black-and-red door were all that had been printed on the front. On the reverse, handwritten in an unfamiliar but elegant script was "Mercy Taylor and Guest," and beneath our names, the message, "Tonight, sunset. Black tie required."

TWENTY-NINE

"Are you ready to admit you need help?" Emmet's voice came from behind me.

"Are you still following me?" I said, turning. Rather than feeling angry that I was being stalked—*again*—I was happy to see a friendly, if taciturn, face.

"Yes," he said and sat down next to me. He leaned in closer, his warm breath tickling my ear. "You must understand. I've not only been tasked with teaching you. It is also my duty to protect you, at least until the families are sure you can protect yourself."

"Or to spy on me and keep me in line until they can figure out a way to do away with me."

He pulled away from me, his eyes wide, and his skin momentarily flashed back to the color of the gray dirt from which he had sprung. "No, Mercy. You must believe me. I believe I have made my feelings for you clear. Even if the families do not have your best interest at heart, you must realize that I would never assist in any effort to bring you harm."

"At least not knowingly," I said and watched his face as the possibility that the families had been lying dawned on him.

"They instructed me to follow you. I have been following you. Practically everywhere you've gone for months."

I stopped and looked up into his stoic face. He had braced himself for a burst of anger, but I still had none. Deep down, I'd known it all along, even before Ryder had attested to Emmet's constant, invisible presence. I'd felt him nearby, and had taken comfort from it. I shook my head and started to go, but he reached out and caught my forearm in his massive hand. "I was there Mercy. There when you encountered the Tierney man. There when your mother took you. And I was there in the Tillandsia house when the skylight crashed in on her."

So it really *had* happened after all. "And you reported everything to the families?"

He shook his head. "Not all of it. Only as much as I felt necessary. That you accidently damaged the old man, yes. That a collector has come to Savannah, yes. That Peter is not human and that you have been meeting with your mother, no. That is why I denied having pulled you from the Tillandsia house. If I had admitted to being there, I might have been forced to share the truth about your interview with Emily."

"So why the editing for my family?"

"Because I don't know whom to trust, and you shouldn't make assumptions regarding anyone's goodwill for the time being either."

"Even yours?"

He scooped up my forearm into his strong hand. "If it keeps you safe, if it makes you vigilant, then yes. Doubt me as well." I tugged on my arm, and he released his grasp. "Show me the paper you hold. Please."

In spite of his own warning to trust no one, I couldn't bring myself to doubt his goodwill. I handed the card and the letter over to Emmet, who examined them minutely, as if they were a palimpsest whose secret text would reveal itself under scrutiny.

"I'm afraid that's all she wrote," I said.

"It would be foolhardy to attend," Emmet said as he returned the papers to me.

"But I must. This could be my only hope of bringing Maisie home. Besides, if any of what my mother has said is true, she gave her life for this."

"Perhaps it is true. And perhaps this letter is from your mother," he said, pausing to consider his words. "But consider this: a woman capable of faking her own death once could certainly do so again." I had not allowed this thought to surface in my mind, but now that it had arisen, I could not deny the possibility, even though I know what it meant. If she had done such a thing, I meant nothing to her. Emmet allowed me no time for reflection, no respite for my conflicted emotions. "I must inform you that your Aunt Ellen has gone missing. Neither Iris nor Oliver is overly concerned, as she has begun drinking again. Evidently, they consider disappearing part of her standard drinking behavior."

I nodded. "That much is true, I'm afraid."

"I am not so sure this time. I know you love her. Your devotion to her is evident, but for your own safety"—he seemed to sense my growing determination to knock down anything he might say against Ellen, so he went for the big guns—"and for the safety of your child, you have to consider that Ellen herself may have arranged Tucker Perry's assassination to throw you off guard and lure you to Tillandsia."

"No," I said. I found it unthinkable that Ellen would do such a thing. When it came down to it, I felt a much stronger need to defend her than I did my own mother. "She loved Tucker, and she would have no motive for hurting me."

"And you once believed that your sister loved Jackson, and that she'd never want to hurt you either." That stung, especially since he was voicing my own repressed fears. "Listen to me," he

228

said, with an anxiety that I'd never heard before in his voice. "If Emily is truly dead—and I still think that's questionable—who would have reason to kill her? Who was harmed most by your mother's actions? Who else has been participating in Tillandsia all these years? Who knew the truth about the power generated by the group? Who would have the power to turn those same forces against your mother? Against you? Who else is a strong enough witch to turn that Ryder buffoon into a collector?"

"All right. Stop." No longer caring that I might be seen, I crossed my arms and willed myself home. I found myself in the garden, Emmet still by my side. How he had managed to attach himself to me was a question for a later time. I scanned the house and garden to see if anyone was home, but we had the place to ourselves.

"I ask that you consider what I've said. Whoever gave the order to cause the dome to fall could at best be considered indifferent to your well-being. Perhaps you are correct in your convictions. Perhaps Ellen is an innocent."

"She is."

"If that is indeed the case, then you should question why Oliver is so eager to get his hands on the power that has been built up by Tillandsia."

"He wants to use it to help Maisie," I said, my growing irritation playing in my voice. "That's his only interest in Tillandsia. And what do you have to say about Iris?"

"Well, your aunt is a widow now. Don't you think it is possible that she may in some part blame you for that? No, it may be that your aunts and uncle love you and want to protect you, but are you willing to bet your life on it? Your child's life?"

I considered his words. Yes. Yes, I would bet my own life on trusting my family, at least what remained of it, in spite of Maisie, in spite of Ginny, and in spite of my mother's accusations against them. But no, I could not, would not, risk little Colin's life by betting on any of them. "You're right. I can't take the risk." There had been too many lies, whether well-intentioned or no. "I'm afraid there's only one person I trust that deeply." His black eyes warmed with hope, and I felt bad dousing their light. "I'm sorry, but I'm talking about Jilo."

He covered his disappointment by tilting his head and trying to look as if he had just learned an interesting clinical fact. "Then we shall request her assistance."

"I'm not sure she will help." I'd never thought anything could frighten Jilo, but she had been terrified by what had happened with the gray rainbow. "And I'm not even sure what it is you are proposing."

"The old woman will do anything you ask," he said, and then added, "I think you are right to place your trust in her." He crossed the garden and leaned over to touch the rose quartz in the flowerbed. It glowed as brightly as a lightbulb. "If I cannot dissuade you from attending Tillandsia tonight, then I propose we do what your uncle suggested, what your mother requested. Reach out and take control of the power of Tillandsia. We'll do it without your family. We will do it on our own."

"Okay, and then what?"

"We drain the power from Tillandsia and store it elsewhere, put it in our pocket so to speak, for use when we have a clearer view of who is pulling the strings and working against us. We use it to protect you. Then, once we know where we stand, I will not interfere with you retrieving your sister, assuming there is enough power remaining."

"Assuming that there is power, and that we can access it, how or where could we store it?"

"Your friend Jilo has vacated her haint-blue cell. She designed it to hold energy."

230

I thought about that. Of all the people I knew, Jilo had the most expertise when it came to siphoning off energy and finding a way to store it. At least since Ginny had died and stopped draining off my own power. "I will contact her and ask her to help. I have to do something."

"I will do whatever I can to support you." His eyes crinkled a bit. "But there's one final aspect we must consider."

"And that would be?"

"Your uncle seemed convinced that the only way to tap into Tillandsia's power would be to enter into a sexual ecstasy."

I had filed that little tidbit away as something to consider only when absolutely necessary. Even though the horse had broken well free of the barn, Peter and I had agreed, at my urging, to wait until after the wedding to make love again. Now I needed to show up and tell him he had to put out as part of a magical rite. I worried more about my own dignity than his willingness.

"Of course," Emmet began, "it would be unwise to expose Peter to this untested magic. It might trigger his awareness."

"His awareness of what?" I snapped.

"That he's a changeling."

"Damn it, Emmet," I said. My head started hurting. I closed my eyes and tried to compose myself. "He can never know."

"I understand, and that is why I am counseling you against bringing him tonight."

Emmet was right. Again. "So what do you propose?"

"I offer myself—"

"Oh, no. You hold on right there." I threw up both of my hands. "That is not happening. I am engaged to Peter. I love Peter. I will not allow anyone else to touch me that way."

"I understand." He drew nearer to me. I took a couple steps back, but then froze when his eyes locked onto mine. "I understand you wish to remain faithful to your fiancé. I won't say that

I would not like to lie with you as a man." In spite of myself and my storming, guilty conscience, the image of our naked bodies straining against each other rose in my mind. "But I respect you and your commitment to Peter. I would never attempt to touch you that way as long as you honor that commitment."

"Good," I mumbled, trying to rid my mind of the thought of Emmet's body, but still transfixed by his intense gaze.

"You must acknowledge, however, that if ensnarement is the intention of whoever sent you this invitation, they will be surprised to find that you have a very capable and coolheaded witch as your escort, rather than your impulsive carpenter." I couldn't deny that Emmet's firepower might come in handy. He smiled, his eyes narrowing, lending a mischievous look to his normally serious face. "Besides, there are so many ways I can pleasure you without even touching you." My temperature spiked as a vibration tingled through my body. "I can bring your pleasure centers to life with nothing more than a word, a thought." I felt a surge rise up through my body, firing up each chakra as it passed into a tangible rainbow. Red, a shock, mercury rising. Orange, I felt a wave of shivering satisfaction swell up inside me. I should have protested what he was doing, but yellow, I felt so safe. Green, I knew I did have feelings for him; this wasn't merely a carnal act. Blue. My pleasure expressed itself in a gasp. A soft moan. My eyes closed, and my head tilted back. Indigo. My eyes fluttered open to see the devotion on his face, the beautiful intensity of Bernini's *David* made flesh, the purity of the feelings he held for me. The world around me turned violet, as he fully suffused me with his power. I fell forward into his waiting arms.

"Ahem." Jilo banged on the top of the gate with her cane. I tore myself from Emmet's embrace, startled and ashamed. "Wouldn't mind a taste of that myself, mud pie." She cackled and closed the garden gate with her stick. Both hands on its handle, she wobbled her way toward me. "Jilo understand you be needin' her." I looked from her back to Emmet, glowing in his smugness. In that moment, I hated him; in that moment, I knew that if it hadn't been for Jilo's arrival, I'd still be lost in his arms, my body demanding his.

THIRTY

"The game is afoot," Emmet said, glancing over at me as we pulled up to the gates of the Tillandsia house. I rolled my eyes, and he smiled. He turned down the long drive, pulling near the oval, which had been a patch of dirt only a few days ago. Tonight, a decades-old magnolia stood there, fragrant in its full and miraculously timed bloom. The scent wafted in through my cracked open window. It intoxicated me, almost as much as the few times I'd allowed myself to glance over at Emmet. His piercing eyes burned, and despite their fire, they were even blacker than the tuxedo he wore. His hair was combed back in thick onyx waves. I fought the urge to run my fingers through them. My love for Peter was all that prevented me from acting on my desire.

I forced myself to concentrate on the matter at hand. Our plan was good, although I was not about to jinx it by thinking of it as foolproof. My job was to unlock the energy, and then Emmet would relay it to Jilo, who had ensconced herself in her haint-blue chamber and would be waiting to take charge of any magic we sent her way.

We pulled around the oval, where attendants were opening car doors and collecting keys. Emmet placed the car in park and turned to face me, a hint of a grin on his lips. "I've never driven before. Did I do okay?"

I laughed even though I shouldn't have. I should have questioned his overly earnest request to act as chauffeur. Tonight, though, I didn't want to ask too many questions of him. I was afraid of the answers. "You did great."

Powerful searchlights crossing beams overhead and smaller lamps scattered throughout nearly turned the night into day. Peter's crew had done no additional work since Tucker's death, but the Tillandsia house shone, the very image of perfection. Only magic could have transformed it so quickly. The sad and peeling paint had been exchanged for a fresh and nearly luminescent white that coated the house's Doric pillars as well as the building itself. The shutters had been enameled black. Only the door remained as it had been, the same black and red that the Tillandsia Society had evidently adopted as its symbol.

The attendant opened my door, and I stretched out my legs, making sure that my much higher than usual heels connected safely with the still fresh pavement. Emmet met me at the side of the car and offered me his arm. I let myself lean on it, enjoying the comfort of his strength. My fingers dug into his jacket as we stepped past the infamous door and over the threshold. My eyes darted nervously around the entranceway, but there was no visible dome overhead. The true architecture of the house fully honored the Georgian preference for symmetry—two stairways curved gracefully up to the top floor, one on each side.

Eyes fell on us from every direction, predatory and hungry—some for me, some for Emmet, and a good number for us both. I recognized some of the faces, including a teacher from my high school and a few business people and their respective spouses. Most of the faces were new, but all, the new and the known, glowed with the same carnivorous delight. Conversation stopped as a servant who was attired in a period costume, complete with a powdered wig, stepped forward. "Your invitation, please." He held out a silver tray to receive it. I looked at Emmet with panic in my eyes. I'd forgotten to bring it. He smiled and produced the paper from his coat pocket. After he placed it on the tray, the servant picked it up. "Miss Mercy Taylor and Mister . . . ?" He paused, appreciating the dark wall of man next to me.

"My name is Emmet Clay."

"Wouldn't mind spinning that clay on my wheel." A stage whisper floated down from a group of middle-aged ladies at the top of the stairs. The conversation picked up again in spurts and stops, soon reaching its previous volume and complexity, even though most eyes remained fixed on the two of us.

"A warm Tillandsia welcome to you, Mr. Clay," the servant said and bowed.

Emmet leaned over and whispered into my ear. "They can't take their eyes off you." His warm breath tickled.

"I think you are the one everybody's checking out."

"No," he said. "You are breathtaking in that dress."

I bit my tongue to keep from turning it into a joke, from saying, "What, this old thing?" Instead I returned a simple "Thank you." I wore another of Ellen's finds, an ice-blue vintage cocktail dress with trails of slightly darker flowers that ran down the fabric in rows. It read as very sweet and demure, and my amplified cleavage was well hidden by the collarbone-high neckline and wide straps. Even with the pleated waist, it still covered me without drawing attention to my pregnancy. The skirt fell a little below the knee. I'd borrowed Ellen's pearls, wearing them for good luck as well as a sign of my faith in her, and had my hair up in a loose bun. The entire effect came across as much more Sunday school than orgy. I surveyed the room filled with high slit

J.D. HORN

skirts and deeply plunging necklines, and realized the seductive power my modest look held simply due to juxtaposition.

Even though I knew the participants were here of their own volition, the house had the feeling of a zoo or prison, each room as a separate cage. I reached up and touched my aunt's pearls, focusing on them, using them to help me hone in on her energy. "Aunt Ellen is here," I said to Emmet. "I can sense her."

"Do you detect that she is in danger of any kind?"

"No, she doesn't seem to be under any stress." In fact, when I reached out to her, I experienced a sense of calmness, as if she were resting or medicated. Waiters walked around carrying glass after glass of Ellen's favorite form of medication.

"Then let us focus for now on the power." Emmet lifted his hand, using it like an antenna or maybe a dowsing rod. "There is much of it here, just waiting for us to tap into it."

"I feel it too." The power did not resonate like the smooth and vibrant energy of the line, nor did it sizzle like the nearly psychotic electricity that had built up at the old Candler Hospital, having fed off the pain and misery of those who had been lost there. It lay somewhere between the two, and it felt something like silk being pulled across a ragged rock. I gave a slight tug to the bond Emmet had helped set up between Jilo and myself. She tugged back.

"The real party is this way," a naked man I recognized as a former state senator said with a grin, using his sex to point to the doorway of what had probably been the parlor or drawing room.

I felt the blood rise to my face as I watched his pasty buttocks pass through the arch of the door. I turned nearly purple when the servant who announced us approached. "If you'd prefer a more private setting, there are rooms upstairs. Although there will be several," he said, giving Emmet a thoroughly appreciative stare, "who will be *very* disappointed if you don't join the festivities."

"We came here to 'participate,'" I said, dreading the thought of crossing the barrier into that room.

"We don't have to stay, Mercy. We can find Ellen and leave if that is what you would prefer."

"If you are speaking of Mrs. Weber," the servant said using the correct German pronunciation, "she is already in there with her friends." He stretched his hand out to indicate the room into which we had just been invited. Emmet and I looked at each other, each reflecting the other's uncertainty. "Don't be shy. Dive on in," the servant said. "The water's warm."

I nodded to Emmet, and he placed his arm around my shoulder and led me from the entrance into what I'd assumed was the party room. Once there, I realized that the old parlor was simply being used as a cloakroom. At one end, a female attendant, pretty close to my own age, stood perfectly naked and totally unashamed. At the other end, a muscular man, nude except for a gun belt, stood guard at the door that led from the cloakroom into what I now knew to be the party room.

"Welcome, y'all," the attendant said, offering us rubber bracelets with numbers printed on them. "Here are your claim numbers when you are ready to head out tonight, so take care not to lose them." She dropped both bands into Emmet's large hand, and then held up two black vinyl garment bags with the corresponding numbers written on them.

"That's all right," I said. "I think we'll keep our clothes on for now."

"Oh, I am sorry. This must be your first time." She smiled congenially at us newbies. "No one gets in without, well, displaying their goods."

"In our case, you will please make an exception," Emmet said in a calm voice. He wasn't attempting to charm her magically, as

Oliver would have done; he was simply stating his wish in his habitual, matter-of-fact manner.

"I am afraid we can't do that, sir. Fair is fair. Besides, I am sure that neither you nor your pretty lady has anything to be ashamed of." She smiled at me, her eyes asking me to talk some sense into my date. "Your lady friend can keep her pearls, if she likes. And her shoes," she offered.

"When in Rome, I guess," I said, and when Emmet looked at me, his eyes were filled with surprise. "We'll only need one bag."

"Oh, sweetie," the attendant said, her shoulders relaxed. She seemed relieved by my surrender. "Don't go making that mistake. You are a true beauty and all, but it's quite a rarity for a couple that comes to Tillandsia together to leave together."

Emmet's face clouded over like a storm about to burst. His eyes narrowed and his brow creased. "I apologize. I believe when I used the word 'please' earlier, you thought I was making a request. I am telling you that in our case, you will make an exception."

The woman lowered the bags as Emmet dropped the bands on her table.

"Listen here," the doorman said, moving his hand to his holster. "Everybody's just here to have a good time. Loosen up or leave."

Emmet turned to face the guard. Even though the man was close to six feet tall and had the muscles of a professional bodybuilder, Emmet towered over him by nearly a foot. I could tell the guard feared Emmet might call his bluff and make him pull his pistol from its holster. Emmet stood firm, and after a few taut moments, the guard drew aside. Emmet placed his arm around my shoulder again and led me into hell's second circle.

The hall, for you couldn't simply call it a room, stretched out much larger than I had imagined it could, or perhaps the sense of size was an optical illusion created by the numerous gilt-framed mirrors that lined its walls and had been suspended from the ceiling. Still, even with the hall's size, it felt close and claustrophobic. It had no windows, and the only perceivable exit was the entrance through which we'd just come. It was too dark to even determine the color of the walls, save in one corner where a bright spotlight illuminated a stage and the wall behind it. It had been painted plum—a good shade for debauchery, I decided.

Deep inhalations and sighs sounded from one end of the hall to the other, answered by soft moans and whispers and the occasional alarming cry of pleasure. I lowered my eyes, trying not to look at anything. But there, all along the floor, writhed piles and mounds and rows of bodies, lying together, caressing one another, in kaleidoscopic combinations. A heaving, groaning work by Bosch. A green scent like acacia in hot sun. Another, seaweed washed up on the damp shore. Tattoos and scars and every shade in the rainbow of flesh. Faces contorted with pleasure or contorted with pain, as per their inclination, appeared from the shadows only to be swallowed again by the darkness moments later. Waiters circled, offering any vice from alcohol to tiny packets of white powder to hypodermic needles loaded with God only knows what. Pillars of smoke floated in and out around us, some smelling sweet—cloying, even—others like vinegar. I tried not to breathe the smoke in, fearing the effect it might have on my baby. I should never have come here. I should never have risked Colin. I should have put him first, before Maisie, before my own selfish need to prove to myself that my mother loved me. I wanted to scream as the truth hit me. Regardless of my reasons, my justifications, that was the true reason I'd come. Well, I no longer cared. All that mattered was proving to my son that I loved him.

I turned and tried to push my way back to the exit, desperate to leave the hall, but dozens of revelers had followed us in and were crowding around us. I started to panic, striking out, slapping, clawing at those who surrounded me. Emmet picked me up and strode away from the center of the room, where we had somehow found ourselves. He sat me down with my back against the far wall, and used his own mass to shield me from those who would have crushed up against us. "I want to get out of here. I need to get out of here," I cried into his ear. "Forget the plan."

"I know, and I will find us a way to do just that."

"Just get us to the exit," I said, not comprehending why this wouldn't show itself as the obvious solution.

"The wall behind us is where the exit was . . . Your back is directly against it."

I felt around behind myself, feeling nothing but wall, but then I turned and saw my own eyes dimly reflected back at me by a mirror that had taken the place of the door. They mimicked the eyes of a trapped and desperate animal. Emmet put his hands on my shoulders and turned me back toward him. "Don't panic," he said. "It's the magic in this room. It is seeking to master us, but we must take control and become its master instead . . . We must continue with the plan. You can do this. We can do this."

His words calmed me, and I found myself unconsciously mimicking his breathing. Deep, slow breaths. My heart slowed its wild beating.

"There is only one way out of here, and that is to capture the magic," he whispered in my ear, his hot breath tickling the sensitive skin beneath it. "And there is only one way to capture the magic." He pressed my back gently against the mirrored surface. His hands reached out and found mine, pressing our palms together, lacing our fingers. His heat consumed me, and again I felt his energy, his power, coalesce at the tip of my spine and climb its way up through me. In spite of my fear, in spite of the

241

revulsion that the gathering had engendered in me, I felt my body give into pleasure. "Picture it, Mercy," he said, his lips brushing against my earlobe. "See the power of this room becoming yours."

I tried to envision the energy coming into my grasp, my control, but I sensed the hall around us changing. A sound, caught somewhere between a human moan and the buzzing of locusts, began to reverberate around the space, although only Emmet and I seemed to notice. The partiers remained blithely unaware of any change in the atmosphere. I struggled to look beyond Emmet's shoulder. A beam of light, cold and uncomforting, bounced from one mirrored surface to the next, weaving a web around all those who were gathered here.

The beam pierced my heart with horror because it revealed that we were no longer standing in the mirrored hall, but in the hexagonal entranceway where I'd seen my mother murdered. The dome hovered over us once again, backlit in a way that attested to its presence, but lent no illumination to the space beneath it. Even though the mirrors had disappeared with the plum walls that held them, I could still see everything around us reflected from a thousand different angles. I looked forward and saw myself from behind, my arms raised and intertwined with Emmet's.

The servants who had been purveying their stupefying substances had dragged one of the partygoers to the center of the room. The shaved head and mangled stump of an arm identified him as Ryder. The participants who had been so intertwined that they'd appeared to be a single mass of writhing flesh began to disengage, each body unknotting from the others, individuating. Some rose to their feet, others only to their knees. The most terrible of all were those who'd abandoned any pretense of humanity, rising up on all four limbs. Faces dotted with black and alien eyes turned to focus on Ryder at the center of the gathering. "His blood for their glory" came from one side of the circle that had formed around him, and then the others took up the cry, chanting it over and over again.

A symbol, like an Egyptian ankh mated with the symbol for infinity, had been carved into Ryder's forehead. It glowed an angry red, but Ryder himself seemed indifferent to the situation unfolding around him. He knelt, too wasted to protest, too intoxicated to care what was happening. The revelers cheered as another man, naked except for a mask of Janus that covered his entire head, stepped forward and slid a knife across Ryder's throat. His body slumped forward as it bled out. The blood defied the laws of physics, running up the walls instead of pooling at the lowest point of the room.

The dome was no longer fixed in place—it started ascending, and the staircase that led to it started to grow longer, level after level. This was no longer the room where I had seen my mother die. It was growing into a tower, and it kept growing ever more quickly, stretching higher and higher and gaining speed as it did so.

The man with the knife removed his mask and cried out. He turned to face me, his eyes entirely black except for glowing crimson dots that had replaced his pupils. I recognized him instantly. It was Joe, Ryder's buddy. The crowd turned their attention from Ryder's exsanguinated corpse to Emmet and me, and they began to advance on us, chanting in a language I could not understand. I screamed and struggled, trying to alert Emmet to what was occurring behind him, only to realize that he was frozen in place, trapped by the power we had tapped into as surely as you can get stuck to an electrified fence. He couldn't move. He couldn't speak. He couldn't disconnect from the power that rose up through him and into me. The black magic filtered into my body, settled in around my solar plexus, and then found its prize, the point at which the line had connected its magic to mine. It had found a vulnerability in the line itself, and I had provided it with an entry point. The full gravity of absolute darkness pulled at me, its source, the power I had been so foolish to welcome into myself, the power of Tillandsia.

THIRTY-ONE

"What the hell is going on here?" Peter's voice caused the world around me to shimmer, and then break apart. He grabbed Emmet by the shoulders, and even though Emmet was by far the larger man, he threw him onto the floor.

I was shaking, a scream still caught in my throat. The tower and its dome had vanished. We stood in the true entranceway of the house. All the other guests were gone, and the room where we stood was still very much in a state of aborted renovation.

Peter turned from me to Emmet, who had managed to sit up, although he was still obviously in a state of shock. "I asked you what the hell's going on."

"Peter," I managed. "It isn't what it looks like."

He spun back to me, his face flushed red and a pulse visible at his right temple. Such anger burned in his eyes. "I don't even know what it looks like, Mercy, so why don't you tell me what you two are doing here?"

"We're here looking for Ellen," I said. That at least consti-tuted part of the truth.

"And what? You thought you'd find her in his coat pocket?"

"We can explain if you'll allow us," Emmet said, managing to stand and regain a bit of his sense of decorum.

"You shut up before I shut you up." Peter's voice quivered. "What's wrong with you?" he addressed me. "I thought we had this settled once Jackson took off, that we had decided it was going to be you and me. Now here I find you doing I don't know what with this guy. I mean, for God's sake, Mercy, he isn't even real. He isn't even a man."

I looked at Emmet, begging him with my eyes not to retaliate with the knowledge he held about Peter. Nodding slightly, he lowered his head and stepped away. "It isn't like that," I said, even though my conscience took little nips at me as I said it. "You don't understand what's been going on."

"Well, how about you break it down for me? Nice and slow and easy so I can get it."

I stood there trying to find the words to say to him, to explain how my life had turned upside down and nothing at all felt like it was under my control. The words would not come. He started shaking, but I couldn't tell if it was from rage or heartbreak. I wanted to say something, to make it right, but a movement in the corner of my eye drew my attention. I looked away from Peter to see my mother coming toward us. I reached out to Peter to get him to turn and look, but he stepped back from me.

"To hell with it," he said and turned to leave, but in that split second, my mother appeared directly behind him and drove a blade deep into his chest. He convulsed and coughed up blood.

"There," she addressed me. "Mama just made it an easy choice for you. That one"—she nodded toward Emmet—"looks good in a tux. This one works my last nerve." She pushed Peter away, and he fell to the floor.

"What have you done?" I broke from my rigor and threw myself down at Peter's side.

"That blade is made from iron, you know," she said. "Iron through the heart is the one sure way to kill a fairy."

I knelt next to Peter and, my hand trembling, pulled the blade from his chest. I threw it aside, and it melted in midair. Emmet tried to run to my side, but Emily raised one hand, palm out, toward him. An unseen magic flung him up and backward, pinning him to the wall. He struggled, but couldn't release himself.

"Why?" I asked that woman, the woman who only seconds before I had still thought of as "Mama."

"Call it 'Plan B' if you like," she said and stepped toward us. She moved her foot gingerly forward and kicked Peter's body. "Go on. I'm curious to see what you can do. There's still a little life in him. Let's see if you can save him. That is, if you *want* to save him." She smiled and leered at Emmet. "Quickly now, before I change my mind."

"I'm not Ellen. You saw what happened when I tried a healing before."

"Yes, I did. Your efforts proved delightfully amusing." She laughed. This had to be a nightmare. Peter couldn't be dying next to me. My mother could not be such a monster. She read my thoughts. "Oh, baby. This *is* real. This whole night has been real. Maybe not on the plane that you're used to, but real all the same. We came so, so close. You and your golem here, with all your beautiful power blending in with mine. It was lovely. Lovely. We came so close to completing the Babel spell. So, so close to building a tower that reaches beyond the line, all the way to the old gods. The line may keep them from coming to us, but it can't keep us from going to them. This one"—she glared at Peter— "caused us to waste a perfectly good demon. Barron's power has been expended, and I can't get it back." She delivered a savage kick to Peter's side. "I knew you'd bring the golem rather than risk your changeling, but he still just had to show up and interrupt. It must be the magic in his fairy blood that allowed him to break the spell." Her eyes focused on my throat, as tightly as if the look were intended to strangle me. "If you'd been wearing the locket I gave you rather than your aunt's tatty pearls, he might not have managed it even then."

She mocked me by pulling her lips into a pout. "That's right. Mama put a spell on her little gift." She shook her head as the exaggerated expression turned into a true frown. "You do have some power in you, little girl. There was enough magic in that locket to charm a normal witch into believing anything I wanted her to. You, it only made a little more amenable."

I was an anchor. She shouldn't have been able to charm me at all, but that was the last thing I had time to contemplate right now. I pressed my palm over the wound on Peter's chest. Half praying, half reaching out for my own magic, I tried my best to close the hole, to will a beat back to his heart. She circled us once, as if taking a moment to consider. "All right, you are a novice, so I'll let you have a little help. Josef," she called into the darkness, "bring her."

Joe entered, dragging Ellen's naked form with him. His hands dug into my aunt's shoulders, bruising the skin around the points of contact. He flung her to the ground next to us.

"There," Emily said. "There's your precious Ellen."

Ellen lay there barely conscious. Blood from multiple needle pricks had trickled down her arm and dried. "A tenth of what's in her could kill a platoon of regular men," Joe said. "It's so nice to have a toy you can't break, no matter how hard you are on it."

"Tick tock, tick tock, my girl," Emily said. "It makes no difference to me if he lives or dies, but your leprechaun's running out of time."

"He isn't a leprechaun."

"And in a few moments more he won't be anything at all."

Ellen lay on the floor, barely able to move. She tilted her head toward me, but I wasn't sure if she actually registered my presence, or if her effort was simply a reflex. But then she reached her hand out to me, and I took it. There shone only a glimmer of awareness in her eyes, but when our hands connected, I watched the aunt I knew and loved surface, like a swimmer breaking through the water. She inhaled sharply and let go of my hand, rolling over and pushing herself to her hands and knees. She crawled to Peter's side, placing her right palm across his forehead and her left over the wound on his chest. She closed her eyes, and then her lips began moving in silent prayer.

As she knelt over him, as her golden light began to spread through him, I focused in on his face, that face I'd loved but taken for granted since I was a little girl. Now that I was at risk of losing him forever, I realized how much I needed him, how much I loved him. Ellen opened her eyes and looked at me. She had difficulty speaking, her mouth still dry from the drugs that had been pumping through her body. "I've found him," she said. His eyes opened a crack, and he drew a breath.

"Brava. Brava, my darling." Emily applauded. "You saved the boy." She turned to face me. "It's a shame you can't do the same for that Negro of yours."

The joy that had reached my heart ran cold. "What have you done to Mother?"

"That darky is not your mother. I am your mother."

"No, not anymore. I guess maybe even never. What did you do to Jilo?"

Emily narrowed her eyes, leaned her head at a coquettish angle. "We dosed her."

"You and Joe drugged her?"

"Oh no. Not Josef and I. You and I. The magic you asked her to collect for you. It had a little bit of something extra in it. Something so fine that your old 'digger' would never notice it," she said and laughed. "All right, it's true that puns are the lowest form of humor, but I couldn't resist. Your Jilo, your 'Mother,' I knew she could never resist tasting the magic you sent her way, so I added a little something special just for her. She was dead within seconds of touching the power. I do hope her passing was *peaceful.*"

The word no sooner escaped her lips than a loud bang sounded on the door. Emily turned, surprised. As soon as she lost focus, out of the corner of my eye I noticed Emmet moving. He launched himself across the room and placed himself as a protective barrier between Emily and—bless his heart—Peter and Ellen.

Another bang. Emily shot a look at Joe, and he took a step toward the door, but halted in his tracks as a third bang rang out, sending a reverberation through the entire house. A final bang sent the black-and-red door bursting open with such vehemence it broke free from its frame. It spun through the air, just missing Joe's head as it flew over him. He fell to the floor as it passed, scurrying over to Emily on his hands and knees. When he rose to stand, he positioned himself strategically behind her, letting her shield him.

"Next time you'll open the damn door when Jilo knock." Jilo crossed the threshold into the entranceway, her walking stick still held high. As she stood framed in the door opening, several bolts of angry lightening ripped across the sky, backlighting this fury in a purple turban, lilac floral-print housecoat, and crocheted slippers.

"You are as hard to end as the cockroach," Emily said, crossing the room to face Jilo.

"That right, Jilo a cockroach." Jilo lowered her cane to the floor and leaned her weight into it as she bent toward Emily. "And she be here long after you dead and gone."

Emily raised her hand in the air, a ball of red light forming at her fingertips. She screamed in anger, hurling the ball at Jilo, who dropped her cane and opened her arms wide the instant before the power hit her. Her anguished face showed that it hurt like hell, but in a moment, her expression changed from one of pain to one of victory. She clapped her hands together, and as the energy danced on her fingertips, it transformed in color from red to royal blue. She pulled her hands apart and shot the ball right back at Emily. It hit her dead on. The smell of singed hair rose up around her, but she remained standing.

"You gonna have to do better than that if you want to take out Jilo." The old woman cackled. Her laughter caused Emily's face to twist with rage. "Jilo been borrowing power all her life, and now she ready to learn you a thing or two for messing with her girl." She motioned toward the ground, and her cane popped up into the air. She grasped the stick between both hands as a delighted gleam lit up her eyes. "Come on, batter up, bitch. Let Jilo see what you got."

Emily howled with fury and drew both hands into claws. Another ball of fire formed at her fingertips.

"Stop it," Iris's voice commanded as she entered the room. "Stop it."

The fire at Emily's fingers dissipated. Iris crossed the room, doing her best to take it all in. Oliver followed on her heels.

Iris stepped up to Emily, reaching out a hand to touch her face. In spite of the violence that had stained the room, her gesture was one of love. "We thought you were dead," she said and tried to draw Emily into her embrace.

"Do not touch me," she said, nearly hissing out the words.

"Emmy," Oliver said stepping out from behind Iris. "What has happened to you? Why are you doing this?" He looked around, obviously struggling to comprehend what exactly "this" was.

"Oh, little brother, I have been liberated. Freed from the tyranny of the line. *That* is what has happened to me." She reached out and tousled his hair. "Wouldn't you like to taste that freedom? Move past any sense of guilt or regret? You too have suffered under the line's yoke. You too have been exiled." Her fingers traced down his temple to his jaw. "We two are so alike, so much more so than you and those two drab creatures. You're not afraid of a little fire. You like having your own way. Join with me. Join with us." She reached up with both hands, her long red-lacquered fingernails tracing down both sides of his face. She tossed her hair back and looked up into Oliver's face, blinking her green eyes at him like an affectionate feline. She smiled and chanted, "Red Rover, Red Rover, send Oli on over."

Oliver's hands grabbed hers and pushed them away. "It's true. I am one selfish peacock of a bastard. I know that, but I am nothing like you. There's something inhuman about you now . . . maybe there always has been."

Emily laughed. "Inhuman? Oliver, if only you knew. You'll have to trust me that the irony is delicious."

"It isn't too late, Emily," Iris said. "It isn't too late for you to stop traveling down this path. Let us help you."

"Isn't it too late?" she asked, her question addressed to me rather than Iris. "I've allied myself with the *rebel* families. I have sworn to help them destroy your precious line." She nodded in the middle sister's direction. "I've tortured your dear Ellen, and I enjoyed every second of it, I might add. Did I mention that Josef and I were the ones who killed her worthless Tucker?"

"You said he was helping you." Ellen looked up at me as if my words would be the straw that broke her.

Emily laughed. "Oh my dear, I lied. I have some of the most powerful witches in the world supporting me. Why on earth would I need anything from Tucker Perry?" Her eyes narrowed, hardened. "I'm not a desperate lush." She tossed a glance in Ellen's direction, and I knew she was looking to see if her barb had hit home. She smiled, satisfied when Ellen winced. She turned back to me. "He was a pawn. I burned his heart out just to keep you off balance."

"And to take him away from me," Ellen said from the floor at Peter's side. Her physical energy had been exhausted. She pressed against the floor with both hands, barely strong enough to keep her upper body from collapsing to the parquet.

"Oh, yes," Emily said, nodding as she looked down at Ellen, "there was that too." She paused. "What about what I've done to you, Mercy? I've toyed with your delicate feelings. I stabbed your fiancé, oh, and speaking of your fiancé, I got you to cheat on him." She raised her chin, looking down the bridge of her nose at Peter. "Do you hear that, Peter? It's true. She surrendered herself to that creature. Maybe not physically, but he inserted himself inside her all the same. My whore of a daughter loved it."

"Shut up," Peter said, trying to sit up, but still too weak.

"That's no way to talk to your future mother-in-law," she said, and then again addressed me. "Tell me, *darling*, is it too late?"

I looked up at her and felt the power of her toxicity. So much anger, revulsion, and hate filled me, but then I stopped and dug deep into myself. In spite of everything, I wanted to find a way to end this. To reach out and rescue her from the darkness. "No, it isn't," I said. "Let us help you."

She snorted. "Living up to the charming name that Ellen hung on you, huh?" Her eyes flashed wide, and her mouth pulled up at one corner into a sneer of disgust. "If I could have named you, it would have been different. I would have called you 'Abomination,' for that is what you truly are." She looked away from me and back to Iris. "I don't need help. I need you to get out of the way. It's time for the line to fall. Our old friends have waited long enough," she said, and then added in a plaintive voice, "and they are so, so hungry."

"Then I'm sorry, dear one," Iris said, her voice breaking. "You can no longer hold the power in your possession." She paused and lifted her head high. "Emily Rose Taylor, I bind you. May the power reject you. May it not claim you as its own."

"Emily Rose Taylor, I bind you," Uncle Oliver joined in as Iris repeated the words.

"May the power reject you." Ellen added her weary voice to the chorus. "May it not claim you as its own."

"Emily Rose Taylor, Mama," I said, the word ripping the outer layer from my heart. "I bind you. May the power reject you. May it not claim you as its own."

"You little bitch," she said, looking at me through narrowed, venomous eyes, her head held back as if she were regarding something distasteful. "Do you really think you can control me? That any of you can control me? I do not depend on your line for my power. It comes from an altogether different source. One that you fools, you worthless ants can't even begin to comprehend."

"You wrong again," Jilo said, banging her cane. "Jilo can comprehend your dirty magic. She smell it on you. The death. The horror. The desecration you have fused with yo' soul."

"'Desecration'? That's a mighty big word for you, Jilo. Don't strain yourself."

"Oh that right. You all high and mighty and just pissing magic, but they also one other thing you is . . ."

"All right, you old hag, I'll bite. What's that?"

"Outnumbered," Jilo said and raised her cane. An arc of electricity shot out of it, bowing out over Joe and Emily's heads. Iris took the hint and raised her hand, shooting another bolt of energy. Emmet joined in too, adding another arc, the powers joining together to form a nearly completed cage.

"Last chance, Oli," Emily said. "You know I was always so fond of you. Come away. Join us. We won't keep each other ignorant of the greater truths. We won't place the real power in the hands of the few. With them you are an underling. With us, you will nearly be a god in your own right."

"Thanks for the offer, sis, but being 'nearly' a god sounds like way too much of a time commitment." He raised his hand to add his energy and complete the cage that the others had formed around Emily, but before he could complete the act, the vile woman descended through the floor and vanished, taking Joe with her.

"Well, I reckon I've lost my spot as the black sheep of the family," Oliver said into our stunned silence.

"Yes," Iris agreed. "It looks like you have."

THIRTY-TWO

"Get me away from here," Ellen said, crossing her bloodied arms across her chest. "I want to go home and shower."

"Of course," Iris said. "We'll get you home right now." Oliver wrapped Ellen in his jacket, and Iris put her arms around her sister's shoulders, leading her toward the gaping hole where the black-and-red door had stood.

"I will alert the families to Emily's return," Emmet said, "and see to it that she is found and taken someplace where the dark magic she has contracted can be controlled." Strange, Emmet made it sound like Emily had a disease. Maybe that's what this type of magic was—a malignancy that ate away at any decency.

"She tricked me into coming here tonight," Ellen said. "She made me believe that Tucker was still alive. She made a copy of him." Ellen stopped and looked at the door that was now laid on the floor. "Burn that damned thing." She looked over at me, her lips twitching.

"I'm so sorry this happened to you. That they did this to you," I said.

Ellen said nothing. She nodded her head and turned away, letting Iris lead her. Peter tried to stand but couldn't make it up under his own steam. When I reached out, he wouldn't take my hand. He wouldn't meet my eyes either. Oliver came and helped him up. "Let's get you to your parents' place," he said.

"No. No. Take me home to my house," Peter said. I reached out again to take his hand, and he pulled it away. "Not now, Mercy. Leave me alone for now."

"He'll be okay," Oliver said to me. "I'll keep an eye on him." Peter allowed himself to lean on my uncle's arm. His eyes—emotionally bruised, hurting—grazed mine and then looked away. He hobbled out the doorway, relying on Oliver's strength far more than I would have liked. He was still in pretty bad shape physically from the injury my mother had inflicted. I couldn't even allow myself to consider the emotional damage I'd caused him. I knew there was only one way to truly set things right.

"Emmet, I want to thank you. I appreciate all you have done or at least tried to do for me. The ways you've tried to protect me and teach me how to use my magic . . ."

"Of course—"

"Wait, Emmet. I need you to hear me." He fell instantly silent, hanging on my every word, ready for anything I might ask of him. Well, almost anything. "I need you to leave Savannah. I can't have you near me any longer. You understand?"

"Perhaps better than you do yourself," he said. His expression was more than stoic—it was emotionless, as if he could shut his feelings down as easily as a normal man takes a breath. He could burn with such passion that I had braced myself for anger, hurt, maybe even hate. I felt shaken by the utter indifference I registered there. He didn't speak another word. The air just shimmered around him, and then he was gone.

"Look like it jus' the two of us, then," Jilo said, her cane thumping with each step she took toward me.

I broke. My legs buckled under me, and I fell to my hands and knees. My hair tumbled down around my face, hiding everything from my sight except the hot tears that dropped from my eyes onto the floor. In one night, I'd undone a lifetime's worth of love. Even if Peter could forgive me, he would never forget the sight of Emmet and me together. I wasn't sure Ellen would ever recover from this second horrible loss, and I feared that in her eyes, I would always be a reflection of my mother. No. That monster wasn't my mother, even if she had given birth to me. "I've messed everything up."

"You can't take all the credit fo' that. You had plenty of help. Here now. You come to Jilo." The old woman of the crossroads used her stick to lower herself to my side, then drew me into her arms. "You go ahead. You cry it out now." I held her tightly and buried my head in her shoulder. "Get it out, girl. You gonna need to pull it together right quick," she said, "'cause something tell Jilo that bitch ain't nowhere near done."

THIRTY-THREE

Dawn broke over Savannah, scraping the night sky bloody before letting the sun rise over the horizon. I hadn't slept at all; each time I tried to close my eyes, another horror was projected on my inner lids. I'd spent most of the night on the side porch, staring east and hoping that by the time morning arrived, I would know how to fix things. Daylight had come, but I had grown no wiser.

"Stand a little company?" Ellen's voice reached out to me. I nodded, grateful to see her up, grateful that she still wanted to speak with me. She came out and joined me on the porch swing. Her face had been scrubbed clean of makeup, and her hair hung damp and unstyled. She wore one of Oliver's terrycloth robes rather than one of her own silk wraps. We sat there for a few moments, the only sound that of the glider rocking easily beneath us. "I don't even know where to start."

"I am so sorry."

"Me too." She raised her face to meet the coming light, to drink it in. "Right here, right now, sitting here with you, I keep thinking it must have been a nightmare. It wasn't though, was it?"

"No. It happened." I leaned into her, and she placed her head on my shoulder.

"Was that really her? Was that really my mother?" I felt a sudden burst of hope that this Emily was only an imposter. My childhood dream turned on its head, and I found myself hoping, praying that my true mother had died at my birth. That she had been resting peacefully in Bonaventure for the last two decades.

"I'm afraid so," Ellen said, and then examined her arms in the morning light. The needle tracks had disappeared, and the bruises had already begun to fade.

"I hate her," I said.

"To tell you the truth, I really hate the bitch too. Sisters, huh?"

"Yeah, sisters." I wrapped my arm around hers, careful not to aggravate the bruised tissue. We clasped hands.

"Iris and Oliver are inside. We need to talk before the families start their inquiry."

"What? Get our stories straight before the long arm of the magical law gets to us?"

"Yes. Precisely that. They can bind us, you know. Iris, Oliver, and me, if they think we have done anything to put the line at risk. They can take away our magic."

"And what about me? If anyone did anything to hurt the line, it was me."

Ellen stood and took the quilt from me. She started to fold it. "You are an anchor. They can't remove you from the line without the risk of bringing the line down, but they could erase your mind. Wipe you clean. Leave your body in place until you expire and the line chooses a new anchor."

"They could try," Iris's voice answered, a cold determination behind her words, "but I will see every last one of them dead and burning in hell first."

"I second that notion," Oliver said. "Come on in. I've made coffee."

We followed him into the kitchen. The largest of Ellen's rose quartz crystals glowed at the center of the table. Next to it sat an old scrapbook or photo album. I suspected that Emily's return had prompted a search through the old photos. Had Iris spent the night going through them, looking at the old snapshots trying to see if there was something about Emily they had missed? Or had Oliver been trying to figure out whether a different action on his part might have saved his big sister?

Any perceived mistakes of the distant past seemed much less important to me than the ones I'd made myself last night. "How is Peter?" I asked.

"Smarting. That's how he is," Oliver said, pouring three mugs of coffee and reaching for an herbal tea bag for me. "I stayed with him until he passed out. He's probably gonna wake up with a hangover from too much whiskey and skinned knuckles from punching the wall, but he'll be okay. You two will recover from this. You have a whole lot more working for you than against you." I wished I could believe that was true. "For now, we need to focus on the matter at hand. There is no doubt that the other anchors felt Emily's efforts to skirt the line with her Babel spell."

"How did she do it? How did she catch me up in her spell? I'm an anchor now. I thought witches couldn't charm me."

"Witches can't charm you with the power of the line," Iris said as she took the seat on my right. "But the magic Emily is channeling comes from a place of pure evil." I thought of the locket she had placed around my neck. How it had clouded my mind, perverted my judgment. Made me more willing to believe the worst about those who truly loved me.

Oliver gave my shoulder a gentle squeeze. "The families will be sending representatives to look into what happened here last night. Maybe you could ask the Sandman if he can pick up any rumblings as to whom they are sending and when."

"He's gone. Emmet's gone," I said. "I sent him away last night."

"Well, Gingersnap, you did the right thing, but you picked the wrong time to do it."

"I'm in trouble, aren't I?"

"We all are," Ellen said and sighed. "I've got to tell you though. If the worst we had to face was losing our powers, I think I could accept that."

"Yeah, well, speak for yourself, sis. Besides, if the families judge against us, they won't satisfy themselves with stripping the three of us of our powers. They'll want to make an example of Mercy."

"Maybe I deserve to be made an example of."

"Bullshit." I had never in my entire life heard a word of profanity come out of Iris. It had the effect of a lightning bolt shooting through the room. Even Oliver kept his trap shut. "Bullshit," she said again, this time with less vehemence, but still with all the fire. "The families can send whomever they want. Ask any questions they want. We have done nothing wrong."

"We have disobeyed . . ." Ellen began.

"Whom exactly? Not the line. I feel it." Her right hand pounded on her chest. "I feel it in here. The line is on our side. It will protect us."

"I wish I could be as sure as you are," Oliver said. "They have been looking for an excuse to bring us down ever since the line chose the first Taylor as an anchor. The Taylors take too many liberties. The Taylors push their own agendas. The Taylors aren't humble enough."

"Well, that last bit is probably true," I said.

"And so what if it is? We let our hearts rule our heads. We like to do things big. We are Celts for goodness sake."

"I agree with Iris." Ellen took a sip of her coffee. "The line chose Mercy. It cut through Ginny's deception. We tried to invest its power in Maisie, and it stood up to us. It wanted Mercy and I have to believe it wanted you for a reason. I say we call their bluff. Tell them exactly what has been going on and let the chips fall where they may."

"That sounds great in theory, but Mercy has a lot more to lose than any of us, right, Gingersnap?"

Iris nodded in agreement. "Yes, she does," she answered for me. "That's why it's time for us to come clean with her"—she looked at me—"with you. It's time for us to share everything we know, and even make a few conjectures, because we don't know everything. I do believe the line chose you for a reason, so it's time for you to learn exactly who you are."

She reached out for the album, but Ellen stayed her hand. "I should do this. He was my husband. I'm responsible for bringing him into the family." Iris squeezed her sister's hand and let Ellen take control of the book. Ellen slid it over to me, but didn't take her hand off it. "This belonged to Erik. To your father," she said. "He always told me that he kept it as a reminder of the evil he'd managed to escape. He led me to believe that it served as a moral touchstone, something to keep him on the right side of humanity. I now believe he thought of it as more of a brag book. A place he could turn when he needed strength to carry out the mission he'd come to complete."

"Mission?" I asked. It sounded like such a tactical term. Military.

"He had come to fulfill the prophecy that said a child born to a union of our bloodlines would reunite the thirteen families and bring down the line. Honestly, I had never heard of the prediction before we married."

"I had," Iris said, "but I thought the story was one of the many fantasies we witches have developed around the line. I said nothing to Ellen. I didn't want to ruin her happiness. I regret that now. She should have gone into her marriage with her eyes wide open."

"I wouldn't have believed it. Knowing wouldn't have changed a single thing. I believed in Erik. I loved him, even after I found these clippings." She took her hand off the scrapbook. "Go ahead."

A shiver of magical energy flooded my fingers as they touched the cover. I could tell that at one time this book had been enchanted to hide what was within it. The magic had long since faded to a mere spark, but I sensed that the spark had belonged to my father. I wanted to stop for a moment. To let myself experience his magic, remembering him the way I did before I opened the cover and had all my remaining illusions shattered. I closed my eyes and felt him, his pride and sense of purpose, and then I opened my eyes and turned the cover.

A photo had been removed from the first page. "That was the picture of your great-grandmother I gave you," Ellen said. "I don't know what possessed me to do that. I guess I did it out of relief that I no longer had to hide that Erik was your father. I wanted us to be relieved from all our secrets."

She was getting her wish today. Below the place where the rectangular photo had been, my father had written my great-grandmother's name: Maria Orsic. "Who was she?"

"She was not a witch, but she was known as a psychic medium. There are a lot of non-witches who have the sight."

"Like Claire," I said, without meaning to say it aloud.

"Yes. I've sensed that about her. Maria was different from most psychics though, in that her psyche had somehow developed the capability to travel outside the line's protection. Out there, where the demons still wait. They began to court her, for lack of a better term. They gave her insights, glimpses of history—hell, they even gave her diagrams for a flying saucer. They convinced her that they were our loving brothers. Aliens from Aldebaran. She, in return, became their evangelist."

"They deceived her?"

"They played into her need to feel special and superior. It's one of mankind's greatest weaknesses—the need to feel superior to others."

"But witches kind of feel that way, don't we?"

"Not the witches in *this* family," Oliver said. "And yes, by that, I mean the four of us sitting here. We may be proud of who we are, proud of our skill with magic, proud of our heritage, but we really don't think that we are somehow innately superior."

"And that is coming from our selfish peacock of a bastard brother," Iris said, a smirk on her lips, but pride showing in her eyes.

"Turn the page," Ellen said and nodded at the book. I found another photo of Maria, this time sitting in a group of women. Beneath the photo my father's script recorded their names: Maria, Traute, Sigrun. I gasped as my eyes shot back up to the picture. One of the faces had been burned into my mind long ago . . . I knew her without needing to read her name: Gudrun. Erik had added "*die Vril-Gesellschaft*" beneath the women's names. I looked up at Ellen, and her expression of sympathy answered my unspoken question. I knew then that Maria had been the leader in an attempt to bring down the line.

I turned back to the album and flipped the page. The next one held two photos of the man I had come to think of as Careu. In the first, he stood next to an old prop-style plane. I felt my pulse thundering in my neck as the face I recognized fell into its familiar context. The next photo showed him, this great American hero, standing flanked on one side by two admiring women, while a man with adoring eyes looked on from the background. Standing before Careu, on the photograph's right side, stood a man in the process of handing over a sword. He wore a lighter suit with a white kerchief in his pocket. A cigarette dangled from his lips. He had a double chin and wore his hair slicked back. I knew this man. I recognized him from history books. "That's Hermann Goering," I said, poking angrily at his face. "He was one of the Nazi leaders." I felt ill.

Oliver came and squatted down next to me. "Yeah, Ginger-snap, I'm afraid it is." He put his arm around my shoulder, and pulled me in for a kiss on the temple. "Do you need a little break?"

"No. I've got to know. How did my great-grandparents meet?"

"They never did," Ellen said. I looked at her, confused. "Your paternal great-grandparents were both great supporters of eugenics and the goal of building, or as they would have it, rebuilding the master race. Goering and his friends created a special project with this aim. They called it *Lebensborn*, the 'source of life.'" My mind flashed back to the file I'd seen among my Grandfather Taylor's papers. I realized his interest in the *Lebensborn* program wasn't a study in historical curiosities, like Iris had told me. The file contained research on his son-in-law, my father.

"Your great-grandparents," Ellen continued, "each of them donated their genetic materials to the cause for study and duplication. Technological schematics provided by the Aldebaran brothers provided the know-how for your great-grandfather to engineer a process similar to what we now know as in vitro fertilization. The Nazis sought to create a master race, but the Aldebarans wanted to create a thousand Marias. The doctors in the project planted Maria's fertilized eggs in the wombs of several of the *Lebensborn* mothers. Erik's father, your grandfather, was one of the children born from this process."

266

I closed the book. My hands felt soiled from having touched it. I wanted to wash my hands. Wash myself. Wash away the filth of the source from which I'd sprung. Now I understood why Ellen and Iris had hidden the truth from me. Paul and Maisie and I, we were all somehow wrong. "We're the children of monsters," I said and pushed the book away.

THIRTY-FOUR

"But that doesn't mean you are a monster," Iris said. "I raised you right. You know the difference between good and evil."

"Maisie didn't," I said. For the first time, I wondered if Maisie could be saved. Rescued, sure, but redeemed?

Iris looked me dead in the eye, her lips pressed together in a tight line. She nodded. "All right. I failed your sister. I'm not denying that, but I did not fail you. You are no more like your sister than . . ." She stopped herself.

"Than you are like yours," I finished for her. I hugged myself, fighting a chill and a sense of self-disgust. My hand felt my stomach. "What am I bringing you into, little guy?"

"I wondered the same thing when I discovered I was pregnant with Paul, and I am going to give you the same answer I gave myself. You are bringing him into a loving family. A flawed family, that's sure, but one that will cherish him."

"Emily said that the families brought about the accident that killed Paul. Do you think that's true?"

"I don't believe it is. I pray that it's not, but I don't think we should take any chances. They can never know the truth, sweetheart," Ellen said. "The families. They can never learn that you and Maisie are Erik's girls. They have to keep believing that Connor is your father. Do you understand?"

"Yes, I do. What I don't understand is how Emily could have been drawn to this darkness. What happened to her to make her capable of everything she has done?"

"I don't know," Iris said. "I have never before let myself confess these thoughts about Emily to anyone, not even myself. Sometimes it seems that a person comes into the world with a missing piece. The piece that makes them human just isn't there. My intuition has always tried to tell me that my sister was born without that piece, but I always buried my concerns before . . ." She paused. "I almost said 'before she died.' I still can't get pieces to line up right in my mind. But before, as I think of it now, it seemed to me that she was playing a role, playing at being a loving sister, a loving daughter. There never seemed to be any true emotion behind it. It felt more like she mimicked others' emotions, but never had any of her own. I think she came into this world broken."

"Do you think she really did love my father?" I asked Ellen.

"At one point, I would have guessed that maybe she did, but not after last night. She couldn't have loved him, or she would never have hurt his child. She would have never tried to channel her evil brand of magic into you."

"She didn't care about me at all . . . I just served her as a means to an end." I'd given it a lot of thought overnight. "She attacked the line by going after its weakest link. She knew that if she could poison me, she'd be poisoning the line."

"I'm not sure about that," Iris said. "First of all, you are not the line's weakest link. Second, even though the rebel families want to end the line, they are still connected to it, an anchor from each family." It hadn't even occurred to me that there were still actually thirteen anchors; I'd only ever heard anyone speak about the ten anchors from the united families. "I am sure they were waiting in the wings, ready to spring into action as soon as the line had been damaged, but if it were just a matter of 'poisoning' an anchor, the rebels would more than happily sacrifice one of their own." She leaned back in her chair, her face tightening. "No, Emily knew this Babel spell she was working wouldn't bring the old ones into our reality. That spell was about taking *you* to old gods' realm. I don't know why, but for some reason the rebel families need *you* to break the power of the line."

"Do you think we caused any real harm to it?" I asked. Even though I was an anchor, all of it was still so new to me. I wasn't sure how the line *normally* felt. Besides, the other anchors had ensured that I couldn't draw on its power. I realized that they were probably controlling me in the same exact way they were controlling the anchors from the rebel families.

"No, sweetheart. It feels like it always has. It's holding just fine."

"But the families will know that someone has been tampering with it," Oliver said. "They will send someone around sooner rather than later to look into what we naughty little Taylors have been up to."

"Well, before they come, there is something I need to do," I said. "I have to talk to Peter. I've got to try to set things right between us. Now, in case the families don't want to give me the luxury of a later."

"Don't you worry, Gingersnap. We will handle the families together. Right now, you get over to that boy's house and put him out of his misery."

"How do I know if he even still wants me?"

"An empty fifth of whiskey and a hole in the drywall told me everything I needed to know on that subject. Go on now."

I showered and stood before my closet, pawing through all the new maternity outfits my aunts had treated me to. What color is best for apologizing to the man who caught you cheating on him? I settled on the simplest of the dresses, a white sleeveless one with a modest scoop neck and a daisy print around the waist. Nothing screams "I'm not a whore" like embroidered daisies.

Peter's house was in Sackville. Before my pregnancy, I used to grab my bike and pedal over, but I'd already been forced to bid a temporary adieu to my faithful two-wheeled friend, and my stomach had grown another inch since then. I didn't want to use my magic. I didn't want to show up on his doorstep suffering from the more and more familiar sense of disorientation. Instead, I called a taxi.

I spent the ride trying to pull my words together. I couldn't take the tack that Emmet and I hadn't truly been together, at least physically. Peter knew better; he knew that I had cheated. In the bright light of day, I did too.

We pulled up in front of the small wood-frame house. Even though Peter only rented the place, he had recently given it a fresh coat of paint, a silvery gray color to offset the pewter shutters and door. The house stood next to a towering live oak that hung over it as if it were trying to keep its companion safe. Peter's truck stood in the drive. I knew he'd be home today. No way would he ever go to the Tillandsia house again, not after what had happened. I doubted that either of us would ever step foot near there again. I paid the driver and got out. Then I stood there and watched as he pulled away, trying to work up my nerve to climb the steps to the door and knock.

"You gonna stand out there all day, or you coming in?" Peter called from the doorway.

"You sure you want me to?" I asked.

He walked away from the door, but left it open. I climbed the few steps and stuck my head inside. He was sitting in the beat-up easy chair he'd bought at Goodwill the day he signed a lease on this place. I stepped in and closed the door behind me, unable to read his expression because my eyes had not yet adjusted to the somber light in his living room. Almost as if I had asked the question, he reached out and flicked on a table lamp.

Dark circles carried his reddened eyes, and sparks of fiery red whiskers lined his cheeks and chin. He still wore the jeans he'd had on last night, but a different T-shirt. Last night's shirt lay on the floor, now a bloodied ball of rag. "How's your wound?"

"I can barely see where she stuck me." He shifted in his seat. "Ellen does good work."

I stepped up closer, moving into the circle of light. "Peter, I am so sorry."

"For the injury?"

"Yes, and for everything else too."

"Pretty convenient summary you got there."

"I'm sorry." I took a breath. "I'm sorry for the wound. But so much more than that. I am sorry for the hurt I've caused you. I am sorry I cheated on you." He looked away from me, tears forming in his eyes. He didn't even brush them away. "I was trying to get ahold of the magic that Emily had stored up in Tillandsia. I convinced myself that we were just performing magic. That it wasn't physical. It wasn't about me, and it wasn't about Emmet. It wasn't sex."

"What I walked in on, it looked even more intimate than sex. The two of you seemed to be bonded together."

My pulse raced as I thought of the union. It had felt exactly like that, and in those few moments before Emily's evil magic had started to flow between us, it had been wonderful.

I knew if I shared this with Peter, I'd crush him. I'd lose his heart forever. "I'm sorry. I truly am. I'll admit, not only to you but to myself, that it was an act of intimacy. That I did cheat on you."

He leaned in toward me, his eyes imploring. "But if you needed sex, if you needed intimacy to do what you wanted with Tillandsia, why wouldn't you come to me? And why would you want to take magic from that place anyway? I felt it, the second I walked in . . . That kind of magic isn't right. It isn't . . ." He paused, as he looked for the word. "Wholesome."

I went and sat on the footstool before him. I'd answer his second question, and pray that the first went away. I could never explain to him why I'd been afraid to expose him to an unknown magic for fear that he'd discover his own true nature and become lost to me forever. "My family has been lying to you. I've been lying to you about Maisie. She isn't in California."

"I suspected something was up. Every time I asked one of you about her, I'd get the same exact information, like it had been rehearsed." He had hit it dead on; it had been. "Where is she?"

"She's trapped. It's hard to explain."

"She was practicing some bad mojo, and it got the best of her, right?"

I nodded. "Close enough. I had hoped I could use the power in Tillandsia to get her out of the trouble she's gotten herself into."

"But seriously"—he shook his head in amazement, and then reached up to brush the copper curls from his eyes—"you're telling me that you and your family, you don't have enough juju to take care of things?"

"We have been . . . forbidden from doing so by the other families. They could sense it if we used the line's power to try to rescue Maisie. They could and most certainly would shut us down, maybe even permanently."

"They'd better not try doing anything to you," he said, the words almost like a reflex. I couldn't help myself. I reached out and touched his unshaven cheek. He took my hand off his cheek, but he didn't push it away. He held it in his own. "So you thought you could get your hands on power they couldn't control. Get the job done yourself."

"I figured it would be much easier to ask forgiveness than permission. Now it looks like I might have been wrong about that."

"Is that what you've done with me? Figured it would be easier to get forgiveness?"

"No." I shook my head. "It wasn't nearly that calculated, at least as far as you are concerned."

"Why did you come here, Mercy? Is it just a pardon you are looking for? 'Cause I'll give you that. I don't understand all this magic, but I do know how much you love Maisie. If it's just forgiveness you're looking for, you got it. I understand that whatever you did, you did for your sister."

"I did come here hoping you'd forgive me, but there's much more than that."

"Okay. I'm listening," he said, still clasping my hand in his.

"I wanted to let you know Emmet's gone. I've sent him away from Savannah."

"Where to?" His grip tightened a little, and he tilted a bit more toward me.

"I don't know. I didn't ask. I can understand if you can't get past the sight of what you walked in on last night. I want you to know, though, that if you will still have me, I want to be your wife."

"If I will still have you? If I will still have you?" He pushed out of the chair and knelt beside me, nearly crushing me in his embrace. "Oh, God. I thought I'd lost you." Our eyes met, and then he kissed me. Any connection I had felt with Emmet was a fantasy; this here, the love I had with Peter, was real. His kiss changed, and the feeling of grateful relief melted under the heat of his growing passion. He stood and pulled me up with him, my flesh molding to the solid contours of his body.

"Wait," I said, pushing away from him. His brow pinched as hurt and disappointment started to show in his eyes. He let go of me and took a step back. "No." I reached out and grasped his arm. "I need help with my zipper." His lips curved into the most delicious bad-boy smile that a good man's face had ever shown. I turned my back to him, and his thick fingers found the delicate pull, his hands shaking. I shivered as he undid the zipper and slid the dress down. I kicked it out of my way, and he leaned in and placed a kiss on the nape of my neck. I slid off my panties and let them fall to the floor beside me, then reached behind my back and undid my bra, tossing it on the sofa. I turned toward him, standing naked before him. My breasts had grown much larger over the last several weeks, and the look in Peter's eyes told me how much he appreciated the change. I leaned into him, my skin pressing against his T-shirt. He began kissing me, trying to pull off his own shirt using a single hand. He growled as he gave up and pulled hard at the collar, ripping it clean down the front. Without ever taking his lips from mine, he slid his second ruined shirt to the floor.

I pulled away to examine the place where my mother had stabbed him with her foul iron knife. The wound had closed over and pretty much healed, but it looked like there might always be a nearly crescent-shaped scar. I suspected that the wound would never fade completely since it had been made with iron. It would serve as a constant reminder of how close I'd come to losing him. I leaned forward and kissed the scar. He moaned and pulled me into his arms, his stiffness pressing into me, the difference in our heights such that I felt it against my stomach. He reached down and swept me off the floor, carrying me toward his bedroom. He kicked at the door to open it, and carried me to his bed, the same bed where we had first made love, where we had conceived our child. He must have been thinking about our baby too, because he laid me down as gently as if I were made of porcelain.

I watched as he removed his jeans and boxers. He laid down next to me, not talking, not moving, just looking at me with so much love, so much hunger. I straddled him and took him into me, leaning over and kissing him, his large rough hands encapsulating my own. This was the first time we had touched each other this way since my powers had been returned to me. I looked at his beautiful, strained face through a witch's eyes, seeing evidence of his otherworldly traits. His eyes changed during his passion, no longer showing the mismatch of blue and green I'd come to love, but glowing silver instead. Pulling my hand from his, I pushed back his hair and saw the point of his ear. I leaned in and gently bit its tip. He groaned. As his passion grew, light began to shine from him, a mild luminescence. No, this was no normal man I had chosen, but I had chosen him all the same. My own pleasure overtook my senses. Everything melded together as my eyes closed. My head leaned backward, and his hand reached out and traced down my neck, my breasts. I shuddered once, twice, as he strained up into me, and then I fell forward into his waiting arms.

THIRTY-FIVE

I didn't wake until late afternoon, nearly evening. Peter was already awake but had been lying there still, so as not to disturb me. I opened my eyes to see his eyes, which had returned to their mismatched blue and green color, trained on me, his gentle love and burning passion wrestling within them. I touched him in a way that would give his passion the upper hand, and once again we made love.

Spent, I laid my head on his chest and kissed his scar again. "Tomorrow," I said. "Tomorrow we'll go get the marriage license. We'll go to the justice of the peace."

"The hell we will." Peter sat up in the bed and took me in the crook of his arm. "That isn't good enough for you."

"It's good enough. Nothing matters to me except that we're together."

He narrowed his eyes and leaned in to peck me on the lips. "Nope. It ain't gonna happen that way. I've dreamed about seeing you come down the aisle to me for too long. You are not going to cheat me out of that."

"You've dreamed about our wedding?"

"Well, honestly I've done a lot more dreaming about the honeymoon," he said. I reached out and gave him a gentle smack. He squeezed me tighter. "But yeah, I've been dreaming about it since we were kids, pretty much since the day I met you. Remember that day in Forsyth, when I let you beat me climbing our tree?"

"I remember beating you; I don't remember you letting me beat you."

"Well, believe what you want, but I let you win all right. I wanted to see that red head of yours surrounded by patches of green and blue. You climbed higher than I did, and when I stopped, you looked down and stuck your tongue out at me. That's when I first thought to myself, 'I am gonna marry that girl someday.' I've been dreaming about that day ever since. So yeah, we'll go get the license tomorrow, but you gotta plan me a real wedding. One with a monkey suit and a white dress, flowers, and too much champagne. Well, for me at least," he said and reached over to rub my stomach. "Oh, and cake." His stomach growled. "I'm starving. You?"

I realized that I was. "Yes."

"Let's go out tonight. Somewhere nice. You can wear that pretty dress you left gathering wrinkles on my living room floor."

"You didn't seem too concerned about it at the time."

"Oh, but I was," he said and leaned in to kiss me. "I was so very concerned." He kissed my lips again and began working his way down my neck.

"Food," I said and pushed him away.

"All right, all right." Another quick peck on my lips, then he pulled his arm out from under me, using his other hand to slide a pillow behind me. "I need to shower"—he ran his hand over his chin—"and shave." He slid out of bed and stood. "Care to join me?" he asked, waggling his eyebrows. I threw a pillow at him.

"Take your shower and make it quick. Colin and I are hungry." He lumbered off, and I closed my eyes as I heard the sound of the shower. I felt so grateful that he loved me, that he had not turned me away. I pulled the blanket up around me and breathed in his scent.

In a few minutes he returned and stood before me, wrapped up in a towel. "You still in bed, you lazy thing?" He started rummaging through his closet for some dress pants and a real shirt.

"My, my. A shirt with buttons, we are going fancy tonight."

"Oh, no. These aren't buttons. They're snaps," he said, pulling the shirt around his shoulders. "It'll make it easier for you later, so you don't have to rip another shirt off me."

"I didn't rip your last shirt off," I said and laughed. "You did."

"Hey, if you get to choose to remember that you beat me fair and square climbing that tree, I get to remember the shirt thing my way."

"Fine." I threw the blanket off and swung my feet out of bed. Peter stopped dressing and watched me, smiling. "I'm going to take a quick shower too."

"You should've just hopped in with me. We could've saved time and water."

"If I'd gotten in with you, we would have saved neither." I got in the shower, at first determined not to get my hair wet, but it felt so good to let the hot water flow over me, washing away the parts of the last twenty-four hours that I didn't care to remember, and somehow reinforcing the sensuality of the parts that I did.

When I stepped out of the shower, I dried off quickly, and wrapped myself in the towel. The bedroom was empty, although Peter had laid my dress and underwear out on the bed. I was just starting to dress when the door opened a crack. Peter poked his head through it. "You got a visitor."

"Who is it?"

"A woman. Says her name is something like Rivkuh."

"Rivkah. Rivkah Levi." I hadn't seen or even thought of Rivkah since the day the line had selected me to be an anchor. She had been one of the three witches who'd arrived early to prepare our house for the ceremony, to search for energy leaks or ingresses that might interfere with the investment of the line's energy in the new anchor. Their efforts had been *wildly* unsuccessful.

"Yeah, that's it. You okay? Should I make her leave?"

"Mercy, darling," Rivkah's voice came to me from over Peter's shoulder. "Get dressed and come talk to me."

I looked at Peter, then shrugged. "I'll be right out, Mrs. Levi."

"Rivkah, please, dear. Peter, do you have any wine?" I heard her opening and closing cupboards. "Ah, here's some red. Corkscrew?"

"I'll be right there," Peter said and closed the door behind him.

I towel-dried my hair and wove it into a single braid. It would be a tangled mess later, but Rivkah was not someone you kept waiting. If I didn't make it out to her quickly, she would invite herself in to join me. I dressed, smoothing out the wrinkles that had collected in the skirt of my dress, and went into the living room to find Peter sitting across from Rivkah at his kitchen table.

"There she is," Rivkah said, rising and waving me into her arms. I hadn't expected such an effusive greeting from someone I barely knew. She kissed my cheek. "Mazel tov on the little one." She released me and reached for her wine glass. "To Colin," she said, holding her glass out to Peter, who clinked with her.

"To Colin," Peter echoed, a certain hesitancy in his voice.

Rivkah sat down. "So tell me, darling. What has been going on here with you and this family of yours?"

"Have you spoken to them yet?"

"No, not yet. I came directly from the airport. I wanted to talk to you first." She leaned back in her chair, stretching into a relaxed and nonthreatening position.

"Who else from the families is coming?"

"No one else. Just me. I insisted it would be better for me to come alone, rather than dozens of us showing up like the Spanish Inquisition. Now tell me what happened last night. What did you all do to set the line clanking like a firehouse bell?"

I sat, trying to gain a little time to get my thoughts together.

"Mrs. Levi, Mercy has been dealing with a lot of stress. It isn't good for her or our baby. I don't want her to relive any of what happened. We're moving on, putting the bad things behind us."

"Again, call me Rivkah, and don't you worry about this young woman of yours or your child. They are both much more resilient than you could begin to imagine."

"All the same—"

"Peter," she interrupted him, reaching out and patting his hand. "Why don't you go out for a little bit and take a walk. Enjoy this lovely evening while Mercy and I have a chat."

"This is my house."

"And it is adorable." She held up both hands, palms up, motioning around the room as if she were a game show hostess. She smiled and nodded, her dark curls bouncing. "We don't need long. Take a spin up to that sweet park I passed on the way here. Daffin, isn't it? We'll be all finished by the time you return."

Peter had to be the most good-natured guy I knew, but even he got a bit peeved when he was ejected from his own home. He looked at me for guidance, and I nodded, doing my best to apologize with my eyes.

He stood. "I'll be back in twenty minutes," he said and gave Rivkah a stern glance.

"That's a good boy," Rivkah said. "Oh, Mercy, you two are going to have such a beautiful child."

Peter frowned, but he headed obediently to the door. "Twenty minutes," he said and headed out the door.

After the door closed behind him, Rivkah reached out and took my hand. "He loves you very much—you know that, right?" I nodded. "Yes. I'm very lucky to have him."

"And he you," she said and then let go of me. She took another sip of wine. "So Emily has come home." She waited for my reaction, but I remained silent. "It must have been a terrible shock for you and your family."

How could I answer that? Seeing the dream of having my mother returned to me changed, bastardized into a bloody nightmare. "How did you know?"

"Emmet," she said. "He came home to me, to his mama."

"Mama?"

"Well, I was the only woman involved in his creation, so if that doesn't make me his mother, I don't know what else I'd be to him." She tilted her head and seemed to be taking a moment to consider me. "He's totally besotted with you as well. You've broken his heart."

"I am truly sorry for hurting him." I had found myself using variations on that phrase a lot lately. "I didn't mean to." Yep. That one too. I wondered if I should aim for the trifecta with "I had no choice." I decided instead to just stop talking.

Rivkah shrugged. "Well, he's alive now, and getting your heart broken is part of being alive. You did the right thing in sending him away. Clean breaks heal the quickest. He'll mend." She paused. "Now back to business. Maybe it's your own fault for naming the boy 'Emmet,' but he isn't gifted at dissimulation. He knows you are in over your head, so he shared with me the truth of what happened last night. The whole story. The complete story. Now I am going to tell you the version that I will share with the families when I make my report to them, so you listen up." She leaned forward on the table and folded her hands.

"Your mother—"

"Please don't call her that."

Rivkah nodded, understanding my horror of the woman. "Emily and this Josef fellow kidnapped your Aunt Ellen and forced you to come to this gathering of theirs. Then they trapped you so that they could attempt to use your power and your connection to the line to complete the Babel spell. You opened yourself up, unwittingly exposing the line, in your attempt to escape. This had been Emily's goal all along. Your Peter stumbled in and forced you and Emmet apart, breaking the hold Emily had on you two." She paused. "How did Peter know to come when he did? Oliver and Iris obviously would sense the disturbance of the line, but him?"

"His mother." I came up with the lie on the spot. I could not let Rivkah know of the connection he shared with the baby. I could not let her learn that Peter was *Fae*. "Claire has the sight. She told him she sensed I was in trouble. That he should come."

Rivkah nodded. "Good. You think well on your feet. That's the story we'll go with." So Emmet had shared the entire truth with her, including Peter's true identity. It felt odd that rather than lying to her as I'd intended, I was colluding with her.

"Why are you doing this? Covering for us? For me?"

"Well, my dear, there has been a lot of talk, foolish and reactionary talk, floating around the families since the line selected you. Some of those speaking most loudly and most foolishly are your own cousins. A few of the Ryans have been campaigning against you. Against your whole immediate family even. They want the Savannah Taylors laid low. I, on the other hand, have always felt a strong affection for your family. At least you keep things interesting."

"Are they all against us?"

"Oh, no, darling. You have many vocal proponents. Especially that charming Taylor woman, oh, what is her name? Abby."

"She always calls herself a white-trash Taylor," I said and smiled in spite of my growing sense of apprehension.

Rivkah laughed. "Well, the 'white-trash' Taylors are all strongly in your corner. However, the fact that Emily Taylor faked her own death and aligned herself with the three rebel families may give even your staunchest supporters pause when the story gets around."

"What can I do?"

"There now," she said and smiled at me approvingly. "That's a good girl, because it really all does come down to you now. Your next few steps are critical, if you want to protect your family and yourself. The first thing you will need to do is make a public abjuration of your mother. Express your horror about her actions and the choices she has made."

"Easy enough."

"Yes, easy perhaps, but still painful. You can handle it. The next step is going to come harder to you. You need to knuckle down. Submit yourself to the will of the other anchors. Be humble. Do as they tell you. Focus on what they feel you have to learn. They have been carrying your weight for long enough. You must thank them and apologize for having been so headstrong." She raised her hand to prevent any protest. "And 'headstrong' is a generous way of putting it. You did put the line at risk last night."

I nodded to acknowledge this truth. "For my family," and by that I also meant the man I would soon marry and the child to whom I would give birth in some months, "I can do this."

"Good. They will also want you to go away for a while, to a place where you can't interfere with the line. They'll want you to train directly under Gudrun."

"No. That I cannot do." I couldn't spend time anywhere near Gudrun, the woman who had worked alongside Maria, the conduit, if not the source, of the darkness that had claimed my mother and taken my sister.

"I am afraid you won't have a choice. If you resist, they will consider a binding. Nobody wants that, especially the other anchors. Show them that you can be reasonable. Besides, the more willingly you submit to the inevitable, the better the impression you will make. I do think we can put this off until after your wedding, though, as long as you lie low and don't make any more waves."

"What about the baby? I won't do anything that will harm him."

"Nor would I ask you to. He'll continue to develop normally while you are with Gudrun. I will personally insist that you are allowed to return home before he's born. At least temporarily." She smiled and wagged a finger at me. "This will constitute the first time in the history of the line that an anchor gets maternity leave. You might have to spend a little time separated from each other, but from his perspective, he'll only be without his mama for a few days." She lifted her glass and polished it off. "Now, I need to know. Are you on board with this?"

I nodded my head just as Peter knocked on his own door, then opened it. "Perfect timing, Mr. Tierney. Now, where are we going for dinner? If I don't eat soon, I'm going to *challish*."

THIRTY-SIX

Dinner with Rivkah ran late, and Peter reluctantly brought me home rather than to his place after we dropped her off at her hotel. I needed sleep. The baby needed sleep. But before slipping between the sheets, I went to my jewelry box and pulled out the ring Peter had given me. I placed it once and forever on my finger, then went directly to bed, drifting off within moments.

I felt more annoyed than worried when the sound of pecking against my window woke me. I stayed still, thinking that it must have been a bug or an insomniac bird, but another strike against the glass sounded, and then a third. I sat upright in bed. A blissful second or two passed during which I thought I must be asleep and dreaming. Joe stood directly in front of me, and instead of opening out to our side yard, my window framed another room, an enormous stone room ripped from the pages of a fairy tale. Joe held his index finger up before his slyly curled lips, warning me to keep silent, and then tugged savagely on a rope he held in his left hand. I barely had time to register that the rope glowed a sickly green and couldn't possibly have been composed of ordinary fiber before Adam Cook's battered face banged on the other side of the glass. The rope Joe held was connected to a noose around the detective's neck. Adam's eyes were bruised and largely swollen shut. His lower lip had been busted. His nose was broken and twisted crooked on his face.

Joe pressed the long, thin fingers of his free hand against the window casing and started to slide the window up and open. Even though I still couldn't help hoping this was a dream, I wanted to yell, to call out to my family, but I couldn't produce a sound. Joe tugged again on his unwholesome lasso, and then both he and Adam disappeared from sight. A sleek and well-fed rat with a human face, just like the vermin I'd set alight at the bar, crawled up over the window ledge and insinuated its body and pink tail through the opening Joe had made. I shuddered, still unable to produce a sound, as it scurried across the floor and up onto my bed. It crept up closer to me, its beady red eyes glinting up from its miniature human face. "Your mother seeks armistice," it said. I grabbed a pillow and swatted at the creature. It dove from my bed and returned to the windowsill, where it stopped and turned to face me. "I am to tell you that you will follow me," it said, "or my brethren and I will eat your ape friend's flesh."

I found my voice. "He is not an ape. He's a man."

"Ah, but then his flesh will taste twice as sweet," it said and rubbed its tiny, nearly human hands together.

"I'm coming. Don't do anything more to Adam." Jumping out of bed, I crossed over to the window.

The creature looked up at me, the pouting of its lower lip showing its disappointment that I hadn't refused. "Very well. Follow." It slid through the opening, its tail disappearing over the ledge last. When I reached the window, I saw the creature waiting for me on the other side, sitting on its hind legs, grooming itself by licking its hands and running them over its head. My repulsion grew so strong that I felt small flames form on my fingertips, yearning to fly from my hand and devour the abomination. It was only his role as my guide that kept me from doing it. I had to save Adam.

I slid the window far enough open to climb out, carefully putting my foot down on the stone floor to confirm its solidity before hefting my full weight over the sill and into open air. I held on to the window's ledge, ensuring that the ground beneath was solid and not merely a mirage before letting go. As I did, my window disappeared, only to be replaced by a stone-block wall. I struck at one of the blocks with the side of my fist. It was as hard as the floor beneath my feet. The exit was gone.

"She is waiting," the rodent guide said. "Her patience is not without bounds."

What I wouldn't have given at the moment for a visit from Jilo's three-legged cat. "And neither is mine," I said, the flame flaring up on the tip of my index finger.

I felt sickened when its face crumpled in fear, and it bowed to me. I loathed the creature, but I hated myself for my readiness to dispose of it. "Forgive me, miss," it said, prostrating itself at my feet.

"Let's go," I said. It rose, its sharp claws clicking across the stones as it moved. It paused every so often to make sure I still followed. We had been walking down the hall for several minutes, and I began to feel like I was on a treadmill. Even though we were maintaining a steady pace, we never seemed to grow closer to the light at the far end of the hall. "How much farther?" I demanded. "I mean, have we even moved?"

It turned and looked up over its hairy back at me. "We have traveled many miles. I do not know how much farther. It is different each time."

We carried on in silence for a while longer. Stone floors, stone walls, and a stone roof above. Light seemed to be held at a premium in this place—there was always a spare circle of it overhead, but it lent little clarity to what came ahead, and what lay behind us was swallowed up in shadow. I sensed something circling us a little beyond the edge of the light. I stopped for a moment, narrowing in on the sound . . . a growling noise, but not from a dog. Eyes came close enough to reflect the dim light. I looked away and hurried forward to catch up to the rodent chimera, its pink tail swishing back and forth as it moved before me. At the sound of my quickened steps, it stopped and looked back at me. Again its face sickened me, and I had to fight the urge to destroy it out of revulsion. Reassured that I was following, it turned and picked up its pace as well. As we continued down the seemingly endless hall, a question needled at me. Finally I had to know. "Did she do this to you?"

It stopped in its tracks and turned to face me. "Do what to me, miss?"

"Did my moth— Did Emily create you?"

"Oh, no, miss," it responded with a slight bob of its revolting head. "The other witches, they made me."

"The rebel families?" I asked feeling the pulse in my neck as my anger grew. She may not have been directly responsible, but how could Emily bind herself to the families who would create such a creature? Its very existence seemed an affront to nature.

"Oh, no, miss. The witches who hold the line, they made me." It turned before it could witness my mouth falling wide open. I was still trying to collect myself when we finally arrived at the end of the hall. An archway separated it from the next room. Blue light, not the brilliant cyan I had grown to associate with Jilo, but a dim and bruised blue, spilled out through the doorway.

"You owe my daughter a debt of gratitude, detective," Emily said as I followed the rodent into the chamber. Adam sat slumped over on a straight-backed wooden chair, barely holding on to consciousness. Taking someone I cared about had been Emily's way of ensuring I would come. I knew that picking Adam as that someone had been her way of punishing Oliver for rejecting her.

Adam lifted his head and tried to look at me through his swollen eyes. I ran toward him, inadvertently kicking the rat. It squealed in indignation and skittered behind Emily, seeking shelter from its mistress.

The creature that had been circling me lunged out from the shadows and blocked my access to Adam. I registered that it was a wolf, snarling and snapping at me. I jumped, but managed to regain control and stand my ground. Lifting its head to howl, the wolf let loose with a human laugh. I watched as it crouched on its haunches and began shaking head to tail. The gray fur slid off, the creature shedding its pelt as if it were a cloak. "Not yet, princess," said Joe, still sitting in a crouched position. I noticed that his backwoods twang had totally evaporated, replaced with a foreign, slightly Germanic intonation. He smiled widely and stood, bowing as if he were actually greeting royalty. Then he scooped up the wolfskin cape and tossed it back into the shadows.

"You are a skin-walker," I said.

Joe tilted his head, stretching his limbs like he was trying to reacclimatize himself to his human form. "Among other things." He turned from me and approached Adam. He took Adam's head between his hands, tilting it up so that Adam would be forced to look into his eyes. Then he tightened his grip, slowly turning Adam's head from side to side.

"Take your hands off him." My voice quivered, and Joe turned to me, his eyes wide in mock terror. All the same, he did unhand Adam. "Let him go," I said, turning toward Emily.

"Oh, indeed, we will," Joe answered for her. "He has served his purpose. Your concern for this ape brought you here."

"He isn't an ape. He's a man, and Oliver loves him."

"Oh, God, men in love with each other, don't get me started on that," Emily said, rolling her eyes. "I had hoped Oliver would grow past that phase, but if my little brother is so enamored of the detective, he should have taken better care not to leave his toy out where anyone could snatch it."

"The sooner he's gone, the better. I cannot stand the smell of him," Joe said.

"Okay, who the hell are you?" I spun back around to him. "You show up like some hayseed with Ryder and Birdy, and now I find you here with my . . . her?" I had almost referred to Emily as my mother, remembering in time that regardless of whether I shared her DNA, she was not my mother.

"This is Josef, darling," Emily said. "He has been the most valuable ally I have had in trying to pull you to the right side of history. To the right side of evolution."

"You mean Ryder was an example of evolution done right?" I asked.

Joe began laughing as if I'd just told the funniest joke ever. Emily held up a hand, signaling him to calm himself. "Josef's relationship with Ryder and his woman proved a convenient arrangement. Josef is one of us, darling, can't you sense that?" She squinted her eyes and gave her head a small shake to show how my ignorance shocked her.

"Why did you sacrifice Ryder?"

"What, did you think him an innocent?" Joe asked. "He sacrificed his wife and unborn child and killed a score or more of humans and at least two witches. He was a collector; he gathered his power, his magic, from his victims' quantum energy—the sum of everything that would have occurred in their lives. He so hungered for power that he quite willingly sacrificed his own flesh and blood to summon Barron and take the demon into himself."

"It was the demon we wanted," Emily said. "Ryder was only a useful tool—a container, if you will. The power he had taken into himself through killing humans had grown great, but once he'd augmented it with the demon's energy, he was ripe for sacrifice. There was enough magic in him to allow me to attempt the Babel spell."

I turned to Emily. "You are the one who gave him the mark and turned him into a collector."

"You say that as if you are accusing me." She took a few steps toward me. "Ryder was a battery, and his death freed his energy so that I could use it toward my own ends. If your fellow anchors hadn't dampened your magic, I wouldn't have needed him. But because you willingly let them limit your power, I needed an extra boost of energy. Furthermore, if you hadn't interfered with Ryder's attempt to collect your golem's magic, it might not have been necessary to summon the demon, so I think it's fair to say that the lives he claimed lie at your feet as well."

Joe faded into the shadows and returned with a plastic grocery bag filled with something about the size of a melon. He handed it to Emily, who opened it up and smiled, folding the plastic back to reveal Ryder's face. "Josef," she said, "let's display our latest trophy."

No sooner had she given the command than an enormous chandelier descended before us. The blue light suffusing the room grew more intense but narrower, revealing that this chandelier was the room's sole source of light. In spite of all the horrors I had witnessed, the sight of the chandelier made my blood run cold. My rational mind fought against a correct interpretation of the image. At first, I merely took in its geometric features. The chandelier was shaped like a cone, its circular base, which must have been at least thirty feet in diameter, at the top, its point facing down.

And that's where my intellect checked out, for the chandelier did not consist of electric lights, gas jets, or even candles. It was made entirely of severed heads, the eyes of each opening and closing independently of the others. All hair had been removed, leaving their pates perfectly smooth. They were pale, bloodless, and each was carved with the symbol I'd seen on Ryder's forehead. Some mouths were opened in soundless screams, others in mad laughs. Some remained closed, dispassionate, stoic. The unwholesome blue light that illuminated the world around us was emanating from the heads' open eyes. The realization that the light falling on my skin was being shed by this nightmare made me want to scream. Would I ever feel clean again? Feeling Joe's gaze on me, I looked over at him. His own eyes glowed, not with the sickly blue light, but with the joy of witnessing my revulsion.

"Feel no sympathy for them," Emily commanded. "They are all murderers, many times over, and they had no empathy for those they killed." She stood and crossed over to the chandelier, where she removed one of the heads. She placed Ryder's head on the newly vacated bobeche. His face shocked to life, the light building up in his eyes before shooting out his irises. His regard fell on Joe, and he silently mouthed the man's name.

"They are aware?" I asked, regardless of their deeds during life, it was a gruesome punishment.

"Of course they are," Emily said and laughed, seemingly amazed that I'd ask such a silly question.

"They were all collectors?"

"Yes. Well, all but this one," she said, lifting the head in her hand so I could see it better. "This one here is Alan. He never actually killed anyone. He would have liked to, but he didn't have the balls for it. Alan," she said, turning the head around so that it would have to look her in the eyes, "was a petty little despot who worked at an airline ticket counter. To make a long story short, he really, really irritated me." She tossed the head into the shadows, and I heard a crunch as it struck against the stone floor. The sound of scurrying and the excited screeches of vermin filled the room as creatures like my guide descended on their prize.

I shook off my urge to vomit. "If you empowered these people to be collectors, you are responsible for the murders they committed."

"They would have killed anyway. I merely took advantage of their natural inclinations." Emily stood back and admired the new addition before waving her hand, signaling that the chandelier should rise. "And now I can turn their evil to a good purpose."

"What good purpose could *you* possibly serve?"

An intricately carved mahogany Gothic throne materialized at her side. It was hideous, but in line with its surroundings. She sat and tapped the perfectly manicured nails of her right hand on the top of the lion's head handrest. Joe came and sat at the throne's clawed feet. He looked up at Emily, his face glowing with awe, and what else? Was it passion? The way he tilted his face up toward her was like a sunflower following the sun. She reached out and lovingly ran her fingers through his hair. "I told you before about how our teachers and guides have been deposed from their rightful place of honor and banished from this world," she said. "I serve them in their desire to eradicate the evil that is the line."

Filled with revulsion for Emily's world, choking on my disappointment, and yes, hate, I lost patience. "I don't believe the line is evil. I believe you are," I said.

The hard look on her face softened, her eyes closed a little and lost focus, as if she were looking into her own soul. After a moment, she pursed her lips and looked up at me. "Evil? Maybe I am. But this is war. Yes, a war. Mercy, I know I've gone about this all wrong. I hadn't intended to make an enemy out of you."

"Then you shouldn't have tried to collapse the world in on Jilo and me."

Her eyebrows arched up. "I assume you don't mean that poetically, but all the same I have no idea what you are talking about."

I ignored her lie. "And you *really* shouldn't have tried to kill my fiancé."

"There are mother-in-laws who have done worse," she said and smiled as if I would find any levity in her actions. "I was angry. I wasn't thinking," she continued. "His fairy blood ruined everything," she said, more to herself than to me, then added, "We were so close when he came and interrupted us."

"So close to what exactly?"

"To returning this world to its rightful owners, and to returning Maisie to us. The anchors and the witches who support the line will never allow her to return. You have to get that through your head. You want to talk about evil? The line has erased your sister from our very reality. Isn't that evil enough for you? If not, think about the creature I sent to fetch you. I wanted you to see one of them up close. His kind are not of my making. No, they are a product of the witches who maintain the line. They developed the foul little beings to serve as spies among the humans, to keep tabs on them lest they seek to overthrow their masters as the witches did theirs. That little bit of history is one that's never taught to the young witches. And so much of what is taught is a confection of half-truths and lies."

"But bringing down the line *will* return us to the control of the demons."

"Stop calling them demons. They are not demons. They are our creators. Our parents. Everything we have and everything we are, we got from them."

"You are out of your mind."

Emily's head tilted to the side and her lips pulled back, revealing gritted teeth. She leaned violently forward, her hands white-knuckled and digging into the arms of her chair. My own muscles pulled taut, preparing themselves if she were to pounce. It may only have been Joe's position at her feet that kept her from doing just that, but he proved barrier enough to slow Emily's building rage. She sensed my body preparing to respond in kind to any violence, and she forced herself back against the chair, loosening her grip on its arms. "I am the sanest witch you have ever met. It is only your willfulness, your ignorance that makes you doubt me." She regained control of herself, righting her head and relaxing her shoulders. "I brought you here to attempt to correct that ignorance."

"All right," I said, holding my hands out before me, palms down. "I'm sorry. I'm listening."

"Thank you for the apology. I accept it," she said, the final traces of tension disappearing from her face. She folded her hands and assumed a thoughtful pose. As she collected her thoughts, I stood in silence, calculating my odds of making it to Adam and sliding us out of here. "The old ones," she said, interrupting my train of thought. "When they found our planet, no humans existed, leave alone witches. The small mammals from which we've descended were millions of years away from even developing prehensile thumbs on their own. We were tree-dwelling mice, doing our best to hide from the masters of this world, but our visitors saw potential in us, and they decided to make a long-term investment in our future. They claimed our world for us. They cleared the land for us."

"You are saying they wiped out the dinosaurs?"

"Yes, they erased the dinosaurs, and everything that took their place until we were ready to rise to supremacy. They were always here to help us. Teach us. Protect us. Change us. Perfect us."

"Enslave us. Even if what you say is true, even if they did play a nurturing role in our early development, they didn't help us out of the kindness of their hearts. They engineered us to be their servants. Food, even. The witches rebelled to give us free will."

"Free will to what? Kill each other in wars? Poison the planet with toxins? Gorge ourselves on chemical foods while millions starve? These are the products of your treasured free will. The old ones, our guides, would never have allowed such madness. There are six and a half billion humans on this planet, and that number is burgeoning by the minute. That's six billion too many for the world to support. Humans are out of balance with nature. They are a virus, spreading, destroying. The human race is the ultimate ecological nightmare."

"So you bring down the line. You let your *old ones* back in. Who decides who gets to live and which six billion people have to die?"

"You could. If you help them, I am sure they will let you determine who are the most worthy of life."

I shook my head in disbelief. "I am not qualified to make that decision."

"No? A nurse who dedicates her life to healing or a drug dealer who murdered his grandmother? Pick one."

She stood, and pushing past Joe, she began to circle me, forcing me to turn. The movement combined with the blinking of the skull lights disoriented me. "That's an extreme example. Life isn't so simple," I said. "It isn't so black and white."

"Oh, my dear girl, it will amaze you how quickly clarity comes to you. How soon you will realize that those shades of gray you worry about are such unnecessary complications." She stopped and stood before me, the bruised light casting nightmarish shadows on her face.

"Those beings you want to help," I said, "they want to enslave the human race."

"Humans need to be subjugated for their own good and for the good of the planet."

"My son will not live as a slave."

"Of course not," she said as she tilted her head toward me, a wrinkle forming between her eyes. "Your son will reign as a king.

He will be truly free, not a slave of the line. My darling, you defend the line, but you know nothing of what it is or the blood that the witches spilled in its creation. Tell me, dear, what do you know about it?"

The dream I'd had a few days ago came to mind, and I found myself remembering it in vivid detail. I watched again as a faceless man slithered like a serpent away from a pyramid. Nearby obelisks lit up as lightning struck them. A whirring moan echoed from stone circles. I shook it off. "Pretty close to nothing, but what I do know is that you used me." I paused and an odd thought hit me. "I have a special connection to the line, one that none of the anchors has," I said, realizing the truth of the words as I said them. "What is it? Why me?" I asked.

"You are the witch of the prophecy. You are the one who was born to end the line and deliver us all from its tyranny. Why else do you think Ginny separated you from your magic? Why else do you think the united families have continued to estrange you from the power that is rightfully yours?"

She had sidestepped my question. I knew I'd never get any truth out of her, and the longer I allowed her to keep us here, the more likely it seemed that things would not end well. "No, you are wrong. You'll have to find another messiah. Now let Adam and me go."

"You are both free to leave whenever you would like, but remember this: They will never bring you into their fold. The anchors are terrified of you, since they know you will be the one to hold them accountable for their sins. Let me help you. Let me teach you what the line really is. How it imprisons you and how it will imprison your son . . . that is, if the other anchors even allow him to be born." She paused and watched my face, making sure that her words had made the impact she'd hoped they would. "Half witch, half fairy? Certainly a challenge to the status quo. A wild card. The anchors, they don't like challenges, especially ones they fear might be out of their control. If they learned the truth about my dear grandson . . ."

"Are you threatening me?" My hands curled into claws, ready to strike.

"No, my dear. Just the opposite. I am warning you. I am explaining to you how best to protect yourself and your child. I would never, ever betray your secret to the others, but you are already enough of an outlier in your own right, and I can guarantee that the anchors will also keep an eye on your little one, waiting to *remove* him from the equation should they ever feel the need. You'll have to find a way to hide his true nature, or they will kill him just as they killed Paul. Just as they would have killed you and Maisie if they'd known Erik was your father." Joe came and took her arm. "And just as they would try to murder Josef if they found out Erik was *his* father."

I stood there dumbstruck as I looked at Joe with new eyes. The hair, the cleft chin, the high forehead. He did bear a strong resemblance to Erik. Leaning in, he placed a passionate kiss on Emily's lips. I watched as animal electricity surged between them. Emily pushed him away and laughed. "Relax. He's only your half brother." He took her in his arms and pulled her near, so that her back was leaning against his chest. He caressed her, his fingers lingering near her hardening nipples, and nuzzled his face in her hair.

I couldn't bear another moment of it. "Adam and I are leaving now," I said. I tried to project confidence and authority, but she knew she'd shaken me.

"Of course," Emily said. "I can see you need more proof than the word of the woman who gave birth to you. I'll see that you get it. Please remember I tried to convince you the easy way first, but you left me with no choice. Now I'll have to force the anchors to show you their true colors."

I pushed past Joe and knelt beside Adam. When I placed my hand on his shoulder, he flinched. "It's okay, Adam. I'm going to get you away from here." He tilted his head up toward me. The look on his bruised face did not reflect gratitude. His swollen eyes narrowed even more, and he pulled back, as repulsed by my presence as I had been by the rodent with the human face. I offered my hand to help him stand, but he pushed it away and forced himself to his feet without my help.

THIRTY-SEVEN

Joe released Emily and raised his hands toward us, but before I could even react, the foul blue light he was generating condensed into a single point, and the stone walls disappeared from around us. We stood on a beach, the moon shining brightly from the western sky, the east beginning to show the first blush of purple. Adam collapsed to his knees, and I reached out for him.

"Do not touch me," he warned. He bent over, his face almost touching the sand, and a wail reached out from the innermost part of his heart, disturbing the quiet of the coming dawn.

"Adam, it's me. Mercy," I said. I knelt down next to him and tried to comfort him.

"I know who the hell you are, and I know what the hell you are. Now get away from me." Even though he hadn't made his way up off his knees, his hands balled into tight fists, his right one higher and ready to strike out, his left one lower, ready to defend. He was prepared to beat his way past me if I didn't do as he said. I stood and backed away. When Adam rose to his feet, his movements were jerky.

"Where the hell are we?" he said as he spun around, trying to find his bearings. He spotted the darkened, defunct lighthouse that loomed nearby. "That isn't Savannah. It isn't Tybee."

"No," I said. It wasn't Tybee, with its motels and souvenir stores. The unspoiled Hunting Island Beach stretched out before us. Even though we had to travel a good hour away from Savannah, Iris had often brought Maisie and me here when we were children. I wasn't sure if we'd landed here by hazard or design. "We're in South Carolina. I can get you home." At least I hoped I could. I'd never tried to slide this far before, and it would only be my second attempt at carrying a passenger. "But I will need to touch you."

"No," Adam said, leaning away from me. His face had contorted itself into a mask of pain. His right eye had now completely swollen shut. "No. I want no more of you people," he said. "Your mother put a noose around my neck," he said, pulling his still clenched fists up before his face. He drew them down and glared at me through his still functioning eye. "I am a black man, Mercy. You can't begin to understand . . ."

"Please. I know she's a monster. I am so sorry for what she's done to you. Please, let me take you to Oliver. Let Ellen heal you."

He continued to shake his head. "I know you mean well. I do. I know you aren't like your mother . . ."

"Please then. Stay here and let me get Uncle Oliver," I said, but Adam just shook his head.

"No. I know what's in you Taylors now. I've seen it." His good eye searched my face, as if he were trying to see through a disguise, but then he turned away. "I know what y'all are now, and I can't bear it."

Beneath the crashing surf, I heard that same growling I'd heard in the stone hall. At the edge of the line of trees, a retreating moon illuminated the wolf form that Joe had once again assumed. The beast padded up within yards of us and settled down, waiting for us to move so that it could give chase. Adam's body vibrated, shivering from cold, quivering from adrenaline. "Don't move," I said, but my words came too late. Adam took off in a full sprint, heading in the direction of the lighthouse. The wolf looked up at me, glee in its amber eyes. Its right front paw shimmered and stretched out into a furry, human-shaped hand. I watched as each of the five fingers Joe showed me bent in toward the palm. He was counting down, giving Adam a head start. The hand shrunk back into a wolf's pad, and Joe howled into the night, then leapt into the air and took off in pursuit.

I ran after them, ignoring the protest of my feet as the soft sand gave way to wood planks and then asphalt. I stopped on the road to get my bearings, but Adam and the wolf had already vanished from my sight. I turned in a circle, trying to hear some sign of them, but any external sounds were drowned out by the beating of my own heart. I was about to send out a psychic ping to see if I could get a fix on Adam when a beam shot out of the decommissioned lighthouse, illuminating the world around me. I saw my mother's figure standing in silhouette on the external catwalk near the black-painted top of the beacon. Praying that Adam had managed to escape and find shelter, I closed my eyes and slid to the lighthouse's white base.

I knew this place by heart, having climbed to the tower's top many times over the years. Tonight, its entranceway stood wide open, and light—every bit as bright as what was shining from the beacon's focal plane—poured out the black doorframe and reflected off the gold "1873" that adorned it. I put my foot on the first step, pulling it away again when I felt a sticky wetness. I looked down. It was blood. More had dribbled down on the next step and the next. I stepped up gingerly, trying to avoid further contact. I entered the tower, only to find more blood inside, much more, a puddle of it having formed at the base of the circular stairs that led up to the external railing where I'd seen Emily. Another drop of blood fell from above and splashed into the puddle. I looked up, but the brightness of the light and the curve of the stairs, combined with the way the tower narrowed as it went up, prevented me from seeing its source.

The silence in the tower was absolute, and the sound of my foot touching the iron mesh of the first of the winding steps echoed as loudly as if I'd hit it with a sledgehammer. "Come on up, darling," Emily's voice rang out in my mind. "We are all waiting for you." I closed my eyes, focusing my thoughts on the ninth landing. When I opened them again, Joe stood there before me in his human form, completely naked. He wiped the blood from his mouth with the back of his hand.

"Adam," I said, feeling my knees start to buckle.

"Relax," Joe said. "I only took a little taste." He squinted and licked his lips.

"Where is he? What have you done with him?"

"He's hanging out with your mother," he said and opened the door that led to the external circular catwalk. "After you."

"No, you first." I would not turn my back on Josef. He shrugged and smiled, then stepped out the door, letting the wind slam it shut in my face. I grabbed the handle and pulled it open, a whistling sound coming through the crack. I peeked through, but could see nothing, so I opened it wider and poked my head out. Adam hung in midair, his head lolling down, his arms being whipped about in the wind. I forced the door fully open and stepped out onto the catwalk.

"Call them. Call them to you." Emily said to me, making me jump even though I had known her to be there. "I want the whole dear family here for this event." I considered a quick slide. Go out. Grab Adam. Get anywhere the hell away from here. Emily floated over to face me. "Don't even consider it, darling. I'll make sure he hits the ground before you can even blink. Now call them."

"Do as your mother tells you. Call them, sister. Call your aunts. Call the ape's *lover*."

"You are mighty brave when you are hiding behind her skirt," I said, my anger overtaking my fear. "You'd better hope I never catch you out alone. I will rip your big bad wolf costume right off you."

He took a step toward me, straining so that his muscles would pop. "I am much more adept at using magic than you are."

"I ain't talking about using magic, *little brother*."

"Enough, children," Emily said. Josef's taut muscles were still twitching even as he took a step closer to Emily. She ran her fingers through his hair and then trailed them down his naked back. "Shhh . . ." She soothed him and then turned toward the sea and leaned against the metal railing. She whistled three discordant notes, then repeated the sequence twice.

From out near the horizon, where by now I knew the sun should soon rise, a furious shrieking came in response to her call. The awakening sky lost all light, fading to a deep purple, the shade of Adam's bruised skin, and then any hope of color was lost, repelled by storm clouds that had arisen from nowhere.

"A few simple sounds," Emily said. "And not much power at all. Just enough to encourage nature to do what it already wanted to do anyway. The water was already so warm, aching for a touch to arouse it. So easy to start, so hard to end." The winds began to whip up whitecaps. "What do you think, Josef?"

"At this rate, it will only make it to a category four by the time it hits Savannah," he said, jutting out his head over the railing to assess the growing storm. "I want a five."

"And so you shall have it," she said. She whistled again, and this time the notes came more quickly, sounding shriller. She kept it up until I thought my eardrums would burst, but then the sound mercifully stopped.

"It's building on its own now," Emily said. "Remember, I tried to avoid this, but you left me with no choice."

"A hurricane with no warning. No time for alerts. No evacuation," Joe said. "The destruction will be spectacular."

The clouds continued to thicken and blacken, and the first flash of lightening shocked the sky. "You have to stop this."

"Oh, no, my daughter. If you want this stopped, you will have to be the one to stop it." She smiled at me. "I know that you can . . . that is, if you are allowed."

"What do you mean *if I am allowed*?"

"Ask the Duvals. They could have turned Katrina away from New Orleans, directing it to a less populated area. Or they could have used their magic to help the levees hold. But the anchors wouldn't allow your cousins to save their home, just as they will not allow you to save yours."

"That's ridiculous. The storm was too powerful. If they could have done—"

"Oh, they could have done," Emily interrupted me. "And they would have done too, but the anchors said that diverting that much power from the line would weaken it. They commanded the Duvals to step down, and they did."

"Well, I am a Taylor, not a Duval," I said, and another flash of lightning punctuated my words, the clap of thunder so near it caused the metal catwalk to sing beneath my feet.

"Oh, my dear, I'm counting on that. Now go ahead. Call your family. I want you to do your best to turn this destruction you've forced me to call upon Savannah back out to sea. My sisters and brother will give you all the help you need." She closed her eyes and raised her hands toward the sea. "Now, I'll give it the slightest nudge." Her lips moved silently, and the horrible monstrosity on the horizon began to move closer to us, toward her outstretched hands. "My work here is done," she said and reached out for Joe's hand.

"Wait. Is it true? Is this just another trick to get me to endanger the line? Will the energy I use weaken it?"

"That's what the Duvals believed. Tell me, do you?" A flash of lightning enveloped them, and they vanished. The world around me stopped as Adam fell.

THIRTY-EIGHT

I reached out my magic toward Adam, but he slipped from my grasp. His body plummeted, limp, but bending in the wind. If I couldn't stop his fall, I could at least cushion it. I envisioned the air between him and the ground condensing, slowing his descent. I watched from above as his fall slowed and he was eased onto the ground. From my height, I couldn't tell if he was still alive. I concentrated on him, and in the next instant, I was kneeling by his side. I felt for a pulse. "Thank you." I sighed a prayer of thanks to the universe.

The howl of the wind reminded me that Adam wasn't my only worry. I needed to find my family, and together we needed to find a way to deal with the storm before the winds found their way to land. Not even counting the damage it could do to Savannah, countless innocent lives lay in its path. It would certainly claim Parris Island and Hilton Head, ravaging on until it had destroyed Daufuskie Island. Didn't Jilo have family there, as well as on Sapelo?

Oliver had closed on his new house yesterday, and today the winds would wipe it from the map. My own house, where Iris and Ellen were probably still sleeping, would be destroyed if I didn't make it there to wake them. I wrapped my arms around Adam and focused, but I didn't feel the tingling sensation that usually hit me before I made one of my leaps. Was Savannah too far away? The usual sliding feeling did not come. Rain began to pelt me like grapeshot. Could the storm be interfering? I opened my eyes. "No," was all I could say. We were still at the base of the lighthouse. We hadn't moved an inch, but the storm had. I closed my eyes again. *Come on. Come on*, I screamed in my own mind.

"What in the hell is goin' on here?" Jilo's voice spat into my ear. I felt her cold hand reach out and spin me around. She stood there before me on the beach, dressed in a fuchsia polyester nightgown, a yellow scarf tied around her head. I lunged forward and pulled her into my arms.

"Adam," I heard Oliver say with a gasp, and looked up to see him drawing near too. He ran up to us, bare chested and wearing drawstring pajama bottoms. He took Adam from me and rolled him over, cradling him in his arms. Iris approached from the opposite direction, wearing a housecoat, and Ellen stumbled a few feet behind her, moving groggily.

"You've brought us here?" Ellen asked. She had arrived fully dressed, wearing the same outfit she'd had on yesterday. I knew instantly that she hadn't slept. She had passed out drunk. Perhaps she was still a bit drunk now. Okay, one disaster at a time. That one would have to wait.

"I hadn't intended to, but . . ." I said and motioned out toward the approaching storm. "Emily," I said before emotion choked me. I swallowed hard. "It is heading straight for Savannah. Oh my God"—I remembered Adam—"Adam's been hurt."

"Let me have him," Ellen said to Oliver. She had been shocked sober by the sight of the two men. Oliver laid Adam's head down gently and slid back to give her room. "They've been bleeding him," she mumbled or maybe said. The wind made it hard to hear without screaming. Either way, the rest of her words were lost.

"We need to do something, push this back out," I said, "but Emily said the anchors won't let us."

Jilo spat on the ground. "The hell you say . . ."

"It's true," another voice came, this one totally unexpected. It was sharper. Northern. "The others would stop us. That," Rivkah said, her dark hair whipping around her face, "is why we have to act now before they register what we are doing."

"How did you find us?"

"From whom do you think Emmet inherited his tracking skills? I spent two years in the Israel Defense Forces. I sensed you were in trouble, so I came. That's why I'm here," she said, anticipating a question I hadn't even had time to consider. "Now do you want to talk, or do you want to turn this storm around?"

"Of course we want to turn the storm," Iris said. "But you can't take part in this. A Taylor caused this. The Taylors will act alone and shoulder the responsibility. This is not your fight."

"I am not going to stand by and let innocent people die. You let me worry about the consequences." The blowing wet sand bit at my ankles. Lightning ripped a seam in the sky and thunder shook us.

"What do we do?" I asked.

"How'd she start it?" Jilo asked.

"I don't know. She just whistled."

Iris nodded. "Well, the classics are always the best. We need to pull the storm back and then bend its course. I will have to descend into its eye to do that." She shed her housecoat, the light silk of her nightgown instantly ravaged by the rain. "Jilo, honey, I am so glad you are here."

"Well, that make one of us." Jilo's frail form shivered.

"If any of us knows how to collect and transmit power, it's you," Iris said. "It's going to take all of us and all of our power to stop this storm. We need someone who can borrow everyone's

310

magic and loan it to me." The two women looked at each other, an unspoken pact forming between them.

Ellen stood and stepped away from Adam. She looked at her brother and shook her head. "I don't know, sweetie, I've done what I can . . . We'll just have to wait and see." Oliver shuddered at the words. "I'm sorry. I caught his essence just in time, but I don't know. He's lost so much . . ."

The wind howled even more loudly around us, drowning out the rest of her words. Iris raised her head to the sky and lifted her arms. Amid the flashes of lightening, she spun up into the air, turning her face into the driving wind. I watched in amazement as her body took to the wind, her flight against it a testimony to her strength.

We all pulled closer, huddling around Jilo. Oliver spoke first. "Jilo Wills, I grant you my magic. All of it. It is my power to give, and I give it to you of my own free will." He paused. "I'm counting on you, you old buzzard. You fix this."

More surprising than watching Iris take to the sky was witnessing Jilo's gnarled hand as she reached out and pulled Oliver into her grasp. She pulled him to her and planted a kiss on his forehead. "She do her best."

Ellen came next. "Jilo Wills, I grant you all of my magic. It is my power to give, and I give it to you of my own free will." Jilo began to glow, the sole point of light now that dark clouds had devoured the sky.

I stepped forward, but Rivkah grabbed my arm. "Not you, Mercy. We need you as Plan B," she said and then turned to Jilo. "Jilo Wills. I grant you all my magic. It is my power to give, and I give it to you of my own free will." Lightning tore at us from the four corners of the sky, merging into a single bolt and striking Jilo as one. At first, I thought she must have been killed, but the old woman of the crossroads shot up and hovered a few feet off the ground. Clasping her hands together, she shot a single blinding arc of energy across the water, transferring what she had collected to Iris.

The wind lessened. The rain eased. Iris was succeeding, I just knew it. Then, the next instant later, she was thrown face down in the surf. Oliver jumped up from Adam's side and ran toward her, but after a couple of steps, he too collapsed. I used my power to slide over to her and pull her out of the water. I knelt over her and felt for a pulse. I couldn't find one. I looked up and called for Ellen, only to witness her weave and collapse.

"We've been found out," Rivkah said, falling to her knees, and then onto her side, her left arm sprawling over her head.

A moment of total silence descended upon us, and then wind roared and snapped back onto its original path. The world around us flashed, and Jilo collapsed to the ground as all the magic was drained out of her.

"Sons of bitches," she screamed and shook her hand at the sky. "You sons of bitches." She looked at me. "Yo' other anchors done cut off the magic. They done worked a binding on yo' family and the Yankee woman. I think they done killed 'em, girl."

I ran like mad from one to the next. No pulses, but I sensed they weren't dead. They had been suspended, frozen. "You stop this," I screamed, knowing full well even a whisper would be heard. They must be observing us after all. "You don't have the right." Feeling a sharp pain in my chest, I fell to my knees. The wind lashed stinging sand across my face, and another, sharper pain stabbed into my solar plexus.

Jilo tread toward me across the wet sand. "They workin' you now. Don't you let them, Mercy. You give your power to them, you ain't never gonna get it back. They take yo' magic. They take you family. Don't you let them. You fight, girl." She knelt before me and grasped my hands.

The pain was excruciating, and I almost gave into the waves of darkness that rolled over me, but then I thought of Colin, and I found the strength to fight back. I screamed, not out of pain, not even out of anger, but out of a mother's primal sense to protect her child. No more. I would be weak no longer. I was no one's victim, and neither was my child. "I reclaim my magic," I shouted into the wind. "It is mine, and you may no longer have it. I revoke any permission I granted you."

As the anchors channeled their combined power together to try to control the magic that belonged to me, my witch's eyes witnessed multiple vistas, different worlds, encapsulating us, as one reality pressed in against another, competing for supremacy. Beyond them all, a pair of monstrous eyes, as large as moons, as large as planets, closed for eons, winked open, and turned toward us. Not yet fully awake, they still reflected the hunger of hibernation. Were the other anchors really so desperate for me to back down? They had risked everything in their attempt to control me. The fools were playing chicken with the line and stirring up the demons.

The hurricane was almost upon us. Waves lapped farther up on shore and washed over the inert bodies of those I loved. If they didn't wake soon, the sea would carry them away, and they'd be lost to me forever. Jilo released my hands and faced the sea. I felt my heart slowing, as the other anchors continued their efforts to bind me without collapsing the line. A wave found me and knocked me flat. I struggled to push myself up. When I managed to force myself back to my knees, Jilo had disappeared, but the entire world around me had filled with the sickly, bruised blue light that I'd come to associate with Tillandsia.

I found my feet and turned toward the sea. The source of the light floated out above the ocean, thirty, maybe forty yards from shore, but I would have known Jilo from a thousand yards away.

She had drawn the energy of Tillandsia into herself and was doing her best to single-handedly drive the storm away. Even though she knew the power had been poisoned, she had chosen to take it into herself anyway. She had put the well-being of others before her own. She must have known that, even with the power of Tillandsia, it would take a real witch to turn the hurricane away, especially when it would require taking on both the storm and the anchors of the line. She had sacrificed everything just to buy us a little time. To buy *me* a little time.

"There's a price for stealing power," I said softly, calmly. "And you all are stealing my power. Return it to me. Return it." A searing pain ripped through me, making me cry out. I tried to block out the pain by turning my mind to the power of the line. It had recognized me once before. It had chosen me. If, as I'd sensed at times, it was something more than a tool, more than a mechanism for controlling others, it would hear me. I called out to the line, wrapping my plea in the single grain of hope that hadn't yet deserted me. I was answered by a pain worse than any other I had felt, a sensation like my solar plexus being ripped wide open, the pain so great that my vision failed and everything around me was swallowed by blackness. During that dark moment, I let myself collapse on the wet earth. It was over. I had been defeated. The line had deserted me; the other anchors had won. For a moment I felt sure my heart would stop beating, but then around me flashed another world, green and cool and lovely. Music trumpeted from every direction, then faded away. The pain in my solar plexus cooled, and my own thundering reality gelled back around me. I felt the line reenergize itself, regain its ground, reinforce its walls, and then I felt a change, a shift, an explosion that felt like joy bursting out of me. Colin had reached out and filled my heart with his own power, one that fell outside any witch's ability to control. *Fae* magic, which the anchors could never touch.

With that added ammunition, I stopped the world. Everything around me slowed. Raindrops stopped in their descent. Trees that had been bent by the wind held their tortured poses, even though the wind itself had lost its power to blow. All motion and sound ceased. With my son's help, I ripped my magic from the hands of the other anchors, pitiful fear-filled souls, and their consciousnesses scurried away from me like Emily's rats. I broke the binds placed on Rivkah and my family. Then I looked out at Jilo, and with a thought brought her to my side, disconnecting her from the lethal force she had taken into herself. There, frozen in its path, loomed the storm I had feared so. I looked at the suspended hurricane and laughed. I claimed its towering energy as my own, turning its force to my purposes. I sent my awareness out to the line, and it zoomed in every direction around the earth at once. Breathtaking. Beautiful. Strong. Stronger, perhaps, than it had ever before been. Silently, I asked its permission to free my sister, and the line acquiesced. I reached out, like a comet burning not through common space but through fluctuating dimensions, and caught hold of Maisie. Then I brought her home.

THIRTY-NINE

"How's she doing?" Oliver whispered as he slipped into Maisie's room. Though she had been home with us for more than a day, she had only opened her eyes once. She hadn't spoken at all.

"The same," I said. I hadn't left Maisie's side for more than a few minutes at a time. I could barely stand to take my eyes off her for fear she'd disappear. I was afraid the other anchors would do something to steal her from me.

"Any news from Adam?"

Oliver's face darkened. "Physically he's fine. He's shut me out though. He's shut all of us out." He tried to muster his patented smile of confidence, but couldn't quite pull it off. "I think Adam and I are through. I don't think he's going to be able to get past whatever it was Emily showed him."

I would have liked to find some words of encouragement to offer, but I didn't want to lie. Adam had been so angry, so frightened. So over us Taylors and our magic. He had said that he knew *what* we were now. I wasn't sure if he meant the magic, or if he had somehow seen deeper into our true nature. Either way, I couldn't lie to my uncle. "I'm sorry," I said. "I think you may be right about that."

Oliver kissed the top of my head. "You should take a break. Get some sleep. Your aunts and I will stay with her."

I shook my head. "No. I can't. I can't give them a chance to take her away."

"No one is going to do that. I promise you." He stood at the foot of Maisie's bed and watched her sleeping.

"Did you know Maisie and I have a half brother?" I asked. Oliver's head bounced like a bobblehead doll in surprise. His jaw dropped, but he said nothing. He had been struck speechless for the first time in his life. "I don't know the details, but Erik had a son. His name is Joe . . . Josef. He's been helping Emily."

"I guess we should tell Ellen, but . . ."

"Yeah, *but* . . ." How much more could Ellen take? Tucker's body remained with the county coroner. We hadn't even had the opportunity to hold a memorial for him yet, leave alone a proper burial. She needed to mourn her fiancé, and hitting her over the head by pointing out another of Erik's infidelities would not help.

Oliver shifted from one foot to the other, and then sat down on the foot of Maisie's bed.

"What aren't you telling me?" I asked.

"You're getting pretty good at that . . . reading me, I mean," he said.

"It isn't magic; you are just terrible at hiding things from me."

He smiled and took Maisie's hand, caressing it as he searched her face for signs of life. "Emmet has returned." His eyes traveled from Maisie's face to my own.

"I asked Emmet to stay away from Savannah."

"The families sent him here to negotiate with you."

"Negotiate?"

"To sue for peace if you will."

"But I am not the one who declared war."

"You, Gingersnap, have scared the holy hell out of them. I don't understand what you did, but you single-handedly *changed* the line."

"No. The line changed itself. It simply used me to do it." I paused, trying to collect my thoughts. "I know it sounds nuts, but I think the line is alive. It's self-aware. I think it wants to evolve, but it can't while the anchors hold on to it so tightly. I think that's why it chose me. I've been an outsider to magic my whole life, powerless and overlooked. The other anchors didn't think I could possibly threaten the way things stand."

"The other anchors *will* view any attempt to change the status quo as a sign that you have aligned yourself with Emily. That you, too, want to end the line."

"That couldn't be further from the truth," I said and stood. My limbs had gone stiff from inactivity. I stretched, and felt the blood begin to pump more freely through them. "I've seen what it protects us from. Still I don't think we should fear change. My gut tells me that the line wants to form a partnership with us rather than acting as our master or our slave." I went to the window and looked out at the gray autumn sky. "Emily's wrong about pretty much everything . . . except one thing. The anchors maintain a power structure that's based on secrecy and misdirection, if not out-and-out lies." I turned back to Oliver so that I could witness his reaction. "To begin with, witches don't get their power from the line. The line gets its power from us."

"I don't understand how that could be," Oliver said, surprised and uncomfortable to have his own worldview challenged. His right hand smoothed down the thick blond hair of his left arm. As he considered my words, his mouth pulled down into a deep frown, and he looked down at the floor.

"I don't know for sure. Maybe it's like an alternating current. I doubt if the other anchors will ever share the details of how the witches created the line with me now, so I don't know if I'll ever be sure. But I do believe that the magic begins as ours and is fed into the line. From there, it gets parsed back out, in a more even distribution. No witch does without, but no witch can rise to his or her true potential either."

"No witch who isn't an anchor," Oliver said, nodding. "I don't like it. Your theory makes me uncomfortable, but that tells me you are more than likely on the right track."

"I don't like it either. I wish there was a clear and easy way to look at the line and the decisions that the families who built it have made. I mean, yeah, the three rebel families are evil. Their evil is Technicolor, in-your-face evil. I worry, though, that the side we have chosen has its own form of evil too. One path is totally wrong, but what if the other is just a longer, more scenic route to the same hell?"

"Then you will blaze us a new path toward sanity," Oliver said. "Frankly I think *that's* why the line chose you. Most people want easy answers to life. They will agree with whatever the echo chamber around them says as long as it means they don't have to think for themselves. Only a precious few can cope with ambiguity and carry on."

A soft knock on the door interrupted us. The door opened a crack, revealing the dark giant on the other side. "I apologize for the intrusion," Emmet said. His black eyes poked holes into me, probing me. Checking to make sure I was truly unharmed. Checking to see if the experience I'd been through had led to a change of heart. I smiled, as I felt happy to see him, but I did my best to convey without words that nothing had changed between us. He turned from me to look at Maisie. "She will awaken soon. I am sure of it." I sensed that he had not intended his words as an actual prognostication. He had meant them more as a comfort.

"Thank you," I said, and he nodded.

"I meant to honor your request," he said, "that I stay away from your home, but circumstances—"

"I know. The families sent you."

"Yes. They hope that you will accept a request to meet with the other anchors. Work through any *misunderstandings* that may have arisen." Oliver harrumphed, and we rolled our eyes at each other. "Please understand," Emmet continued, "that even though I agreed to act as emissary of their message, I am in no way neutral, not after the crimes they have committed against you. I have chosen a side, and you, Mercy, have my full allegiance. The families are aware of this, and that is why they asked me to approach you. They hope to prevent the deepening of any schism between you and the other anchors. They ask that you meet with them to see if you can work out your differences in a way that will not harm the line. In return for this meeting, they will make an oath not to *interfere* with your sister."

As I considered his words, I listened to Maisie's steady breathing and turned to look at her beautiful face, blessed in sleep with a serenity I hoped she might one day feel upon waking. I wanted many things from the other anchors, starting with this oath to leave my sister alone as we worked through her issues. For once, though, I found myself in a place of power, and I had every intention to take full advantage of that. "Tell them I agree," I said. "But I will pick the time and the means."

FORTY

I learned that the line's anchors rarely met face-to-face. Of course, due to their duty as anchors, they could not physically venture too far from the places they had been chosen to anchor. Because of this, when they gathered together, they did so virtually, leaving their bodies at home and projecting their minds to the meeting space. I knew the perfect place for the gathering they had requested, one that would allow all of us to meet, perhaps for the first time in the history of the line, in the flesh. I opened new entrances to Jilo's haint-blue chamber over each anchor's home. We could all meet together without anyone leaving their territory.

I bent these entryways, though, so that each entrant would have to pass through the world of the endless living shadows, the minor demons that folk in the low country called boo hags before reaching the chamber. These creatures held no fear for me now. I could almost pity their lust for a skin that would allow them to walk in the world of light. Almost.

I laughed at the thought of the other anchors seeing this place, a place that had once terrified me, built by a woman who had once scared me out of my wits. Again and again I found myself taking comfort in the smallness of my past horrors. My skin prickled and turned to gooseflesh as I wondered if there might arrive a tomorrow when I looked back from the vantage point of even greater terrors, feeling nostalgic for today. That kind of thinking would get me nowhere.

The chamber had collapsed to half its previous size, bending and twisting in on itself. The endless cyan was now punctured by bruised plum stains left by the poisoned magic of Tillandsia. I had to maintain my focus and my confidence. Thoughts of Emily and Josef were a threat to both, so I pushed away any remembrance of Tillandsia and took my place at the portion of the room that bent upward. I would claim the higher ground. It might not lend me any true physical advantage, but it would help a lot psychologically. I claimed Jilo's abandoned cerulean throne and sat in it. This would count as the final time I'd come to the haint-blue room. At Jilo's request, I'd close the chamber down after this meeting, collapsing it until it became merely a dense, dark point in space. In the quiet before the others came, I allowed myself one long last look.

Just as I finished taking the room in, its edges began to shimmer. A fluctuation in the air here, a quiver there, vibrations announcing the arrival of my magical colleagues. *Disappointing* was my most prominent thought as they resolved into their full physical forms. They were not as tall as giants, and not one of them had a sunbeam crown or a quiver full of lightning bolts. No, the pantheon of anchors looked like plain old regular folk. African, European, Asian, Middle Eastern, and combinations of all the above. True, all of them were witches, and if they were not truly the most powerful witches in the world, they were at least the witches with the greatest access to power. All the same, I swear one of them looked like she had come from dropping her kids off at soccer practice, and another like he had been working in his garden. Calm. Nonthreatening. None of them would even arouse a sense of disquiet, leave alone danger. I suspected this was by design, but this calculated attempt to disarm me brought Hannah Arendt's phrase "banality of evil" to mind.

Smiles from some, heads lowered in deference from others. Each person's pose screamed, "We are all friends here!" In spite of that, my intuition shouted at me. I feared that maybe I was growing paranoid or jaded. Maybe the way my own mother had turned on me had colored my perception of the world. I considered the possibility that perhaps these witches weren't my enemies, but then I remembered how they'd tried to sacrifice the innocent individuals of my hometown in a misguided attempt to look out for what they considered to be the greater good. "All right. Y'all wanted to talk. Well, I'm listening."

A middle-aged man with an average build and thinning mousey brown hair that framed a friendly and guileless face stepped forward. In my mind, I labeled him Mr. Beige. "If it is all right with everyone, I will volunteer to speak for the group." The fact that no one protested or even spoke up told me that this decision had long since been made, and that this was in fact nothing more than a show, probably intended to demonstrate how well the rest of the anchors played together. Yep. They were all about the collaboration. All about the team. Individuals need not apply. "Even though we each represent our respective families, we anchors like to think of ourselves as a family in our own right. A family of anchors." He smiled, holding his hands out toward me. "On behalf of all of us, it is a pleasure to welcome you." He didn't introduce himself; no one did. I said nothing, letting the silence thicken around us.

"I regret that our first meeting should occur under the cloud of the regrettable circumstances *your mother created.*" He accented the last three words, an obvious attempt to goad me, but I didn't bite. My failure to respond as expected affected his confidence. He seemed a little less sure of himself when he began to speak again. Small beads of sweat started to form on his upper lip. "It's unfortunate that we had to step in. We merely did what we felt necessary to protect the line. We hope that you will understand that and put aside any ill will you may feel about the actions we felt compelled to take."

"Tell me," I said. "What is it you want from me? Are you looking for pardon? Because I have to tell you, I'd only consider forgiving you if I thought you wouldn't follow the same course again."

"Well, no," Beige said, pulling himself up, the air of congeniality slipping away, "we are not looking for forgiveness. We did what we felt we had to do to protect the line."

"And that makes the fact that you are *all* attempted mass murderers something I should overlook?"

The other eight began shifting, looking at one another. "I didn't want anyone to come to harm," a diminutive Asian woman said. The illusion of cohesiveness crumbled. "I didn't want to interfere with your efforts."

"Then why did you?" My own voice surprised me, a venomous hiss pinning the woman to the spot as I leaned forward and struck her with my eyes. "Why did you allow them?"

"I, I was outvoted," she said, lowering her eyes.

"Listen," Beige continued, trying to regain momentum, "none of us wanted harm to come to the people of Savannah. Remember we didn't start the storm."

"No. Emily did. She did it to prove a point to me. The point that you all would be willing to see an entire city wiped off the map. That you would be willing to bathe in blood, and would pat yourselves on the back for doing so."

Beige looked around at the others. "This path will get us nowhere. We came here today because we want to put what happened behind us. Yes, you defied us, but we were perhaps in the wrong."

324

"*Perhaps* in the wrong?" I spat back at him.

"Yes, from your perspective, we were wrong. Evidently from the line's perspective as well," he allowed, a trace of humility in his voice. "We don't understand what happened. We know you don't like the stance we took, but it's the same stance we anchors have been taking since the creation of the line. And that stance is to protect the line at *all* costs."

"Costs that others are left to pay. Well, this time the line kept you from standing on the sidelines and letting people get hurt. The line doesn't seem to want the kind of protection y'all have been offering."

With this, Beige's bluster faded, and the real man stood before me. Middle-aged, balding, dressed in a tan suit and loafers, and suddenly faced with the possibility that for a good portion of his life he had been working under the wrong set of assumptions. "You seem to have a deeper connection to the line than any of us. You *communicate* with it. It interacts with you as if it were a living entity in its own right."

It surprised me that my experience of the line was not common to the rest of the anchors, but I did my best to feign disinterest in his disclosure. It would not do to give too much away. "I never assumed it *wouldn't* communicate with me."

The other anchors looked at one another, and I could hear a buzzing of communication between them. They blocked my full comprehension, but I could still pick up snatches of their conversations. The words *dangerous* and *control* popped out at me. When the buzzing stopped, Beige addressed me. "We understand that for some reason the line has chosen you to enjoy a special relationship with it. We would like to better understand this relationship, but you must have your own concerns that you would like us to address. Perhaps you can tell us what you would like from us?"

I took a moment to consider. The truth was, all I wanted was for these witches to go away. To leave me and my family alone. To let us live out our lives in peace. But I knew that even if they promised that to me, they would be lying. The line had used me—no, it had used my son—to loosen these people's stranglehold on it. They would grant me no peace until they could understand what had happened and find a way to dig their claws back in. I could read it in their eyes that this false promise of security was exactly what they wanted me to ask for. They thought I would trade what I knew about the line for their promise to leave me be. They could not have been more mistaken. "Just tell me the truth about one thing. What is the source of the line's power?"

"I believe you already know the answer to that."

"I'd still like to hear it from you. Come on. I'm an anchor now. I thought I had earned the right to learn the secret handshake."

"The sharing of knowledge follows the gaining of trust," Beige said, stiffening as if he had suffered a personal affront. "And sharing what you know about what happened to the line will go a long way toward gaining our trust."

"What do you think happened?" I asked.

"Now you are just being childish," exclaimed a heavyset woman with a thick Russian accent. Whatever she saw on my face silenced her. She stepped back.

"We don't know," the Asian lady spoke up. "We know that the line is stronger than before, but the magic has been modified. There has been a foreign strain added to it. It is somehow less *ours*."

Less in their control, she meant. Beige glared at her, willing her mouth to close. "This foreign magic," he said as he turned to face me, "it is not unknown to us, nor is it totally unrelated to our own. We encounter it occasionally in a burst here and there, but never in such a quantity or concentration as last night."

Now he had my attention. "How is it related?" I leaned forward, straightening my back and tilting my head. My posture had betrayed my interest. That meant they would never tell me. I felt one pair of eyes pin me with more intensity than the others. Instinctively I turned toward a waiflike young witch, impossibly pale and fair, nearly androgynous with the scale leaning almost imperceptibly toward male. His eyes, white and devoid of either iris or pupil, fell to my stomach.

"The sharing of knowledge follows trust," Beige repeated. His words were almost drowned out by the buzzing unspoken communications of the other anchors. Beige continued his soliloquy, but I tuned him out. I focused intently on the thoughts of the others, until the words *Fae* and *infant* and *study* twined together and became the common thread. The boy had made the connection between the magic and my son.

"We thank you for this meeting." Beige's words broke in through my panic, and shimmers at the edge of the room announced that many of the anchors had already begun to take leave. My heart raced. They had tricked me. They might not completely understand, but they knew the line had tapped into fairy magic, using my baby as the conduit.

"No," I said, slamming the exits closed before any more could fade. "You will not harm my child," I said, feeling the intensity of my emotions build. "You will not study my child." I flew up from Jilo's throne, grasping it with my magic and hurling it at them. "You will not use my child."

Beige threw up his arm, and the throne burst into flames in midair, falling as a rain of ashes. "No?" he asked. "And how do you intend to stop us?"

I began shaking, fear and rage combining to tear reason from my grasp. How could I stop them? How could I prevent them from taking Colin from me? Locking him in a laboratory and sacrificing him to *the greater good*? My feet made contact with the floor, and I was no longer myself when I strode toward Beige. I approached him like an angry lioness, transformed by fear into a living, breathing embodiment of Durga, the very spirit of a mother's drive to defend her young. Beige's confident smile slumped, the corners of his mouth turning down as his brow furrowed. As I neared him, he tried to take a step back, but my hand shot out of its own accord and pierced his skin, above the navel, below the heart, right at his solar plexus, right at the point where the line connected its magic to his. I ripped that connection out of him. He screamed, from pain and from powerlessness. I held the ball of light, bright and shimmering, before his eyes and then shoved it back into him and closed the wound.

His knees gave way, and he tumbled forward. "That," I said as the other anchors rushed in to catch him, "*that* is how I will stop you. Do we understand each other?"

"Yes," he said, nodding furiously as the others helped him balance.

"Good," I said and reopened the haint-blue room's exits for the last time. "Now, get out of here and tell the families to stay away from me. Stay away from my child. Stay away from my husband. Stay away from my family. And stay the hell away from Savannah." The anchors who had remained fled the chamber and rushed into the realm of the living shadows, comforted, I am sure, to face the kind of adversaries to which they felt more accustomed. I made one last turn in the cerulean light, and then watched as Jilo's chamber folded in on itself, sliding away only at the last possible moment before it disappeared for good.

FORTY-ONE

A truly vintage wedding dress from the 1940s, ivory silk with a cowl neckline and a low-draped back. A bouquet of white roses and blue hydrangeas. Both from Ellen. Iris had loaned me the pendant necklace I was wearing, which had been passed down through more than a hundred years of Taylor women, a diamond-encircled cabochon emerald above a drop-shaped emerald. Iris had also made me a gift of a new pair of emerald and diamond earrings, the emeralds' color an astonishingly close match to the antique ones in the necklace. From Maisie, I stole a kiss, as she continued to live in her dreams.

Oliver, of course, would give me away. His other contribution to the event was that he'd convinced the justice of the peace and the parks authority with just three days' notice to let us perform the service in Forsyth Park, where Peter and I had first met. Peter had the idea that we should marry at the foot of the oak we'd always called "the climbing tree," the one with the lowest and sturdiest branches. No groomsmen, no bridesmaids. Just the two of us before God. Iris had balked at first when Peter and I had said we wanted a simple wedding, no fancy reception, just cake and a band in the park. In the end, she'd capitulated and had even taken out a full-page ad in the *Savannah Daily News* welcoming the whole darned town.

We had taken over a suite of rooms at the Mansion, and a team of hair and makeup artists were surrounding me, turning me into a fairy-tale princess, an image I'd never re-create under my own steam, even with magic. I loved every minute of it, though, because this day wasn't just for me. It wasn't even just for me and Peter. It was for the whole family. My aunts and uncle had arranged everything, devoting their attention to even the smallest details, although I had a surprise to spring on them as well.

"Shame on you," I said as that surprise trudged into the room, dressed in chiffon the color of blue morning glories and a purple hat large enough to shade half of Savannah.

"Why shame on Jilo?" she asked, scanning me to try to find a place to land a kiss without messing up my hair or makeup.

I popped up and kissed her instead. "You know you aren't supposed to outshine the bride."

"Well, darlin', Jilo can't help it if the Lord has bestowed such blessings on her. Wouldn't seem right to hide them." She laughed, and took a seat on the foot of the bed. "Are you happy, girl?"

Tears started welling up in my eyes just as Ellen and Iris entered the room. "Yes," I said. "Yes. I am very, very happy." Jilo nodded in reply.

"Oh, now, now," Iris said reaching for a tissue. "No waterworks until after the photos," she said. Then she noticed Jilo. "Oh, Jilo. I am so glad you liked the hat. I knew it would suit you perfectly."

"I love it. Thank you," Jilo said softly and smiled. So much for my ability to surprise anyone. I looked at these three beautiful women. Each of them, in her own way, was a mother to me.

"Let's loosen her hair a bit," Ellen said to the stylist. Then she turned to me. "I've got a crazy idea," she said. "It's only that the thought of you and Peter marrying here in the park reminds me of when you were still a scrawny little tomboy. Well, since you aren't wearing a full-length gown, how would you feel about doing this barefoot?"

A knock at the door interrupted the decision. "May the future mother-in-law come in?" Claire asked. We hadn't seen each other since the day Ryder and Josef had barged into the bar. I hadn't been purposely avoiding her, I had just been *busy*. I knew from her tone that she was concerned that I might actually turn her away.

"Of course," I said, waving her in. "Would y'all mind if Claire and I had a moment alone?"

The assistants dropped everything as soon as I made the request, but my aunts exchanged a look before moving. Jilo grumbled a little under her breath, but then she worked her way off the foot of the bed. Once the room had been cleared, Claire stepped closer. "You, my dear girl, are breathtaking."

"Thank you," I said, reaching out to take her hand. "I am so sorry, Claire. For what I did to Peter—your natural son Peter, that is." Heck, I should probably apologize for what I'd put her adopted son through as well, but I would spend the rest of my life doing my best to make it up to him.

"No, I am the one who's sorry. It was only my grief and confusion talking. I know that you tried to help him and that he was already dead when you put your hands on him. I know," she said, tapping her hand against her heart. "Listen, I have realized that the Fae did live up to their promise, just that time must move a bit differently in their world than in ours." She paused. "When the police found him outside the powder magazine, he was wearing a heavy overcoat."

"Yes, I remember it."

"A fortune in gold and jewels had been sewn up in its lining. A fortune befitting a prince."

"Yes, Jilo picked up on that and told me."

"Well, Colin and I have been discussing what we should do with the proceeds from this unexpected windfall. We have decided to donate everything to the research of children's cancer, because that, in the end, is really what took our Peter from us. We are donating everything he carried with him except this." She opened her purse and pulled out a silver baby's rattle, monogrammed with the initials PDT, Peter Daniel Tierney. "This belonged to him. We sent it with him," she paused. "I cannot explain why—I don't understand it myself—but it would mean the world to me if you'd carry this with you today, if you could find it in your heart to include our other Peter in your marriage to my adopted son."

"I would consider it an honor," I said, taking the rattle from her.

"I love you, Mercy Taylor," Claire said, tears bursting from her eyes and rolling down her cheeks.

"That's Mercy Tierney," I said.

Claire smiled through her tears and reached out with both hands to grasp my stomach. "And you too, you little monkey. Grandma loves you." She stood and walked to the door. "I'll send your entourage back in." She smiled at me once more, then left.

I'd experienced the magical warping of time many times over now, but it couldn't begin to compare to the way natural time moved on my wedding day. One moment I was sitting in the hotel, getting the final touches to my makeup and hair, and the next I stood in the park beside Oliver, waiting for the musical cue to start toward the climbing tree. "You good?" he asked, leaning back and taking in the full view of a niece so done up he could barely recognize her.

I lifted my bare foot and wiggled my newly polished toes. "Never better."

Iris took honors as the first mother-of-the-bride. I watched as her new boyfriend, Sam, escorted her up the aisle. Ellen followed her as the second mother-of-the-bride. I had expected Peter's buddy Tom to serve as her escort, but as I squinted against the sun, I realized that Ellen was holding on to Adam's arm. It shocked me to see him there. He'd told me he was done with us, all of us, and I had believed it to be true. I didn't know what had led to his change of heart, and frankly I did not care. I squeezed Oliver's hand. "You good?" I asked.

His eyes were wide with surprise. "Never better," he said, his face beaming.

Finally, Jilo, the third mother-of-the-bride, proceeded between the rows of white folding chairs on the arm of her great-grandson, Martell. As she settled into her seat, I heard big Colin call out to the band, "Strike 'er up, boys!" "Haste to the Wedding" came from the temporary bandstand Peter himself had helped build. Oliver looked at me with questioning eyes. I nodded once, and we wound our way through the open field. There, waiting beneath its sheltering limbs stood the man I loved, the man I had always loved, my Peter. I looked into his mismatched eyes and everything else faded away.

Next thing I knew, music was swelling up all around me as Peter spun me in his arms and the party officially began. The happy faces of well-wishers whisked in and out of view. I danced from Peter's arms to Oliver's to Colin's. And then Adam stood before me. He bowed to me and extended his hand. I took it gladly.

I was pleased it was a waltz, and a slow one to boot. It gave me a chance to catch my breath and find out why Adam had changed his mind about us. "I'm so happy you're here," I said. "But what changed? I thought you'd seen too much, been pushed too far. I thought we'd lost you forever."

"I thought so too," he said, sadness creeping into his eyes, even though he was still smiling. "Emily showed me the worst side of you all. She showed me things I don't think the rest of you know about yourselves."

"Like what?" I asked, forgetting all about dancing.

He laughed and led me back into the dance. "There's plenty of time to get into all that, but today is about celebrating. Like I said, Emily showed me the worst side of witches. But you and Iris and Ellen, and hell, even Oliver, y'all have shown me the best. You risked your life to save me. Besides, in spite of it all, I love that impossible uncle of yours. No matter what."

Peter had been pulled aside by his buddies and was being fed whiskey chasers for the champagne he'd already been downing. "Not too much there, buster," I called as Adam waltzed me past him.

"Just married and she's already calling the shots," one of Peter's friends said and slapped him on the back.

"That's fine by me," Peter said and stole me back from Adam, but not before I'd placed a kiss on the detective's cheek. Adam surrendered me to my husband, and Peter smiled down at me, holding me tight in his arms. And I, well, I had never felt more love before in my entire life. I knew toasts had been made, I knew we'd cut cake at some point, and I had vague recollections of being pulled in one direction and then the other by a photographer who was bound and determined to capture every moment. But I knew those moments would be the ones I'd always remember—standing in Peter's arms, enjoying a golden, happy blur with everyone I loved around me, and the fine people of Savannah, even those who would not truly call themselves my friends. Before I realized it, the sun had slid to the western sky and was sending its light down at an angle that announced twilight would follow not far behind. And as the jigs had given way to waltzes, in fine Celtic tradition, with the setting of the sun, the waltzes gave way to a few tearful laments.

"We should get going soon," Peter leaned in and whispered in my ear. I nodded my agreement. As an anchor, I couldn't travel too far from Savannah for a honeymoon, so Oliver had arranged for us to enjoy a week's stay on Sea Island. No one in their right mind would complain about that, but I would have settled for Tybee as long as I had Peter with me.

"The only thing left," I said, "is to toss the bouquet." I loosened the ribbon around the flowers and removed the baby rattle Claire had wanted me to carry.

"What's that?" Peter asked, reaching to take it from my hand.

"Just something old from your mother. You go find her and give it back to her, okay? I'm going to go hunt down Jilo. She'll never forgive me if I toss the bouquet and don't aim it in her direction."

"I think you are right about that," Peter said and leaned in to kiss me. "I'll meet you beneath the climbing tree?"

I nodded. "Always and for the rest of my life." He had a hard time letting go of me, but my hand finally dropped from his as he headed toward the bandstand in search of his parents. My eyes followed him, not wanting to lose sight of him, but finally I turned my mind toward finding Jilo. I had little trouble picking her out as I scanned the field. She had moved away from the crowd, and was sitting in a white folding chair that had been moved into the shade of a live oak.

Her eyes were partially closed, giving her the appearance of a napping cat. "You sure are a beautiful girl," she said, raising her head as I neared. "You Jilo's girl, you know. Don't you ever let anyone tell you otherwise, you hear? Jilo, she love you as sure as if she'd carried you." I hiked up my skirt a little and knelt down before her. "You get up now," she scolded. "You gonna ruin yo' pretty dress." She reached out and traced her hand along my cheek.

"My dress will be fine," I said to her. I took her hand. "Peter and I need to leave soon. I'm going to toss the bouquet. Thought you might like a shot at catching it."

The old woman of the crossroads laughed. "Girl, the last thing Jilo needin' is another man to take care of. She done had more than her fair share, so you keep those flowers of yo's good and far away from Mother." She scanned the park, taking in the dappled light, the lingering crowd, and the last few strains of music. She drew a deep breath and sighed it back out. "You gonna be all right now, girl," she said and shuddered. Her eyes glazed over; her hand went limp in mine.

FORTY-TWO

Out of all the stories people tell about Savannah, the one that truly embodies the spirit of the place is this: Sometime around 1800 a fire broke out during a Christmas party at the home of Josiah Tattnall. By the time the servants discovered the fire, Josiah realized it was too late to save the house, so he took his guests outside to continue the party by the fire's glow. To me, the moral is that even though life will take the things and the people you love from you, you should never, ever stop celebrating that you are alive. Josiah's guests toasted life and each other and shattered their glasses against a large tree to show that they planned to move on and not hold on to a past that was gone.

The place where Josiah's house once stood is now part of Bonaventure Cemetery, where stones mark my grandparents' final resting place as well as the newly dug grave where Tucker lay. The morning had been spent memorializing Ellen's lost love. Now, a mere spitting distance from the plot where he rested diagonally across from my birth mother's empty grave, we Taylors, Tierneys, and a sole Cook gathered to honor the memory of Mother Jilo Wills.

Jilo's actual burial had been a Wills family–only event held out on Sapelo Island. I'd wanted to attend, but after decades of rancor, her people hadn't quite been able to wrap their heads around the way she and the Taylor family had bonded at the last hour. Martell had promised to say a prayer at the service on my behalf.

Oliver had a picnic basket filled with champagne flutes, and he set it down as we neared the part of the cemetery that had been laid out in a pattern representing the All-Seeing Eye. He opened it and handed a glass to each of us. Peter followed behind him, filling everyone's glasses but mine with champagne. He paused before me and fixed his eyes on mine. My soul leaned in and touched his strength. His soul touched back, and then he moved on. Adam opened a bottle of cider for me and filled my flute.

"No," Ellen said to Peter when he reached her. "I'll have the cider as well." I tried not to let my relief show. I prayed turning away from alcohol would be easier for her this time than the last.

With all our glasses filled, Peter returned to my side and put his arm around me. I leaned into him and wrapped my arm around his waist. I'd manage to stand on my own tomorrow. Today, I was just happy to have him there to hold.

"Who would like to begin?" Oliver asked.

"I would," Iris said. She bit her lip for a moment. "Jilo, I know you can hear this." Her voice broke, and she cleared her throat. "I am sorry our friendship blossomed late, but I am so glad that it did."

Iris lowered her head, a signal that she had finished, and Ellen stepped forward. "Jilo, I thank you for looking out for all of us. Most people will never know what a debt Savannah owes you, but we do, and I, for one, will always be grateful to you." She stepped back and placed her free arm around Iris's shoulders.

"Oh, hell," Oliver said, reaching down and pulling out a bottle of scotch from the picnic basket. He opened it. "Listen up, you old buzzard," he said, emptying it on the ground. "This is 1937 Glenfiddich. Just don't haunt me, okay?"

I laughed in spite of myself, and then all eyes turned toward me. "Mercy?" Iris prompted me. "What would you like to say to Jilo?"

What did I want to say? I had been struggling to find the words that would sum up how I felt, but the right ones would not come. I wanted to say I loved her. That there would be a hole in my heart forever where she had once been. That she had scared the hell out of me, irritated me beyond belief, and I didn't know how I could possibly face the weight of the magic that was now mine without her support, her strength, her churlishness. I felt my hand shaking, so I raised my glass. "To Mother," I said.

"To Mother. To Jilo," the voices echoed around me. I drank the cider in a single draught and hurled the glass against the nearest tree.

Acknowledgments

I would like to thank my spouse, Rich Weissman, for his loving support and encouragement, my agent, Susan Finesman of Fine Literary, and the amazing team at 47North, especially David Pomerico and Angela Polidoro. Thanks also to my literary midwife, Kristen Weber. Finally, much love to my furry co-authors: Duke, Sugar, and my little Quentin Comfort. (Daddy misses you, Bug.)

ABOUT THE AUTHOR

© 2013 LEVY MOROSHAN

J.D. Horn was raised in rural Tennessee, and has since carried a bit of its red clay with him while traveling the world, from Hollywood to Paris to Tokyo. He studied comparative literature as an undergrad, focusing on French and Russian in particular. He also holds an MBA in international business and worked as a financial analyst before becoming a novelist. He and his spouse, Rich, split their time between Portland, Oregon, and San Francisco, California.

31901059491292